I am a child of the Goddess Morrigan…
I was born in the land of Éire…
And my heart blazes with its fury…
I have lived through the ages…

I seek to right those who have wronged…
I am the Maintainer of the Balance…

The Balance must be maintained

triscelle publishing

presents

shards of light
morrigan's brood book v

by

heather poinsett dunbar
& christopher dunbar

map of story locations

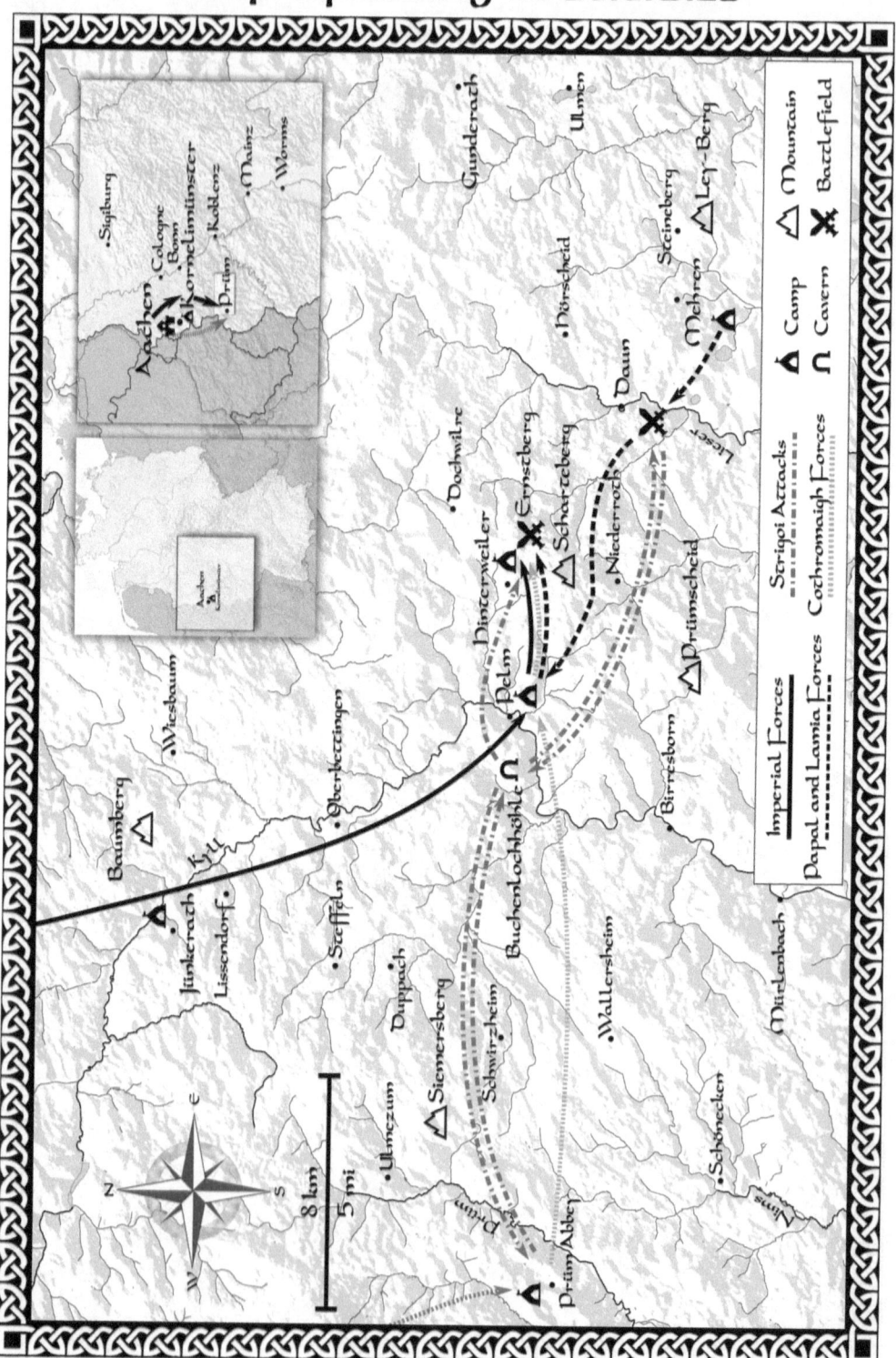

map guide

West Roman Empire, Circa 801 CE

Location Name	Modern Country	State Name
West Roman Empire / Frankish Empire / Carolingian Empire		
Aachen	Germany	North Rhine-Westphalia
Buchenlochhöhle	Germany	Vulkaneifel, Rhineland-Palatinate
Daun	Germany	Vulkaneifel, Rhineland-Palatinate
Ernstberg	Germany	Vulkaneifel, Rhineland-Palatinate
Gunderath	Germany	Vulkaneifel, Rhineland-Palatinate
Hinterweiler	Germany	Vulkaneifel, Rhineland-Palatinate
Jünkerath	Germany	Vulkaneifel, Rhineland-Palatinate
Kornelimünster	Germany	North Rhine-Westphalia
Mehren	Germany	Vulkaneifel, Rhineland-Palatinate
Pelm	Germany	Vulkaneifel, Rhineland-Palatinate

References refer to the map on the opposing page.

Battle for Ernstberg

Strigoi Northern Attack
Battle of the Gods
Strigoi Western Attack
Cothromaigh Counter-Attack
Strigoi Southern Attack

Legend:
- ✖ Battlefield
- ◯ Lookout Boulder
- ▨ Mirror
- ⌂ Camp
- ∩ Cavern
- ×× Fortification
- ▬ ▬ Strigoi Attacks
- ▪▪▪ Cothromaigh Forces

Dedication and copyright page

For You

April, 2021

Shards of Light

Morrigan's Brood Book V
Print ISBN-10: 1-937341-40-2
Print ISBN-13: 978-1-937341-40-4
by Heather Poinsett Dunbar
and Christopher Dunbar
Published by Triscelle Publishing
Edited by Ruth Davis Hays and Sarah E. Aalderink
Front Cover art by Alexandra Rena-Wagner
Back Cover art and website artwork by Khanada Taylor
Maps created by Daniel Feher
Triscelle Publishing Logo by Dayna Hartley
Copyright © 2021 by Triscelle Publishing. All rights reserved.

Printed by permission in the United States of America, the United Kingdom, Australia, or another other country designated by the Publisher. See back page for printing information. For any issues with print or binding quality, please contact the company through which the purchase was made and give the code number on this book.

Visit our website and find us on WordPress, Goodreads, Facebook, the Library Thing, LinkedIn, Twitter, and many other places on the web.

www.triscellepublishing.com
triscellepublishing.wordpress.com

Also available in several eBook formats

acknowledgments

Heather's Acknowledgments

It's been too many years. My apologies for our lateness in getting this book out, though I'm certain many people are familiar with the effects of life happening. I left a library position, feeling overwhelmed with the four hours of daily driving it involved. I stopped working and then went back to writing slowly. I also found a new part-time job as a librarian and discovered that I really do like helping people research and find books; I just really hate driving four hours a day.

We lost our elderkitty, Lucius, during that time and adopted another older cat, Lily. Together she, Brigid, and Clyde decided to continue plotting against me typing. Yet, despite their interruptions for noms and attention, book and story ideas started to flow again.

I owe thanks to many for encouragement and inspiration. Special thanks go to Ruth Davis Hays for kicking my backside on the edits. Many thanks also to our cover artist, Alexandra Rena Wagner, for dealing with our wishy-washyness about colors and who belonged on the cover (Chris talked her and I out of a cover displaying the secret and elicit feelings between two male characters, but I'm not gonna go on further about that!)

A huge round of thanks to Heidi Bowles Ellis, Tracy Angelina Evans, Kara Hash, Khanada Taylor, Sarah 'Sally' Aalderink, and the other writers who prodded me to continue. According to Chris, I've become quite the Lamia. Mandubratius would be proud, but even Marcus would admit that sometimes a little manipulation to get things done isn't entirely bad. So, lets get this late party started.

Christopher's Acknowledgments

This book really didn't take five years to write. Things came up, like shiny keys dangling in front of a toddler's eyes. The pressure of working long hours coupled with the strain of having to find new consulting gigs every few months put a strain on my creativity and my drive to finish this book.

In order to break the monotony, Heather took over some of my pre-editing duties and worked directly with our editor, Ruth Davis Hays, to get things moving again. She also guilted me into commencing with the book design and coordinating with our new cover artist, Alexandra Rena Wagner, to get working on the new cover art. Heather is quite the manipulator.

So, here we are, the long awaited sequel to Curse of Venus is here in print and in eBook form. I want to thank Heather for kicking my arse, Ruth for not one but two passes on this book's manuscript, and Alexandra for pertaining this beautiful cover art. Please enjoy the culmination of our works.

Lines of Blood-Drinkers

Algul – A line of Arabic blood-drinkers created by their God of War, Verethragna. Their known abilities include the power to create visual hallucinations in both mortals and in other immortals. However, their vulnerability lies in strong smells. Their numbers are small, due to a genocidal war between themselves and the remnants of the Ekimmu.

Deargh Du – An ancient line of blood-drinkers from Éire (Ireland) that trace their ancestry to the Goddess Morrigan. Their true talents lie in their magical skills and their fae-like beauty, known as glamoury. They can fly, create glowing light, heal mortals as well as other immortals, and draw down darkness and shadow. Their major weakness is the metal gold. After the creation of the Ekimmu Cruitne, the Deargh Du withdrew back to their native land and ceased interacting with other blood-drinking races.

Ekimmu – A group of blood-drinkers originating in Assyria from Zaltu, God of Strife. They grew in strength and power, eventually dominating the Middle East. However, other races, such as their enemies the Algul and the Lamia, began to hunt them down, decimating their population.

Ekimmu Cruitne – The Ekimmu, fleeing a genocidal war, removed themselves to the northern regions of Alba (Scotland). After meeting some of the Deargh Du, who traveled with the Scoti tribe, an Ekimmu and a Deargh Du conspired to tip the balance by creating a new being. Morrigan, in her rage, sought to confine them to their lands. Ekimmu Cruitne are struck by illness whenever they try to cross the ocean. Their greatest talent is their olfactory sense, making them excellent trackers. They can also heal others, fly, read minds, and enjoy manipulating games of chance. In addition, they can create the sensation of pleasure as well as pain in themselves and in their victims.

Chiang-shih or *Jiangshi* (殭屍) – A Chinese line of blood-drinkers that originated from Shenlong, a dragon God. Shenlong created the Jiangshi to protect His earthly treasures from greedy mortals. While the Jiangshi can control storms like Shenlong, they can only fly, in the form of a dragon, when the moon is full and have difficulty crossing water. Little else is known about them, as they choose not to interact with most of the western lines. Their true talents lie in their medical knowledge and their gifts. Both Jiangshi and Kyonshī share the same blood-lines, but they are distinct. They also cannot tell one race from the other by smell. The Jiangshi and Kyonshī are at war with one another.

Kyonshī (キョンシー) – A Japanese line of blood-drinkers that originated from Shinryū, a dragon God. Shinryū created the Kyonshī to protect His earthly treasures from greedy mortals. While the Kyonshī can control storms like Shinryū, they can only fly, in the form of a dragon, when the moon is full and have difficulty crossing water. Little else is known about them, as they choose not to interact with most of the western lines. Their true talents lie in their medical knowledge and their gifts. Both Jiangshi and Kyonshī share the same blood-lines, but they are distinct. They also cannot tell one race from the other by smell. The Jiangshi and Kyonshī are at war with one another.

Lamia – According to legend, Lamia was a Queen of Libya who seduced Zeus. In retribution, Hera killed all of her children. Heartbroken, Lamia began feeding on the people of Greece, and before long, she had many new immortal children. The Lamia infiltrated Roman society, and soon Rome became their seat of power. The Lamia's skills lie in mind-bending, or manipulation. They even have an ability to enter dreams and influence the dreamer.

Ouphe – An ancient Saxon line of blood-drinkers that moved into Britannia during the Saxon conquest. Their strength is in their monstrous lycanthropic nature; many blood-drinking races can die from the wounds given by an Ouphe. Yet, the Ouphe are severely affected by silver. Their origin is a mystery.

Pacu Pati – Blood-drinkers from India that originated from Kali. The Pacu Pati tend to cloister themselves with their new families of other Pacu Pati and do not meet with the other lines. When other lines have witnessed the celebrations of the cycles of life and death, they tend to misunderstand the celebrations, and a lack of a common language generally adds to the confusion.

Strigoi – A line of blood-drinkers that began from a cursed Greek beauty named Iris. Aphrodite's curse did not grant Iris and her victim's immortality; instead, they only survive fifty years after their transformation. The Strigoi are telepathic and unleash uncontrollable madness upon mortals and immortals alike. Affected mortals tear at their eyes and puncture their eardrums to escape the onslaught of sights and sounds. Despite their talents, Strigoi are physically weak, stunted, and are the ugliest of the blood-drinkers.

Sugnwr Gwaed – A British group of blood-drinkers created by Cernunnos, the Horned God of animals, wilderness, and the wild hunt. Their strengths include enhanced communication with animals and their talent for vocal persuasion. They can convince their victims of almost anything. They also fly, like the other Celtic lines, and have an aptitude for healing others.

Other lines will be revealed in future works.

character guide

Marcus Galerius Primus Helvetticus	Marcus

Long ago, Marcus forced himself to forget the true source of his Cognomina ex virtute, "Helvetticus"; a name which Caesar bestowed. Yet, the Strigoi forced him to remember the blood of the women and children he butchered. How heroic he was...

Mandubratius	Awvarwy (a-war-wee)

Mandubratius couldn't be happier. He successfully merged the Lamia with the Children of Ares, he converted hundreds of papal soldiers into Lamia, and he has Pope Leo III dangling from strings. What could be better? Having Máire.

Máire Ní Conghal	Máire (moya)

Máire has won her duel against her aunt Talia in order to prevent her hostile takeover of Heloise' and Julien's lands. With Talia dead in the eyes of Emperor Charles' court, will her aunt seek reprisals, or will she cower in Awvarwy's embrace?

Claudius Metrius Sertorius	Claudius

Claudius never had a son before. While coitus with whores, slaves, and the women of his slain foes probably yielded offspring, until Horatio came into his life, Claudius never had someone he could call "son". But, will Cernunnos welcome him?

Arwin Mac Alpin	Mac Alpin

Marcus has Máire, Edward has Amata, Mandubratius has Talia... and possibly Máire, and Claudius has his "son" Horatio. But who does Arwin have? That Irene looks ravishing enough. Too bad she has eyes for Emperor Charles. Oh well.

Tertia Amata Antonia	Amata

Mandubratius' malignant machinations made Amata mightily miffed and mortified! Mischief that malcontent misogynistic menace manufactured made Amata march merrily to Marcus, Máire, and Mac Alpin. Mead makes memories and mind mend.

Téa Uí Cennedi Uí Máine	Talia de Burgundy / Talia de Époisses

Defeat! How could she have lost? All her plans for taking over Francia, for gaining real power, are lost to her! She is dead in the eyes of Charles. Now, she must crawl back to Mandubratius and receive whatever punishment he feels she deserves.

Patroclus Statilius Messalinus	The Legate

Patroclus sacrificed much to maintain the Lamia, whilst Mandubratius recovered following his defeat so many centuries ago, and supported the co-consul through many trials. Now, the Legate is rewarded for his service by being replaced by Sextus.

Edward	Edward, Edwina, Edgar, Edna

Edward still cannot believe that he would fall in love with a Lamia who also loved him back! She sacrificed so much politically to be there with him! She must love Edward a lot. So, what is next for two blood-drinkers? Marriage? Really? Hmm.

Sáerlaith Ní Adhamdh	Sáerlaith (saer-la)

As Sáerlaith lay bleeding from the vicious attack in the catacombs of Prüm Abbey, she remembers the scrolls she was given to take to Máire. Not only will the exiled Deargh Du have a new home in Vézelay, they will also have new gifts to wield.

Caoimhín of Ard Mhacha	Caoimhín (kev-een)

The true Deargh Du have a home again: Vézelay. Sure, it isn't Ard Mhacha, it isn't Éire, but it is home. Caoimhín has the honor of building a new Deargh Du stronghold. Yet, he wishes he could accompany his friends... and especially Sáerlaith.

Irene the Athenian / Basileus	Empress Irene / Ειρήνη Σαρανταπήχαινα

Irene decided to remain with Marcus and his friends rather than traveling with Mandubratius so she could visit an old flame. If only she could have wed Charles... what a good husband he would have made. Now, she just wants Charles for sex.

Karl der Große / Carolus Magnus	Emperor Charles / Charlemagne

The best hope for the empire to continue has died with the discovery that his favorite son and only worthy successor is a Deargh Du who cannot father children. Charles had placed so much hope in Julien. Now, the empire will die with Charles.

Pope Leo III	His Holiness

Leo finally has an army capable of taking on the demon scourge, but at what cost to his soul? With the aid of the Lamia leader Michael Tolomei, or rather Mandubratius, many papal soldiers became "angels". May God forgive him for his devilish decision.

Julien de Divio	Julien

Forgiveness is the reward a man or woman gives themselves when they wish to ignore the transgressions of another in order to forge what they hope to be lasting peace. Should Julien forgive his brother Reginald, or should he seek retribution?

Heloise de Divio	Heloise

She knew that Talia was trouble! Oh, her poor son Reginald, who fell for Talia's feminine wiles and her Lamia manipulation. Even if he had something to do with that brutish attack on Sáerlaith and the others, she knew she could forgive him.

Reginald de Divio	Reginald

Released from Talia's Lamia influence, Reginald is left with the memory of what he tried to do to his mother and to his brother... or rather half-brother. He had watched and listened as another controlled his speech and actions, yet he still blames himself.

Horatio di Reate	Horatio

Horatio always had a strong sense of his role in society and in the cavalry. He knew where he stood and what was expected of him. Since becoming Lamia, however, in fact, since joining Claudius' troupe, Horatio has no clue how he fits in with them.

Seosaimhín Uí Turrlough Uí Niall	Seosaimhín (sho-siv-een)

Such power we have now, praise be to Nagirrom! We shall use our shrieking horde to upset the Balance and spread fear in the hearts of mortals and immortals alike! The wolves howl their ecstasy as they hunt the stag to feast upon its fear and flesh.

gods and goddesses of the series

Irish Pantheon – Tuatha dé Danann (People of Dana)	
Aine (*An-ya*)	*Goddess of Love and Fertility*
Aongas Og (*An-gus Og*)	*God of Love and Youth*
Brigid (*Bri-jid*)	*Goddess of Healing, Writing, Water, and Cats*
Dagda (*Dah-dah*)	*The 'good' God of Many Skills*
Dana (*Day-na*)	*The Mother Goddess*
Lugh (*Loo*)	*Multi-skilled God of Battle, Light, Writing, and the Harvest*
Medb (*May-v*)	*Goddess of Sovereignty*
Manannán Mac Lir (*Man-nan-awan Mac Lir*)	*Guide to the Otherworld and God of the Wind, Travels, Sea, and Sailing*
Morrigan (*Mor-ee-gan*)	*Goddess of Death, Battle, Blood, and Rebirth*
Nuada (*Nu-a-da*)	*God of Healing and Weaponry*
British Pantheon	
Cernunnos	*God of Animals, Wilderness, Fertility, and the Wild Hunt*
Greek / Roman Pantheon	
Aphrodite (*af-rə-dy-tee*) / Venus (ˈwɛnʊs)	*Goddess of Love, Beauty, and Sexuality / Goddess of love, Beauty, and Fertility*
Ares (árɛːs) / Mars (*Mārs*)	*God of War and Manly Virtues / God of War; part of the Archaic Triad*
Hera (*Hēra*) / Juno (ˈjuːnoː)	*Queen of the Gods and Goddess of Marriage, Women, and Birth / Patron Goddess of Rome and Goddess of Women; part of the Capitoline Triad*
Zeus (*Zews*) / Jupiter (*Joo-pi-ter*)	*King of the Gods and God of the Sky, Thunder, Lightning, Law, Order, and Justice / King of the Gods and God of the Sky and Thunder; part of the Capitoline Triad; Patron Deity of Rome*
Hindu Pantheon	
Kali (*Kālī*)	*Goddess of Time and Change; "She Who Destroys"; "Redeemer of the Universe"*
Chinese and Japanese Pantheons	
Shenlong (*shén lóng*) 神龍 / Shinryū (*sheen-you*) 神竜	*A dragon God in Chinese and Japanese mythology known as the "Master of Storms"*

prologue

"*Granddaughter. Granddaughter! Wake up! Wake up I say!*"

"*Wha... what? Grandfather? Am I dead? How is it that I can see you?*"

"*You're not dead, Talia, but you deserve to be. After all, you failed to reacquire our family lands twice, as I recall.*"

"*But you lost them in the first place, grandfather.*"

"*Ha! I was betrayed by your cousin. He allowed the Franks into the stronghold. I gave my life to make sure you escaped. Which is more than you've ever done for our family.*"

"*I tried to take back our lands. I had not even seen twenty cycles—*"

"*It was an utter failure. You only escaped because you disguised yourself as a peasant boy. Here again you failed. Even with your abilities as a Lamia, you couldn't rebuild our legacy.*"

"*That's not my fault, grandfather. I'd been acquiring territories from different sources. It was only due to Deargh Du interference that I was exposed. Also, I never received education in combat.*"

"*I'm not talking about that, you whelp. The best way to attain power is to manipulate circumstances, so it's given to you freely. You had an opportunity early to seduce the emperor. You could have received those lands out of the kindness of his loins. I think your sponsor, whatever his name is, saw the true objective that you were blind to. Not only would you hold Burgundy, but the emperor's ear as well. You could have had power to influence him!*"

"*How could I have—*"

"*Talia, you are small-minded. Perhaps it would have been better for me to flee from the Franks, but no. I threw my life away for a poor excuse of a grandchild. I hope you find nothing but failure. If I find you in the afterlife, I will punish you for all your misdeeds!*"

"*I will redeem myself, grandfather!*"

chapter one

801 CE - Aachen

Talia drifted through a linen-hazed dream. Voices whispered, calling her name. Pain tore through her torso as a sword ripped through her chest. She cried out and opened her eyes. Cold dampness greeted her. She shivered, surrounded by darkness. Something soft covered her face. More material bound her hands to her hips. Talia struggled against the bindings, frustrated. She gasped as she managed to tear her arms free of the cloth and rip aside the material limiting her vision.

"Funeral linen?" she uttered, her voice harsh with disuse. She had been abandoned in a cold, damp room without the assistance of a surgeon.

The circumstances of her battle with Máire replayed in her mind. Such a stab wound through the chest would have been fatal to mortals. Now, everyone believed her dead, everyone of significance.

Talia turned to the side and noticed that her wounds still lay open. She heaved a soft cry and then stifled her unconscious utterance, fearful a mortal may witness her animation and attempt to destroy the evil spirit that possessed her cadaver.

Rage caused her to forget caution, and she hissed, "You stupid, worthless, waste of a blood-drinking, devil-worshipping bitch," wishing Máire could hear her words.

That interloper, Marcus, quelled my niece's rage. Damn him, too.

Biting her lip as she rose from the table, Talia glanced around the room.

Feed, find clothes, and then escape. That is what I must do. Mandubratius must be with the papal forces. Why else would he not be there to witness a battle he would have dearly loved to see?

Talia took a few uneasy steps to the door. She grabbed a long stick and began to hobble with it, fighting pain at every movement. "All for revenge," she whispered, while leaning her cheek against the smelly wood.

Lucius awoke from his slumber curled up in a warm spot between Máire's knees and her belly, as she slept on her side, and began to groom himself. As he raised his left hind leg and started licking it, he glanced around the dark room and dwelled on his situation.

I have a warm, soft bed and a fairly warm companion. Now, if only my dinner would arrive, everything would be in perfect balance.

Lucius lowered his leg and studied Máire's sleeping form for a moment.

After witnessing the battle, he wished he could have bards tell the tale of this Deargh Du. Unfortunately, most of the bards disappeared with the mist, as Christianity pushed through Éire.

Lucius' ears twitched at the annoyance of that memory. Humans had the right to choose how they wished to live their lives. The ancient immortals gave mortals these opportunities. At times, however, mortals made bad decisions that seemed quite comical. The fairy cat purred at that thought before yawning, stretching, and then plopping down on his side.

Yes, mortals could be most amusing.

The sound of footfalls interrupted his intentions to return to his slumber. He could sense the guards outside the door snap to attention as if someone of rank waited beyond the door.

Máire awoke but feigned sleep. She patted him gently and whispered, "I think we have company."

Lucius sniffed the air. "Yes, a mortal," he said. "Is it someone you know?"

"Yes, I believe that is the Emperor himself, Lugh."

"This should be most entertaining." Lucius rose from his position next to her and fixated his gaze at the door.

"Indeed," Máire replied, while continuing to feign sleep.

The door opened and in walked the Emperor. "Wait outside," he commanded before closing the door behind him with his left hand while grasping a candle in the other. The Emperor neared the bed and pulled up a chair. He ignored Lucius' piercing gaze and stared at Máire as if trying to decide what to think of her. The Emperor set the candle on a table behind him and, in a soft tone said, "Máire, wake up, Máire."

Lucius saw Máire's eyes open. He hoped she would remember to act as though she were wounded.

"Oh, Imperial Majesty," Máire acknowledged in a strained voice while opening her eyes. She smiled weakly at the Emperor. "What day is it?" She sounded as if she were in poor health.

"Please don't play this game with me," the Emperor demanded while staring down at her. "I know you are no longer wounded. Your strength returned to you earlier this evening. What I wish to know is what you have done to my son."

Máire's face revealed her discomfort. The shadows from the flickering candle exposed rage and guilt.

"I beg your pardon," she whispered. "I was wounded, and I am recovering. As far as this accusation about your son, I have no idea who or what you are speaking about. What son, Imperial Majesty?"

"Do not pretend that you are still weak. I know the truth, Deargh Du."

Lucius crept to the foot of the bed, allowing for a better view of the two combatants in this amusing battle of wits, when he felt Máire shift as if she planned to sit up. He noticed her hand rest at her side, under the blankets where her blade lay hidden.

"So," she began, dropping the charade of recovery, "Julien is your son. I should have recognized that. Now I can see you in his eyes." Máire stared at Lucius for a moment, as if gathering her thoughts. She looked back to the Emperor, her emotions lay bare. She confirmed the rest of his accusation. "Yes, I am Deargh Du. If I'm not mistaken, it was Julien who told you what I... what we are."

"Yes," the Emperor answered. "You are quite astute in these matters."

Lucius began to purr. The drama unfolding in this room and the emotional intensity entertained him.

This will be a thousand times better than chasing a quick hare.

"Did you give him a choice?" The Emperor's voice grew tight with ill-concealed rage.

"Yes, I asked Julien if he wanted to live or die," Máire answered.

"Did he even understand the consequences?" The Emperor exhaled in an impatient hiss.

"No, there was no time. In fact, usually there are many years of observation and interaction with a candidate before offering a chance to become Deargh Du. However, Julien possessed many of the traits desired in a candidate for this honor." Máire paused to let the Emperor mull over her words before she continued. "Even after the transformation begins, one has an opportunity to die."

"An opportunity? What do you mean?"

"Those going through the transformation meet Morrigan. She evaluates them and judges their worthiness. Not just anyone can be Deargh Du, Imperial Majesty."

"Who is this Morrigan?" the Emperor asked. "That name sounds familiar."

"Perhaps your bards, poets I mean, spoke of Morrigan. She is the Irish Goddess of blood, battle, death, and re-creation. She is the matron of all Deargh Du."

"Matron?" The Emperor's brows raised.

"Yes, Imperial Majesty, she created the Deargh Du."

"So, Lady Máire of Ulster was a human once?" The Emperor studied her again.

"Yes, Maél Muire Ní Conghal Uí Máine, Chieftain of Béal Átha an Fheadha was a mortal. Marcus transformed me over two hundred years ago, the Goddess named me Máire, and I have been Deargh Du ever since."

Lucius lied down and studied the Emperor as the elder mortal's eyes widened at these truths.

"I assume Julien did not mention that we are immortal, for the most part," Máire added.

The Emperor began to breathe heavily and squeezed his eyes shut.

Lucius turned towards Máire and spoke to her mind. "You told him too much, too soon. You are shattering his reality. You must learn to be patient with mortals who cannot fathom the idea of beings such as us wandering the earth."

Máire leaned forward and held onto the Emperor's shoulders with her hands. "I realize all this is overwhelming to you, Charles."

Lucius made note of Máire's use of the Emperor's given name in a familiar manner.

The Emperor opened his eyes, shook his head for a moment, and shut his eyes again. "I've seen with my own eyes the strange miracles and magics that my son can conjure. I also see with my own eyes that you are not weak from your wounds." Emperor Charles exhaled. "I'll even wager that your wounds have healed completely."

Máire pushed off her blankets and revealed her bare arm. She then peeled away layers of bandages.

From his vantage point, Lucius could see her fully healed translucent skin, as well as the Emperor's expression as he leaned forward on one knee to get a better look at her now absent wounds. The fairy cat observed him reaching for his candle, but he stopped once Máire's glamoury illuminated the room.

The Emperor touched her shoulder and said, "The first commandment says that we should have no other Gods before our God. Yet, what you say contradicts that commandment."

"No," Máire answered. "Your God says for His followers to honor no other God before Himself, but I'm not Christian. I've spoken to Morrigan and the Goddess Brigid. I've seen them with my own eyes. In fact, Morrigan's blood courses through my veins. Her vitae flows through your son as well."

"Blood?" The Emperor looked away from her shoulder and into her eyes.

"It is how our gift is passed from one Deargh Du to a mortal who wishes to become one. There is a transference of essence."

"And that is what my son had to do in order for you to save him?"

"Yes." She stared back into his blue eyes.

The Emperor leaned back in his chair. "My perception of the world as I know it is now a shattered clay pot. Perhaps your cat knocked it over." The Emperor gazed at Lucius for a moment.

Lucius watched the Emperor grapple with his emotions and then stare at his hands.

"I believe what you are saying. I know there is more you can tell me about yourself, but I am buried beneath this avalanche of new insight. New insight on my son, and who and what he is now."

Máire leaned in and patted the Emperor's hand. "Imperial Majesty," she said before adopting a familiar tone once again. "Charles, you should rest and contemplate these new observations. Please do not speak of them to anyone."

The Emperor stretched and yawned. He rose from the chair and began dragging himself towards the door, like an ancient mortal suffering under the weight of age and cares. He stopped and rested his hand on the handle of the door. He then looked over his left shoulder and asked, "La... Máire, I would like to speak to you again if you are willing."

"I am available to speak with you anytime, Charles," she answered.

"I look forward to asking you more questions." He walked out, the door closing behind him.

While Lucius started towards the opposite side of the bed, Máire slid in, arranging her feet so as not to disturb him. He found himself in between her calves.

"So," he said, feeling a sibilant purr tickle at his throat, "your son-in-darkness is the son of the Emperor. You must be very proud, young Deargh Du."

Máire grumbled a bit before sighing. "I cannot fathom what Julien is going through. He must have just learned this himself."

"Because he cannot produce children now, he cannot be the Emperor's heir," Lucius commented before walking up closer and stepping onto her stomach. He preferred lying on her chest or belly. Deargh Du tended to become cold at their extremities during their sleep.

"This means that my gift, and Morrigan's, saved Julien's life, yet these gifts also ended it."

Lucius flopped down on her abdomen and stared into her green eyes.

Deargh Du and mortals alike can be most entertaining.

Máire said nothing more to him, although he could feel her gentle fingers rub his brow. Lucius closed his eyes and purred.

Julien waited for the guards to open the door and allow him past them. As soon as he cleared the threshold, he placed the plate of food on the floor and gazed up at Máire, who looked at him and smiled. He became so distracted with her radiance that he nearly fell, but then Lucius knocked him over and leapt at the food.

The fairy cat cried out, "It's cold! My champion's portion is cold!" He whined and uttered a frustrated meow, but despite his protests, he began to eat.

"I did my best," Julien stated. "I was preoccupied when the Emperor called me and my mother to speak to him privately after our meal." He looked back at Máire expectantly.

She scooted towards the opposite edge of the bed to make room for him.

As soon as he sat down next to her, Máire took his hand and said, "Your family is safe. Your home is safe." She brought his fingers to her mouth and kissed them.

Julien jumped as she grazed his index finger with a sharp tooth and sucked at it. Overcoming the shock, he said, "Things are considerably more complicated now. Apparently, I'm not the third son. I'm the eighth bastard son."

"Yes, Charles told me." Máire laughed before adding, "He accused me of forcing you to become Deargh Du."

After extracting his finger from her mouth, Julien kicked up his feet and slid back next to her in the bed. He leaned against her shoulder and inhaled the scent of her hair, wondering how she managed to smell so clean. "Were you able to convince him that I had a choice, and this is the choice I made?" Julien stared into the darkness for a moment before watching Lucius gnaw on the lamb. He smiled at the fairy cat's single-mindedness.

"Yes, I did, but he seems somewhat reluctant to accept what you have become," Máire answered.

"He wanted me to become his heir and give him grandchildren," Julien admitted. "He's been grooming me for leadership all my life." He chuckled without mirth. "I always wondered why I managed to achieve more than most third sons… why I had the opportunity to find favor with the vassals. He wished me to be known and respected, I think. Yet now, that life is not to be."

Máire moved in closer and embraced him.

He turned to meet her green eyes.

"If I had not–"

"Don't second-guess what happened," Julien whispered. "If you had not acted as you did, I would be dead. I would not know the Emperor is my father. I wouldn't have known about my daughter and sons. I could have missed out on experiencing the truth about the other Deities and you, my mother-in-darkness. I enjoy my new life. I do not regret it. Please don't regret what you did." He leaned in and kissed her. "I thank you for saving my life and giving me an opportunity to have you, my beloved, and my new family." Julien pulled away and turned his eyes to the wall. "I will need my new family in the eternal nights. My fath… the Emperor wishes me to leave the Empire when our duties are complete."

"I'm so sorry, Julien," Máire whispered.

"Exiled," Julien muttered. "I am to leave my homeland and be sent away from my mother, sister, and daughter," Julien paused and then whispered, "and my father."

"And your brother," Máire added.

Julien felt his jaw set in anger. "My brother," he hissed. "Why do you bring him into my thoughts?"

"Do you feel that his punishment is just?" she asked.

"Yes," Julien roared. However, upon hearing the shuffling from the guards outside the door, he lowered his voice. "He threatened my mother, Máire. Of course this judgment is fair!"

"Are you certain that those actions weren't controlled by my aunt?" Máire asked.

"My brother has free will and can make decisions on his own."

"You know very well about the talents that the Lamia wield, Julien." Máire bent her knees and crossed her legs. "Their manipulation techniques are superb. Many have been at their mercy. My aunt learned her skills from a master. She already had much talent for these lessons as a mortal. Talia manipulated Reginald. Perhaps he experienced jealousy at your success, but she brought it forth and made the ridiculous seem righteous, Julien."

"How can I accept that the person who arranged the attack on my mother and members of my new family is not the aggressor, Máire? He perpetrated these horrors."

Lucius jumped on the bed and began grooming himself with vigor.

"Did you notice a difference in his behavior before he met my aunt?" Máire asked.

"He was still a rude and dangerous annoyance to his family," Julien answered. He sighed. "Perhaps."

He watched Máire stare at the opposite wall for a moment as if contemplating something grave while Lucius sidled towards her and settled himself in her lap, looking sleepy and satisfied.

As Máire stroked the cat's brow, she appeared to have made up her mind. "I may have told you this before, but Mandubratius manipulated me even after I became Deargh Du," she stated. "He climbed into my dreams with an expert's skill and made me pity him several times. If a Lamia can manipulate a Deargh Du with such ease, a mortal would have no chance."

"You think I should forgive Reginald for what he did to our family," Julien asserted.

"I think you should do what you feel is just," Máire said. "In looking at Amata, Patroclus, and Horatio, I wonder if they were manipulated into their current state. Well, we know Horatio was." Her eyes began to glow. "I wonder what would have happened if my strike had not been so lucky," Máire fell silent for a few seconds as if reliving the event. "Several nights before our fateful battle with the Lamia in Éire, I was bathing in a river when Mandubratius found me. If I hadn't stabbed him in the heart, I may very well be a Lamia now. Foolish mortal that I was, I forgot I had to behead him to destroy him." Her eyes became their normal intensity. "I just remember seeing the look of realization in Reginald's eyes after I stabbed his sponsor through the chest. You should speak with him before you come to a decision."

Julien met her eyes. "I will consider talking to him. Where do you think I will find him?"

"Many victims might find themselves wishing for sunrise," Máire stated. "I would bet that Reginald remains where the guards dragged him." She then embraced him.

He relished the feel of her arms around him. He kissed her again, feeling strong urges to join her in the bed first, yet these thoughts disappeared upon hearing an annoyed grunt from Lucius.

"You two move around too much," Lucius complained before sitting on the corner of the bed.

Julien turned his gaze to Máire. "Why does this matter mean so much to you?"

"My aunt did this. Where I come from, family members are often held accountable for the actions of their family. If I had eric to offer for this, I would."

Julien was confused. "What is 'eric'?"

"Eric is a compensation for misdeeds. It is an ancient Brehon law," Lucius stated before crawling over to Julien.

"Thank you, Lucius," Máire quipped, "I was going to explain it to him."

"I understand," Julien responded. "Thank you, Lucius." To Máire, he said, "You battled your aunt for my family. That seems adequate compensation. Rest now." He kissed Máire's brow. "Lucius, Champion of Fairy Cats, please continue your protection of my beloved champion."

The fairy cat stared at him for a moment. "I have fed, and I have a suitable bed-warmer. Yes, I will protect her."

Julien rose and looked back to Máire. "Rest well. You have nothing to feel guilty about."

Charles closed the door to the bedroom partway, allowing the guards to complete closing it. He marched down the hall muttering and whispering as he waved away the guards. The candlelight flickered, yet its feeble light still illuminated the walls of his palace.

"How am I supposed to feel about these people?" he whispered to himself. After all, Rome and her Pope would see them as demons. Yet, these would-be demons fought for his empire against the murderers of his subjects. "Is my judgment of these Deargh Du flawed, or does the error lie within Papal doctrine?"

A sudden and unexpected vision of a beautiful woman waiting for him in one of the rooms along this hall made his head swim with bizarre and carnal thoughts.

Is this a memory or a premonition? Who is this woman? Is she still in that room? I must find her!

He scampered down the hall until he found the doors he had seen in his mind. No guards stood nearby, so Charles paused at the doors with heightened anticipation and opened them himself.

No lights greeted him from within the room, but the faint scent of exquisite perfumed oils wafting through the doorway hastened his heart. His candle, when stuck into the room, failed to illuminate the murky darkness to Charles' satisfaction. However, the bed appeared to be occupied.

The image overwhelmed his mind again, but this time, the figure became clearer. A brunette woman with long, unencumbered tresses, blue eyes, and an ample bosom waited for him in that bed. He could swear he smelled her intoxicating wetness.

Charles rushed through the doors and closed them behind him. He then dropped the poor candle onto a table next to the door and began to undress, nearly tearing his clothes in his exuberance. Once nude, he grabbed his abused candle and willed it to illuminate the beauty waiting for him in bed, but sadly, the candle merely sputtered. Still, he could discern a shape reclining in the bed, as well as two pinpricks of red light that must be reflections of his candle's flame.

As Charles walked around the bed, his meager light revealed a feminine form draped in blankets, yet the face remained shadowed. No other light, not even the red pinpricks, could be seen.

The female form stirred as if awoken from slumber.

"Who are you?" he asked the female under the covers.

"Don't you recognize me by my scent, Charles? You should remember your lover who wears the finest of perfumes."

He found himself a bit annoyed at her use of his name. Very few women could refer to him in such familiar terms.

The candle's light did not reveal the face of the mysterious woman, but through shadow he could discern a slender and graceful hand tucking thick strands of hair behind her left ear. Charles moved in closer, but his eyes alone could not penetrate the gloom. "Your voice is familiar, but I can't see your face."

"Oh, come now, Charles." The woman leaned forward into the candlelight, illuminating her features.

Charles felt a deep sense of shock and dread upon recognizing the woman before him.

"I thought you would recognize me. Such a pity," the Empress Irene cooed.

"What are you doing here, Basileus? What are you doing in my quarters?" Charles tried to control his temper.

The Empress smiled at him and pulled back the covers, revealing her naked form.

"I just wanted to see you. It has been awhile since we were intimate. Regarding your other question, I've visited here before and I remembered the secret passages of this palace."

"You… are not welcome here." Charles reached for his dagger, unsure of Irene's true motives, but then he cursed himself upon realizing it lay in a pile of his clothes next to the doors.

"Do you know why I did not marry you?" she asked, her eyes and voice lost their seductive allure.

"No, but I am curious about that," Charles replied. The Empress had been very interested in a political and marital alliance, once.

Irene stared at him in what seemed like a moment of reflective silence. "It was not my choice, Charles. My ministers hired mercenaries to kidnap me. I was on my way to Aachen when they stopped me and carried me back to Constantinople. I managed to wound a few and save a few dear companions of mine, but I could not fight them all. My ministers thought the idea of reuniting East and West would be a foolish one."

Charles witnessed a growing sadness in the Empress's features.

"I tried to correspond with you," she continued as regret tinged her features, "but my letters were interrupted. After a few years, I gave up and ceased writing to you."

Charles put down the candle on a night stand. "Your story is plausible, and I would like to believe it."

Why did she still have to be so beautiful in the soft light?

He sat down on the side of the bed. "I take it this visit is not official," he stated.

"Charles, can't we stop talking like lawyers? I've been hungering for you all this time," she purred, sounding as she had during her last visit.

Charles chuckled and leaned in closer. "I'm not as desperate for alliance as I was last time, Empress. Tell the truth."

"Fine," Irene murmured while beaming at him. "I do wish to enjoy pleasures with you again, but as you've surmised, that is not my primary reason for being in Aachen. I assume you know your guests... Marcus, with that incredibly long Latin name, and his traveling companions?"

Charles pulled back at the mention of that name. He felt his smile fade away. "Yes, we've met," he commented. "He and his associates work as mercenaries for me."

Irene's eyes revealed her curiosity. "Mercenaries? For you?"

"Yes, I hired them to take care of the murderers attacking my... our people. Have you noticed anything odd about Marcus and the others?"

"Hmmmm." Irene pursed her lips in thought. "That Marcus seems to wish to do right, but something troubles him, or so I believe. Some old guilt, perhaps." She shrugged. "Or perhaps it's just that I don't know him very well."

"And the others?" the Emperor asked, prodding her for further information.

"That Máire, she is odd. She fornicates with goats with the frequency of raindrops. However, I will say that she is capable with a sword," the Empress continued. "I have a feeling that she and Lady Amata are lovers."

The Emperor watched the Empress's eyes twinkle with that bit of naughty and probably untrue gossip. Such tales disgusted him somewhat but were still intriguing. The merriment faded as the Empress talked about the others.

"There is a lost soul in that young soldier, Horatio," she quipped before pausing. "Moving on to the others, Claudius seems deranged. He and a few of the others speak to this cat they found on our journey here. I've also witnessed him chatting to many animals in the manner that you and I are speaking now." Irene made a face. "Still worse is that Mac Alpin character. He's nothing but a brutish Anglo-Saxon... Briton... whatever he is, some kind of Celtic mix-breed, no doubt. And that Julien de Divio is nothing more than a loutish ruffian. Why did you give him such power, Charles? He displays the very worst of your people. Though, he is quite handsome." She smiled into the distance and then began to lick her lips suggestively.

Charles frowned at Irene for her insult against his son and for her attempts to distract him with her overt sexuality.

Keep focused, man!

"Those are interesting descriptions, Empress, but what I really want to know is whether you've noticed anything..." he paused searching for the right word, "otherworldly."

Irene chuckled. "Nothing beyond flying, sleeping during the day, and feeding on the blood of the living," she quipped.

Charles shushed her. "Don't you find these things to be sacrilegious?"

"Well, from the view of the Eastern and Western church, anyone of culture and learning is considered sacrilegious," Irene retorted.

"But you said these people drink the blood of the living," Charles hissed. "That's demonic!"

"Calm yourself, husband," the Empress demurred.

Charles felt his eyes widen at her phrase and the familiar term of affection.

"In my heart, we were wed, Charles," Irene whispered. "I've always considered you my husband." Her eyelashes fluttered.

He found himself lost in Irene's eyes.

There are those red pinpricks of light again, but are they a reflection off her eyes, or—

Charles felt his will ebb, as her body beckoned to him. He felt animalistic passion well up within him upon witnessing her leg move, revealing her engorged sex.

Don't stare, man! Look away! Anchor yourself in the conversation!

Charles shook his head to focus on the matter at hand. Her femininity seemed almost overwhelming. He felt powerless to protest such a provocative and inappropriate display. "Don't you think that what you described is demonic?" he asked her again, wanting to ignore the rest of their conversation and the mad feelings of lust rushing through him.

Irene stretched herself, causing her breasts to become more obvious, and hummed for a moment. "Charles, anything that doesn't agree with your chosen religion, you consider demonic. Sleeping during the day and drinking blood is a necessity of life for those people."

As if to accentuate her point, Irene rolled forward onto her hands and knees facing him and smiled, revealing her teeth. She swayed a bit, side to side, as if she were a serpent about to strike her prey. Her breasts dangled playfully, almost hypnotically, caught up in the rhythm.

He scooted away a little, intimidated with her aggressively seductive intensity. Even Máire, who demanded respect and strode through the palace in flimsy clothing with uncovered hair, did not display such wantonness. Bile made him feel a touch of nausea at the thought of pleasure with that demonic Deargh Du.

"Empress, I can't believe you find this acceptable. It's unholy and it's murder," he gulped out, fearing she intended to kiss him… or worse.

"Charles, innocent donors are not harmed, and they don't even remember it. At least, that's what I have been told."

Irene stopped swaying. She sat down with her legs curled beneath her. The Empress then leaned back on her elbows and kicked out her legs, crossing one over the other. She rubbed the toes of her right foot against his knee. With the outstretched fingers of her left hand, she traced a line from her left nipple, outside of and down her left breast, down her abdomen, along the cleft of her thigh, and down to her clitoris.

He realized she now attempted to distract him from his questions about these beings. She must know more about Marcus and the others. A terrifying thought entered his brain.

If Julien could be one of them, surely his former betrothed could be a demon as well.

Charles rose and pointed at Irene. "You're a Deargh Du!"

Irene laughed. "Charles, you insult me. I am Lamia, thank you... not a tree-worshipping backwards Deargh Du from Éire." She scooted back against the wall. The seductive aura surrounding her faded into candlelit darkness.

The Emperor sat down on the bed again. He could not fathom what Irene meant. As he rubbed his brow, he recollected something Julien had mentioned about Lamia in the same context as the Deargh Du, as if they must be similar. He stared at his former wife-to-be.

First Julien and now her? They were not human. They claimed to not be demonic, yet I have no understanding of what to consider them to be.

"To those few mortals who witness what we are, we inform them that we are angels. That way they do not burn us," Irene added. Her laughter faded, and now her entire form radiated purpose. "Of course, we Lamia can't fly, and we can't do those tricks with light and shadow."

Charles closed his eyes, remembering Julien's demonstration of his skills. He recalled that he could almost see angel wings and a halo on his son. Julien had seemed so serene, yet Charles knew from the scripture that angels were never mortals... ever.

Could the scriptures be wrong about angels? After all, my son... the others like him... surely, they are not demons.

He opened his eyes and stared at her. The blue eyes of the Empress glowed for a moment with a strange, red intensity in the candlelight, and then faded. "Angelic is an apt description for those of us who are mortals," he commented. "Can you become mortal again, if you chose so?"

Irene laughed and covered her mouth. She dropped her hand and continued chuckling as she leaned back. "Why would we want that, Charles? I didn't become Lamia to grow older. I wanted to preserve what remained of my beauty and youth. Besides," her voice lowered into a throaty murmur, "there are other gifts given to the Lamia." The Empress rolled forward onto her hands and knees again. She crawled towards him. "Gifts that can make men as malleable as clay."

Charles took an unsteady breath, trying to control his growing arousal. He wanted to grab her. He closed his eyes, forcing himself to ignore the scent of her and the strangely intoxicating perfume that exuded from her body. "If you did wish to change and become mortal again, could you?" he asked.

"No," she answered. "I will be like this till the day I bake in the sun, or lose my head."

Charles backed away from Irene again and shook her body out of his mind. He stared at the door, feeling a profound sadness grow. "Then my son is lost from me forever." A powerful urge to lock eyes with Irene overwhelmed him, and he obeyed.

"Which son?" Irene tipped her head to the side while boring into his soul. "Louis? Karl, Pepin? One of the others?"

"No!" Charles blurted, unable to resist telling the truth. "Julien!"

"Julien de Divio?" Irene's eyes twinkled.

He tried to resist confirming the answer, but her gaze wrenched it out of him. "Yes," he said in supplication.

"Oh," Irene murmured. She seemed to mull over his answer before responding. "So, because he is Deargh Du, you cannot think of him as your son?"

Her gentle question surprised him, and his sadness threatened to swallow him. As Charles continued to stare into her eyes, he felt his earlier distrust fade. He loved her, once. If circumstances had allowed it back then, she and he might have wed... might still be married now, perhaps with better children who could rule someday.

Would Julien still have been born? Would he have been my heir?

Charles felt encouraged to reveal his thoughts to the Empress. "I wished... he was to be my heir," he admitted. "My other sons are better suited for other careers than leadership."

Irene backed away and slid under the covers and blankets. Her features became demure. "Well, you cannot make him your heir now," she said. "He is Deargh Du, and children are not possible in our state. I'm so sorry, Charles."

Her tender sincerity astonished him.

"I'm also sorry for saying what I said about him earlier. I find the Deargh Du to be righteously annoying and sanctimonious at times," she admitted. "I lied about him. He and his family are most honorable." Irene shrugged a little. "He is still your son, Charles, and I'm certain that he still loves you as a father."

"I don't know if I can love him as a son," Charles whispered.

Irene moved to his side and embraced him.

"You still will love him," Irene whispered. "I cannot help but love my Constantine, even if he plotted my demise. You just don't understand fully enough to know who and what Julien is now. Granted he could not be your heir, but he's still your child."

The Emperor blinked back his tears. "Yes," he answered. The next time he saw his son, he'd tell him how he felt. A gentle hand slid through his hair. Her body felt chilled, yet her closeness became a renewed distraction. He could remember the last time they coupled, her giggles and moans were unforgettable. Then again, she wielded formidable skills in the bed. He found himself smiling and stared into her deep blue eyes.

"Would you like to-"

"Shhhh," Irene placed a finger over his lips. "I thought you'd never ask." She kissed him. Charles forgot all that plagued him as he pulled her closer.

Heloise sat up in bed and condemned her sleeplessness. She thought that perhaps joining the blood-drinkers again would be suitable entertainment. They were gathered at several tables in a feasting hall adjacent to Máire's room, playing dice and other games, as well as planning their upcoming battles.

She had spent most of her time engaged in watching Marcus and Claudius match wits in some game called Fidchell.

Yet, Reginald's actions drove her to distraction. She thought it best to drink wine and sleep. These guest quarters were pitch-black inside. However, she could not escape thinking over his deeds. She blinked away her angry tears. He did not deserve any emotion, other than rage.

Heloise touched the top of the small table near the bed. She felt the cold metal of the candlestick, but the wine cup hid from her reaching fingers.

"Damn it!" Heloise cursed. Her own child went to such lengths to seize control of Burgundy, without thinking about the pain his family endured. Then again, it was the doing of that treacherous, golden-hued, beautiful snake named Talia.

"It must have been that woman!" Heloise lunged for her drink, still frustrated at her lack of success in finding wine, as well as Reginald and Charles' stubbornness.

"Yes, it was."

Heloise looked around the chamber. She knew the door remained shut. The room had been empty upon her arrival. How did Julien manage that?

Perhaps his new abilities allowed such tricks.

She cleared her throat, hoping her surprise was not apparent.

"How did that woman ensnare him and make him betray us?" she asked. "We are his family!"

Julien leaned in. Light spread as he allowed himself to be surrounded in soft illumination. "The Lamia are masters at changing our perceptions," he murmured. "Máire says that Mandubratius manipulates her even now, and he has manipulated me as well. Once he mocked me for loving Máire, just to get a reaction from me."

Heloise fell silent, considering his words.

"In understanding what may have happened to Reginald, should we forgive him and welcome him back to the family?" Julien asked.

Heloise stared at Julien, as her rage rose. "What?" She hissed through her clenched teeth.

The illumination in the room, centering on Julien, intensified. He kneeled next to her bed, holding her wine cup. She snatched it from him and began drinking. Heloise did not want to hear him repeat his question.

"Mother, should we forgive Reginald?" Julien asked again. His eyes radiated a calming certitude.

Heloise slammed her empty cup on the table. Her emotions warred within. She could see her eldest drunk on his own powers, blinded with the thrill of harming his family and taking their property. Her earlier resolve to rein in her feelings faded away and she began to sob.

"I don't think I can!" She cried.

Her youngest sat down next to her and embraced her.

He began to shush her as if she were a weeping child or skittish horse. A gentle calm exuded through the room, and she found herself quieting. A strange magic made her nervous. The glamoury grated on her.

"Please don't use that to calm me, son," she bade Julien. "I can find my own peace without your help."

Julien sighed, and she felt the magic slip away.

Heloise wiped her face with the blanket. Perhaps the effort of crying calmed her. Julien pulled back and smiled.

"Mother, I'm sorry, but I don't think that Reginald could control his actions entirely."

"But he was weak to allow himself to be manipulated," Heloise answered then she pursed her lips in thought. Máire seemed to be the exact opposite of a typical Frankish woman. She and Julien shared the blood of a Goddess. Neither would be described as weak, despite moments of weakness. If a Lamia could affect a Deargh Du, then how could a mortal escape their tactics in exploitation?

Heloise met her son's eyes. Reginald's jealousy could have made him an easy target.

"You are right," she admitted. "Reginald is not entirely responsible for all that happened."

Julien clasped her hand. "So, we will offer him our forgiveness."

Heloise closed her eyes for a moment. "I can forgive him," she admitted. "However, I don't think I can look at him again so soon. After all that has happened, but yes, I forgive him." Heloise opened her eyes and squeezed Julien's hand.

"I will inform Reginald that his mother and brother forgive him, and I will try to find some duty for him. Perhaps that will make it possible for you to wish to see him. He can make you proud of him again." Her son paused and dropped her hand.

"Mother," he began. "Why didn't you tell me who my true father was?"

Heloise turned to face him. The room chilled and she pulled up the blankets around her. "Because the Emperor wished it," she answered.

"But, I wouldn't have told anyone," Julien asserted. "I kept your secrets about our ancient familial faith secret, did I not?"

"I know you would have kept this secret, Julien," Heloise replied. "But your attitude may have changed, and it would have given all away. People would have found out and they might have provoked you into telling the truth. You could have been killed, like Pepin. That would have broken my, and your father's, heart."

"I understand," Julien answered. "I forgive you for not telling me this truth about my true father." He took a deep breath and looked older. Heloise found herself growing sleepy. The light in the room dimmed as peace took its place.

She reclined in the bed and watched her son pull up the blankets around her. Her eyes closed as she felt a gentle kiss on her brow.

A voice sounding much like her father's echoed in the chamber. "Go to sleep, princess," Julien said. The door opened and closed.

Julien peeked through the doorway at the gathered blood-drinkers. Several appeared to be half-asleep. The others were watching a Fidchell match between Mac Alpin and Claudius. Fidchell being one of the few games an Ekimmu Cruitne could not exploit. He turned away, ignoring his wishes to join them and attempt to learn the strategies of that game.

He headed towards one of the palace exits. He sensed a sentry of guards posted in front of the exit.

He saluted the sentry.

"Inspector General," the ranking guard bowed his head. "How may we be of service?"

"I desire to speak to my brother," Julien stated. "Where might I find him?"

A guard stepped forth. "I aided in the removal of your brother. I can take you where you may find him."

Julien nodded and signaled the guard to lead him.

The guard walked around Julien, heading towards the rear of the palace.

Soon, they walked through the palace kitchens, past the cooks and butchers preparing the morning meal.

The guard motioned to a back door.

"Inspector General, when you wish to rejoin us. Knock three times."

The guard opened the door. Julien stepped out into the back grounds. A dark alley led to an outer gate and a silent guard saluted him and let him through.

"You will allow me through when I request it," Julien said to the guard.

The guard's gray countenance lifted for a moment as he nodded his head, before he grew serious again.

The gate closed behind Julien.

Julien found himself amongst the trash and rubbish of the palace. He sniffed the air and found the trail of a Lamia. A short distance away, a figure sat between the piles of rotting meat. Julien gagged at the stench.

His brother stared into the darkness, oblivious to Julien's presence. Reginald's arms encircled his knees and he seemed to be slowly moving back and forth.

Julien crouched down, feeling as though he were addressing a child again. His anger faded into pity. "Brother, I forgive you."

His brother did not seem to hear him.

Julien placed a hand on Reginald's shoulder. His brother stopped moving and turned to face him.

"That..." Reginald paused, "everyone warned me, and I didn't listen. She knew my secret thoughts and made things seem so plausible. I had control over myself, yet I could not." His brother blinked and then swiped at his eyes.

"I know," Julien admitted. "Their manipulation skills are extraordinary, Reginald." He sat down next to his brother and patted a shoulder.

He heard his elder brother begin to sob into his hands.

Julien leaned in and hugged him for a moment. The last time they'd embraced had been over two decades ago, when he'd had nightmares and mother had been at one of her grove's celebrations.

"I understand what happened, Reginald. I forgive you. The Lamia manipulate other races with ease, a mortal is no match for them."

"I'm not worthy of forgiveness," his brother hissed. "Because of me, our mother almost died. Talia wanted you dead as well. I'm going to wait for the sun. I shouldn't be alive."

"No, don't say that," Julien sighed. "It's not true, everyone has a purpose as a mortal and in these new lives of ours."

Reginald laughed. "Perhaps you have a purpose, Julien. I have nothing.

You always had a purpose, as a mortal gendarme and now as a Deargh Du," Reginald fell silent. "Yet, I do not fault the Emperor for turning my possessions to you, Lirienne, and our mother. After what I allowed to happen, it is only fitting."

"Reginald, I can give you purpose. Join my new family," Julien answered.

"You wish me to join your friends after what I did?" Reginald uttered a dry laugh. "I think you attempt to speak for them, when they probably wish nothing to do with another Lamia."

"If you prove yourself to be worthy, they will be happy to accept you," Julien answered. His brother seemed to calm down.

"It looks like you were right about my parentage," Julien said. "I am a bastard, the Emperor's bastard."

His brother tilted his head to one side. Reginald chuckled and shook his head. "That makes sense."

"It matters little," Julien added. "The Emperor wants nothing to do with me. He wishes me to leave the Empire once our duties are complete."

"Why not?" His brother looked confused. "Look at all you did, Julien."

"It is because I am Deargh Du, because I cannot father children, or be seen in the light of day. I have been exiled in effect. That is, I will be once our business with the Strigoi is done." Julien stared into the distance.

"And my sponsor manipulated and abandoned me," Reginald smirked. "You may only be my half-brother by birth, but we are full brothers in circumstance."

Julien nodded his head. "I think that you need the assistance of my new family. Join us."

"Your friends and you," Reginald murmured. "Much of what I know about you and your friends, family, whatever you call them now, came from Talia. I doubt she was truthful."

"We can learn together. There are several of us involved that have become blood-drinkers in the last few months." He smirked at Reginald. "Even the elders seem to find themselves lost in dealing with the Strigoi. They are the monstrous demons that have been attacking the two empires. The Empress Irene gave us a mirror that wields a strange power over the Strigoi. It allows them to witness their beauty, and they sometimes become this transformed being."

The overwhelming smell of rot faded a little. Julien stared at the horizon in the distance. The skies turned dark purple.

"You would join a party of many seeking knowledge, Reginald. Would you like to join us?"

"If they don't mind my presence, I will join you," Reginald said.

"Good."

"Has mother forgiven me?" Reginald attempted to rise from his seat amongst the trash.

"Yes," Julien admitted, "but her heart is broken over what happened. She needs time to recover." He stood and helped his brother to his feet. "Perhaps soon she will be prepared."

Reginald exhaled and gagged a little. "I stink, little brother. However, I think it's too late for a bath in the springs."

"Yes, it's too late now. We'll go inside. You can sleep, clean up at dusk, and meet my family," Julien said. He started to help Reginald towards the door.

"How can I get back into the palace?" Reginald asked. "The guards dragged me out."

"They will think seeing you enter the palace is nothing more than a dream," Julien answered. He neared the door and knocked three times. "The Empire always needs new gendarmes."

"I don't believe I deserve such a title," Reginald answered.

Julien chuckled. "It's yours, like it or not."

"I will earn the title then."

The door opened, and Julien stepped within the palace, pulling his brother in with him. He concentrated on enhancing his glamoury. The guards appeared to ignore his brother and merely closed the door behind them.

chapter two

áire stared at Lucius as he exhaled in sleep. The fairy cat had finally curled across her ankles in an attempt to keep her feet warm. She could hear noises down the hall. The rousing sounds of dice scattering across the table, as well as bets placed on a round of Fidchell. Of course, they had not even visited her with an invitation to play; Fidchell required concentration, and she had little of that to spare this morning. Sunrise was coming quickly. Then she'd be stuck in this bed for another eight to ten hours. Eight to ten hours without an embrace. Granted, she could only enjoy so much from an embrace. However, her bravado from her earlier battle faded, and even though she could protect herself, she wanted to feel defended.

"I'm all alone," Máire muttered.

She heard a soft rustle. Lucius looked up at her.

"I'm here with you," he uttered. He stood, stretched, and climbed on top of her left leg. Lucius reached her stomach and flopped down.

"I know. I didn't mean it to sound like that, Lucius. However, it would be nice to have company, especially a male visitor." Lovely, now she sounded desperate.

"I'm a male visitor," Lucius trilled. He twitched his tail about in an irritated fashion.

"Yes, very true." Máire stroked his brow. "Yet, sometimes a human male is very nice."

"What on earth for?" Lucius scoffed. "I'm furry, warm, and I purr! Amata and Lady Heloise say I'm adorable. What more do you need?"

Máire chuckled. "Seriously, do I need to explain matters of human intimacy to you?"

"Intimacy?" The cat smirked.

"Yes, intimacy. You know very well what I'm talking about."

The cat uttered a mirthful laugh. "Yes, but I love seeing Deargh Du become flustered."

"Behave, Lugh, or you'll find yourself outside my... the princess's door," Máire warned him.

"I'm a fairy cat, I don't behave," Lucius replied. He patted her mouth with a soft paw.

Máire smirked. "How can I ignore you when you're defiant?"

She began to rub his chin.

"It is a character flaw," the cat sighed and arched his chin towards the ceiling. "Yes, yes, scratch right there, sweet Máire."

The door opened. Máire jumped a bit, as talking to Lucius had distracted her from all other sensations.

She noticed Julien and a Lamia enter the room. Máire sat up in bed. She could tell this was not Horatio or Patroclus, and Amata exuded a graceful demeanor missing in this Lamia. Perhaps Julien had forgiven his brother. She decided that would be a good guess.

"Reginald and Julien." She smiled, hoping her surprise would not be too obvious. "It's nice to have visitors." She continued rubbing Lucius' chin. The scent of rotting food made her gag a little. She settled her gaze on Julien and smiled. He still looked beautiful, even with a few nights of scruffy beard growth. In fact, it suited him. She illuminated the room with glamoury and stared into Julien's sea-colored eyes.

Máire turned her eyes to his brother. She'd tolerate Reginald, simply because Julien wished for peace within his family. She wished that her own mortal family of the past could have experienced peace. Perhaps her own character flaw was that she would settle for discord instead of harmony. Besides, Reginald's earlier actions towards her and the others could not be forgotten.

Reginald took a few steps towards her, moving outside his brother's shadow.

"I have no excuse for my actions and words toward you before I was sponsored," he began.

Máire studied him, seeking genuineness and honesty in his features. After all, he could be attempting to peruse her thoughts, or manipulate her. Only one Lamia ever successfully entered her mind during her dreams. Surely Reginald lacked the skills of his grand-sponsor. His eyes seemed to reflect nothing but candor, and a little fear.

"I also appreciate your suggestion to Julien, about an opportunity for my redemption," Reginald continued.

Máire glanced at Julien, for a moment, and then settled her eyes back on his brother. "I must admit that was not my idea, Reginald." She worried that the others might not accept an apology as easily as Julien might. "I'm pleased that Julien offered you a new path. I'm just not so certain that it will be easy."

She noticed Lucius sniff the air and twitch his nose at the smells exuding from the brothers.

Reginald nodded. "I know it will not be easy. Yet, I feel indebted to you and Julien." He moved in closer and kneeled on both knees.

"I vow to God… and your deity as well, to serve you both to the best of my abilities." His face expressed a keen determination.

Máire pulled up a leg, in the hopes of not disturbing Lucius, but she found herself in an uncomfortable position and nudged the fairy cat. She rose from the bed and walked over to Reginald, helping him to his feet.

"I accept your vow and welcome you to my family," Máire said. She realized afterwards that this should have been left to Marcus, but she could not deny Julien's need. Leaning in, she kissed Reginald's cheek.

She found herself surrounded when Julien embraced her. A kiss touched her brow and she heard him whisper into her ear, "Thank you."

One unpleasant smelling man was tolerable, but two sent her senses reeling. Máire pushed both of them back and covered her mouth. The two brothers stared at her with confused expressions.

"You two reek of rotting meat and fruit!" she hissed. "Go to the hot springs, bathe, and burn your clothing!"

Julien gave her a sheepish half-grin. "It's almost sunrise, and I'm afraid mother doesn't want to see Reginald this morning. I'm sure, things will improve with nightfall."

Máire sat on the bed and tried to wipe away the stinky smells from her léine.

"Sorry." Reginald reddened. "I was thrown out after your magnificent battle with Talia. I wandered towards the pit."

Máire blinked for a minute. "Now I stink as well, we'll all need a bath tomorrow night," she chuckled. "I suppose you two wished my protection and a chance to share this large bed."

"What!" Lucius sat up and stared at them. "The bed isn't that big!"

"Yes, it is, we'll all fit, Lugh. Besides, I can't turn out my family."

"But, they smell of disgusting rot, no matter how entertaining disgusting smells are," Lucius grumbled. "First, Julien serves me cold food, and now he expects me to share my bed?"

"There's a wash bin with clean water and some oils," Julien suggested. "We can all wash up, Lucius."

Máire watched the cat close his eyes in thought while waving his tail from side to side. She glanced to her left and noticed Reginald's bewildered stare.

"Who are you talking to?"

"Lucius," Máire answered, extending a hand towards the cat.

"Yes, that is apparent, but is he talking back?"

Julien coughed. "Yes, sorry Reginald. There are many strange things in our world, besides us. Lugh, or Lucius, is a fairy cat. A few races of the blood-drinkers can communicate with Otherworldly beings. Apparently, the Lamia cannot."

Reginald stepped over to the bed and knelt again to study Lucius and stretched out a cautious hand.

"I feel a little silly, but this is probably necessary. Lucius, may Julien and I share your bed? We need Máire's protection."

"Really, that means my protection," Lucius clarified. "Tonight, I am her champion, and she is under my protection."

Julien grinned. "Lucius says that he is Máire's champion and protector tonight, therefore we will be under his protection as well."

Lucius stretched his nose out to sniff Reginald's hand.

"Oh, stinky," Lucius said, "but he's harmless. Please tell Reginald that he may share my bed, and Julien as well, but the blankets are mine, and I may lie on whomever I wish."

"He says we can share," Máire patted Reginald's shoulder and helped him back up.

"Now, I insist on all of us cleaning." She looked for her supplies bag. Máire picked it up and began to empty it out. "I have a few clean léines. You may touch them and wear them, after washing." She chuckled and wandered over to the wash bowl. Julien followed her.

"Léine?" Reginald looked confused.

"It's a long tunic," Julien explained. He started tossing off his clothes.

"I highly suggest we burn these garments," Máire added. She threw aside her léine and began to wash herself. She noticed Reginald look a little sheepish again.

"Sorry," Máire shrugged. "I live with a pack of men who are not modest about nudity. Think of it as practicality, not impropriety, Reginald." She motioned him over, turning to splash some water on Julien's back. She smiled at the memories of their first time near the stream.

Reginald gave a nervous laugh. "I'll do my best." He undressed and began to clean himself.

Máire kicked their clothing out the door and grabbed a linen léine. "Are we acceptable now?" she asked Lucius.

The cat opened his eyes and murmured in assent.

She tossed the léines over to the brothers and climbed into bed. Lucius grunted and moved in between her feet.

Julien and Reginald lay down on her opposite sides. Julien nuzzled her neck and moved in closer as if to smell her hair.

Reginald seemed afraid to be too close.

"I understand you're worried about touching me, but I won't chastise you," Máire turned her eyes to Reginald. "You'll relax when you fall asleep, it will happen." She patted his arm.

She noticed a small smile on his face.

"You are not the monster that your aunt told me you were," Reginald said. "Thank you and sleep well."

"You three as well," Máire answered, hoping sleep would claim her soon.

Reginald could remember bits and fragments of stories that involved a personification of hope. However, his hope presented itself as a beacon of light, a promise of purpose and possible respect.

He inhaled as they approached the room. He could sense a large number of blood-drinkers. A moment of fear overwhelmed him. His brother and Máire had offered forgiveness, yet these blood-drinkers could be different.

His brother walked through the door first. Máire's hand patted his back, and they marched into the feasting hall together. The smell of wine and blood clung to the room. Reginald tried to ignore his hunger. The speech died away and angry stares met his eyes. Reginald scanned the room for his mother.

Mac Alpin shouted something guttural, shaking a fist at Reginald then switched to grumbled Latin.

"What is he doing here, youngling?" He addressed Julien. "His sponsor tried to kill your mother-in-darkness. Remember?" The blood-drinker's eyes settled on Máire.

"Banbh Ceanúil, explain this," Marcus said, sounding calm and rational, yet there was something in those strange eyes that brought forth fear in Reginald. Mac Alpin could be noisy and rude, yet he had the feeling that Marcus might be far more deadly.

"He's manipulated you both," another blood-drinker accused.

Reginald gulped. He was expecting rage from the other blood-drinkers. They would be suspicious. He hoped his fear and their mistrust would fade soon.

He heard Máire inhale a breath to begin speaking.

Julien held up a hand. "May I speak, please?" He turned back to Máire. She nodded her head, a plait swinging back and forth.

Julien turned his stare on the others.

"My brother is here to tell you something important. I think you should all give him an opportunity to speak," he stated.

"Nothing that one utters would please my ears," Horatio stated. "His grand-sponsor is the father of all mistruths and misdeeds!" Horatio reddened and looked over in the direction of Amata. "Sorry," he murmured.

Amata smirked. "Do you hear me denying your claims, Horatio?"

"I think that title is a bit grand for a third-rate chieftain who killed his way into a consulship," Claudius stated. He, Horatio, and a few of the others laughed.

"You will listen, all of you." Julien's eyes burned with a determined gleam. The laughter in the hall died as the room faded into a strained silence. The other blood-drinkers stared at his brother for a moment. A slow half-smile passed across Marcus' features.

Reginald watched the elder give Julien a slight nod of the head. The other blood-drinkers relaxed. Máire gave him a wary smile. She sat down next to Patroclus.

Julien cleared his throat. "Brother, I believe you have leave to speak now."

Reginald felt their eyes seize him. He pushed aside his apprehension and bit his lip, trying to find the best words and then gave up.

"I followed Talia because of weakness," Reginald began. "I committed horrible wrongs against my family. I even conspired with Talia to kill the woman who gave me life."

Hearing his own confession of this misdeed made his eyes burn. Reginald continued eye contact with the others.

"I have no excuse for my actions before my sponsorship or afterwards. I beg for absolution and acceptance. Please allow me to join this gathering. I can help. I feel it is my only opportunity to redeem myself." He concluded, hearing quiet mumbles of that guttural language again.

"Have you asked Lady Heloise for forgiveness?" Claudius asked, resting his chin against the palm of his hand.

"What of the wounded Deargh Du and Sáerlaith?" Mac Alpin queried.

"How can we trust you?" Edward inquired.

"You believe yourself to be worthy to join us?" another asked.

Reginald inhaled, prepared to answer the first question, when he sensed the heartbeat and gentle scent of a mortal and turned to find his mother staring at him from the doorway.

He ducked his eyes to the floor, wishing to fade into a mist. He sensed his mother move in closer. A gentle hand touched his arm and wrapped around him.

Reginald met her eyes, still fearful of what she would say. The silence in the room seemed deafening and all-consuming.

"I forgive you," his mother said. "It is hard for me to see you now and remain angry with you." She turned to the others. "I asked the Lamia here about their talents, and what I have learned has surprised and shocked me. I hope you will allow Reginald to earn your trust and respect, and perhaps clemency."

He leaned in and kissed her cheek.

"However, it will take some time for me to fully trust you again," his

---

mother stated.

Reginald nodded his head and noticed the other blood-drinkers looking amongst themselves.

Marcus stood after a few moments of shared glances between himself and the others.

"We grant you our protection in exchange for your service," Marcus stated. "Julien, he is your responsibility."

"He's my gendarme, I will keep an eye on him," Julien answered.

Marcus ambled towards them. "Do you have any traveling gear?"

"No, these are not even my clothes," Reginald admitted. "Thank you for allowing me to join."

"We've given you no favors," the Deargh Du stated. "You will earn your keep and you may not like the experience. You may regret this decision."

Reginald met Julien's eyes. "I go where my little brother goes. I deserve no favors."

Marcus said nothing for a moment. "We were about to begin packing again. However, I think it's time we discuss what our next steps against the Strigoi should be."

Reginald felt his mother lead him toward the tables and sit him down in between Máire and Patroclus. She began to pace the room.

Amata cleared her throat. "Well, we do have the mirror." She drummed her fingers for a moment. "Where is its mistress?"

"She's probably still asleep." Claudius propped his feet up on the bench. "But I don't think she'll have any secrets to tell about the mirror's use."

"Doubtless she knows little of the magical properties of the mirror," Edward added. "The problem with the mirror is that the field of healing reflection produced is so narrow. Am I correct?" Edward looked over at Julien and then regarded Máire.

"Yes, it is useful, but it does not seem to be effective in large-scale battles," Máire answered.

"Not to mention, the wielder of the mirror is exposed to attacks," Julien stated.

"Yes. I have found that the Strigoi's attacks increase in strength with every battle," Patroclus murmured. "Their mental attack is more precise and debilitating, now."

"And the symptoms are still hallucinations, visions, smells, and auditory experiences?" Heloise stopped pacing for a moment.

"Correct," replied Marcus. "Yet, I know the attacks last longer, and the dreams and visions are disturbing."

There were grunts of assent around the table. Reginald felt relieved that he'd never experienced such horrors.

"Excuse me. I think I have something that may aid you all," his mother said. "I'll return with it." She left the room.

"Máire, weren't you supposed to still pretend to be sick?" another blood-drinker asked.

"I had a miraculous recovery." Máire smirked.

"I'm hungry," Amata said. "Let's meet back in an hour. It will give Lady Heloise time to find this treasure." She looked over at Marcus.

The Deargh Du shut his eyes for a moment. "That sounds good. An hour for feeding." He frowned as he turned away and left the room. Lucius trotted after him.

"Máire, what is wrong with your father-in-darkness?" Amata asked in lowered tones.

"I think he suffers from the Strigoi attacks." Máire shrugged.

"He never seems to pass out from the attacks," Patroclus stated.

"So, that means he does not have the luxury of recovering from the attacks," Máire answered. "He will be well once these trying times pass." She rose from the seat. "Then things will be back to normal."

Reginald watched the other Deargh Du leave the table.

"The mortal General always acted in this manner before battles." Claudius shrugged in a nonchalant fashion. He left the table to follow Máire.

Julien stood up and patted Reginald's shoulder. "We should feed now, before the hour has passed."

Julien and Reginald returned to the feasting hall. Their mother paced around the room again.

"Sorry, we all were hungry," Julien told her, noticing the scroll case that swung back and forth with each of her steps. "Are those the Druidic scrolls?"

"Yes, they are."

"I thought you burned them," Reginald said.

Their mother laughed. "I burned scrolls that were nothing but gibberish."

He sensed others gather around her again. He heard Marcus cross the threshold. Máire and Claudius followed. They both looked pale, while Marcus seemed in better spirits. He walked around the main table and leaned forward onto his fists.

"So, Lady Heloise, I gather these are useful tools that we can wield?" Marcus asked.

"Yes, these are ancient scrolls of magics. I'm not exactly clear on these magics. Sáerlaith suggested the well-traveled Deargh Du may be able to read them." She looked over at Marcus and extended the case towards him.

A growing uncertainty surrounded Marcus, as the elder Deargh Du studied the case for a moment.

"Máire," Marcus said, pulling away from the case. "You are the one Deargh Du present with the most Druidic training. She has traveled as much as I have, and she knows more about these matters. Go on and take it, chroí."

Julien watched his mother-in-darkness beam. She snatched the scroll as a child might grasp at a treasured gift. Máire sat down, already impatient with the case. She pulled out the scrolls.

Máire began to mutter, and Julien had the feeling Máire might be talking to herself. "These pre-date the majority of the materials I've read at the stronghold in Ard Mhacha." She continued reading.

His mother sat across from her. "Yes, these are older than most ancient works."

Máire dropped the scrolls and turned away, covering her mouth. She uttered a strange squeak.

Marcus placed his hands on her shoulders and leaned in.

She rose with a leap and wrapped her hands around his arms and began speaking in Gaelic.

Shock registered on Marcus' face. He sat down, as did several Deargh Du.

"Well, what is it?" Lady Heloise asked.

"Máire says that these are the original copies of Adhamh's personal papers," Marcus said.

"They contain knowledge that the library in Ard Mhacha refers to, but our Arch Druid could never find. Ruarí thought that it might have been stolen back to the Otherworld as punishment for various misbalances," Máire added, as if annoyed with questions and talking. She returned to reading the scrolls.

"And yet, they've been here in Francia," Fianait answered. She swallowed and then inhaled. "Our progenitor knew we would be here."

"Time in the Otherworld passes differently," Julien added. He wondered why that sounded so familiar, and why he felt the incessant need to say it out loud. The other Deargh Du nodded their heads. He noticed Máire seemed to be bouncing in her seat.

"My family tells a tale that they found this knowledge in Éire." Julien watched his mother stand as she spoke. "We started copying the scrolls and hiding them out of fear that some over-zealous Christian would find them and destroy the knowledge. My father said that what happened in Alexandria could happen anywhere and that these scrolls were to be protected, as they were the eldest of any of them, perhaps even the originals. Druids took these scrolls and copied them. They passed these copies to chieftains and their students, so the future generations could have access to the knowledge. There are some new notes on these original materials behind the first set, in Latin and Greek." She straightened her back.

"And how does this ancient knowledge help us?" Claudius asked.

Máire made a hushing sound and held up a hand, saying, "This scroll contains information in another that Edward found in Bath. Edward, it was that clumsy stranger who bumped into you after we bought those scrolls, before Patroclus and Amata arrived." Máire's voice increased in pitch and speed.

Everyone turned to study Edward. He and Amata had been sitting next to each other in silence. The blonde Ekimmu Cruitne nodded his head.

"This contains the complete story of Iris, the creation of the Strigoi, and Aphrodite's mirror." Máire looked up from the scroll. "This has something about a substance that may lessen the symptoms from the Strigoi's attacks. It includes certain plants and mushrooms."

"Yes, I'm certain all present know that plants and mushrooms can create disturbances in what one sees, hears, smells, and tastes." His mother looked around the room. "Too much would be poisonous, however small quantities would merely create these sensations."

Máire rose again and took off a small bag from her belt. "Heloise," she tossed the bag towards his mother. "What do you make of this powder? I thought mushrooms and other herbs, but you are an expert."

His mother opened the small bag and took a pinch of the substance. She rubbed it between a finger and her right thumb and smelled it. She dabbed her fingertip on her tongue and immediately spat it out.

"This is mostly redcap mushrooms, Psilocybe," Heloise said.

"If someone is taking redcaps," Amata began, "They will experience these sensations, as Heloise said. Perhaps if someone takes this mixture, the Strigoi's mental attack will be useless."

"Yes, the mind is already under the effects of the substance," Máire said. "Or at least that is what I remember from my training."

"Máire found that substance in that cave in the Eastern Empire," Marcus added.

"Someone must be living amongst the Strigoi. This substance will offer protection from the madness." Julien's mother closed up the pouch.

"Ladies, do you believe that this powder could protect the blood-drinkers, as well as the mortals?" Edward turned a blue-eyed stare to Julien's mother.

"I don't know how becoming what you are changed how you react to herbs and plants," she answered. "I would wager that you all would need a stronger dosage than what a mortal would take. Your dosage would be dangerous to a mortal." His mother paused mid-thought as a rather pleased Empress wandered into the hall.

Heloise cleared her throat. "Perhaps a small dose would allow a mortal to survive the Strigoi's attack."

"From what you three have said thus far, we must find some of these mushrooms, at least enough for a test. Then perhaps more," Claudius said.

"My, everyone is so animated. So vocal," the Empress intoned.

The other blood-drinkers, excepting his mother-in-darkness, stared at her.

"Fear not, I'll be silent and learn what has transpired later," the Empress twittered with a seductive smile.

She took a seat at the table between Marcus and Máire after nudging Máire to the side. Máire seemed lost in the scrolls, but pulled them away from Empress Irene. The Eastern Empress leaned over Máire's shoulder, trying to read the scrolls as well. Her Imperial Majesty appeared to be distracted from the ensuing conversation.

"These mushrooms are common, but we must get enough to give to the imperial army, the papal army, and to us. It will require the diligence of all to gather the mushrooms and prepare them," his mother stated.

"How do we convince the Emperor and Pope to give their soldiers this medicine?" Julien asked.

"As far as the Emperor is concerned, if you give a convincing argument, he will encourage the troops to consume the mushrooms. As for His Holiness..." His mother closed her eyes mid-thought.

"I am sure we can rely on Mandubratius to manipulate His Holiness into consuming it," Marcus chuckled.

Julien noticed the Empress's brows rise for a moment. Then her face grew calm.

Mac Alpin laughed. "This should be an interesting project. Warriors picking mushrooms?" His demeanor turned solemn. "This will be a massive undertaking. Where should we dry and grind the mushrooms after collecting them?"

"Prüm Abbey," Edward answered. "Besides, we must return for Sáerlaith and the others. They will have recovered by our arrival."

"Alright," Marcus moved away from the table. He gathered the remainder of his belongings and set them on top of his traveling bag. "Fianait, tell the rest of the forces outside Aachen to meet us at the abbey. Arwin, send a small party for Caoimhín and the others in Vézelay. I know most of our forces know little about mushroom gathering and we will need their guidance in selection. We still have half the night left, and we should make the most of our time."

The men and women stood and began their duties. Only Máire and the

Empress remained seated.

Máire rolled the scrolls and returned them to their case. She held the case out for Heloise.

"No." His mother gently pushed back the case. "Sáerlaith asked me to give them to you. She felt you would make the most use of them."

Máire appeared stunned at that statement. "Thank you so much." She blinked away tears.

"Banbh Ceanúil, I have a special duty for you," Marcus took Máire's arm. They walked away.

"So, are you prepared and packed?" His mother slid an arm around him.

"I just need to retrieve my sword," he answered. "I shall return." Julien left the feasting hall, hoping he would not find the room he slept in occupied.

A hand touched his shoulder as he marched toward the room. He found himself face to face with the Emperor. Now he could smell the scent of blood and hear the pace of a heartbeat.

His father held out Julien's sword.

"Thank you, Imperial Majesty," Julien said, trying to remain calm.

"Inspector General, a word if you will."

"Yes, Imperial Majesty."

The Emperor led him towards a column. Julien felt a moment of grave concern overwhelm him. What would his father say? Emperor Charles' expression remained unreadable.

"I thought about what I said to you earlier." Emperor Charles' staid visage seemed to fade and become the face of a father.

Julien decided to allow him to speak.

"I wish to rescind my earlier orders that you leave these lands when you're done with your service. I think I… I was rash in ordering your exile."

Julien remained silent, watching the Emperor struggle with his thoughts and words.

"I am convinced that what you are is not demonic or evil," his father concluded.

"I am the same that I have always been," Julien stated.

Emperor Charles nodded his head, forgetting to chastise him for the interruption. "Yes, you are still my son."

"Thank you, father."

The Emperor paled for a moment. "For now, please do not address me in that manner."

Julien tried to remain tranquil. What could be wrong with acknowledging him? He knew the Emperor acknowledged many of his 'natural' children.

He must have made a disgruntled noise. His father shushed him.

"I need time to think through what our public relationship will be, Julien. Come speak to me when you return from your duties, Inspector General." The Emperor's voice became louder and officious.

"Yes, Imperial Majesty. I shall report back to you upon my return."

Julien took the sheathed sword from his father and turned away, returning to the feasting hall.

As he left, he could hear the Emperor whisper.

"Go forth and make me proud, my son."

"I shall indeed, father," Julien whispered as he neared the vociferous party within the room, as their final packing preparations continued.

Prüm Abbey

Horatio closed his eyes as the Druids, Priests and Priestesses, whatever they called themselves, continued blathering on about these mushrooms. He attempted to keep himself from yawning. Horatio's eyes snapped open, and he nearly jumped, as the large black cat wound its way around his legs.

The cat known as Lucius stared at him with utter disdain for a moment, then turned, wandering towards Claudius.

Horatio turned back towards the speakers. What was it about this sort of gathering that made him feel tired? Perhaps it was the soothing monotone voices of the Druids. Priests always sounded that way as well, when they weren't talking about damnation and hell. Suddenly, everyone fell silent. The two Druids turned towards the shadows.

Marcus trudged out of the darkness, a strange martial gleam in his eyes. He cleared his throat and paced across the corner of the room.

"We have scant hours of the night left, so I'll be brief," the Deargh Du scanned the room. "The head of the Deargh Du council requests more time to rest. I shall assume temporary leadership over the Deargh Du line, as well as our brave friends and allies, until tomorrow night. There must be a chain of command for these duties, but fear not, I'll be stuck in the forests harvesting mushrooms with the rest of you. It will give all the lines a chance to decide who they wish to report to." Marcus paused and rubbed his hands together, staring at the crowd with silvered eyes. "I led an army of the Celtic lines once before. I believe a majority here were in that army."

Horatio watched heads nod in assent. He believed that there would be some sort of fight over leadership. However, perhaps this group of warriors worried so much over the Strigoi that they believed disagreement and squabbling to be a waste of time.

"My friends, thank you." Marcus stopped his pacing. "We Deargh Du lost our home, but at this moment we cannot change that fact. We've been offered a new home here in the empire. Sugnwr Gwaed and Ekimmu Cruitne still have their homes in the north. The Lamia have their homes in the south and east, yet if we do not take care of the Strigoi soon, their homes will disappear too. Our lands and our people are threatened by an enemy only some of us have faced. This enemy is quite formidable. They number in the thousands. These Strigoi attack us viciously without warning, using their madness as a weapon. In the past, this weapon was uncontrollable. Most mortals died from these attacks, and we suffered as well, immobilized during our fearful hallucinations. We were easy prey for the Strigoi."

Marcus studied the faces before him. His eyes settled on Horatio's for a moment.

"Someone has taught the Strigoi new skills," the Deargh Du stated. "They know how to stun mortals, so they can transform them into more Strigoi. We have witnessed them increasing their numbers."

Marcus began to pace again. "I am certain many of you know that my associates and I went to Constantinople to acquire a device. We have used this device to change the Strigoi into something else. Through this device, they become another kind of blood drinker, which was previously unknown to us. Perhaps they are now Aphrodite's Blessed." He smiled.

"You may find them amongst our party. Do not fear them. They travel with us now as our friends and have expressed a desire to help us change as many Strigoi as possible.

"However, this device, this magical mirror, is limited. It can only lift the curse from a few Strigoi at a time. The transformed Strigoi realize these limitations, and they know that this may keep us from changing the Strigoi in great numbers. Yet, that matters little now. The Strigoi are massing in number and we must face them in pitch battle. This will not be an easy task, for they will outnumber us. If they immobilize us, we cannot stand against them."

Mumbles echoed through the corridors of the lower levels of the abbey.

"Yet, we believe we've found a way to negate the effects of their madness, at least enough so we can fight them."

Marcus pulled out a small bag from his belt and poured a dark substance in his hand. "Can all of you smell this?"

Horatio strained his neck and sniffed in the direction of the substance. He watched the other blood-drinkers sniff the air and nod at each other, all except the transformed Strigoi. Perhaps they lacked the olfactory skills of the Celtic lines.

"These are redcap mushrooms. They grow in the forest." Marcus glanced at the room. "Well, we've all seen them. They're very common. We need to gather as much of these mushrooms as possible by the end of tomorrow night. Then we must dry these mushrooms in the sun for a day. After that, they will be ground, and we will drink it in a broth."

Someone Horatio did not recognize raised his hand.

"Maon?" Marcus nodded towards the other blood-drinker.

"What are the effects of this mushroom on immortals?" Maon asked.

"I figured we should all witness that first-hand," Marcus said. "I ask that everyone form a circle around me. An hour ago, I requested two volunteers to test this substance, so we could see if their fighting abilities are restricted by the mushrooms."

Horatio felt Mac Alpin pat his back. "I'm itching for a battle. Don't look so worried, lad. This promises to be fun!" The elder laughed and charged into the circle. Other blood-drinkers joined in the laughter. A burly warrior came forth from the crowd.

"Well done," Marcus grinned. "Now, remove all your weaponry and armor."

Horatio heard huffing protests from the two blood-drinkers as they relinquished their swords, knives, and armor to others.

"Honestly, you two whine worse than some mortals," Marcus stated. "Now, are either of you experiencing any of the affects that Máire explained when she dispensed the mushrooms?"

"Other than my usual annoyance with your constant jabbering, Marcus, I feel like a thousand sou," Mac Alpin answered.

"Tiarnán?" Marcus looked over at the other Deargh Du.

"I agree with Mac Alpin; your voice grates on my nerves. Let's get on with this." The Deargh Du rubbed his forehead. "Yet, something is strange. The room is becoming bright, as though Lugh brings the dawn early to warm the dead here."

Mac Alpin scratched his beard at the statement. "I see no sun. Yet, I do hear the strangest song in my head."

Whispers grew. The others studied the two blood-drinkers. Claudius seemed a bit bemused with the conversation.

"Can the two of you fight?" Marcus queried.

Both warriors turned towards him. They nodded silently and returned to staring at each other.

"Then fight," Marcus said. He backed away, motioning for the other gathered blood-drinkers to give Mac Alpin and Tiarnán room.

Horatio watched the two blood-drinkers shrug and hold up their fists.

The opponents swung at each other. Their eyes gleamed with the pleasure of a fight, yet something seemed to hold them back.

He noticed Marcus motion to the Greek priest to join them. There were a few whispers as the rather tedious fight continued.

Suddenly, the fight seemed charged. Tiarnán growled and kicked Arwin in the stomach.

The elder's face grew red with rage. Arwin staggered towards Tiarnán and threw a punch. Tiarnán shook off the blow and concentrated on his opponent for a moment, before successfully pushing him towards the outside ring of blood-drinkers.

Will either of them manage to stand upright? How could they fight without some balance?

The warriors lurched in each other's direction.

Mac Alpin threw another punch, hitting Tiarnán's chin. The Deargh Du wobbled and appeared stunned at the attack. Tiarnán grabbed Arwin's shoulder and punched him in the stomach.

"Alright, stop! That's enough!" Horatio heard Marcus bellow in Latin, then in what he assumed to be Gaelic. Neither Tiarnán nor Mac Alpin appeared to hear him.

The gathered lines began pulling the two fighting blood-drinkers apart and restrained them.

Marcus stepped into the center of the room. "Alright, before this became a true battle, I asked Father Xofer to try to interfere with them, to create insanity within them. As you witnessed, their focus on the battle increased. Maon, does this answer your question about the effects of redcaps on blood-drinkers?"

"How would these mushrooms affect a mortal?" Fianait asked.

Marcus turned towards Máire.

"In smaller doses, the effects will be the same," she answered. "However, a mortal will die if they took the dosage I gave to Arwin and Tiarnán."

"I believe that this may give us a small opportunity to battle the Strigoi. We need to gather as many of these redcaps as we can. I will dispatch a small group to gather mortals to aid us in grinding these mushrooms during the day. We shall sleep in the catacombs. Feed carefully on the neighbors, they need their strength. Are there any other questions?"

The Roman Deargh Du scanned the silent, chilled room. "Then let us begin."

The blood-drinkers moved towards the exits.

Marcus motioned Horatio and Amata towards him. "Please watch Arwin," he said, passing the elder Ekimmu Cruitne's arm to them.

Arwin turned to face Horatio. "Edwina, when did you become so short?" Mac Alpin roared.

chapter three

Outside Prüm Abbey

Julien crouched next to an expanding elm and closely examined the ring of mushrooms. He inhaled, trying to judge the smell of the ones available.

"Can I ask again how you can tell that these mushrooms are the right ones?" he asked.

"Well, you could just pick them all and let Máire or your mother sort through them," Marcus called out, hearing his mumbles. The elder Deargh Du leaned in to sniff at the grouping of mushrooms.

"These are right," Marcus pulled a few from the ground. "Those are not as mature." He grabbed the cloth sack hanging from Julien's right shoulder and dropped in the choice mushrooms. "You will learn to do this sooner or later." He shrugged. "Like most of the Deargh Du here, you were not trained in selection of plants, herbs, and mushrooms."

A sleepy-eyed Lucius stared at Julien from his perch on Marcus' shoulders. The cat stretched out his legs for a moment. Dark claws began to knead on the Deargh Du's muscle.

"Lucius, must you show affection by clawing me?"

"This is not affection," Lucius answered. "You have an undesirable odor this evening and I'm trying to keep that stink of mushrooms away."

"Then go use Julien as a resting perch. He's picked fewer mushrooms," Marcus smirked.

Julien yawned and pulled out of his cramped position. Lucius leaned closer. His nose and whiskers twitched for a moment.

"He exhibits the same unpleasant odor as you. Besides, your shoulders are warm and comfortable. Not to mention that you provide me a high perch from which to reign."

The fairy cat smiled his mysterious grin.

"I'm not smelly, Lugh," Julien raised his hands towards his nose to double check. "Alright, so I do stink a bit."

"Are you chieftain or king now, Lucius, or perhaps you are emperor of all you survey," Marcus asked the cat.

"I'm no mere emperor, subject."

"You are more than an emperor indeed," Marcus added.

Lucius proceeded to purr and closed his eyes.

Julien listened for more of a conversation. Silence grew. He gathered the last of the mushrooms in front of him and dusted off his hands.

"Have you noticed a change in Máire?" he asked. "She spends all her free time reading those scrolls."

"Mmmmm," Marcus murmured. "I suppose she seems more exuberant since those scrolls appeared. She's always enjoyed the process of learning new things. Usually she displays the emotional attitude of a dead fish. However, when there is war of one sort or another, or learning involved, she finds some passion. Yes, most of the time, she is like a dead fish." He grew silent and frowned.

Julien smirked a bit and uttered a mirthless laugh. "Dead fish, yes."

The other Deargh Du set down his bag of mushrooms and frowned at him as if any laughter could be inappropriate.

"She believes herself cursed, and I've witnessed her depression firsthand for over two hundred years." Marcus turned away and stared at the vast forest. "I'd do anything to allow her to feel happy emotions again. That is primarily why we gave her the quests and missions before the Strigoi threat. It was not so much to gamble on her talents, but to give her something to learn. It would anger her, but we witnessed passion then."

"There is a visible spark now," Julien said. "This upcoming battle with the Strigoi and the scrolls, they can make her forget the curse. Maybe then she would realize that she allowed the curse to fester and it is time to continue... across the bridge instead of staring at the river."

Marcus turned back to regard him. "Yes," he answered. "That was a very good allegory." He grinned. "We should encourage this. The more sparks that ignite, the greater chance there is in rekindling the fire."

"What encouragement should we give her?"

Lucius heaved a sigh. "You two are utterly brainless sometimes. Show an interest in the scrolls and encourage the translation, Marcus." He turned his sleepy-eyed stare to Julien. "And you, ask her questions about the ancient works of the Druids. Her passions lie in the pursuit of knowledge. When she learns these tools, she will understand that she can step away from the curse. I am one who believes that curses are two-fold. He or she who is cursed must accept the curse and allow that curse to continue affecting them. When Máire can control a skill, she may realize that she is able to love and feel love. Then she will accept that the curse is not strong itself. She made it strong."

The fairy cat hopped off his perch and settled on soft grass. He stretched his legs and curled himself up to sleep.

"I hate it when cats do actually know it all," Marcus said. "He makes it sound so easy."

"It is easy, it is just in the nature of Deargh Du to believe things to be difficult," the cat said. "Now, shut up and get back to work."

"I believe there are more mushrooms down the path to the east," Julien said. He mused over Lucius' suggestions. Máire admitting love for him without a persistent denial afterwards or excuses detailing that she cared for him because he was her son-in-darkness would be truly extraordinary.

Lamia Camp outside Mehren

Mandubratius looked across the tent and sighed. "Gaius, are you asleep? I am mulling over our activities in the last few nights. While I am pleased at the progress of our newly sponsored younglings, I cannot sleep."

"You mean their feeding exploits this past night?"

Mandubratius pushed back the blankets. "Who would have believed that just those three mere babes could drain a horse?"

"Indeed," Gaius chuckled. "I wish we could see the owner's face. His prized stallion dead of an unknown wound, when all that his guards witnessed were strange nocturnal squirrels."

Mandubratius smirked. "They must have been very hungry squirrels."

"They had huge teeth, I'm told," Gaius chuckled.

Mandubratius chuckled. "Stop making me laugh. It keeps me awake. Do you ever wonder if we take advantage of our gifts too much?"

"Don't tell me you've taken up that whole balance ideal like the Deargh Du speak of, Mandubratius. Mars, no! I've never considered such an idea."

Mandubratius rolled onto his back. The cot creaked, and he longed again for a comfortable bed and cushions. "I suppose I am being a bit sentimental. Perhaps, I long for a soft bed and gentle feminine embrace. Missing such things makes me think inane thoughts." He closed his eyes for a moment. "You've traveled from Constantinople to Vézelay with the Empress. Did you enjoy the journey, or find her to be pleasing company?" Mandubratius asked, rolling his head to stare at Gaius' cot on the other side of the tent.

Gaius coughed into his hand. "I found her coupling demands to be tedious, repetitive, and unfulfilling. She was interested only in her own self-gratification at my expense. She took my right hand once when I made the mistake of climaxing before she did." The general smiled. "It was made more annoying when she would call out for you. In order to even the score during my performances, I would call for Amata or the lovely Fianait, that golden-haired Deargh Du. That infuriated Her Imperial Majesty to no end."

Mandubratius laughed. "Gaius, you lead a challenging existence fraught with peril."

"Frankly, I must ask how you stand copulating with her," Gaius said. "The Empress, I mean. Not that glorious blonde or Amata."

"Through most of the journey, I had little choice," Mandubratius replied.

"But, how could you stand to have such torture? I mean, that bitch removed your manhood, Mandubratius."

Mandubratius stared at the ceiling of the tent. "I cannot lie to you, Gaius. The first time was a tremendously painful experience. Then, I actually began to enjoy it." He glanced back at Gaius, who turned pale.

"Please, do not let the others hear you say such a thing, Mandubratius."

"I truly do not consider that a sign of weakness. When you are with a woman such as the Empress Irene, and she enjoys your company, sometimes pain and near death are truly pleasing. Do you remember the strange, heightened pleasure when your sponsor took you to the very edge of death?"

Gaius sighed. "I have tried to forget that. I only experienced fear in my transformation. I cannot understand finding pleasure in pain, especially when engaged in coitus with Irene."

"It is like those strange insects that devour their mates. The male mates willingly with the female, even though he knows that she will consume him, sometimes during their own climax of coitus, if they experience such a thing." Mandubratius answered.

"Were you an avid student of insects and their activities as a child?"

"Not any more so than any other animals," Mandubratius admitted. "I heard these tales from traders when I was a mortal, though. I never forgot them." He became silent.

"Please excuse my interruption of your thoughts, but where should we travel with our troops tomorrow night?" Gaius asked.

"Hmmmm, perhaps a few miles north of camp," Mandubratius suggested. "It will give them an opportunity to travel at our speed, and give them some sport. The Emperor can stand to lose a patrol or two while we train."

Gaius grunted in assent. "I will tell Sextus that after sunset. I am about to fall asleep. May droves of women experienced in the arts of love pleasure you in your dreams, and I hope that they do not harm you."

Mandubratius grinned. "And may you encounter a broken Empress in your dreams, and may she plead with you for mercy."

"With that thought in mind, I cannot sleep, consul." Gaius laughed.

"Then, I will leave you two alone." Mandubratius turned over to his other side and yawned.

Prüm Abbey

Máire could sense someone lean over her shoulder. She assumed it was Marcus again, urging her for a snippet of the translation? She decided to ignore the interloper and concentrate.

However, her interloper turned out to be Julien, and his voice proved to be a distraction. "I've never seen such a mass of mushrooms set out to dry like that."

"Yes," she answered.

"I do hope the millstones will arrive on time. I know that our group will be separated. Some of us will join the mortal millers. The others will continue on our mushroom hunt."

"Yes." She rolled up her current scroll and unrolled another. The wooden bench creaked a bit as Julien sat next to her.

"I do hope that we will have enough wine to dissolve the mushroom mixture in." Julien's finger traced over hers.

She paused amidst her reading. "Yes."

"I am tired," he leaned in closer. His finger moved to play with a dangling strand of her hair. "Will you share my blankets?"

Máire sighed. The constant interruption furthered her growing annoyance. "No." She tossed her hair and it settled in place.

Julien's hand moved to her throat.

"Have I ever told you how exquisite you look in the moonlight?"

"Julien." Máire felt her mouth twitch into a smile. "It is morning and we're inside."

"Yes." His fingers slid down her neck, "but at nighttime, when the moon graces us with her light, you are beautiful in her radiance."

"Beauty is a gift for the Deargh Du from Morrigan," Máire answered. She tried to return to reading and ignored the movement of his digits over her skin.

"Still, you are exceptionally beautiful under the moon and stars. I wanted to make sure you knew. I was not certain if I told you before." He twirled a curl of her hair around his finger.

She grumbled under her breath as, within her peripheral vision, she noticed a seductive smile spread across his face.

Julien pulled back and said, "I've watched you perform your exercises when you believe yourself alone. Your body moves with such grace. Then again, my favorite time is when you are bathing. It's such a naughty little thrill. It's almost as much fun as catching you staring at me."

"I think you just like to watch me," she answered, feeling his weighty stare.

"Yes, I do. Can you fault me for that?"

"I suppose not," Máire chuckled. She returned to reading. She felt growing warmth spread through her. She heard her son-in-darkness sniff the air.

"You smell lovely. You smell of lilies, roses, lavender, mistletoe, and the sweetest of honey." Julien's eyes closed as he continued to inhale the air.

"Your fragrance knows no equal."

"Julien, what are you after? I'm trying to read!" She raised her voice.

Julien opened his eyes. The dying torchlight made his blue eyes turn the color of gleaming azure. He laughed. "I thought the purpose of this conversation was obvious. I already said what I wanted."

Máire's eyes moved back to her reading. Julien's hand moved under her chin. His fingers turned her to face him. He pushed aside the scroll.

"I'm reading. I'm not interested," she informed him.

"Yes, your lips say that, but you're trembling, and you smell of readiness," he whispered. "I could kiss you for an eternity. Your lips are so soft." His thumb moved over her lips, caressing them with a gentle touch.

Máire closed her eyes, hoping she would not find herself succumbing to his advances when there was so much work to be done. She felt her lips part, and the tip of her tongue darted out and teased at his thumb for a too-brief moment. She stopped and asked, "Will you continue this prattle all morning?"

"All day if I must," Julien replied. "I even memorized poetry for you. Shall I commence?" His gaze challenged hers.

"Fine," she answered, trying to not sound excited. "Let's hurry before I change my mind."

"Truly?" A finger dipped inside her mouth.

Máire forgot her impatience and nipped at the digit playfully, sucking at the blood from the scratch. She pulled back. "You heard me. I can no longer concentrate on my work," she answered.

Julien laughed again and pulled her in closer. "I know." His lips were perhaps an inch away from hers. Her eyes closed a bit as she leaned into him. Her mouth caressed his in a tender exploratory kiss. His hands moved to her tunic and pulled it over her head without pause. Her mouth moved back to his.

His beautifully swollen lips moved over hers with a growing intensity. Julien suckled her lips for a moment, and then parted his mouth to taste her. His tongue twined with hers in a delirious fervor. A cold and gentle hand slid through her hair.

Before she could think, he lifted her from the bench. She found herself atop the blankets. She moaned as he pulled her down to further explore her throat with his mouth. Julien's left hand sought and caressed an eager breast. Her fingers worked at unfastening his belt. A moment of sheer delight shuddered through Máire as he stroked her. She tossed aside his tunic.

Julien exhaled and, in a quick flurry of movements, settled her underneath him. Her tightly beaded nipples rubbed against his torso in a most pleasing fashion. She stared up at him and smiled. He clasped her wrists. She laughed and rolled Julien onto his back, straddling him.

"You are at my mercy now," Máire whispered in a sibilant purr.

"I want none of your mercy," Julien answered. He traced a hand over her breasts. He growled playfully and wrestled her beneath him again. She giggled until he leaned in, whisking at a nipple with his tongue. His phallus teased at her wet entrance with a gentle stroke.

Crying out in utter frustration, she slid her legs around his waist, and he entered her fully with one deep thrust. She arched toward him in a wild response. They began to writhe together. She lost track of everything but the building pleasure. Máire closed her eyes, hearing Julien begin to groan with each blissful thrust. She heard herself start to moan.

She took a moment to stare up at Julien before clenching her eyes shut as she strained against him. Her shallow and fast gasps grew as she began to allow herself to voice her pleasure louder. Then that faded as all thought ceased. She heard Julien cry out in blissful agony and satisfaction.

He shuddered as he came, and she felt her body clench his.

Máire rolled Julien over onto his back and continued. Some strange energy within demanded that she persist. He remained erect.

His moaning grew louder, and she felt Julien's hands rest on her hips.

Her body erupted in waves of pleasure. Máire closed her eyes. Every other sensation melted away. All she could concentrate on was the feeling of her pleasure as she writhed. With the thrill starting to fade, Máire regained a sense of herself. She stared down at Julien. His eyes were shut and he looked as though he were in some amount of pain. He opened his deep blue eyes and stared up at her with a silly grin.

"You've exhausted me," he whispered.

She pulled off of him and slid down his body. "That was the point," she whispered in Julien's ear.

He rolled Máire onto her side and held her. "Don't go."

"I must continue my studies." She started to sit up. Julien's arm fell to his side. She cleaned herself off with the edge of the blanket, wishing she could take advantage of the river. Yet the sun kept them all indoors.

Máire wandered back over to the table to continue reading. Halfway there, she stopped. A realization struck, and she inhaled a gasp of air so deep, she began coughing. She ceased it, trying to understand how she managed to climax. She did not even feel as though she needed to feed. She turned back and rushed over to Julien. "Julien, wake up!"

Her son-in-darkness remained silent. He appeared to smile as she sat down next to him.

"Julien!" Máire shook him.

"Mmmph! Sleeping," he whispered, pulling the blanket over himself.

"Julien, you just helped…" Máire paused and smiled for a moment, until a strange panic set in.

What if I can never experience that again? Nearly three hundred years without satisfaction is not a way I want to live again!

She rose to her feet and began to wander down the hallway, thinking that surely someone had heard them. Máire felt a small amount of horror.

Everyone will be making jokes about it tonight.

Máire noticed a figure under blankets, lying on his back. She moved in closer and noticed Horatio twitch a little.

He must be pretending to sleep at this point.

Máire sat down next to him. Sliding her hand under the covers, she found him. She could see Horatio begin to smile as she caressed him.

As the novice ran through the vineyard laughing, Horatio caught her blue eyes studying him in the brief moments of her stopping to catch her breath. She raced out of the vineyard into the golden fields, which soon became a dense forest. She giggled as she tossed aside her veil. Long, golden tresses flew behind her. She motioned him to continue chasing her.

Horatio paused as a large, gilded bed appeared in the distance. The young woman stopped and paced to the other side of the bed.

Fine linens moved in the breeze. This was a bed truly worthy of a king.

The novice sat down and patted the space next to her.

Horatio raced towards the bed.

"I'm so glad you followed me." The golden voice filled the forest.

Horatio felt his cheeks bloom. He'd deprived himself of the earthly delights all his life. He'd planned on always waiting for marriage, but this wouldn't count, or so he convinced himself.

The young woman with blue eyes appeared to be older than him. That just meant she had experience, and he needed to learn these things.

"I'm glad as well," he murmured. He studied her graceful form, feeling himself become hard. The novice returned his stare.

Horatio found himself embarrassed, yet with every passing moment, the desire to have her touch him grew. His self-consciousness melted away.

"Are you ready for me to attend your needs?"

"Yes," he whispered.

The young woman slid off the bed. She began to disrobe, revealing pale skin and a lovely, petite figure. Her movements turned to a dance, and Horatio could not decide what to do.

"Do you want me to touch you?" Blue eyes demanded his attention. A mischievous

grin slid over the novice's face.

A strange relief overwhelmed him, and he found himself breathless. Yet, she had not touched him. He knew he should be inside her before this happened. The novice did not even remove all her clothing. Horatio felt flustered and ashamed.

"Shhhh. Don't worry," she murmured. "You've done nothing wrong. Is this your first time?" She took his hand.

Horatio nodded his head, still upset for his lack of experience.

"Many men would be pleased to be so virile," she said, kissing his fingers. "May I undress you?"

"Yes," he whispered, knowing he could not say more.

She started on his tunic as he continued to stare at the slight contours of her body. "Am I beautiful?" she asked. Her skin seemed to glow with the radiance of the sun.

"Yes," he said. He wished to caress her, but it seemed inappropriate.

Her hands slid over his bare thighs. He realized he wore no clothing now.

"Do you wish to enter me now?" She leaned in closer. He could smell her. His hardness became painful.

"Yes," he moaned.

The novice pushed him gently onto his back.

Horatio felt some shock at the request.

Is this how experienced women train men such as me? Besides, why would a woman in preparing to dedicate her life to worshiping our savior lie to me?

Horatio lay down in the middle of the bed. The golden-haired beauty climbed onto the mattress. She walked over the blankets and stood above him. Horatio felt her feet on either side of his thighs.

"Prepare yourself." She beamed at him with the radiance of the moon. She lowered her body, and he could sense her adjust herself and him. Soon, he could feel her body encase his. She felt so moist and warm.

Chills moved up and down his back.

How am I managing not to climax now?

As she began to move, an unnamed energy within him began to build. Horatio heard the young woman begin to moan. He could see that her eyes were half-closed. He still could not take the thought of touching her. To touch such perfection seemed sacrilegious in their coupling. Horatio felt her hands slide over her and him. He reasoned that this woman had no qualms about touching herself. Her fingers rubbed them both.

She began to move faster.

The movements allowed Horatio to plunge deeper within her body. Horatio closed his eyes for a moment. Yet, they refused to remain so, as he felt a desire to see her. He stretched up his hands to feel her breasts. He stroked them. Odd how voluptuous they felt. The pleasures grew so intense as she increased her speed again that the forests seemed to echo her growing cries.

The novice tipped her head, looking at the canopy of trees.

Horatio found himself losing control. He grabbed her hips and began to thrust as much as possible into her.

Opening his eyes, all he could see were red curls and a familiar face.

Máire found herself breathless as Horatio grabbed her hips. The promise of pleasure grew again as the potential of bliss increased.

He delved deeper into her, and she felt him utter something and looked down at him.

"Máire." He squeaked her name, and she felt him begin to release.

Final gratification neared. She lost control of herself and began writhing faster. After a few moments of utter delight, she heard a vague moan of pain in the distance, and she began slowing down. She felt Horatio attempt to physically move her from his body, and she stopped.

Horatio stopped struggling and tried to catch his breath.

Strange how immortals still found themselves needing to draw air.

He stared up at her. "You were my first," he whispered in a throaty voice.

She stared back down at him. She'd never been with a virgin before. She leaned in and stroked back a few strands of his sweaty hair. "I had no idea," she murmured. "I thought you wanted this, Horatio. I'm so sorry for taking this from you." She felt shame for taking his purity.

He smiled into her eyes. "I had a dream. At least, I believed it to be a dream, but it was really you. You need not be hard on yourself. I did want it. It was…" He paused. "I really enjoyed it." His smile widened.

"I'm glad you enjoyed it." Máire slapped his chest with a gentle hand. "This is the second time I've experienced an orgasm since becoming Deargh Du."

"Truly?" He revealed his teeth and stretched a hand to caress her again. "When was your first time?"

"About ten minutes ago," she admitted. The demand for more pleasure rose again. "Would you like me to be your second? You can take control this time. However you wish to have me."

"I've not the stamina for another moment of your pleasuring." He traced his finger around her naval. "Sleep here with me."

"I'd love to, but something within is not sated yet, Horatio. I don't even need to feed. I can't explain it, but I've got to experience this again." She watched Horatio's forehead crease. He appeared to be annoyed, or perhaps even a little jealous.

"I don't understand," he pouted.

She leaned in and kissed his brow. "Horatio, you're a man. You have no idea how painful it was for me to not climax for over two hundred years."

"I've truly only had one."

"Yes, and you're what, eighteen perhaps? I am over two hundred years old! Besides, it's so easy for men to experience satisfaction. You can do it yourself."

"But, that's a sin," he said.

Máire tried not to laugh. He looked so serious. "You're Lamia, chroí, and you lost your virginity to a non-Christian. You need to open your eyes, Horatio, and see that not all pleasure is sinful."

"I don't know if I can," he admitted.

She could feel his hands stroke over her legs and thighs. "You've brought me satisfaction for the second time in over two hundred years. You can do anything, Horatio." She looked around, hearing people yelling at the disturbance. She could hear the noisy Pict over them all. Perhaps Mac Alpin would be next.

"Well, this is your last chance for me to be your second, my sweet. Are you certain you can't handle another time?" She smiled at him as she rose.

His hand stroked over her left calf. "I must rest," he said. "I don't think I can again so soon."

Máire stepped over him and crouched down. She kissed his lips. "You may come to me when you have the energy." She stroked his hair again and watched his eyes flutter a bit. Perhaps a nap would do him good. She wiped herself, again wishing for the opportunity for a quick bath.

Marcus woke up and stretched for a moment. Then the odor of too many unwashed bodies hit his nose, and he gagged. He pondered if the stench was his own and sniffed himself, but he smelled well enough. He was not clean, but he did not smell of disgusting putrescence either. He rose from his blankets, gaining a sense of the time. He began to nudge and kick bodies. "Wake up!" He shouted. "On your feet!"

Nobody moved, save Mac Alpin, who pulled the blanket over his face.

Marcus marched over to Arwin and began to nudge him. "Why aren't you getting up, you lazy arse! Did I miss some race befitting Mhacha herself or some Bacchanalia this morning?" He kicked Mac Alpin again. "Get up! You reek! This whole place reeks!" He pushed away the blanket and saw a pair of sleep-deprived, brown eyes staring at him from the floor.

"Where were you this morning?" a hoarse voice enquired, sounding very little like Mac Alpin. "Didn't you participate?"

"Participate in what?" Marcus felt his impatience growing.

What could I have missed?

"Our glorious early Beltane festivities and orgy, general," Mac Alpin chuckled. "Are you so hung over that you forgot it?"

"Orgy!? I heard no orgy! Why wasn't I woken?"

"Oh." Arwin coughed for a moment. "I assumed you were involved. I had no idea that you missed out. I myself slept with seven women. Yet, our Banbh Ceanúil was the most fun. She had her first orgasm in over two hundred years."

A swell of disappointment made Marcus' head swim. His earlier ire faded.

Why hadn't Máire nudged me awake?

"I was her third," Mac Alpin chuckled. "Then I think Claudius pulled her out of my blankets. You can ask him. I smell him... I think."

"I... how many?" he asked.

"How many what?" Arwin yawned and covered his mouth.

"Men!"

"I saw her with twenty different men before I collapsed from exhaustion. I heard there may have been forty," Arwin answered.

Marcus sighed and sat down for a moment, trying to curb his disappointment. "She may be in danger of incurring Medb's wrath for exceeding her exploits this morning," he muttered. He was used to Deargh Du enjoying their sexual adventures, but not this forty men orgy. He glanced back at Arwin. "How did this dalliance erupt into an orgy?" he queried.

"Hmmmm?" His old friend opened his eyes and blinked a few times. "We heard her ecstasy. At least, I did. I suppose the other women didn't wish to be outdone. After she jumped me, I left my bed and hunted the other ladies. It was utterly glorious. I felt as though I could dance in the sun. I had no need for blood and had boundless energy. Then the exhaustion hit, and we all fell asleep."

"Let me get this straight," Marcus began. "Máire has a climax, then starts having coitus with whatever man she can find. All the other women join in and all this while I'm asleep?" He threw up his hands in anger. "I cannot believe you," Marcus finished. "Yet, the stench of an orgy and wine is here."

"It happened," Mac Alpin verified. "What time is it?"

"Dusk. It's time for us all to get to work."

Mac Alpin grumbled and threw the blanket over himself again.

"First, we will all take a bath."

He witnessed the blankets shake as Mac Alpin laughed.

"Good luck on getting everyone to get moving, Marcus."

Marcus stood and kicked Arwin's leg.

Fine, if they were going to be lazy…

He suited up in armor and grabbed his swords. "Everyone wake up! It's time to wake up!" He began slapping people and blankets with his swords. "Our rest is over. Do not think the Strigoi will let you sleep, you lazy cowards! Get on your feet!" He watched the army rise slowly. "Now that you're awake, the first order of business is to go to the river and bathe! Then you will feed from the livestock here and from the villagers! Do not overfeed from them! Finally, you will return here and start working, you slugs!"

Marcus watched more rise from their beds. "We need to grind these mushrooms. We don't have much night, so get to it!" he shouted. "Do not, I repeat, do not get dressed! Do not even touch your clothing. You smell like the cheapest whores in Rome now, and I will not deal with these unpleasant smells the rest of the night. Get to the river. Now! Now! Now!" He began hitting various people again, including Claudius and Mac Alpin.

"Somebody didn't get laid," he heard.

"Nobody woke me up! Now you will suffer!" he shouted in the direction of the voice.

As they ran for the exit, he looked around and sighed. Long curls of red hair caught his attention. There could be no mistake in who had such hair.

He held his nose to stave off her reeking. He nudged her and then kicked Máire in the rump.

"I'm sleeping!" Máire grumbled. "Must you be so rude and martial?"

"Yes!" he said. "You had your first orgasm in over two centuries without me."

She sat up and blinked her green eyes. "Well, you're being rather selfish, aren't you? You should be happy I found some relief, Marcus."

"Well, yes, I'm happy for that, but I wanted to be the first!"

Máire sighed. "The first and second times felt like they might have been a fluke. In the back of my mind, I almost felt as if they were a dream. I tried to wake you, but you did not respond. I thought you were exhausted, so I left you alone."

Marcus bit his lower lip.

How could I have slept through the ruckus that would have come from an orgy? I know well enough that nobody in this party of three thousand are the type to be quiet.

A flash of that same nightmare crashed through his head. He closed his eyes, willing the dreadful vision to fade away. He heard the sound of Máire standing. He felt her hand touch his shoulder and gently rub.

"Are you alright?"

He opened his eyes and witnessed the worry and fear in her. "I could have used the distraction," he said. "Do you still have dreams… from your encounter with the Strigoi?"

Máire stopped rubbing him for a moment. "They have faded, but I still remember them with fear," she admitted. "Perhaps they lessen if the Strigoi that created the apparition and experience is transformed or killed. Maybe the one that created yours is not dead yet."

"Perhaps," he whispered. He pulled her in closer, ignoring the stench rising from her form. "My dreams and visions are so vibrant and lucid. I ask the Tuaths for balance, yet they do not aid me."

"Their aid is sometimes confusing to us here in this existence. Their influence occurs on a different schedule than our own sometimes." She rested her head on his shoulder and murmured something.

"Hmmmm?" he asked. His thoughts remained on the strange and terror-filled nightmare involving himself as boy in the Helvetti tribe and himself as a bloody-minded mortal general.

"Maybe you and I could take a bath together." She turned her face to the side, studying him. "Remember our first time was in a river." He watched a sly smile move over her face.

"I don't need a bath."

"Ah, but I do," she purred. "You can clean me. Then you can get me dirty again." She nipped at his throat before pulling away. Máire stared at him over her shoulder with an impassioned and bold gaze. Her eyes beckoned as she tossed her hair over her shoulder.

He became aroused. After a second of indecision, Marcus chased after her.

She laughed and began to run.

Fond memories of a race towards a river overtook the outlandish and dreadful memories of his death as a boy at his own sword. Why worry about a dream when the promise of sweet release awaited them at the river?

chapter four

Lamia Camp Outside of Mehren

fter shifting in her sleep for what seemed like hours, Talia awoke to find herself surrounded by dirt. Hunger gripped her as a squeak and the pitter-patter of a rapid heartbeat drew her attention to the rat investigating her hair. She pushed her right hand through the loose, muddy dirt and grabbed it.

As she drained its small body, she realized her bed swam with cold, sludgy water. Talia sensed that her flooding hole would only become worse.

Surely the sun has disappeared behind the clouds by now.

She tossed aside the scant morsel and clawed her way towards the surface. Rain began to pelt her, and torrents of water threatened to drown her. Even though she knew she couldn't drown, she still panicked. Talia flailed about, trying to grab hold of something to pull her out of the slosh pit, when she managed to grasp a tree trunk and finally pulled herself from the sucking hole.

"Damn this cold and rain!" she yelled at the skies, while getting to her unsteady feet. "Burgundy was never this cold." Her feet felt as though they were encased in ice. Talia gritted her teeth.

That Maél Muire will suffer for this! Now I must seek my sponsor's mercy...

"Then that little insufferable bastard son of Charles', then Marcus, then the rest. All of them shall suffer and die!" Talia growled. In her heart, she wished Mandubratius would kill them... or, better still... allow her to do it! She could bathe in Maél Muire's blood. She sniffed at the winds, wishing her nose could reveal the direction of her sponsor, when a mild, instinctive sensation pulled her northward. However, before she could take two steps in that direction, a dense object collided with her, pushing her face down into the mire. A great weight rested on top of her shoulders and hips, pinning her.

"Who are you?" a voice demanded.

Talia attempted a reply, but all that came out were gargled words. When a hand pulled her head back out of the muck, she spat, "I'm Talia of Époisses, and Mandubratius is my sponsor!" She looked the man, whom she assumed to be Lamia due to his strength and lack of the beauty more common in the Celtic lines, and snarled.

He rewarded her outburst by shoving her face into the mud again. "You've been expected," he said as he continued to hold her down. "Before I let you up, if you wish to reach whom you are wishing to see, you must first go through a small trial." He then released her.

"How dare you!" Talia accused.

The Lamia shoved her face back into the mud. "The question you should ask is 'what trial'. I am assuming that is the question you wished to ask. Your sponsor wishes for you to appear broken and in desperate need of his assistance. He also wants you to bend completely to his will."

She mumbled a response through the mud.

"You wish to answer?" the Lamia asked before pulling her from the sludge.

"So, I must be in utter submission to please his ego?" she queried.

"He says it's for the morale of the troops."

"Troops? What troops?" Talia scoffed, trying not to laugh.

"He has troops now," the stranger answered. "The general commands a detachment of Pope Leo's army."

Talia sighed. "What is it I'm supposed to do?"

"You are to be escorted back to our camp in chains, naked, with the appearance of being beaten and raped."

Talia did not like the sound of the Lamia's proclamation.

Mandubratius can be so cruel to me. Why does he do this?

"And if I do not agree?" Talia strained to get a better look at the Lamia, Child of Ares, or whoever he claimed to be.

"Then I can kill you," he answered. A sharp pain stabbed at the back of her neck. "Or, I suppose, I could let you go. However, if you choose to leave, Mandubratius will hunt you down and kill you himself. So, it is really your choice. What would you like to do? Submit, die now, or die later?"

After a careful consideration of her options, she relented. "I will submit to your terms. How will you make me appear to be beaten and raped?"

A whistle, followed by numerous footsteps, heralded the arrival of several Lamia. The number of her kind increased by sevenfold.

Talia steeled herself for the pain, deciding then to not cry out. "Very well. If this is what must happen, I accept this as the consequence of my choice." She then craned her neck to look the man who pinned her in the face. "May I have your name, so I can know who to curse?" she hissed.

"I am Sextus Marius Severus Germanicus, or just 'Sextus', if you like." The soldier's voice echoed in her ear. "Feel free to curse me as many times as you wish. Of course, I am just following orders, and… as you said, this is just a consequence of your choice."

Mandubratius paused while trimming his beard to take in Talia's presence as he felt her draw closer to his tent. He looked away from the mirror and dismissed his assistant. Closing his eyes, he focused on the footfalls immediately outside. He heard the partition flap rise and knew that Gaius stood behind him.

"She has arrived," said the former Children of Ares general.

Mandubratius turned towards Gaius and, in a calm voice, commanded, "Assemble the men into formation."

The corners of Gaius' mouth turned up in a smirk. "They are already in formation. These Angels are well-trained."

"They are indeed," he responded. "Let's take our positions. Perhaps she'll learn not to stray from the Lamia... from me, now." He then exited the tent, with Gaius following a few steps behind him. When the generals arrived at the formation, Mandubratius heard Sextus barking orders.

"Inten... te! Quattuor Ordinem Faci... te!" At Sextus' commands, his soldiers stood at attention and then formed into four ranks, though they appeared a little sloppy. "Apparetis inordinatus, cinaedum vobis inertibus! Dextrorsum vos Disponi... te!" Once his men cleaned up their spacing, Sextus faced Mandubratius and saluted.

"Sir, we found the lost Angel and punished her."

The sound of chains creaking echoed through the shadowed glen. Mandubratius suppressed a strange pang of sympathy upon seeing Talia. Her mud-crusted hair hung over her eyes. Her bruised form smelled of the other Lamia. Hoping to drown out any misplaced emotions, Mandubratius strode over to her and snarled, "Look at me!"

Talia raised her chin to meet his gaze. Her sodden, yet golden tresses parted away from her eyelids. Talia's blue eyes told a tale of strange and serene acceptance. Her gaze remained steady.

As Mandubratius continued to stare at her, he had to admit a little surprise. He knew Talia was smart, but she had never shown any strength before.

"Turn around and kneel," he ordered her.

She lowered her face and turned away from him. Talia then stooped down to the ground with a grunt, planted her knees in the dirt, and leaned forward, while bracing her upper body with her outstretched hands.

"Orbem Istrui... te!" he heard Sextus order. Upon completion of the command, the soldiers formed a circle facing outward around Mandubratius and the officers who stood with them. Sextus then ordered the men to face the middle. "Ad Tergum Verti... te!" Finally, he ordered them to stand at ease. "Quie... te!"

With everyone looking at him, poised behind Talia, Mandubratius prepared to deliver the little speech he had composed in his mind while walking to the parade grounds a moment ago.

"This Angel has fallen. She must be punished so she can seek redemption," he bellowed to the gathered forces. Silence greeted his announcement.

He knelt behind Talia and pushed aside her ripped clothing. He heard a strange gurgle of shame from Talia as he loosened his belt. Lowering his clothing, he began to subdue her as he did to Amata in front of the Lamia senate, so many years ago, after killing their sponsor Felician. However, that situation had been something altogether different than this one. While punishing Talia, he looked at each soldier's face and dared him to say anything. He felt pleasure at seeing fear resonate from every newborn Lamia.

With his body finally at climax, Mandubratius uttered a muted cry of pleasure at dominating Talia, and then he shoved her face forward into the mud. Afterwards, he stood, pulled up his leggings, tightened his belt, and planted his left boot on her backside. "Any questions?" he asked the crowd while scanning their reactions.

The soldiers said nothing.

Mandubratius then nodded to Sextus, who shouted, "Inten… te!"

In response, the soldiers stood at attention.

"Ab Signis Discedi… te!" Sextus ordered, dismissing the soldiers.

Mandubratius removed his boot from Talia's backside, grabbed her shackles, pulled her to her feet, and dragged her towards the tent. He could only hear the sound of her chains clanging together as he escorted Talia to his command tent. He could sense Gaius following in a strange procession.

Prüm Abbey

Edward carried another load of mushrooms to the mill and dumped them into a basket next to the grinding stones. When he looked up from his work, he noticed a lone figure standing in the distance making strange motions in the air.

Without warning, he felt himself pushed forward, nearly knocking over the baskets. He looked up and saw an embarrassed Amata smiling at him.

She apologized for not paying attention and helped him to his feet. Her bright grin and her clumsiness seemed to indicate the last evening's activities had been something of a breakthrough for them.

"Perhaps it's time for us to rest," she purred.

Edward scanned the workers and noticed his father-in-darkness, who looked rather annoyed with his current duties, bagging mushrooms and herbs. However, the others near him, including Marcus and Claudius, appeared to be quite content with their lot.

"Arwin would give us all grief if you and I decided we needed a respite. Perhaps, we can switch duties with someone there," he suggested before leading her towards the table.

Just then, a loud explosion from the distant west made everyone jump.

"Was that our Banbh Ceanúil?" Claudius asked, looking in Marcus' general direction.

"Yes, that is Máire," Marcus acknowledged as he stared off into the distance, looking unconcerned with the entire process.

"Shouldn't we-" Amata began, while staring in the direction of the noises, before Arwin cut her off.

"Yes, if you value your hair, you should remain here. She demanded that we do not disturb her."

"Indeed?" Amata retorted. "What is she doing?"

Marcus glanced at Amata and answered, "She found information in that scroll about how to call forth lightning. Best that we stay as far away from her as possible. She's not sure about how to control anything she releases."

Edward sniffed the air. "I smell burned flesh. We should ignore her demands in favor of her safety."

Arwin chuckled. "Goddess help you if you do. Amata, you have small hands. If you help the others pick and sort, I'll take your duties." Before she could reply, the Ekimmu Cruitne ran for the woods, though not in the direction of Máire.

Amata laughed in that delightful way Edward loved. She then walked over to the table and started pouring the mixture into bags.

"Well?" Edward asked the other blood-drinkers still near him. "Let's go see what's burning. Besides, dawn will be here in an hour."

"I don't want to incur Maél Morrigan's wrath," Claudius remarked. "If we upset her, she may not be in a good mood later." He smirked and went back to work.

Marcus laughed. "Edward is worried that our Banbh Ceanúil will replace him as our champion fire starter. Go find her, if you are so concerned, Edward."

"Cowards," Edward muttered under his breath before walking towards the west. With every step he took, the smell grew more noxious. He eventually gave in and took to the air.

The lightning had not behaved. Then again, lightning never acted with a predictable nature. Even though the smell of burned hair lingered and served as a distraction to her commands, the wind now asked for release.

Máire inhaled and exhaled as she felt the passion of the old knowledge consume her. The thrill of channeling energy from the opened path to the Otherworld made her experience a strange giddiness she had not felt in ages. She rolled up the scrolls and placed them within the leather case.

Máire scanned the valley, looking for a safe place to unleash the wind. She soon found a gentle slope where the vortex of wind could settle. With her spot selected, Máire concentrated on summoning thunder and gathering breezes.

Animals in the valley below screeched, annoyed with another one of her interruptions, and began to race for the forest.

Máire studied the point where she wished the tip of the vortex to touch and then dissipate. A simple chant came to her thoughts, and before she could think over the words, they pushed past her lips in a fevered hurry.

Máire closed her eyes, envisioning clouds coming together, blotting out the stars and moon. She sensed the center of the windstorm gather speed and lower towards the ground. She opened her eyes and stared at the vortex. Trees whipped and began bending to the ground as if in obeisance to the force of nature.

The sound of shattering limbs and trunks made Máire cringe in fear. She could no longer concentrate on controlling the vortex. It veered towards her. The debris within its many arms of wind churned and whipped about, raining stones in her direction.

"Go back through the passage," she murmured, hoping that her words would be enough to send the energy back through the gateway to the Otherworld.

A sudden, searing pain tore through her body. Máire felt the winds lift her and toss her about like a dry leaf. A heavy thud resonated around her, and she realized the winds had forced her into the dirt and rocks. A tremendous roar echoed in her ears. "Please," she whispered. "Return to your home."

Whether through command or coincidence, the storm began to dissipate and lose its integrity.

Did it hear my request?

Máire rolled onto her back and closed her eyes.

Máire awoke to hear the sounds of licking and slurping. She felt a rough tongue brush over her curls.

Is Lucius grooming me now?

Soon, a warm weight rested on her chest, and the coarse tongue began to lap over a sore spot on her forehead.

She finally opened her eyes and found the land bathed in sunlight. She attempted to bring her right hand up to shade her eyes, but her palm could not move past soft fur.

Máire blinked a few times, allowing her eyes to grow accustomed to the light. A glance to where she felt the furry mass pressing against her revealed a black cat, which leaned in closer, nosed her hand away, and then returned to tending her wound. Its delicate purr grew louder.

Lucius has a throaty purr, so perhaps another cat has found me.

As she patted the cat, it looked up and studied her with bicolor gold and green eyes.

Definitely not Lucius.

When it flopped onto its side, she followed her compulsion to rub the cat's belly. The cat purred louder with each stroke while Máire studied the large, white clouds above. Soon, she discerned the sounds of other animals echoing through the air.

She pushed herself up off the ground, and the cat squeaked a meow as if disturbed that Máire had deigned to move her. Once on her feet, she surveyed her surroundings and discovered an impressive dun set in the distance. Sun gleamed from its white stone walls. It stood as the tallest building of her memory.

"A truly mighty fortress," she whispered.

A shadow fell, offering immediate shade. Máire looked up to find the source… and into a graceful face with black eyes… then lurched to her knees upon recognizing who blocked the sun.

"Phant… Morr… grandmother? Have I passed into the Otherworld?" she asked as a warm hand stroked her hair.

"Arise, my granddaughter," Morrigan sang in a gentle voice that soothed Máire. "Fear not. Yet next time, be mindful of Brigid's place in your lap. I do not think she liked being tossed to the ground when you moved to your knees."

Máire turned and studied the black cat, which narrowed its eyes at her. While Máire watched, the graceful feline figure changed, transforming into a blonde woman who stared at her with a strange smile.

"You are most fortunate that you give good rubs," purred the blonde woman, who pouted as She spoke. "I felt like clawing you when you cast me aside. Well, stand up and close your mouth, Deargh Du. Honestly, you and your father-in-darkness tend to gawk at me in the most amusing fashion."

Máire found her feet and rose. "I am sorry. I am confused. I was flung to the ground, and I lost consciousness. I awoke here, and I'm not sure of myself."

"Have no worries, granddaughter, for you have not passed. I simply-"

The clearing of Brigid's throat interrupted Morrigan.

She chuckled. "Fine, Brigid. We decided to bring you here, Máire, to discuss your new knowledge."

At that moment, a strange wind began to roar, assaulting Máire's ears, forcing her to cover them. Thunder rumbled and lightning blinded her. Máire nearly fell back to her knees as a God appeared from a beam of radiant light, which had come down from the maelstrom above.

"Ladies, stop proclaiming your actions in this matter. I am He who called this one forth. I wished to see she who dared to ask for my energy." The God tipped His head to the side to study Máire.

"True, but we planned on speaking with her," Brigid countered.

Morrigan reached the God of the Sea in two long strides, placed Her right hand on Máire's left shoulder, and said, "Now Manannán, this is no mere mortal. She's my granddaughter… and one of my Deargh Du."

"She's an excellent druid," Brigid added.

Máire studied the ground, feeling her face redden at the compliments. When she looked up, she could see Manannán Mac Lir smiling at her with a crooked grin.

"I was surprised," said Manannán. "It has been… at least as the mortals perceive it… a very long time since one has called for my energy. I feared that the knowledge of such matters had died with the growing popularity of Je and Hovah's son. Sometimes, I fear that my name has melted into obscurity."

Morrigan patted His shoulder and stated, "Well, we have made sure that our names will not be lost. We gathered all the mortals' knowledge from before, and we entrusted it to a group of mortal druids. They have been passing on the knowledge from generation to generation. They secreted away copies, in case that knowledge was discovered by those who might destroy it."

Brigid slinked Her way towards Manannán in a manner most befitting a cat. "By a strange twist of fate…"

Morrigan cleared Her throat.

"Oh fine," Brigid grumbled. "Morrigan felt it was time to release a set of scrolls in Vézelay. The scroll moved into this Deargh Du's hands."

"Part of that knowledge involves invocation of your name to call forth the tornado," Morrigan said.

"Tornado?" Máire whispered. The three deities stared at her in a strange manner. "I am not familiar with that word. Please excuse my interruption." She felt like a small child surrounded by knowledgeable and somewhat frightening adults.

Morrigan laughed. "For Dana's sake, Máire, you may speak. In a different time, the vortex you created is called a 'tornado'."

"I wish I could have witnessed it first hand," Manannán sighed. "I imagine it would have been so beautiful."

A small feeling of dread grew in the pit of Máire's stomach. The vortex, or tornado, had been so destructive and so hard to control.

"Máire, call forth another one," Morrigan suggested.

Máire could see Manannán's sea-colored eyes gleam at the thought.

"Yes, please do so, Máire. I want to see it," He said.

"I don't feel as if I could control it."

"Are you disobeying your grandmother?" A playful grin lit Morrigan's face.

"No, no," Máire said, feeling a large amount of nervous energy grow within. "However, the experience of calling down such a great force has humbled me."

"And so it should have," Brigid said.

"In order to master this knowledge, you must practice it," Morrigan stated. "Then you can learn to control it. Who best to help you in this than the Lord of Winds, Sea, and Travel?"

Manannán scoffed. "My duties are more than merely that!"

The Goddesses smiled at Him.

"My apologies," Morrigan purred. "I was merely teasing you."

Máire studied Their faces, wondering what games occurred between the Tuaths. They turned back to her with somewhat patronizing grins, as if she were a young child learning to take steps.

"Alright," Máire said. "I will summon the vortex." She closed her eyes.

"Ah, ah." A hand gripped hers, and she felt a soothing heat. Máire opened her eyes, feeling Manannán's stare.

"You must not think of the size of the storm, young Deargh Du," the God whispered. His fingers unfolded her hand and He raised her palm towards the warming rays of the gentle golden orb above. "Rather, you should think of this vortex fitting into your palm. Then, you will control it by closing and opening your hand. The vortex will abide by your thoughts," Manannán continued. "If you think of it as a larger being than what you can contain in your hand, it will revert to its own nature. The vortex's destructive force will unlock, and you will not be able to direct it."

Máire nodded her head. "I will try."

"Trying will not work with nature. While you cannot fully control the energy you summon, you may guide it," Brigid said.

"Then, I will do so," Máire said, sounding more confident than she felt. Steeling herself, she closed her eyes. The simple chant came to her lips again, summoning the vortex to the glade in the distance. She closed her hand, envisioning the clouds joining and blotting the sun.

Máire slowly spread her hand open again. The spiraling windstorm gathered speed and lowered towards the ground. She opened her eyes and stared at the center of the vortex. A strange realization came to her mind as it grew in strength. It seemed more willing to listen this time. A voice within begged her to release the full power of the storm, but she ignored the urge.

A strange sound echoed near her. She noticed the God and Goddesses hitting Their hands together and looking pleased.

Máire turned away from the minor distraction. Her focus centered on her right palm. She closed her hand and whispered for the energy to return to its origin.

A warming force surrounded her as she felt arms envelope her. Morrigan patted her back.

"Just remember to put these skills to good purpose, granddaughter. Do not abuse them, for they are not toys."

Morrigan kissed her forehead and pulled away. Manannán's eyes engulfed her, and she found herself unable to speak. She could vaguely remember her nights of mortality and feeling overwhelmed by the Deargh Du. This seemed a thousand times over that engulfing beauty.

"Thank you for calling my name. Do so again when it is necessary. Seldom do I hear it. I relish it."

"I will do so," she murmured, feeling foolish for not finding words.

"Ladies, I feel someone calling for my boat," Manannán said.

Máire watched His smile linger on the Goddesses for a moment before His body melded with the winds. He faded into a small vortex.

Brigid yawned. *"After that fine display, I could use a nap."* She stretched Her form and reverted into the black cat. The Goddess leapt up towards Máire. Máire inhaled as Brigid landed in her arms. A rather insistent purr echoed. *"Now, I want the attention you normally give Lucius,"* the cat demanded.

Máire stared at Morrigan in disbelief that she cradled a Goddess in her arms. Stroking the black fur, she found herself yawning.

"You are sleepy and need to rest," Morrigan said. *"Remember to maintain the balance. Do not abuse the knowledge, or else the balance may seek you."*

Máire sat down on the green grasses. *"I promise, grandmother,"* she whispered. *"I love you."* She leaned back, enjoying the cushion of the Otherworld as it cradled her.

"I'm so glad you realize that you have that power as well." Morrigan crouched down. *"I love you, too. Now, please tell Marcus that he has the power to overcome his nightmares. They are visions, not reality."*

Brigid's resounding purr soothed Máire as she closed her eyes.

Máire felt a heavy, warm weight upon her chest and a tickle from a strange rough, wet object being drawn repeatedly at the hair that lay alongside her neck... as if something were licking her. A cat! She must still be in the Otherworld with Brigid. Máire opened her eyes and called out the name of the Goddess, only to see that she addressed the wrong cat.

"No, not Brigid," Lucius answered. His green eyes settled on hers. "Thank you for saying that I am as beautiful as She, Máire. Now, rub my forehead."

"Where is the sun?" she asked, feeling a sudden tear at her heart. "Where is the beautiful, blue sky?" She started to sit up. Learning from her experience with Brigid, she gathered Lucius into her arms as she moved.

"Sun?" Lucius stared at the starry, night sky. "I would think that the sun would incinerate you. Poor Deargh Du, you must have hit your head very hard. We should go back to the abbey, Máire. The sun will come soon."

Another voice echoed in the distance, and she witnessed Edward walking toward her.

"There you are," Edward said, looking fearful. "I smelled burning skin and thought you may have incinerated yourself." He pulled Máire to her feet.

"What?" She felt confused.

"Starting fires is what I do," Edward stated.

Máire caught a strange twinkle in his eyes, but she felt too perplexed with her own condition to acknowledge the joke. She turned away and began walking.

Edward joined her. "I worried when you did not return. The others are not as concerned, but these last few nights have brought forth much change in you. I couldn't find your scent, and it made me anxious."

Máire smirked. "So, things are well between you and Amata. This gives you time to worry about me?"

Edward grinned back at her. "I suppose so."

"How long have I been gone?" She hefted Lucius as he wiggled, seemingly uncomfortable with the way she had been holding him.

"Most of the night," Edward admitted. "Many of the party were a little upset that you weren't there to assist in the gathering and preparation, but Sáerlaith said it was your duty to translate and study the scroll, in preparation for guiding and teaching the skills to others."

The memory of creating the vortex stood forth in her mind. "The sun is rising soon, let's go," Máire suggested.

Lucius grumbled and squirmed his way out of her grasp. He settled around her neck. "Such a fine chariot I have now," Lucius murmured in her ear. "Go faster."

She stopped and examined the looming landscape. The valley appeared to be resplendent once again. "This isn't right. Those trees were not like this a moment ago."

"What are you talking about?" Edward asked. "We need to move faster." He grabbed her arm, and they began walking faster.

"Those trees were pulverized," Máire said. "I called a vortex, or tornado, that destroyed those trees, Edward."

"You are not talking sense, Máire. What does that word mean? I have never heard of such a thing as tornado. I see no destruction. We can investigate it tomorrow. I believe that you simply hit your head."

"The Otherworld," she whispered. "Edward, I woke up in the Otherworld. Brigid, in the guise of a black cat woke me up."

"Lucius woke you up. He grooms many of us." Edward chuckled. "You were dreaming, Máire." He continued dragging her. "We'll speak of this inside the catacombs."

Máire winced as Lucius' claws dug into her shoulders as their walk increased to a jog. "At the end of my time there, Morrigan said something."

"And what did she say?" Edward's strides lengthened.

"She said..." Máire shook her head for a moment. "We must fly. Hang on, Lugh." She took to the air. They flew towards the catacomb doors. The blinding, white light of oblivion hit them as they reached the entrance to the dark basements.

Máire slammed into a stone wall, her shoulder dislocating. Yet, she noticed Lucius on the ground, grooming his left rear leg. Not one hair out of place.

"I said that we needed to hurry," Edward chided. The smell of burnt flesh reinforced his point.

Máire embraced him with her good arm. "Consider me chastised," she said. She sensed and smelled Marcus near them.

The interior door opened, and he appeared frantic.

"Where have you been?" He took her arms before studying Edward for a moment. "We started to become concerned when we heard Edward calling for you. He has a good nose and can find nearly anyone. We sent others through the forest, but no one could locate you." He stepped away and examined her left arm. "Best we do this now," he said, before taking it and forcing her shoulder back into place.

The shooting pain made Máire dizzy. She sensed the warmth of healing.

"Where was she, Edward?"

Edward sighed. "I think Lucius would know better than I. I know I walked through that portion of the forest before, and yet I didn't smell her," he muttered, giving his head a quick shake. "I hate that sound of bones moving into place, no matter how often I hear it. However, before I forget, Máire hit her head and said she went to the Otherworld, Marcus."

"Edward, I was not seeing things," Máire sighed. "I created a vortex of winds, and it turned on me. Morrigan brought me to the Otherworld, or perhaps Brigid did, or perhaps several thought it best I come there. Manannán..." She paused and stared at Marcus. "I woke up in the sun with a black cat in my arms," she explained. "The cat transformed into the Goddess Brigid after Morrigan's arrival. Then Manannán Mac Lir arrived and taught me how to create and guide the storm."

She paused, allowing the healing warmth to flow through her body. She began talking anxiously again. "My summoning of the vortex alerted them that someone pulled energy through the mists into our world. Morrigan warned me about upsetting the balance with the storm, and I fell asleep holding Brigid... the cat. Then Lucius woke me, and I found that all the damage I caused had been repaired." She watched Marcus look over at Lucius.

Lucius twirled his tail about, looking satisfied at receiving the attention. "Máire was unconscious, I found her, and I decided to wake her. I have no idea if she was in the Otherworld."

"Mmmmm." Marcus rubbed her shoulder. "Perhaps Morrigan restored the natural order. Your vortex was not a natural occurrence. She amended things, and therefore you have little recollection of it." He stroked her hair and placed his hand over a sore spot on her scalp. "You do have a bad bump on your head, though."

"Well, head injury or visit to the Otherworld. I was nearly incinerated by something that was not my own doing," Edward stated with a half chuckle. He rose. "I'm going to find Amata and go to sleep. Please do not release a vortex here, Máire."

Máire watched Edward walk away. "Morrigan warned me," Máire repeated, feeling exhausted as well. She leaned in and rested her forehead against Marcus' chest.

"Heed Her warning," he said. "She wanted to destroy me, once. Do not think, for a moment, that you can disobey Her. She does not allow Her brood such luxuries." He exhaled noticeably.

"She said something else, about you," she added. Pulling back, she stared into his graying eyes. "She said that you can overcome the visions from the Strigoi. They are not reality." She watched Marcus withdraw and stare at the dirt for a moment, as if measuring the weight of Morrigan's words.

"Easier said than done," he murmured, sounding as though it were nothing more than a small issue. "Perhaps if you shared my blankets today, I could find some peace."

She took his hand. "As long as you do not toss and turn too much, you will have my protection. I was chieftain once, I remember those duties well."

"I'm sure you do." Marcus guided Máire towards the large gathering of blankets and supplies.

She watched him smile. "Don't forget Her words," she whispered. "You can control the fears. I love you." The last phrase was a strange jumble. She turned back to Marcus. "After this is over, we'll go back to Bath for awhile, and the horrors will fade away like the mists."

"Bath," he murmured with a smile. "Yes, after this, we can return to our home there, all of us. I love you, too." He squeezed her hand.

Lamia Camp outside Mehren

Talia awoke in the tent and attempted to move her right foot. The cold chain moved about her leg as she sat up and stared at her surroundings. The tent seemed sparse with two beds, and she could smell the guards outside. A flickering lamp and glimmering objects caught her attention. She wrapped her arms around her knees and finally caught sight of Mandubratius watching her from the shadows. She tried to judge his mood by his appearance, yet she could not gage his disposition.

Usually, such an intrusive stare would annoy her. However, this time, Talia found a reserve of patience. She waited for him to speak. He remained contemplative and scratched at the beard on his chin.

After a half an hour interval, he unlatched the chains that did nothing more than symbolize her confinement. It had all been for show, after all.

Talia rose and stretched, wandering to the washbasin. Cloth and perfumed oils awaited her. Then, she realized that a set of combs and brushes lay to the side of the oils.

Most men would never carry such luxuries. Then again, my sponsor is most unusual about some things.

She dipped one of the cloths into the water and began to wipe herself down. A few minutes later, Talia's skin glistened, her hair was no longer tangled, and she dabbed on a touch of fine perfume. She heard movement and turned. She saw Mandubratius presenting a small, bronze mirror and a package wrapped with a silken ribbon.

Her sponsor turned away, remaining silent, and sat down in his wooden chair again as she continued her cleaning.

Talia pulled at the ribbon and found a bundle of silken robes. She closed her eyes as the silks flowed over her skin. Yet, the fact that he would not speak needled at her. She must have some value to him. After all, he could have given these gifts to another.

Talia turned to study him. She sashayed towards him, swaying her hips, knowing the movement of the silk over her limbs would be overwhelming to almost any man. Talia moved to sit in Mandubratius' lap, but before she could maneuver herself, his right hand lashed out, and she felt a hard blow against her cheek. She found herself flying backwards and landing a few feet away.

"Are you done now, Talia? You do not seem to realize the predicament you are in. Yes, I allowed you to clean yourself, and I've gifted you with expensive clothing, but you may not try to seduce me as an equal. You lost that privilege when you squandered the gifts I gave you. I may yet decide to kill you. However, until then, we will return to the ancient ways of the Lamia. I initiate, you acquiesce."

"Then, why didn't you kill me?" she growled, rubbing at the sore spot on her cheek.

"Why didn't I, indeed? You certainly deserve it. Oh, but you are so entertaining. You can be the toy I originally intended you to be."

Talia felt her face tighten in rage.

"This surprises you? I sponsored you to be a plaything and nothing more. You were so limited in your usefulness. I merely wanted someone easy to manipulate by leveraging promises for favors and tokens of wealth. I realized a century later what a bore you were. I decided it was best to leave you to your own devices. Eventually, I thought you'd realize how pointless taking over a mere slice of the Empire was. Then you would return when you needed me to do something for you. However, things have changed, my sweet. You have become a little more interesting."

Mandubratius leaned forward, his eyes gleaming. "I will allow you to accompany me and be my plaything for now. That, or I could kill you. I have the Empress, and she's amusing and strong, stronger than I believed her to be. Not to mention that Irene is our key to Constantinople. Then there's Amata, and she's intelligent, knows how to act as a useful co-consul, and is beautiful. Then there is that intriguing mystery known as your niece. She is so fun to chase."

She watched him smile. He could kill her. Her will fought the idea of her becoming his toy.

Perhaps I can bargain with him.

"Mandubratius, I know that it is important to you that you show dominance over me to the others."

"Yes," he hissed. "That is necessary, so the troops see that I will punish those who disobey."

"Then, I have two conditions I wish to bargain."

"Hurry and name them, then." Mandubratius waved an arm. "However, I do have the right to ignore them and simply take what I wish from you."

"Hmmmm, the first condition is that you help me seek revenge on Julien de Divio and his family."

Mandubratius stared at her. "Any sort of dealings with that pup smell of boredom, Talia. I will consider it, but he's beneath my worry. You should forget the second condition. I fear hunger has made you lose your intellect." He stretched an arm to her. "You may feed."

Talia felt her eyeteeth elongate. She turned over her sponsor's hand and bit into the underside of his arm. He was such a manipulative bastard, but she could take comfort in knowing that she could kill him herself at some point very soon. Until then, she would merely acquiesce to Mandubratius and pretend to be the good slave. After his death, she would return to the destruction of the Franks. Self-doubt concerning her success began to rise again, so Talia closed her eyes and lost herself in the taste of his vitae.

God, he tastes of absolute deliciousness tonight.

chapteR fiue

s Seosaimhín knelt in front of the effigy, scattered and dry bones cracked beneath her knees. She presented the silver bowl of a mortal's blood to Nagirrom. Seosaimhín then turned and motioned the Strigoi away.

How annoying those things could be at times. Yet, their army grew numerous. Nagirrom must be thanked. After all, only Nagirrom could give these brainless beings a brain.

"Oh, great Nagirrom," she intoned. "How powerful and large your army grows, like a bear who finds plentiful prey. We thank you for your favors upon us. We feel we are ready to strike. Yet, we await your command. We are the blossom that waits for the wind's pleasant gust to carry us." A cry in the distance captured her attention. She growled at the remaining Strigoi. "Bow before your Master!" Seosaimhín sank down, resting her face against the cold floor of the cave.

A flapping of wings echoed through the hushed chill. Nagirrom landed on His statue. "You say you are ready?"

Seosaimhín looked towards the snow-clad crow. "The cub is no longer a cub, for she has shed her first blood."

"I have witnessed many of the smaller battles, Druid of Dementia," Nagirrom murmured. She heard the soft choking of strange laughter. "How large is your force?"

"Five thousand," Seosaimhín answered. She smiled, revealing her teeth.

"Impressive," her avian associate stated. "Since they are obviously ready to fight, take your army to the southwest. There is an army led by His Holiness nearing us. His soldiers would make powerful Strigoi warriors."

"His Holiness," Seosaimhín chuckled. "Such a lofty title for a mere mortal, Nagirrom. The pack shall become whole and the alpha female shall lead them into the night to find plentiful game."

"It will not be that easy, my Druid. An army of Lamia is near this Papal feast. An army led by your associate Awvarwy."

"Awvarwy... or Mandubratius." Seosaimhín smiled and shook her head. "We will enjoy meeting with either. Perhaps our former alliance will spring forth sweet apples, and our appetite can enjoy his pleasing taste."

"If his army can be bargained or bought, ally yourself with him," Nagirrom urged. "Yet, you must be persuasive. He is a most stubborn blood-drinker."

"Even the slightest trickle of water can carve canyons from mountains," Seosaimhín purred. "Our words to him will be sweet, as a lover's."

"The Emperor has also sent an army. They will arrive in the next night. Obliterate his army. He destroyed sacred forests. This Charles needs a lesson."

"This pack is ravenous with blood thirst." A strange compulsion urged her to touch the pallid and fair feathers. Seosaimhín bit her lip and glanced at the ground in front of her knees. "Your will shall be done." Seosaimhín stared at the crow as He rested on His statue.

The bird's unsettling gaze fixed on her. "The mists of magic shroud the Emperor's army. Yet through those mists, I can see one you call 'soulless'. That child of Hers, the Roman one. You know of whom I speak, Seosaimhín."

"The wind blows through the cave and whispers his name: Marcus," Seosaimhín answered. "He has not been far from our thoughts. Our pull on his child has faded through the effect of time. Then we thought it best to make her miserable another way. We have been twisting his mind. Your children have helped us in bringing forth his nightmares. She hates to see him in pain." Seosaimhín could not help but smile at that.

"You are obsessing over those two again," Nagirrom warned. "They matter little in our plans. Forget them. Your son learned from his errors in the Otherworld. Connor chose to move forth into another life. You had your revenge against Maél Muire. She suffered for many lifetimes."

"Does Nagirrom desire the Soulless One and his child to continue to exist in this world?" Seosaimhín asked. Incredulity sparked her words. "This soulless one gathers his own pack, Nagirrom, and it is not enough that Maél Muire suffered several lifetimes. She must be miserable always! She dared to thwart our curse! What better way to send her to the Fields of the Judged?"

Seosaimhín considered moving to her feet to pace, yet remained on her knees. She glared at the bird, feeling a seething, defiant rage within. "The Soulless One doesn't deserve to exist either," she growled. "The rest of his party has as much right to exist as the ants do!"

There was a soft sigh. "I believe I understand your perspective, Druid. However, you see the world through the eyes of a mortal. There is so little earth-bound immortals understand. I wish you to destroy this pack's bonds, not the pack. We have need of them. You must present Marcus to me, not just his head."

Seosaimhín ground her teeth. "It will be done."

"Go forth tomorrow night. All shall happen as I have seen it."

She heard a caw-caw and the flap of wings.

"The Druid of Dementia shall quench her desire," Seosaimhín answered. "That desire burns greater than the sun itself. The alpha wolf goes forth with Nagirrom's army."

Outside Prüm Abbey

Máire listened to the others in the distance. They made a ruckus as they continued their mushroom harvest for the creation of the herbal mixture. She had left to gain some quiet time and think over these new tools. She nearly jumped, sensing a Deargh Du approach. She smiled at Julien.

"You aren't planning on staying here, are you?" he asked.

She continued watching him. "No, I just needed peace to concentrate."

"So, will you teach me these skills?"

"Yes, when I master them." She moved in closer and inhaled the scents of the evening. "However, you need to go or else you will only serve as a distraction." She chuckled.

He gave her a boyish grin. "I would never attempt to divert you from your studies. I will stay a mile or so away from you. You tend to become distracted when you study these spells."

"Tools," she corrected him. "I think we Deargh Du were meant to know these as tools. For a mortal, they might be magic. For us, I have a feeling that this is something we were meant to know, and our kind lost the knowledge through our own decadence and over-indulgence."

"Still, Marcus said..." Julien inhaled and exhaled, and removed all traces of his smile. "... 'Julien, you must watch over our Banbh Ceanúil. She loses herself at times to Sophia, the lady of wisdom.'"

Máire chuckled. "Take care that he doesn't hear you attempting to mimic him." She slapped his arm. "Fine. Give me an hour to work on this alone." She leaned in and kissed Julien, before heading towards the lake, whispering the words that allowed her to walk across the water. The water became solidified with every step of her feet. She could hear Julien shuffle his feet behind her. "Go," she called out before turning back towards him and waving him away.

He stared at her but made no move to leave.

"I promise to teach you these things." She then faced forward and continued towards the center of the lake. Máire could hear Julien return to the sylvan trails.

She closed her eyes to concentrate on creating a cylinder around herself. She heard the sound of water rushing around. Mists caressed her face, and Máire opened her eyes to find a circular wall of water surrounding her. The wall rose higher and, after a moment of pleasure at her success, she noticed the walls bend as they began to lose integrity. She willed the walls to reform, and they became straight and strong again.

Afterwards, Máire concentrated on increasing the diameter of the walls. The walls shimmered and slowly started to grow. The maintenance of keeping the walls up became a strain, so she allowed the water to rejoin the rest of the lake. Cold water moved over her boots and she took to the air.

"One last tool," she murmured as she landed on the bank. She wished to create a thin, reflective wall of water. She sent her energy towards the water.

A new wall rose. It began to shimmer and reflect back a moonlit view of the forest. Starlight seemed to magnify towards her.

The sound of padding footsteps trotted towards her.

Máire closed her eyes, finding a store of strength to keep the wall in place, so her concentration could move elsewhere. She heard a tensing of muscles. Máire sensed a shape leaping towards her and rotated in time to catch a black, furry mass. "Hello, Lucius. Did you come to help me?"

The cat stared up at her. "How disappointing, young Deargh Du. I thought you could tell us apart now."

"Brigid?"

The cat's mouth moved into a mysterious smile. "Do you like the wall of water? I find it most beautiful."

Máire rubbed a hand over Brigid and heard more footsteps. Before she could prepare herself, another black and furry creature propelled himself onto her shoulder.

"Well, well," he purred. "Do I have the honor of addressing my Patroness?"

Brigid uttered a somewhat annoyed mew, and Máire released Her.

The cat disappeared and became the human form of Brigid. She then plucked Lucius from Máire's shoulder and rubbed her cheek over his brow. "Hello, my sweet. I have missed your most beautiful eyes."

Lucius purred. "What brings you to this reality, my Lady?"

Máire began to wonder if she needed to leave.

"Do you see that wall of water, Lucius?" Brigid asked the cat. "That is what brought me here. I heard Máire's call, and thought I'd visit her and you, of course." She kissed Lucius' brow.

The fairy cat turned his face to the wall of water. "Máire did this? Why, it's splendid. Brigid, let me down." Lucius squirmed for a moment, and Brigid released him.

"I believe Brigid aided me, but yes, I did bring it forth," Máire corrected. She watched Lucius jog towards the wall, on top of the water, without a second thought. She gazed at him in silence as he approached the barrier of water.

He tapped the wall with a paw and then leaned in for a sniff.

Brigid tutted and chuckled. "Try not to coo over Lu… Lucius. It's very hard to avoid the desire to cuddle him."

Máire smiled back at her. "I think we have all accepted that Lucius decides when and if to give affection, Goddess."

Brigid smiled. "That is the nature of cat-kind." She turned back to examining the wall. Her blonde hair lifted in the winds. "Do you realize how strong and sharp that wall is?"

Máire shook her head.

Brigid picked up a large rock. "Lucius, could you rejoin us?"

The fairy cat ambled back to them.

After his arrival, Brigid threw the boulder towards the wall.

Máire winced at hearing a loud crack and then realized that the rock lay in pieces. The wall remained steadfast, as did the reflection. The wall did not even buckle. She found no words and closed her open mouth.

Brigid walked a few paces to Her left and pulled a sapling tree from the ground. In its place, another grew from the soil. She motioned for Máire and Lucius to follow Her. They tread towards the wall. When they reached the edge of it, Máire leaned in to slide her finger over the sharp side of the wall.

A hand grabbed hers.

"Before you touch the edge, let me show you something," Brigid said. She hefted the sapling and touched the trunk against the side of the wall.

Máire felt her mouth open again, as the trunk split into half as it hit the shimmering edge. It seemed that the side of the wall could slice into anything with just the briefest contact.

"You cannot see it, but the water in this mirrored wall is moving at the edge. It is compressed into a fine line. Go back to the shore and reassert your control over this wall."

Máire heard the scuffling of claws and found herself in the possession of Lucius again. Returning to her spot on the shore, she released the cat and whispered her will to the water. "I have it now," she said to Brigid, feeling her efforts at concentration increase triple-fold.

Brigid rejoined them. "Lucius, can you summon a ball of light for me?" she asked.

"Certainly," the cat acknowledged, while staring at the Goddess for a moment. "Where do you wish it to be, radiant Lady?"

Máire wondered why Lucius hadn't offered to light their paths earlier.

"About fifty yards away from us, Lucius," Brigid instructed.

Lucius raised a paw, and Máire witnessed a growing ball of light glow at the right side of the wall.

"Look over your left shoulder and you will witness a perfect reflection of the light source. That is the nature of the magic you've wielded." Brigid turned to face Máire. "Now, you must alter the wall you've created."

"In what way, Goddess?"

"I want you to change the properties of water so that the light from the single source bathes the entire valley in its brightness."

Máire tried to remember the lessons within the scroll. "I do not know how to do that," she stated, feeling rather ignorant.

"Instead of water reflecting what is within the liquid, the water can absorb the light and amplify it in all directions. This tool will allow you to turn night into day, Máire," Brigid explained.

"I will do so," Máire answered, catching herself almost say 'try'. She wrapped her mind around the wall of water. She sensed she could almost touch the structure of the water, and the water became nothing more than chains of some strange material, chains that could be manipulated. The wall began to shimmer.

A screeching noise grew as the water started to vibrate. The screeching became a thunderous blast. The wall shattered and collapsed under its weight into the lake.

Máire fell to her knees and then sat. How would she ever get these tools to work? Then, she noticed a soft, yet firm hand rest on her shoulder, as Lucius curled into her lap.

"Do not fret," Brigid said. "You have done more than any non-Tuath has done in centuries. The feat you attempted has never been used by a non-Tuath. You must continue studying this skill if you wish to proceed. You are a quick study, Máire, but don't expect to master every aspect of this knowledge with the first attempt." Brigid studied the water. "Allow me to show you what it will look like when you have mastered it."

As Máire stood up, a disgruntled Lucius followed her.

Brigid closed her eyes and murmured the same words to the water.

The wall began to grow, solidifying into an unyielding structure. The surface of the water began to glow. The wall seemed to become a permanent edifice.

"Lucius," Brigid began, "can you make your light source brighter?"

"Yes," Lucius said.

Máire watched the cat simply close his eyes for a moment. His furry brow furrowed in contemplation, and the light became brighter.

Máire turned away from the fearful bright light. She covered her eyes with her arm. She sensed the light fade away, and she stared at the glowing structure.

The structure stopped glowing after a minute, and the reflection faded. The towering wall poured into the lake.

"That was beautiful," she said to the Goddess and the fairy cat. "How can

I hope to master that?"

"Even what is instinctual for many of us still requires practice," Brigid answered. "However, I do have a connection with water, so I cannot remember a time that I could not construct a wall of it. Let's move on to a different aspect of this tool. If you need to create a wall, and there is no water, how do you form a wall?" She smiled at Máire, her mouth moving into the expression of a satisfied cat's.

Máire glanced at the lake for a moment. "My aunt spoke of water in the air," she answered. "It makes sense. After all, that is where mists are born."

"She taught you well." The Goddess stared at the lake. "I think you need to return to the abbey. The sun rises soon, and Julien will turn frantic."

"Lucius, do you plan on jumping on my back again?" Máire chuckled.

"Unlike you, I'm not hindered by the light of day." The fairy cat turned to Brigid. "If the Patron of cats does not have to return to the Otherworld, I was hoping to spend some time hunting and rolling in that patch of wild mint I found. There is more than enough game for two."

Brigid grinned at them. "How could I miss out on such frolics and entertainments?"

The Goddess' eyes revealed a feline cast. Then, the rest of her body contorted into the form of a black cat.

Máire felt as though she could not leave.

Brigid nuzzled her leg, and Máire crouched down to look at her.

"You need to leave," the Goddess said. "Practice your new skills."

"I see Lucius found a friend," an unexpected voice over her shoulder stated.

Máire jumped as Julien stood next to her.

"Yes, he wants to play in the sun," she said.

"Speaking of sun," Julien said while taking her arm, "we need to leave before we are missed."

Máire nodded, and then they took to the air, flying towards the catacombs.

Lamia Camp outside Mehren

Mandubratius drifted in and out of sleep, mulling over his decisions of the evening. The entire process of dealing with Talia left him perturbed, so he consoled himself with too much wine. He shooed away Sextus, after relaying a single message and orders to not disturb him. One went to His Holiness detailing joint training to prepare mortal soldiers for working with the 'Angelic' forces. They would meet late tomorrow evening or the night after.

He could hear Gaius yelling at the soldiers. They slept in the ground this morning for the first time and found it somewhat distressing.

A gentle hand stroked his shoulder.

He opened his blurry eyes. A lovely figure became visible in the dim light. The preternatural darkness foretold the presence of a Deargh Du. His heart swelled, despite the warnings in his head. Máire came to into his view. He could see an oddly happy expression on her face. He'd finally have the opportunity to enjoy her and please her. What a strange thought that was. He had not been in the frame of mind to please any woman in the last few weeks. Mandubratius extended his right arm, wishing to touch her.

"Máire?" His voice croaked her name.

Damn that wine.

"Not Máire," a voice replied, sending shivers up and down his spine.

He scooted away from the figure and fell onto the ground. The voice opened a memory. "Seosaimhín?"

How could that even be possible?

"As true as the cycle of night and day, Mandubratius," she answered. "It is we before you."

The lights illuminated the tent, and the irrational fear that she somehow brought the sunlight with her overwhelmed him. He blinked at the stunning woman before him. Her skin remained as black as a moonless night.

"What are you?"

"We are like the Soulless Ones," Seosaimhín announced. "Yet, we have a soul. We were given this gift long before Maél Muire received hers that fateful night. We hid our age and skin, so we could pass as an old mortal woman. We also found herbs to hide our true nature from the Soulless Ones and their friends. We fooled them all. Maél Muire believed us dead and so did you." The woman tipped her head to the side and smiled. "Then again, perhaps she sensed us once. We allowed you to see us to make a deal with you."

The light dimmed to a comfortable level. Mandubratius found himself blinking again. "What kind of deal?"

Seosaimhín offered her hand to help him up.

He felt some fear at touching her, but the fear of insulting her and instigating her wrath engulfed his original anxiety. Mandubratius took her proffered hand. A strong grip pulled him to a standing position.

Seosaimhín sat down on his cot and patted a spot next her. She had the strangest expression on her face, a dreamy smile that did not engage her eyes. Her eyes appeared focused and remained on him as he sat and faced her. Her dreamy grin lingered on her face. "We have a secret to tell you, Mandubr... Awvarwy, whatever you call yourself these nights." She leaned in and stroked her hand over the left side of his hair. Her dark thumb settled on the hollow of his cheek. Her other hand moved to his thigh.

"And what is this secret?" He felt he sounded confident enough to speak with this woman who resided in a body that seemed to house too many.

Seosaimhín chuckled and leaned in closer. "We are the mother of the Strigoi. We did not create them, but we have given them new direction."

"And what direction is that?" he asked.

"The will of Nagirrom."

He considered her words. Her skills revealed a Deargh Du nature.

Why does she refer to her matron as 'Nagirrom'? Perhaps it is some backwards confusion in Seosaimhín's mind.

"Morrigan?" he asked.

The hand on his thigh moved at lightning speed, forming a painful vice on his testicles. For some reason, it sparked fear this time instead of excitement. Her other hand scratched at the side of his face.

Rising welts itched as they began to heal.

"You will not utter that name in our presence again. To do so is blasphemy. We would kill you."

Mandubratius considered the dagger under his pillow. However, the growing insanity in Seosaimhín's eyes made him reconsider that plan. "My apologies," he said, hoping sweet words would soothe her. "I will do as you bid. So, why does the mother of all Strigoi wish to strike a bargain with me?"

"We wish for alliances," Seosaimhín answered. "Nagirrom is wise in understanding that the Strigoi need strong friends such as the Dark Ones. Nagirrom also remembers the travesty the Soulless Ones caused. Nagirrom desires vengeance, and so does Seosaimhín."

"And if I refuse?" Mandubratius asked, forgetting his earlier dread of this woman. He did not find the idea of forming an allegiance with an insane Deargh Du and her army of Strigoi to be exactly favorable.

"So, chief of the Dark Ones, is your mind not as open as the sky? If it isn't, we will consider you an enemy, now."

Mandubratius said nothing for a moment, while staring into her eyes, which told him that she only needed a small excuse to kill him. Everything about Seosaimhín seemed to be ice. "My mind is open," he informed her. "I will seriously consider this offer." He knew the consequences for saying 'no'.

A smile spread over Seosaimhín's face, like the ripples of icy water breaking through a frozen pool. "We are fawns at play, then." Seosaimhín rose from her seat and meandered to stand in front of him. "Good that your mind is open, chieftain of the Dark Ones." She crouched and stared into his eyes. That unnamed fear rose in the pit of his stomach again.

How could she do this so easily?

"So taxing to be the queen bee of the Strigoi," Seosaimhín whispered. She leaned in towards his left ear. "It forces us to feed more than usual." She began to sniff around his neck, making her intent obvious. "So hungry."

He tried not to shudder, as her breath chilled him. He could not reveal his fear. He needed to tell her that he could not serve as her meal. After all, he did not feed this evening. However, before he could find words, Seosaimhín's mouth locked on his throat. The pain became overwhelming. This was not the gentle and tender blood kiss of most blood-drinkers. They wanted feeding to not be invasive. It made the process and aftereffects easier to hide. This painful feeding felt like an attack. Mandubratius tried to push her away, but Seosaimhín's arms locked him in place, and he could not move.

She pinned his legs down with her own.

He heard a weak protest in his throat. He sounded as weak and as pitiful as he did when Felician and the others found him. Yet, this was a thousand times worse than his transformation. Every moment in her grip made him even weaker. He could no longer endure the pain.

Then, the images came and the pain dulled. The inescapable visions of strange creatures flayed apart made him wish to run, for reasons he couldn't understand. He witnessed a dark figure pull forth the gore-drenched innards of these Strigoi as they wriggled in torture. A truly disgusting revelation dawned on him that Seosaimhín experimented on these beings in an attempt to improve their talents. His own torture techniques and games seemed so ordinary and mundane in comparison.

Soon those visions faded, and he began to hear screams in his ears. Mandubratius opened his mind's eye and witnessed the process of transformation. The fear in the mortal's eyes seemed so eerily similar to his own during his elevation to Lamia. He experienced strange growing warmth of external pleasure that made him wish to vomit. Seosaimhín's laughter echoed in the din of screaming mortals, begging for mercy, their wailing resonated of the cries of his own victims. Awvarwy wished to escape, but then Seosaimhín turned to face him in this nightmare.

How could that be possible?

The remaining shred of his rational mind speculated that perhaps this was how that insane Deargh Du viewed herself, or this was her balance.

She snarled at him, and all became black.

Mandubratius awoke and immediately felt agony radiate through his entire body. The pain seemed concentrated on the left side of his neck. He longed to sit up, but weakness kept him pinned to his bedding. He groaned and started to blink his eyes, but his blurry vision kept everything out of focus.

"Don't try to sit up, General. You are too weak," a distant voice called.

"What happened?" Mandubratius asked the gray figure fast approaching.

"We found you here, sir. Almost completely drained and we found no signs as to who did it."

He heard other voices around him. The memory of the evening came back to him in a flash, and he moaned at the recall of the event. The pain increased so much that he felt his entire body become immobile. His vision faded and that overwhelming fear took him again.

"General, we've fed you," the figure advised while drawing closer. "What can I do to help?"

Mandubratius focused his mind on the present. He was weak, but not as weak as he had been in Seosaimhín's grasp. He concentrated on his motionless limbs and he forced himself to relax. He opened his eyes and finally recognized Sextus. He could hear Gaius yelling at the new troops.

"How many know of my state?" he asked Sextus.

"General Gaius, myself, and the five officers that contributed to your feeding. If anyone asks, we say that you were attacked by the Strigoi during a scouting mission. We have kept Lady Talia away from your tent."

"Very good," Mandubratius whispered.

"Sir, the others and I wish to inquire what happened two nights ago, if it is not inappropriate for me to ask."

Mandubratius sighed and stared at the ceiling of the tent, trying to decide how much he should he tell. He didn't want to admit to the fear, but there was something about Seosaimhín. Some aspect of the officer's question caught him by surprise. But then the time frame Sextus mentioned caught his attention. "Yesterday? Two nights? How long has it been, Sextus?"

"It has been two nights since we discovered you, sir. Did a Strigoi enter the camp?"

He heard worry creep into the Lamia's voice. It would look poorly on the guards and the others if the infiltrator had not been seen or sensed.

"You have nothing to fear regarding repercussions, Sextus," Mandubratius replied. "I believe that this was a rogue Deargh Du from Ard Mhacha in Hibernia. She flew in, cloaked herself in darkness, and I didn't know she was here until she revealed herself."

"Why would a Deargh Du do such a thing?" Sextus asked.

"She wished to make a deal with me that I could not accept. I informed her that I would consider it. However, I believe the reason that I'm alive, for the moment, is because I did not tell her 'no'."

"Yet, she will want an answer," Sextus reasoned aloud.

"Yes." Mandubratius mulled over his options. He needed to leave camp as soon as possible. "I will leave tomorrow evening, Sextus. I will join our allies near Prüm. I can draw this Deargh Du away from our forces and toward a number of its enemies."

Sextus nodded his head. "Sir, His Holiness has arrived with his armies."

"Excellent," Mandubratius said. He believed he could sit up, now. He felt his fear fade as his plans came forth for the larger Papal Army and his escape. "Tell Leo that I'll meet with him before I leave tomorrow night. I am certain that this Deargh Du will be watching, so we will send a number of decoys dressed in similar clothing in all possible directions. After the decoys and I have separated, begin breaking camp. I assume Seosaimhín and the Strigoi will follow me towards Prüm. Therefore, take the combined Lamia and papal forces northwest towards Pelm. I will send word then of what to do next."

"That is a good plan," Sextus answered. He headed for the tent flap and then stopped. "May I ask you something else, sir? When this rogue Deargh Du fed on you, what was it like?"

Mandubratius sat up on his cot. "I give you leave in private to ask questions, Sextus. However, on this subject, I will remain silent. Do not ask me about this again."

Sextus nodded, saluted him, and left.

Mandubratius slid back down, feeling his strength fade.

Mandubratius paced about the tent, sensing her eyes on him, despite the fact that many waited outside the walls. He contemplated what kind of protection youngling Lamia could offer against a monster such as Seosaimhín. In his current agitated state, he did not even call for Talia for relaxation.

He paused and stared at the western side of the tent. Six Lamia and a mortal approached his tent. He allowed himself a quick study in the bronze mirror. His features radiated calm. At least everything in his face remained tranquil and composed, except for his eyes. He concentrated on making them serene as the soldiers outside addressed Leo.

A rather deceitful plan came to his mind. Perhaps by concentrating on this, he could push his fears regarding Seosaimhín to the back of his mind. Mandubratius looked at the mirror again and concentrated on appearing fretful. "You may enter," he said.

A soldier raised the tent flap, and Leo walked into the tent, looking weary from his day.

"Leave, and take your men with you," Mandubratius addressed the new Lamia.

The Lamia saluted him and filed out of the tent.

Mandubratius waited in silence, wishing them to move faster. Their interference might prevent the success of his plan to ingratiate himself to His

Holiness again.

"Your men said that this was urgent." Pope Leo watched him. "I was most surprised that only your generals greeted me earlier."

Mandubratius closed his eyes and raised his hand, as the sensations emanating from the six other Lamia faded with every step. He met Leo's eyes.

"The leader of the Strigoi came into camp several nights ago. She entered my tent and demanded that I form a separate alliance with her, or she would kill me," he said to the Pope. He would need to leave a letter for Gaius if his plan worked. He allowed Leo to consider the information.

"You either accepted her offer, or you did not have to make an immediate choice. Since I am not dead, I believe you did not ally yourself with her. Something in your countenance says that you know this being." The Pope stared at him with dark eyes.

"You are most astute," he answered, finding pleasure in his skills at manipulation. "I met her over two hundred years ago in Éire. She is a thousand times more dangerous, now. The truth is that this woman is a blood-drinker, has hidden it from her own kind, and wields a dangerous insanity."

At least that statement rings with veracity.

"And this blood-drinker is even more frightening to you than the de... Strigoi."

"I believe that the Church created a majority of demons to scare the simple-minded." Mandubratius smiled for a moment. "I aided the Church in this matter. It meant more money for us and the Holy Church. Yet, when I looked into Seosaimhín's eyes, there was a demon."

The Pope nodded. "Your candidness is most unexpected. I am honored with this confidence. I must admit that I was fearful that you would decide to feed from me, or transform me tonight."

Mandubratius shrugged, thinking the Pope did not understand that he was more useful as a malleable mortal under the effects of Lamia mind-bending.

"I cannot tell my officers. I believe that they would not panic, but our younglings would. I plan on leading this monster far away from camp. The plan, at first, is to confuse her. Eight of us, including myself, dress in the same cloaks and go in different directions. Hopefully, that will give me the time to head towards Prüm. My associates are at Prüm Abbey, making preparations for battle against the Strigoi. There are Deargh Du there, and I believe this blood-drinker to be Deargh Du. It is best that they deal with her."

"So, we are all in danger now, because you are here, and this Deargh Du wants an answer," Leo ascertained.

"I believe that is correct," Mandubratius replied. "Gaius will be in charge, and he will continue the training between the combined forces, but after he moves the encampment to Pelm." He paused for a moment. "Once our allies and I come to a decision about Seosaimhín, I will inform my subordinates there about the truth. They know there is a rogue Deargh Du chasing me. However, they do not know the truth about this blood-drinker. She's truly insane, Your Holiness. I fear that one of Seosaimhín's victims may be in danger as well."

Mandubratius paused. It was time to give more details and pretend some form of tenderness. No mortals were immune to tales of woe. "I wanted this victim dead once, but she nursed me to health during many of our recent battles with the Strigoi. I must give her the truth, for I care for her." He left it at that. It would be enough to further manipulate the Pope.

"I doubt Máire will believe me, but I don't have the luxury to worry about that." Mandubratius paced about trying to look confused, morose, and somewhat lovesick. "Granted, I am still quite fearful of Seosaimhín, but if I cannot make Máire believe me, I must protect her. Also, if I bring forth Seosaimhín to these other blood-drinkers, we may be able to destroy her, and then annihilate her army. I will leave directly." He tried not to gag at the way he put forth these arguments. This speech sounded too much of Marcus and his ilk. Yet, the Pope looked motivated with his words, and yet still frightened. Mandubratius tried to not look too pleased with his success.

"Then, may God protect you." Leo made the sign of the cross. "Be fleet of foot."

Mandubratius merely nodded his head and pulled the cowl of his cloak over his head. He then walked around the Pope and could no longer hold back a satisfied smile.

Seosaimhín hovered over the camp. It looked less and less like the chief of the Dark Ones would agree to her terms. "Word-drenched coward," she mumbled. "Awvarwy loves his games and the sound of his voice too much."

She noticed a large party of black-cloaked figures exit a tent. They reached the center of camp and all eight began running in different directions.

"Which way, Nagirrom?" She studied the running figures. Burgundy lay to the west. The Emperor and his fighting forces dallied in the north. The Soulless Ones and their associates waited in between, perhaps.

Seosaimhín closed her eyes. Nagirrom remained silent for now.

"Go in the direction of the Soulless Ones and their friends," she murmured. This would be useful to her minions. "He seeks protection," she stated as she noticed three travelling the direction towards those lands.

Best to see where each of them stops.

She steeled herself for the chase and the kill.

Talia wandered towards the tent for her usual evening debaucheries.

Mandubratius seemed so frustrated these nights that he simply requested she arrive before they broke up camp. Their coitus was usually nothing long, but it still felt somewhat degrading. Then again, what else could she do? Mandubratius remained her sponsor, and his assertions that she wasted the gifts of the Lamia rang true.

Talia lifted her flimsy, silken gown to keep it from becoming muddy. She entered his tent and searched for Mandubratius, but the tent stood deserted and cold. She took a blanket from his bed and wrapped it around her, relieved for an opportunity to cover herself.

She sensed another Lamia approach.

"Where do you think you're off to?" asked the intruder.

Talia took a moment to turn her head and look at the intruder.

General Gaius dropped the tent flap behind him and unfastened his sword belt. "I need a good, quick turn with you," he said.

"Where's Mandubratius?" she asked.

Gaius walked towards Talia. "He isn't here," Gaius replied. "However, he left me in charge. Now, get on your knees, or we can make this painful for you."

"I refuse to get on my knees unless you tell me where my sponsor is and why he didn't take me," Talia purred, trying a feeble attempt in order to sound seductive.

"Mmmmm, why play at being coy, Talia? Your sponsor left, and now I must deal with the entire army and His Holiness. I need release." Gaius moved in closer.

"Soon," she purred. "Tell me where Mandubratius went."

General Gaius grinned at her. "An old friend of his stopped by. After seeing her, Mandubratius decided to leave for Prüm Abbey and seek the Angels as well as the Imperial Army."

Talia felt herself pout. "Why didn't he take me?"

"I'm not sure why he didn't take you. He did leave in a hurry. He was so worried about being seen that he sent seven others as decoys in various directions to protect himself. Only a few have returned." Gaius' eyes turned away from her. His face revealed worry and concern.

Talia wondered what or who could have frightened Mandubratius. As annoying as he could be, Mandubratius seldom displayed cowardice. She studied Gaius, who looked as though he had lost interest in her company. She turned away and got on her hands and knees, dropping the blanket. She decided to submit, in case his appearance proved deceiving. She glanced back at him.

Gaius returned her stare. "It would seem that I'm not in the mood for pleasure anymore. I should check on the night watch and see if more of the decoys have returned."

Talia sat back on her bottom and grabbed the blanket.

Gaius turned away and left.

Talia fumed as the tent flap swung shut.

How dare Mandubratius leave me in this situation! For all my humiliation, he simply abandoned me without a word!

She stood on unsteady feet and stumbled towards the box where Mandubratius kept his extra clothing. Talia ripped off the silken dress and pulled on a tunic and pair of breeches. She snatched a small dagger from the bottom of the box. She then took a long, woolen cloak and stomped out of the tent barefoot.

The soldiers, packing away tents, ignored her.

Talia flung the remains of her tattered, silk dress into the mud and headed into the woods, deciding to leave the noise of the camp far behind.

chapter six

Prüm Abbey

andubratius slowed to a jog as he approached Prüm Abbey. The entire act of keeping his senses focused on finding Seosaimhín made him weary. The Strigoi would be too slow to follow him, so that left Seosaimhín. She would be the only blood-drinker attempting to follow him.

Nearing the abbey, he could discern the arrival of a blood-drinker ahead.

How in the name of the Gods did Seosaimhín get around me?

He stopped in his tracks and drew his sword, hoping the sound of the blade did not give away his location. Mandubratius crouched in preparation for an attack, ignoring the muddy road. He sensed her move closer to him.

Mandubratius began to scan the skies. Seosaimhín's invisibility in the darkness consumed him. He could feel her approaching fast! He swung his sword, hearing the blade slice through the air. A miss! He swung his blade through the atmosphere again, when the reverberating clang of metal echoed around him. He stepped away and brought up his blade to guard himself against an attack.

The figure dropped out of the darkness, but it wasn't Seosaimhín who greeted him... It was Marcus!

Marcus studied him for a moment, with his gladii held protectively.

"Be careful! You nearly cut me!" Mandubratius accused the composed Deargh Du. His current mood left him without much in the way of humor. He kept his sword at the ready.

Marcus tipped his head to one side and lowered his gladii. "You aren't meaning to swing that at me again, are you?"

He stared back at Marcus. If there were no alliance, this would be the perfect opportunity to strike. Mandubratius sheathed his sword. "Must you sneak up on me in such a manner?" he asked.

"I had to make sure it was not our enemy," Marcus replied, before sheathing his gladii.

Mandubratius tried not to roll his eyes. "That is a load of sheep excrement, my friend. You know very well who approached you. You wished for entertainment."

The Deargh Du smiled, revealing his teeth. "So, what are you doing in the woods alone?" Marcus asked. "Don't you have an army now? Or are you their scout?"

"Oh, ha ha ha!" Mandubratius found himself in a foul mood, yet Marcus wanted to verbally spar. "I... we do not have time for these so-called witty amusements of yours. There is a rogue Deargh Du that wishes to kill me."

"Now, why would any Deargh Du want to do that?" The other blood-drinker smirked. "Certainly, he or she would not carry out such a despicable act for your invasion of Éire."

"Marcus, your sarcasm is better suited to drunks and nincompoops. I don't fit in either of those categories."

"So, who was this rogue Deargh Du?"

"Who IS this rogue Deargh Du, you idiot! Didn't they teach you to conjugate at the Grammaticus?" Mandubratius began to pace in his impatience. Marcus' attempts to use games annoyed him.

"I know how to conjugate my first language," Marcus answered. "I used 'was' because you either killed the rogue, or it happened in the past, wherever you ran from. That is why I used past tense."

Mandubratius bit back his rage. "For a moment, old friend, let's pretend that you and I are of comparable intelligence, despite how distasteful that is for me to say. That Deargh Du still follows me, therefore present tense is appropriate!"

"If you say so."

Mandubratius opened his mouth to reply when he heard movement around him. Marcus did the same. His hands rested on his gladii.

"Did you sense anything?" Mandubratius whispered. He felt quite shielded at the moment.

"There is someone following us," Marcus admitted, "or rather, someone on the edge of my senses. They are not moving close. I can't tell what race they are. Let's go to the abbey."

The Deargh Du turned away and began to run towards the distant gate.

Mandubratius followed him. He could sense movement above and around himself. Every noise ignited his fears, as if he were nothing more than a mouse scurrying past the trap of a hungry and gleeful cat.

They ran past the gates and through the yard, past the gardens and fields of new grain that the monks tended with care. The thick, noxious smell of mushrooms and herbs infused every breath. Marcus seemed impervious to the stench. Perhaps he was used to it.

His guide slowed down as they neared the center of the grounds. Blood-drinkers lined up to deposit more mushrooms that others, including Amata, studied closely. He noticed the oblivious Empress Irene even carrying a basket; granted, she looked somewhat annoyed with her present duties.

"You made the Empress join in this mushroom hunt?" Mandubratius blurted out, forgetting his earlier fear.

Marcus nodded before waving an arm at a large oak.

Edward and Mac Alpin flew towards them.

"One sou," Edward held out an empty hand towards Mac Alpin. The Ekimmu Cruitne nodded in his direction. "It was Mandubratius under all that grime and dirt, not Horatio."

Mac Alpin ignored Edward's extended hand and began sniffing the air.

"Later, if you two don't mind," Marcus interrupted them. "Arwin, what does your nose tell you? Do you smell something not quite right?"

"Yes," Mac Alpin answered. "There is a Deargh Du, but a strange smelling one that I don't recognize."

"Is it coming closer?" Mandubratius asked.

"No, it is leaving, turning away from our location, at the least."

"Should we sound the alarm?" Marcus asked.

"You should. That rogue Deargh Du is a madwoman. She's been hunting me since I left my camp last night." Mandubratius coughed for a moment, gagging on the smell that permeated the grounds.

"Mandubratius, who is this rogue Deargh Du?"

Marcus had that smug look on his face again. At least, he finally remembered how to ask him the question in proper Latin.

"First, I need to tell Máire," Mandubratius answered.

He heard sniffing again.

"The scents are gone now," Mac Alpin stated. "The wind could have changed. We should tell everyone to keep their eyes open. Edward and I will keep our noses to the sky."

"Edward, could you inform the leaders of each group?" Marcus asked. "From the gatherers to the examiners?"

"Ave, General." Edward grinned and attempted a salute.

Marcus laughed and shook his head.

"His salute is nearly as bad as Máire's," Mac Alpin added, joining in the laughter.

"Back to your duties, soldier," Marcus said to Mac Alpin.

Mandubratius watched the Pict laugh even harder.

"I'm not a mere soldier for you to order about," Mac Alpin answered. "However, I will go back to watching the skies and grounds, because I've never seen Mandubratius look so worried in all my nights."

"Are you going to take me to Máire, or do I have to find her myself?" Mandubratius hissed. "And yes, I am worried."

"Máire is working on something by herself and doesn't like to be disturbed," Marcus answered. He started walking towards the tables where the others were looking over the mushrooms and herbs.

Mandubratius could hear the voices chattering about poor quality and dubious properties. "There is a rogue Deargh Du who may be after your child-in-darkness!" he shouted at Marcus.

Marcus turned back to face him with a prominent frown. "Well done, then, Awvarwy. You brought this enemy to Máire."

"You Deargh Du can surround and take care of this one," he said. "Whatever happened to strength in numbers?"

"That only works with superior strength," Marcus answered. "I hope this is only a mere scout from the army of the Deargh Du in Ard Mhacha."

"All the more reason to find Máire and protect her," Mandubratius answered. He tried to not laugh at that noble statement.

Marcus' face turned to a half-smile. "You wouldn't want to sneak up on Máire, if this is only a game, Mandubratius. The last person who did that is still healing."

"Gutted?" Mandubratius asked.

"No, singed," Marcus chortled.

"I will take my chances," Mandubratius replied.

"She's about three miles northwest, near a lake on the river Mönbach," Marcus answered. "Roll towards the water if she sets you aflame."

"Thank you," Mandubratius answered, revealing his impatience. He turned and began walking towards the gate, then looked back at Marcus. The Deargh Du rejoined one of the tables next to an old mortal woman and began examining the stinky mushrooms. "You're not joining me?"

He watched Marcus blanch. The Deargh Du turned away from the fungus. "I'd rather face this rogue Deargh Du than disturb Máire now."

"Oh, I understand," Mandubratius said with a smirk. "You still haven't pleased her in bed. She's cranky."

Marcus raised a redcap mushroom and began examining it. "Go, before I break your legs," he said. He then dropped it in a large sack to his left.

Mandubratius paused for a moment, wondering if he needed to respond in kind, yet the matter of telling Máire about Seosaimhín weighed on him. He started to run towards the western gate.

Heloise watched another group of blood-drinkers move towards her with a bag of mushrooms. It became easier to tell one group from the other, after working with them for a few nights. She found the Lamia there to be personable and quite human-ish. Then again, that was only Amata, Patroclus,

Reginald, and the sweet youth, Horatio. The Empress Irene was not friendly at all. The Empress obviously found being amongst a large gathering of unfamiliar blood-drinkers somewhat frightening, and she was an Empress. Such unfriendly behavior should be expected, even if Empress Irene's sponsor would soon be gathering mushrooms with his co-consul.

The transformed Strigoi seemed skittish but diligent in their duties. They made the appearance of putting forth a peaceful hope. They spoke softly most of the time and gave the impression of finding the other races confusing.

On the opposite side from soft and gentle lay the Ekimmu Cruitne. Heloise found them to be a loud and affable bunch. They would bring gifts, such as wild moonflowers, to her. They enjoyed their storytelling and spoke of ancient battles. The majority brought simple, musical instruments with them.

A lovely, blonde Sugnwr Gwaed presented a bag of mushrooms to her. This line was quieter than the Ekimmu Cruitne and Lamia. Not as beautiful as the Deargh Du, but they possessed a sweet innocence. At times, animals of the forest trotted through the gates and would stare at the Sugnwr Gwaed with gentle intensity. They brought no musical instruments, but Heloise found their singing to be enthralling and their voices seemed to swell half in song.

The voice of the blonde blood-drinker interrupted Heloise's thoughts.

"Will this do?" the Sugnwr Gwaed asked.

Heloise opened the bag and dumped the contents on the table.

"This is an excellent selection," she informed the young woman, who may have been far older than her. Heloise held out the bag.

The woman smiled and took the bag. She walked a few steps away and took to the sky.

Heloise pushed all but a few mushrooms into a larger bag destined for the grinder. She then heard a throat clear, and a beautiful but impatient Deargh Du stared at her.

They rarely spoke... at least, the ones she did not know. They had an air of superiority at times that she found most annoying. It seemed as though they had lost most of their humanity. The ones that spent time with her in the basement in Vézelay seemed to regard her and Julien with respect, gratitude, and something similar to worship. Yet, the remainder that joined them in Aachen seemed suspicious of them. Perhaps they found themselves obsessed with loneliness. They left their home behind and found foreigners to be feared. However, there were many that seemed to think themselves as Gods, or at least lesser Gods.

The impatient Deargh Du dumped the bag of mushrooms on her table and left without a word.

Heloise heard another throat clear behind her. She turned and found Sáerlaith behind her.

"I must apologize for my line. We have the reputation of being rude know-it-alls for good reason." Sáerlaith smiled. "You have been sorting mushrooms and herbs for some time. Let me take your place. You rest or have a meal."

Heloise smiled back at Sáerlaith. "Thank you. I do need a break." She scanned the cloister and witnessed Julien pacing in a corner by himself, instead of sorting or bagging the ground mixture. She approached him. "Is something the matter, Julien?" she asked.

Her son stopped pacing and stared at her with a strange intensity. "No, nothing is the matter," he answered. "Whatever made you think that something is wrong?"

Heloise motioned to the ground. "You've worn a track through the grass, my love."

Julien tried to smile at her. He looked down at his feet. "Why, yes. There is a path." He uttered a strained chuckle.

"If this is about Reginald, he and I have made our peace. He is my son, even though I'd like to punish him for some of the things he's done. He is trying to make up for his errors."

"Actually, I was not thinking of Reginald. What bothers me is that you're here while there is a rogue Deargh Du near the abbey. Not to mention the Strigoi could strike at any moment. Why haven't you gone home to Vézelay?"

"Because I'm helping with the organization of mortals that grind the mushrooms during the day," Heloise answered. "Besides, your mother did come up with the idea of the herb and mushroom mixture in the wine, remember? I may be old, but I have knowledge." She smirked at her son.

"I realize that you've assisted us in many ways, but you're in danger. Reginald and I feel that if things do not go as planned, we need you to be safe at home."

Heloise studied her son. "Who wouldn't feel safe with over three thousand immortals protecting them?"

"I know, but I feel it would be best for you to be in Vézelay," he insisted. "The battlefield is the last place I'd want to see you."

"I'll go home when the time is right. I won't set foot on the battlefield. Don't worry."

"I will try not to." Julien scanned the western wall of the abbey. "You should request an escort for your trip home. I know brigands wandering the night are nothing, in comparison to the Strigoi, but the roads are still a danger."

"I will request an escort." She noticed her son's face remained pinched in displeasure.

"What else troubles you?" Heloise asked Julien.

"Nothing else, mother," he answered.

Heather Poinsett Dunbar & Christopher Dunbar

"Yes, there is. I've seen that look on your face before."

"Look? What look?"

"I remember you making that face when you found out that Flor's father promised her to Reginald." She took his chin between her fingers and further studied Julien's face. "You tend to wear this face when Máire runs off to her studies involving those scrolls."

"It's not the studies that worry me," Julien admitted. "Mandubratius left here over an hour ago to find her, even after she forbade interruptions. The first few nights, I was allowed to go make sure she did not become slave to her new knowledge, but then she told me I was a distraction." He pulled away from her and began to pace again. "Why does he get to visit her?"

"Are you worried for her safety, or are you jealous?" Heloise asked.

"Jealous? I'm not jealous, mother, but when that bastard is about, he constantly demands her attentions."

Heloise watched Julien continue to pace. "That is jealousy. In your mind, you see her spending more time with him than you."

"I'm worried for her safety," Julien grumbled.

Heloise covered her mouth as she chuckled. "After seeing that poor former Strigoi get singed for trying to protect her from her experiments, I would think that you would be more concerned for that Lamia's safety. Your love will be fine, I'm sure."

Julien stopped pacing and turned to face her. "I suppose I do feel jealous of Mandubratius. However, it's rather selfish of me, considering that we were speaking about your safety, earlier."

"I don't believe he's spent half the time with her that you have. Besides that, you don't annoy her in order to get her attention." Heloise smiled again. "At least, I think you don't."

"Yes, well returning to the former subject." Julien studied the western wall again. "When do you plan on asking for an escort and returning to Vézelay?"

"I'm not quite ready to go home, just yet. There is much left to do." Heloise followed his stare. Julien's distraction seemed to fade.

"What is left?" he asked, meeting her eyes.

"We must finish preparing these mushrooms and herbs for the mixture. Perhaps, instead of concentrating on Máire and that pitiful Lamia, you should join me. We do have our duties."

Julien nodded his head. "I have herbs to gather."

"And I'm most pleased that you do well in your selections. I have mushrooms to examine in the meantime, before they start affecting me again." Heloise stood up on her tiptoes and kissed his cheek.

The crack of lightning startled Mandubratius as he neared the figure in the distance. Máire's form reflected in the moonlit water. At least, it seemed to resemble her.

A steady thrum of energy pulsed in a moment of power. That power pushed him aside and cracked the earth's surface. Mandubratius landed face-first in soft grass. He pushed himself up and found a crater in the earth about five feet away.

"Isn't it enough that I was almost stabbed earlier?" he asked the sky.

He heard a soft rustle and turned towards the noise. The figure moved towards him in somewhat poor-looking traveling garments.

"Máire?"

She stopped and stared at him. "Mandubratius, is that you?"

"May I approach you?" he asked.

"What are you doing here?" She sounded irritated.

"Looking for you," he answered. He began to walk towards her, deciding to give up on waiting for permission.

She said nothing and just continued to stare. Her arms moved across her chest and her features revealed impatience. He could have sworn he heard a tapping foot.

Mandubratius grinned at her. There was just something about her when she allowed her annoyance to emerge. "What are you doing here away from the abbey?" he asked.

"I wanted to be alone."

"But why?" He could no longer sense Seosaimhín, Marcus refused to join him, and Máire's puppy probably toiled in the mushroom gathering. The wish to play another round of their wits-matching game returned.

"I'd rather not discuss it," Máire answered. "Why are you looking for me?"

"I have some bad news for you," he began.

"Well, get to the point! I don't have time for a game tonight!"

"The mother of your former betrothed is alive."

Her features became paler, like beautiful alabaster. Her annoyance faded. "Seo…Seo…Seosaimhín?" Máire stuttered. "That's impossible! I killed her myself." The Deargh Du started to back away from him.

He took a few steps closer and felt his smile fade away. "I am sorry, but she is not dead, Máire. She's a blood-drinker, some variety of Deargh Du or perhaps she's one of a Celtic line that I do not know. She revealed many of the traits that the Deargh Du display, but in some ways, she was not Deargh Du."

"What traits do you mean?" Her voice revealed fear.

"She flies, does that thing you and the others do with darkness and light," Mandubratius answered. "She's strong, stronger than most blood-drinkers."

Máire looked about to faint. This may have been amusing many months ago, but now he regretted giving this truth. He watched Máire's eyes widen.

"You've seen her?"

"She surprised me in camp... near Mehren," Mandubratius admitted.

The Deargh Du wrinkled her face in thought and put a hand over her eyes. "Why did she come to you?"

"She wanted the Lamia to join her army."

There was that beautiful frustration again.

"Army? What army? Can't you just tell me the entire truth at once, Mandubratius?"

He took another few steps closer and moved her hand covering her eyes. She pulled her hand away from his and stared at him.

"Máire," he whispered. "Seosaimhín leads the Strigoi."

Her eyes widened again, before falling backwards into leaf litter and grass.

He felt a strange urge of concern grow. She didn't hit her head or anything, but still, she did not move. He crouched down next to her. The Deargh Du's new mascot, that black cat, bounded over to her and began to nudge Máire's shoulder and neck with his nose.

Mandubratius grabbed her shoulders and gently shook her. "Máire?" No response. He raised his hand and slapped her. It was a gentle slap. At least he believed it to be gentle, yet a fist collided with his head, and Mandubratius landed on the ground a few feet away.

"Damn it all, woman!" He hit the ground with opened fists. He sat up and witnessed Máire rise to a sitting position.

"What happened?" she asked, while watching him with accusing eyes. She sounded groggy.

"You hit me!" he yelled. "I was just trying to rouse you."

"I doubt that," she responded. "You were taking advantage of my condition and were about to have your way with me."

"I swear that thought never crossed my mind!" Mandubratius said. "I was merely trying to revive you." He stared at her, experiencing a growing annoyance with her. He watched her calm.

The black cat climbed into her lap, and she began to pet him. "Fine." She stroked the cat's brow with a gentle hand. "Let's assume that you tell the truth for once. Seosaimhín leads the Strigoi, and you were not about to defile me."

"Let's assume that I tell the truth when I'm sincere," Mandubratius said, pushing aside his own annoyance. He hated to admit that he did deserve some of her fury. "I'm very sincere," he added, finally allowing his face to reveal his fear of Seosaimhín. "Look at me, Máire. Seosaimhín is alive."

Máire studied him for a moment. She exhaled, looking down at the cat before she met his eyes again.

"Alright," she said. "I believe you. This is a rare moment of sincerity for you. Did you say that Seosaimhín was a Deargh Du?"

"Yes, but still unlike any Deargh Du I have ever seen. Perhaps she is related to Deargh Du, or is something else altogether. She does things that you and your line do, but her skin.. it's as black as her heart. She looks young. Much younger than the last time I spoke with her in Éire."

"How can she look younger?" Máire whispered. She lowered her face. "How beautiful is she?"

Mandubratius smiled. "Do I detect a hint of vanity? Are you concerned that your archenemy is more beautiful than you?" He felt a slight sting as a rock hit his shoulder. "Ouch!" he exclaimed. It wasn't that painful, but it hurt enough. "Why did you do that?"

Máire stroked the cat again. He heard a loud and insistent purr. "You deserved that," she said.

"What did I do to deserve you throwing rocks at me?" Mandubratius grumbled. "I came here to warn you of Seosaimhín. Is this the thanks I am to receive?" He was surprised that she did not look annoyed with him.

"We are talking seriously about a person who is leading our enemy, Mandubratius. We knew her over two hundred years ago, and you're joking about a serious and reasonable question. I need to know if she's beautiful. It may aid us in understanding what she is."

He lost his smile again. "Yes. She was beautiful, like a radiant statue of ebony."

She studied his eyes and nodded her head. "I believe you. The last time I saw her though…" Máire grew silent. "I… threw a sword at her. It impaled her. She should have died, but obviously she did not."

Mandubratius scooted in closer to her. "She claimed she was transformed before you."

"Impossible. She lied," Máire said. "I remember when I was mortal, I witnessed Seosaimhín walk in the sun, and she was old." She turned away for a moment. "No, I'm mistaken." Máire met his eyes again. "I never saw her during the day. I know I never witnessed her eat or drink. Strange." Máire patted the cat and became mute again. "She must have been Deargh Du for many years before you knew her. Perhaps, she fooled her own son. I almost feel sorry for him." Máire sighed. "She looked to be so old when I saw her. How could she hide her age?"

"She informed me that she used herbs to hide her age and status as a blood-drinker." Mandubratius leaned in and scratched the cat's chin for a moment. "At least, that is what she told me before she tried to drain me dry."

"That must have been frightening."

"And very painful," Mandubratius admitted. "Even my transformation was not quite as terrifying."

"Why is her skin black, though?" Máire asked. He sensed it was a rhetorical musing until a voice answered the query.

"Seosaimhín was and is still obsessed with death. She would experiment on plants, animals, and even Deargh Du to find answers to death's secrets."

Mandubratius searched the field and the surrounding lands, looking for the source of the voice. Then he realized that Máire was looking at the cat.

"She learned to extract the Deargh Du's blood and simulated the process of transformation against the poor creature's will. The transformation made her mad, yet not in the typical way. As you know, the first night is the night of madness, and yet that madness never left Seosaimhín. Another side effect of this false transformation was that her skin became as pitch. Morrigan was furious."

"Who just said all that?" Mandubratius asked.

"I did, you blind Lamia!"

Mandubratius looked around the landscape again.

"You're looking away, closer, closer," the voice taunted him. "There we are. See the kitty? I am speaking to you."

"But, only the Celtic lines hear animals," he said. "I must be going mad."

There was a loud, belly laugh, and he watched the cat roll onto his back and kick his stout legs.

"Mandubratius is Lamia, how can he hear you or any fae?" Máire asked, rubbing the cat's belly.

"Silly child," the cat answered. He rolled back onto his feet. "Despite the gifts of the Deargh Du, you are still stuck with a mortal's eyes. I stretched the truth a bit when I said only the Deargh Du and Sugnwr Gwaed can hear me. I choose for Mandubratius to hear me, so he can. Yet, your line and the Sugnwr Gwaed can hear me, whether I choose it or not."

The cat's green eyes gleamed in the night. He studied Mandubratius with an all-knowing smile.

"Why do you choose to communicate with me... Lucius, was it?" Mandubratius asked.

"Must I divulge those reasons?" the fairy cat asked. "Just accept it. I am fae. At times, there is no reason for anything I choose to do!"

Mandubratius heard Máire giggle and start snorting. He couldn't help but grin a little at the snorts.

The cat strained his neck around to look at Máire. "And why are you laughing? You need to return to your studies. I get to play. You have to learn."

"But Lugh, what about Mandubratius and Seosaimhín?"

"Seosaimhín is gone, now. She is not your worry at the moment."

Máire rubbed the cat again. "But she cursed me," she muttered. "What if it becomes active again because of her presence?"

The cat closed his eyes at the gentle caresses. "You were never cursed to begin with, Máire. She tried, but you allowed it to manifest within. You felt as though you weren't ready for the transformation, so you wanted an excuse for that anxiety you experienced."

"I was ready," Máire answered.

Mandubratius watched Máire pout.

"You were only ready for a short term transformation to suit the needs of your revenge against your betrothed and Mandubratius. Of course, it doesn't look like you managed to kill Mandubratius. Oh yes, Morrigan stopped you." The cat purred.

"I thought you only hurt me to stop me," Mandubratius said. "Why would you want to kill me, Máire? You like me."

Máire's eyes began to glow. "How can you ask that? You know very well what you—"

"Máire," the fairy cat's voice revealed an authoritative tone now. "This is beneath you. You need to concentrate on your studies. You can speak to the others later about Seosaimhín."

"Fine!" Máire gently lifted the cat from her lap and stood. "I will return to my studies. You can deal with the leech. He can tell the others about Seosaimhín."

"I came here with the best of intentions to warn you that Seosaimhín is alive, and you call me names, bring up the past, and want me to leave?" Mandubratius frowned. He felt slighted at Máire's behavior. He deserved a show of gratitude, at least, if not more. Mandubratius heard a chuckle and found the cat winding its way around his legs.

"You could show him what would happen if you decided you wished him dead again." The fairy cat gave him a feral grin.

"But that's uncalled for!" Mandubratius sputtered.

The cat snickered. "You deserve far worse for your misdeeds, Awvarwy. Máire, why don't you show Awvarwy—"

"How did you know—"

The fairy cat ignored his interruption. "Demonstrate your last skill."

"But he'll—" Máire stared at Mandubratius.

"What harm will there be?" Lucius asked.

Mandubratius could not imagine what they discussed. However, he had a sinking feeling that he would have to experience something painful.

"Alright." Máire turned away.

He watched her face line in concentration. The air grew charged with a strange, pulsing energy.

Lightning?

Everything exploded in a blinding flash of light. Mandubratius tumbled backwards into a pit of darkness. The strange image of painful whiteness burned into his eyes. Only the excruciating ringing in his ears distracted him from the burn in his eyes. He could smell his own singed hair.

That is not a good sign.

Then something heavy leapt onto his stomach. The weight seemed to crawl to his chest.

Mandubratius blinked a few times as the image of the flash faded, and then noticed Lucius staring down at him. The cat's tail waved back and forth like a strange, black banner. As the ringing in his ears diminished, the cat's purr grew louder.

"I must apologize for Máire," Lucius said. "She is concentrating on her work, now."

"Máire?" He wondered if he did more than mouth her name. Mandubratius could hear nothing but the cat's voice and purr.

"She must work on her aim."

"What was her target?" he asked, hearing his voice creak.

"You'll have to ask her, but if I was a mischievous fae cat, I'd say she was aiming for you." The cat chuckled again before sniffing Mandubratius' face.

"How did she do that?" he whispered.

"Some things, Awvarwy, are best not known." The cat hopped off him. "Now, run along back to the abbey and ask for healing."

Mandubratius propped himself up on his elbows. "What's wrong with me?" he asked the cat.

"Half of your body appears to be burnt," the cat announced.

Mandubratius studied his lower torso and legs. He resembled seared meat. "That should be more painful than it is," he said to the cat. He stood up on shaky legs. "Why isn't Máire here healing me?"

"I think her message to you was clear," the cat stated. "She wishes to be alone, now. There is time to play your games later. You should return to be healed soon, or else my assistance to you will fade and the pain will increase." The cat turned away.

"Fine. I'll go back to the abbey, but tell your associate that she owes me an apology and some gratitude for my concern. I ran here because of that concern, yet she refers to me as 'leech'. That is so unkind and hurtful."

"Of course, Lamia, Máire is most unkind to you." The cat's words lilted in a sarcastic tone. Without another word, the fairy cat trotted away.

Mandubratius started to jog back to Prüm Abbey, wondering how Máire managed that trick of bringing forth lightning.

Marcus blinked a few times, trying to keep some of the strange hallucinations at bay.

"Damn these mushrooms," he heard Lady Heloise mutter. She turned away from the table and the sacks. She started sneezing.

He heard mutters over his shoulder and sensed Reginald leading her away from the table. Every day, mortals would ingest the mushrooms by accident. Lady Heloise swallowed some mushroom dust earlier this morning, and her sons took turns watching over her as she mumbled things about the past. She soon recovered, yet now Julien and Reginald's concern doubled. Any healing had no effect on those affected by mushrooms. They could only wait for the hallucinations to pass.

Marcus lowered his head to finish sacking the powders. The strange scent of singed hair drifted towards him, soon mixing with the smell of Lamia. He looked over his left shoulder and found a rather displeased Lamia storming towards him. "I see she didn't appreciate your interruption," he said to Mandubratius. "I warned you."

"Quit smiling and heal me!"

"Why didn't Máire heal you?" Marcus tried to stop smiling, but he found it very hard to not start laughing.

"I'm not in the mood for a battle of wits," the Lamia answered. "I'm in pain. Heal me! Please." Mandubratius uttered the word through gritted teeth.

Marcus wondered if the mushrooms created this scenario. He bowed grandly. "I will gladly heal my illustrious nemesis."

"Don't be so smug about this!" Mandubratius uttered.

"Gerrae." Marcus placed a hand on Mandubratius' shoulder and closed his eyes for a moment, concentrating on healing, instead of amusement.

"Nonsense indeed," Mandubratius muttered.

Marcus squinted at him and watched the Lamia's face relax. The level of burns were superficial but must have been painful. He opened his eyes. "There. It is done."

"Thank you for healing me without further witty exchange," Mandubratius stated, sounding somewhat reluctant.

Marcus returned to the table. "It was not my desire for you to come to harm. I did warn you that Máire is not herself, and she has accidently harmed several who interrupted her meditations."

Mandubratius grabbed his arm and began to tug him away.

Marcus gave in and allowed himself to be led into a corner of the cloister. He had to wonder why Mandubratius would feel this would give them privacy.

"Meditations, my arse!" Mandubratius hissed. "What is she doing?"

"Doing? Whatever do you mean?" Marcus did his best to hide his smile.

"Don't play with me, Marcus. I witnessed her wielding magic. She did something to me." The blood-drinker shook a finger as he spoke.

"Magic, you say?" Marcus gave up and smirked. "Aren't we all magical in some way?"

"You know very well that I don't mean the gifts we gain during transformation. She is conjuring things."

"And what could my Banbh Ceanúil possibly conjure, Awvarwy?"

"I witnessed your piglet call down lightning, Marcus. Stop smiling, this is serious!"

Marcus shrugged. "Druids have the power to ask the Gods to affect weather. She's called down storms with Their aid. Just ask Amata."

"No," Mandubratius shook his head. "This is different. She nearly struck me with a bolt of lightning."

Marcus lowered his eyes to keep from laughing. Mandubratius must have said something to annoy Máire.

"I can see by your face that you know of the magic of which I speak."

Marcus made a face, as he considered telling Mandubratius the entire truth. Then again, everyone else knew of Máire's activities and Mandubratius would learn it sooner or later.

"Máire received scrolls of ancient magics as a gift," he began, deciding to leave out the aspect of her instructing other druidic Deargh Du in its uses in the future. "She spends her nights learning to wield those tools. She sleeps little these days. As soon as the sun sets, sometimes before it clears the horizon, she flies to her sanctuary. At sunrise, she rejoins us. Frankly, I think she is obsessed and gone a little mad. That is why I suggested that you not see her."

Mandubratius' features calmed. "I appreciate your concern for my well-being. I should have taken your warning to heart."

"No apology is necessary. Now, I must return to my—"

Mandubratius grabbed his arm. "I must share intelligences with you. The intelligences I gave Máire." Mandubratius released him and stared at the mushroom dust on his hand. "What in Hades is covering you? You smell of the stench permeating this place, Marcus. No offense." He sniffed at his hand

and made a disgusted face.

"It's redcap mushrooms and some other herbs," Marcus explained. "We've ground them into a powder to be mixed with wine."

"Blech!" The Lamia made a gagging sound. "Why would anyone drink such a vile concoction? Bacchus would be most displeased with this adulteration of his blessed beverage."

"This vile concoction creates a hallucinatory effect on us and mortals. It cancels out the mental attack of the Strigoi. It will protect us, and I'd prefer to fight sober, at least this way we can fight."

Mandubratius grinned and nodded a bit. "Well, that is most impressive. Not all hope is lost for us in repelling these vermin."

"Now what is the intelligence?"

"Oh yes, it slipped my mind, Marcus, my apologies."

"Yes, well?" Marcus felt a rising impatience. Earlier Mandubratius complained of the game. Now he instigated it.

"Seosaimhín is the rogue Deargh Du that chased me."

Marcus felt his bile rise. "Why, in Morrigan's name, did you not tell me this when you first saw me? Here it is, several hours later, and I find Seosaimhín is alive after two hundred years, and she's also Deargh Du! Why go to Máire first, Mandubratius?"

Mandubratius raised his brows. "Because Máire was once family to Seosaimhín, Marcus, and I believed that she deserved to know first." His calm tone seemed a little patronizing.

"If you had told us this news when you first encountered me, we would have had more time to mobilize. You deliberately wasted time! For once, tell the entire truth!"

Mandubratius leaned in to whisper. "Now, Marcus," he purred. "I never tell the truth because I don't accept that there is such a thing. Calm down. I doubt our delay will cost us much, old friend." He moved back and his voice grew in volume again. "The Strigoi could attack the Papal Army and the Lamia forces with them tonight, tomorrow night, or a week from now."

"Those hours could mean the difference between victory and death for your fellow Lamia," Marcus replied, trying not to grind his teeth.

Mandubratius met his stare and said nothing.

Marcus pushed away his rage. It was a somewhat valid reason to allow Máire an opportunity to prepare for the sight of seeing Seosaimhín. Yet, he believed that Mandubratius would not shed a tear over the loss of these forces. He reasoned it was a calculated loss, that Mandubratius might be planning to rid himself of a troublesome Pope and army. "Is there anything else that I need to know?" he asked Mandubratius.

The Lamia gave him a crooked smirk, and he knew there would be more bad news. "Seosaimhín leads the Strigoi." Mandubratius continued to smirk.

Marcus could feel his face heat.

How could that… Briton keep this news to himself, as if it were nothing more than a bit of court gossip?

The smirk remained on Mandubratius' face, and Marcus felt the urge to beat him senseless.

Seosaimhín in charge of the Strigoi? Seosaimhín a Deargh Du?

He knew in the back of his mind that reacting with anger would please Mandubratius far too much. He reined in his temper as he studied the tables of workers and bored blood-drinkers. Marcus summoned his most even voice. "I appreciate you sharing this with me." He watched the smirk disappear.

"You are most welcome."

"So, she chased you here?"

"Yes, I sensed someone following me. No large gathering though, just one blood-drinker."

"Do you know where her camp is?" he asked Mandubratius.

"Well, our camp was in Mehren to the east, but I ordered Gaius to move the camp northwest to Pelm. We suspect the Strigoi are based in different cave systems in the vicinity of Pelm."

"How many are there in your camp?" he whispered.

"Eight thousand mortals. Perhaps two thousand Lamia," Mandubratius answered.

Marcus closed his eyes. "They'll all be killed… the Lamia, that is. The poor mortals will become Strigoi. We will have a greater army to defeat." He turned away from Mandubratius. "Mac Alpin! Claudius!" he bellowed. In moments, he was joined by the other blood-drinkers. "We must depart for… what town was it, Mandubratius?"

"Pelm… or southeast of Pelm. No telling how slow the Pope's forces will travel."

"To Pelm, as soon as possible!" Marcus started to pace.

"Why there?" Claudius asked.

"Because the Strigoi are poised to attack the combined forces of the Pope and Lamia."

The warriors nodded their heads in understanding.

Marcus pointed at Mac Alpin. "I want to be ready to leave by sunset tomorrow, Arwin."

"But, all the powder isn't ready."

"It must be ready," Marcus said. "Take the grinder in the catacombs and we'll take turns grinding during the day if necessary."

"Yes, sir."

"On your way." He pointed to Claudius. "You need to speak to Emperor Charles. He needs to mobilize his army, which is camped in Kornelimünster, southeast of Aachen. Take Julien with you."

Claudius saluted him and left.

"Is there anything I need to do, general?"

He turned back to face Mandubratius and tried to think of something to keep Mandubratius busy. "Go speak with the Empress."

"The Empress? Why would you suggest that?"

"I'm well aware that you have feelings for her."

Mandubratius chuckled. "Do you, now?"

"Again, this is not the time for a battle of wits. It's a fact, and I suggest you visit her because she mopes and complains. It's most tiresome. I think Irene may actually miss your questionable company, though it escapes me why she would. So, I suggest you speak with her."

Mandubratius beamed. The smile revealed a series of ensuing calculations in the Lamia's head. "Why Marcus, I believe you've become a romantic." He chuckled and embraced Marcus while patting his back. "Thank you for that rather generous suggestion. That you would consider my well-being and Irene's is truly kind. After all, your own beloved piglet is struggling with her madness. Why are the beautiful ones always so misguided? I take my leave." The Lamia practically ran towards the gate.

Marcus recognized Irene's figure in the distance. "After this battle is over, we will have a battle of our own, Mandubratius," Marcus whispered to the Lamia's departing form, before returning to the tables.

chapter seven

Southwest of the Imperial Encampment Outside of Kornelimünster

s the band of Celtic blood-drinkers flew towards the northeast, away from the Prüm Abbey, Julien noticed that his traveling companion seemed lost in thought. "What has your attention?" he asked Claudius.

"I can see the lights of the Emperor's forces in the distance," Claudius said. "Every time I see a sight like this, I remember the first time I witnessed such a camp." He met Julien's eyes. "This army is much smaller in comparison to the forces Rome wielded against her enemies, of course, and smaller still than the hordes of enemies we fought." He fell silent for a moment. "As a Sugnwr Gwaed, only once have I glimpsed anything remotely similar to the Roman armies. That was in Éire against the Lamia. I suppose, I was reminiscing. That battle seemed so straightforward then. Train the local Deargh Du to fight as the Lamia did and repel the advancing Lamia army."

"What was that like? Living in the heyday of Roman might?" Julien asked.

Claudius gave a derisive laugh. "What was it like? We committed brutal acts against our enemies. Not only did we kill them, we tried to wipe them from the recollection of time. We burned, murdered, tortured, maimed, raped, pillaged our way through, and I remember that I reveled in these acts as I participated in them, but somewhere I found myself horrified by what I did."

Claudius' dark eyes focused on Julien for a moment. "I do not tell many associates this, but perhaps you should know. Part of my transformation forced me to reflect on those transgressions. Cernunnos even said that greater foes than Rome would arrive in Britain, and it was time for many to join forces within His hunt." Claudius chuckled. "You'll have to excuse this babbling of mine. Whenever I think of great trials such as this upcoming battle, I do reflect on the past."

"You should share this with the others," Julien said. "Marcus could use such tales, I think. He seems a little—"

"So you recognize it as well," Claudius said. "Your mother-in-darkness and I have noticed some changes. When Edward and Arwin saw it, we started to worry more. I think it has something to do with the fact that he never gets the opportunity to escape into unconsciousness when we are attacked. He's awake, and he suffers during the entire event. When the Strigoi attack me, I go back to my days of soldiering, and I find myself instigating horrors. Sometimes, I return to that endless night with Cernunnos, feeling all my trials and successes were useless. I'm banished to the great pit in the Otherworld, and the Strigoi are my torturers. What nightmares do you see when you are attacked?" he asked Julien.

Julien bit his lower lip. "I see my family destroyed. Sometimes I see myself as the judge, and I kill the woman I loved and our children. Yet, most of the time, a faceless judge in a cloak with a cowl sentences my mother, sister, Flor, Clotilda, and I to burn at the stake. There is nothing I can do but feel the pain of the fire."

"You are lucky in that you have done little that deserves punishment," Claudius stated.

"Every brigand and murderer I chased as a Gendarme deserved their fate," Julien answered. "I don't understand what you mean by punishment. You and Marcus surely have done penance enough for your misdeeds."

"Perhaps," Claudius said. "He is a good person now, but I wonder about what he sees when the Strigoi attack us. Remember those atrocities I spoke of? Marcus orchestrated those atrocities. I grant that Julius Caesar gave the orders, but Marcus inflicted death and destruction that went beyond Caesar's orders. Sometimes, I believe if he had not drifted to Éire and become Deargh Du, he would have murdered Caesar, Mark Antony, and Octavian and become emperor. That, or the Lamia would have found his talents useful and sponsored him. What a merciless Lamia Marcus would have become."

"He experienced something in the transformation that changed him," said Julien.

"Yes, he was transformed in more ways than one, but I think Morrigan may have seen Herself in him, if one can guess the motives of a Goddess. There are times, Julien, when Máire, others, and I have seen glimpses of a dark persona within Marcus. I believe he's more powerful than he lets himself appear to be. He may not need to recover as much as you and I."

"More powerful?" Julien asked.

"Perhaps Morrigan perceived something within him that She wished to nurture," Claudius replied. "I don't know, but I do remember once in Bath, he managed to manipulate a Lamia into telling him intelligences about Mandubratius. I know what Deargh Du can and cannot do, but sometimes he demonstrates manipulative talents beyond most Lamia. Have you noticed that he is hardly fatigued after a night of flying? He pretends to be, but you can see it in his eyes."

"I have not noticed that," Julien admitted. "I just assumed it was because he was older, and somehow that…" he paused. "Yet, you and he are the same age."

"Exactly," Claudius said. "I fear something will break through his calm demeanor soon. And I worry about you and Máire."

"Why is that?" Julien asked.

Claudius paused in the flight and sniffed the air. "I thought I smelled

Strigoi. Now, nothing."

"I smell nothing either," Julien confirmed. "But again, why do you worry?"

"I worry because you are his grandson-in-darkness, and you may have strengths that may destroy you. Just look at Máire. If she is not careful, she might annihilate herself. Yet, I still love our Banbh Ceanúil. I shall be her friend, and yours, and Marcus' as long as I remain in this life."

"And I'll endeavor to deserve that friendship, but I truly doubt you'll have anything to fear from me," Julien said. He gave a nervous laugh. He could not remember the last time Claudius ever looked this serious.

Claudius nodded his head and then studied the expanse of lights before them. "Ah, there is the camp. Let's land outside the perimeter. Should we sneak in to see the Emperor, or wait to be announced?"

"I don't think he'd mind if we went past the guards, as long as we don't startle him or the others by dropping shadows and coming out of the darkness," Julien answered.

"Alright, then, you lead and I'll follow," Claudius said. "Let's not take too long. I was almost singed by Máire a few nights ago. I don't want the sun to complete the process."

Imperial Encampment Outside of Kornelimünster

Claudius looked around the encampment, trusting his nagging senses that a Strigoi or rogue Deargh Du haunted this land. The threatening and silent forests brought the painful memories of his nightmares again.

Why do I have to think about those things?

He shook off the fears and continued following Julien towards the camp. The darkness surrounding them allowed them to move past the exterior borders. A large, ornate pavilion in the center of camp loomed in the distance. However, Julien moved past that towards a medium-sized, plain tent, west of the center. No guards stood in front, but Claudius could see through the murky darkness of the shadows and saw several guards watching the tent. Claudius inhaled and could tell two mortals drowsed within the canvas walls.

They landed as quiet as death outside the doorway. Julien opened the stays and inclined his head into the interior of the tent. A dimmed oil lamp lit the center of the space.

"Should we wake them?" Claudius whispered. No one could mistake the sound of snores.

"Dawn's close," Julien replied. "We need to wake them now." He moved into the interior, towards his father.

Claudius moved to the secretary's bed, prepared in case someone overreacted. He looked over the tent. They would have to leave soon, for this tent would offer little protection against the sun.

Julien kneeled next to the Emperor. Leaning in close to his father's ear, he covered the Emperor's mouth with one hand and shook the elder mortal with the other.

"Father?" Julien whispered.

A shiny flash of metal lit the tent as the Emperor revealed a dagger from his bedding and stabbed Julien.

Julien released him in shock. "Father! It's me, Julien!" Julien gurgled in some amount of pain.

The Emperor stared at his son in speechless horror.

The secretary woke, and Claudius kept the mortal's mouth firmly shut.

Julien pulled the dagger out of his chest with his right hand. He then handed the bloody blade to his father and began to heal himself.

"What are you doing here?" the Emperor asked.

"I have a message of grave import to give you," Julien began.

"Get on with it then." He turned to Claudius. "Release him." He nodded to his secretary. "Ercanbald will stay quiet."

The secretary nodded his head vigorously, and Claudius lowered his hands.

"The Strigoi nest is close to where the Papal Army will be camped in Pelm," Julien began. "If we are to prevent the total loss of His Holiness' army and the Lamia forces helping him, we need to mobilize as soon as possible."

"How did you hear about this?" the Emperor asked.

"Father, we have little time. Sunrise is upon us. You need to pack and go. In fact, you may wish to leave the tents and travel light."

"What about the army of your associates?" The Emperor's eyes moved from Julien to settle on Claudius for a moment. "They will join us, correct?"

"They are at Prüm Abbey," Julien answered. "Once the sun sets tonight, they will mobilize and catch up to you."

The Emperor seemed to silently pondered his son's words.

The purple skies of fading night began to surround them.

"We must go, father, and you must assemble your soldiers. We will meet you at dusk on the road to Pelm," Julien said.

"If we rally to the Pope and his troops, what will prevent us from madness and annihilation?"

"I can't explain, but we have a mixture of wine, herbs, and mushrooms that will protect us."

Claudius could take no more of the conversation. "We must go now!" he reminded Julien.

The Deargh Du held up a hand. "Promise me to mobilize," he said to his father.

Claudius blinked, wondering if he might see a repeat of what happened between Marcus and that Lamia in Bath.

"All right, you are as insistent as your mother can be." The Emperor smirked. "I will mobilize my men this very moment."

No manipulation occurred. Claudius felt a little disappointed, but mostly relieved.

"Thank you," Julien answered.

They both raced into the ending night. Claudius could hear Emperor Charles telling Ercanbald to gather his generals. They would leave very soon. "There! A plowed field." He pulled Julien towards a field to the north. They started digging as the skies grew brighter. "Next time, I'll talk," Claudius informed his traveling companion. "You, Máire, and Marcus all talk too much." He chuckled as he dove into the hole and began covering himself.

"I have given them one hour to prepare to move out." The Emperor turned to his generals. "Anything that is not packed is left. That includes tents and gear. Perhaps we should leave those tents," he muttered to himself. "No," he retorted. "I'm sure the men will be timely." He studied the soldiers as they readied their packs. They seemed very nearly ready to go. He took a look at the distant, plowed fields in the north, hoping his son did not suffer from the dagger wound. Charles then scanned the skies for a moment.

"I judge we have a good eleven hours of travel," one of his staff members commented.

"Imperial Majesty, we are ready to leave," his senior general bowed.

Charles nodded his head. "Then let's leave. I should like to be twenty miles or more to the south, so we can meet the Papal forces soon."

Imperial Encampment Outside of Jünkerath

Charles dismounted his horse and studied the circled carts. It became too dark to travel further with torches and even his stomach growled.

"Imperial Majesty, when do you expect these mercenaries to arrive?"

Charles turned to study the young lieutenant on his staff. "Perhaps in a few hours," he said. "Tell the cooks to prepare food; some roasts would be appreciated."

Damn those doctors trying to moderate my diet of roasted meats!

"Yes, Imperial Majesty." The lieutenant scampered away.

Another one of his staff approached him. "Shall I send out any scouts?"

the general queried.

"No, but keep two sentries posted between each wagon," Charles ordered. He dusted off his hands, and then suggested to another general, "Have the men open a wine barrel and let everyone enjoy a cup. We need a few hours to rest." He had a feeling that their time to relax may be short.

"Sir!"

The Emperor turned away from his conversation with a young soldier when he witnessed a guard running towards one of his general's lieutenants.

"Sir, a group of men and women have arrived, claiming to be in the Emperor's service."

Charles rose from his seat. "How large is this group?"

"Well over three thousand, Imperial Majesty," the soldier uttered.

The Emperor attempted to control his shock. He had no idea so many blood-drinkers would be in his empire.

"Are you certain about that number, soldier?" he asked the guard.

"I think so, si-Imperial Majesty."

"Is there anything else, soldier?"

"Yes, their leader waits at the perimeter."

"You should have told your lieutenant that immediately. Now, take me to your post! Run!"

The Emperor followed the young soldier and heard the boots of his generals after him. As they reached the cart, he recognized Marcus on the other side of it. He could never understand why that man always carried such odd looking short swords.

"Greetings," he said, nodding to the Deargh Du.

Marcus bowed for a moment. It seemed almost to be a mere head bob. "Imperial Majesty."

Charles scanned the landscape, expecting to see all the warriors. Yet, all he could see now was a strange darkness. He concentrated on hearing the invisible forces.

Wouldn't so many make a great clamor?

The night animals chatted amongst themselves, as if not bothered.

"My apologies for being late, Imperial Majesty," Marcus said, interrupting Charles' thoughts. "We could not travel with wagons or carts. We had to share the load."

"Load? What load?" Charles experienced a strange brush of confusion. Part of him could not help but fret over what they may have done.

Marcus met his eyes. "I understand that Claudius and Julien informed you of the wine, mushroom, and herb mixture that would protect us from the Stri-demons." The ancient corrected himself.

A flash of memory reminded Charles of that segment of the conversation with Julien. "Oh yes. You carried all of that? From Prüm Abbey?"

A hint of a smile lit the Deargh Du's features. "Yes, Imperial Majesty, we collected, dried, ground, and bagged the herbs and mushrooms, and we also removed all the wine from the abbey's cellars. If you don't mind, my men and women are a little tired. Do you have wagons and carts with extra capacity?"

"Why, I believe we do." The Emperor turned towards his staff as they stood behind him. "General Gausboldus, have the quartermaster help load these extra supplies."

"Excellent." Marcus looked over his shoulder. "Claudius?"

Another figure moved out of the darkness and replied, "Yes, general?"

"Please coordinate the loading of our supplies onto the Emperor's carts with General Gausboldus. I know I'm not looking forward to being a pack mule again."

Charles watched Claudius smile.

"Yes, general." The other immortal walked towards the Frankish general.

Marcus turned back to the Emperor. "We need to begin rationing and distributing this elixir out to your men."

"Of course," Charles replied. "I would like to know more about it though."

"My apologies for interrupting, Imperial Majesty," Marcus began. "However, may we set up the logistics of this distribution? My men need to drink it as well." He turned and motioned forth another of the blood-drinkers.

The Emperor motioned to another one of his staff. "Take this man to the galley squad and tell them to do whatever he says," Charles said to General Gausboldus.

"Yes, Imperial Majesty." His general motioned for the other warrior to follow.

Finally, Charles could see a stream of people moving out of the darkness with many large casks and bags. The weight looked considerable.

Marcus moved in closer and steered them away from his staff. They walked towards the opposite side of the circle, leaving everyone behind.

"Where do you intend to quarter your personnel?" he asked Marcus.

"I will have them form a circle around your encampment as an outer defensive perimeter should we be attacked," Marcus said. "However, I would like to discuss our strategy with you in private."

"Of course," Charles said. "Does private mean with my staff?"

"Do you wish them to know the truth about us?" Marcus' silver eyes began to glow a little.

"Which truth is that?" Charles chuckled, feeling nervous about the entire situation. "Is this the truth that you and yours are angels, or something else?"

"Which do you prefer?" Marcus asked.

"I think, for the safety of both our armies, I would prefer this angelic truth," Charles answered.

"I'll gather my officers, then," Marcus said.

"Marcus, do you consider the Empress Irene to be an officer?"

Marcus' mouth twitched, as if he attempted to hold back laughter. "No, Imperial Majesty. I plan on leaving her with the other soldiers that I do not consider vital. What about your son?"

"I presume you mean Julien," Charles replied.

"Yes."

Charles considered his options. "I'll mention that he's my liaison to you, but please be certain to tell him to exhibit no angelic powers in front of my staff and soldiers for now."

Marcus nodded. "That may have to change later in battle or training, Imperial Majesty, but for now, Julien de Divio is your mortal Inspector General."

Charles thought over another question about the women on Marcus' staff. He planned on asking about them, but decided that might be dangerous.

"Excellent," he said. "We shall meet again with your staff and mine in half an hour." He turned away.

"Imperial Majesty?" He heard Marcus' voice over his shoulder. "We don't have much time. Let's return in a quarter of an hour."

Charles turned back to face Marcus. "Agreed."

Marcus bowed again and ran into the darkness.

The Emperor turned to his exhausted soldiers and motioned his staff in closer. "Gather the rest of my generals and the essential staff."

Marcus led his staff towards the Emperor and then spread the map of the Empire on the ground. Claudius, Mac Alpin, Julien, Máire, and Sáerlaith followed him. He observed the Emperor and his entourage while waiting to begin his briefing.

Several of the generals stared at the women as if in shock. However, the Emperor turned back to glare at his four generals, and secretary and said nothing. The generals stared down at the map in silence.

Ercanbald busied himself with appropriating a chair for the Emperor. The generals crouched down to the dirt.

Marcus remained standing and walked around his staff to the opposite side of the map. He took a long stick from Ercanbald. "This is where the Papal Army was, this is where they are heading, and this is where the Strigoi may be hiding," he said, pointing to the three locations with the stick.

"Strigoi?" one of the generals asked, appearing confused.

"That is the name of our enemy," Marcus answered. "I will explain that in a moment."

"Please continue, Marcus," the Emperor said. He gazed at his staff as if willing them to silence.

"Thank you." Marcus moved the birch stick towards Jünkerath. "This is our current position. We need to meet with the Papal Army, which is moving from Mehren to Pelm, with as much speed as possible. We do not know where they are along the line from Pelm to Mehren. We must bring our cargo with us, which will slow us down, and we also need to travel by night. We will leave in approximately two hours."

He heard a series of grumbles in the Franks' native tongue.

General Ebroin met his eyes. "You wish us to travel at night? We cannot see the road. These demons hunt at night, and we had a grueling march to get this far. How can we go any further? The men need rest, as do the horses and livestock."

"We are carrying an elixir that we created," Marcus explained. "It will protect us from the attacks of the demons. In addition, you and your soldiers will not feel fatigued after imbibing this concoction. If anything, they will wish to march faster. I suppose we can try to feed the livestock the powder. Although, the horses may not react in the best manner," he remarked, looking over at Claudius.

The Sugnwr Gwaed gave him a shrug. Perhaps his line could talk the beasts of burden into a long night of work.

"Are you certain this will work?" General Cassyon asked.

Marcus decided to tell a half truth. "We've had several engagements with the enemy. Those protected with this substance survived."

"So, we'll march day and night with a few breaks for meals?" another of the Emperor's staff asked.

"Something not so harsh," Marcus answered. "We can protect you from sundown to sunup, but you should take half the day for marching and sleep the other half."

"This sounds feasible," stated the fourth general, "but how will we see in the dark?"

"Yes, we can only travel during the day," another said. "You should accommodate your schedule to ours."

Marcus chuckled for a moment. "We would, generals, but you see, my army and I would burn in the daylight. Perhaps it's time that I introduced myself properly. As you know, these demonic beings originally came from hell." Marcus bit his tongue at the mistruth, but continued as the Emperor's staff murmured awestruck muttering again in Frankish. "These demons found ways to possess others. In response to these demons that walk on earth, God..." Marcus attempted to swallow his dislike of this tale. "God sent an army of angels to combat the demonic horde. We," he motioned to his staff and himself. "We are that army. We are called the Cothromaigh." He thought the other lines would sooner be called the Cothromaigh than be referred to as the Angelic Army or Angelic Forces.

Laughter from the gathered mortals greeted his ears.

Marcus expected disbelief, but not the laughter.

Perhaps a show of some sort would be in order.

He brought forth glamoury, and the light around the meeting area grew.

The staff's laughter became silence.

Marcus noticed the Emperor smile for a moment. "This is how we intend to guide the Imperial army at night," Marcus explained, allowing himself to levitate off the ground. "You see, we are angels." He motioned for the others to join him in the air.

Julien remained on the ground and instantly went to his knees and began to say some prayer. The Emperor joined his son and went to his knees. The generals and rest of the staff followed suit.

Marcus met Máire's eyes, remembering her own mortal great aunt and uncle's response to his appearing from their grove. He felt a little shame for such a display. Marcus landed on the ground and allowed his glamoury and illumination to fade.

"Get up," he told the crowd. "We have a job to do. This isn't about worship. We are here to help you defeat the demons that call themselves the Strigoi."

The Emperor rose, as did the others.

"For all our gifts," Marcus said, "we do have three weaknesses. The first is sunlight. The second I won't tell you, that is between ourselves and th- God. The final is that we need to feed from you and your soldiers."

"Feed?" General Gausboldus whispered.

"We feed on blood," Sáerlaith said in gentle and low tones.

The gathered staff fell silent and appeared horrified with the news.

"I wouldn't ask this of good Christians if it was not necessary," Marcus stated. "Besides, whoever donates their blood will not remember their experience, the amount taken is small, and their deed will not be forgotten. Now, may I have you all ask for volunteers?"

There were more dissenting grumbles, this time in Latin as well as the Frankish vernacular.

"Let's pass on that matter for now," the Emperor said. "We can pose this matter to the soldiers after they have a dose of the elixir."

Marcus nodded.

"What does this drink taste like?" General Cassyon asked.

"It's a powder mixed in red wine," Marcus explained. He watched Edward near the circle.

"General," Edward addressed him. "The two strengths are prepared."

"Thank you, Edward," he replied. "Could you," he turned to the Emperor, "ask your staff to divide their men into queues?"

The Emperor turned his eyes to his staff. "Go now. We will meet again in an hour, after everyone receives their share."

Marcus turned to his staff. "I believe it's time for us to drink as well. Go take the others to their queue."

Sáerlaith, Claudius, Máire, Mac Alpin, and Julien walked towards their forces.

"Are you that disgusted by our feeding necessities?" Marcus asked the Emperor, meeting his eyes.

"I'm having a difficult time with the idea of my men willingly submitting to having their blood drained," the Emperor replied.

"Perhaps, if their Emperor shares a personal experience on the matter, they would be easily persuaded." He wondered if the Emperor might remember Máire or Empress Irene feeding on him, though he thought it was doubtful.

"Are you suggesting that I experience a feeding?" The Emperor appeared to be horrified.

If only he knew the truth.

"I can do it or one of the others on my staff."

"Do you expect me to willingly allow you, or any of the others, to sink your teeth in me and draw forth blood?" The Emperor's voice turned incredulous to cover a thin trace of fear.

"You'd feel no pain. In fact, the experience is a pleasant one. I only take a little from each donor. It protects you and me both. Then I'll heal your wound. If I didn't allow you to remember this, you'd think it was just a lovely and sweet dream."

The Emperor did not look convinced.

"How large is your army?" Marcus asked.

"Almost twelve thousand," the Emperor answered.

"And you feed them every day and night?"

"Yes, or we forage the forests for game."

Marcus nodded his head. "Well, I have over three thousand soldiers that I must feed every night, or they have to forage. Sometimes that foraging takes them miles and miles away from the rest of the army."

"What are you getting at?" the Emperor asked, aggravation creeping into his tone. His pale features turned pink and red.

"Should all my forces have to forage, your soldiers will have no Cothromaigh escorts to aid them in the Strigoi-infested forests."

Marcus watched the Emperor consider his reply. The elder mortal sighed in resignation. "You have the negotiating skills of a seasoned diplomat. I shall submit to this feeding and see for myself if it is all you promise it to be. How do we proceed?"

"Let's walk behind the carts," Marcus said. "I'll draw down the darkness to give us a little privacy."

He walked with the Emperor until they were about one hundred feet from the perimeter of the camp. Marcus pulled down the darkness and allowed his glamoury to light a path.

"If you try anything," the Emperor began.

"I swear on my matron, Morrigan, that you will not feel more than a moment of pain, Imperial Majesty." Marcus stopped and turned to face him.

The Emperor's pale features glowed in his light. "How do we—"

Marcus took the Emperor's left arm. "I presume you are right-handed?"

The Emperor bobbed his head, still looking frightened at the prospect of the feeding.

Marcus raised the arm and rolled up the loose sleeve. He leaned in and felt the Emperor shudder for a moment. He bit into the Emperor's arm and began to feed. He sensed the elder mortal begin to relax after the initial pain. The blood tasted of strength, vitality, and fierce battles. Yet love and loyalty swelled within, with a hint of wine and roasted venison flavoring the vitae. Marcus made himself pull away from the delightful aromas. Sometimes, he found it hard to pull away from the blood of the powerful.

The Emperor opened his eyes and exhaled. "Is that—"

"Not yet, Imperial Majesty." Marcus placed a hand over the wound and began to heal him.

"I have no words," the mortal whispered.

"Not many do," Marcus answered. "We are done now." He released the Emperor's arm and allowed the darkness and his own light to fade away.

"Would you recommend that experience?" he asked the Emperor.

Emperor Charles' face revealed some confusion. "I have some memory, but most of it is just a strange fantasy, like the tales from the Irish poets," he whispered. "I thought you said that I would have no memory of the experience."

"The truth is that I don't erase memories. I plant the idea that the truth is too crazy to be the truth. I also thought it best to leave you a shard of the memory," Marcus answered. "How else could you explain it to your soldiers?"

"I see… thank you," the Emperor drawled. "I suppose I expected pain and blood loss."

Marcus chuckled. "There is some pain involved, Imperial Majesty, but not more than a person can withstand. Besides, this is not the first time you've been fed upon."

The Emperor's eyes widened in shock. "Whatever do you mean?"

"You spent a night with the Empress before we left your palace, and you spent some time with Máire once. I am certain they fed from you and removed the memory of the event," Marcus explained. "The Empress is Lamia, so she simply told you to forget the event. Máire made you believe the event to be a lovely dream or fantasy, as I did."

The Emperor shook his head and smiled for a moment. "I do remember something." His back became straight as they neared the perimeter. He stopped and turned to Marcus. "I was planning to speak to the men about the feeding after they receive and drink their provisions. However, I think that the explanation would be better handled by you."

Marcus raised his brows. "Imperial Majesty, would your forces believe a stranger?"

"But Marcus, you are not a stranger. You're an angel of the Cothromaigh army." The Emperor smirked. "If you and your forces present themselves as angels, the men would willingly take part in any activity you recommend."

Marcus grumbled and closed his eyes for a moment. "Imperial Majesty, I do not like pretending to be something I am not. I did it once already."

"What you are is the closest thing to an angel that we have," Emperor Charles replied. "I am certain you and your forces can be angels for us."

Marcus gritted his teeth. "Fine!" He closed his eyes and tried to regain his calm. "We will give a final show, Imperial Majesty."

"Thank you. I agree with you. I hate processions myself," Charles said. "I always found them false and pretentious, but the common people love them."

Marcus felt Lucius wiggle around a bit and poke his head out of the pouch under his right arm. The fairy cat uttered a squeaky yawn as he woke up.

"Is it common for Deargh Du to travel with cats?" the Emperor asked. "I believe I saw this one with Máire earlier. Yes, the eyes, that's the same cat."

Marcus glanced down and watched Lucius stare at the Emperor and radiate glamoury. The cat had a smile on his face, realizing the Emperor could do nothing more than admire him. Marcus rubbed the fairy cat's ears.

"In camp, when I was a soldier," Marcus explained, "we kept cats as pets and to lower the vermin population, although Lucius is not a normal cat. He's very special." He scratched the cat's brow.

Lucius mewed and then leapt out of the bag. He meandered over to the Emperor and rubbed up against the mortal.

The Emperor chuckled and picked up the purring cat. "I usually don't like cats, but this one has a very regal aspect about him. Would you like to sit on my chair while Marcus and his friends perform?"

Marcus heard the cat's purring increase in volume. "That sounds like a yes."

The Emperor chuckled. "Alright, Lucius, you get a seat of honor." He looked back over to Marcus. "What time will this vision occur?"

"We will be ready in one hour."

"One hour." The Emperor nodded his head and walked towards his chair.

Mandubratius found himself trying to dodge Irene. She always seemed to be in his path, demanding attention.

Perhaps a little honesty would be best with her.

"Irene," he called out, meeting her blue eyes. She returned his stare and appeared to be worried. "I'm going to be spending a lot of time with the Emperor and his mortal staff," he continued. "It may not be a good idea for you to accompany me."

Irene's face revealed her hurt. "So, you don't want me about? Why not? I offer you much pleasure, don't I?"

"It's not that my sweetheart, it's just..." He paused for a moment, attempting to come up with an answer that would allow them to both save face. "It is common knowledge that the Empress of the East lives in Constantinople. She would not join soldiers in a war against demons. Emperor Charles' staff may recognize you as the Empress, or at the very least, a woman of nobility marching with common foot soldiers in common traveling attire. It's just not done, don't you agree, Irene?" He watched her mull over his answer.

"I must bow to your logic. It would be unseemly for me to be recognized," she uttered in a stilted voice. "So, why must you associate with Charles? Take your place as Consul with me, and what's-her-name."

"I am the emissary to His Holiness," Mandubratius replied with a bemused chuckle. "I must be seen in Emperor Charles' association."

"But, how will I hide, and who will protect me?" Irene demanded.

Mandubratius studied the field of soldiers. "Amata—"

Irene interrupted him. "She'd just as soon have me dead, Mandubratius!

You can't be serious."

He sighed, "Marcus, then."

"That Roman brute?" Irene queried. "I don't like his kind. Besides, won't he be with the Emperor as well?"

Mandubratius considered the other options available. Máire would take care of Irene, but only to poison his child against him. He then noticed singing and harp music in the distance, distracting him with their lovely tune, until a sour note turned the song into a painful cacophony.

"That's not how to play a harp, Horatio!" he heard Mac Alpin rally. He noticed a group of the Ekimmu Cruitne and Sugnwr Gwaed playing together. Every time Mandubratius tried to think, Arwin Mac Alpin's voice would carry through the night air and interrupt him. "Mac Alpin!" he yelled at the loud blood-drinker.

"Hmmmm. Yes, he will do well," Irene replied.

Mandubratius turned back to Irene, who wore a most beguiling smile while tapping her foot to the music. "Did I hear you correctly?" he asked.

"You suggested him."

"Who did I suggest?"

"Mac Alpin." Irene smirked.

"Empress, I did not recommend him."

"However, you did say his name, Mandubratius, and I agreed."

"But why?" Mandubratius asked. "He's loud, brutish, and vile."

The music and songs stopped. Brash laughter interrupted his thoughts.

"Thank you for such pleasant compliments," Mac Alpin yelled out.

Mandubratius grabbed Irene's arm and dragged her away, outside of Mac Alpin's earshot, or so he hoped.

One could never tell with these Celtic lines.

"I know he's barbaric," Irene commented. "However, there's just something about him that's very..." She paused with a smirk. "Besides, he'd defend me, and no one would dare attack me. I'm sure all others fear him."

Mandubratius mused that she'd grow tired of that graceless Scot soon enough. Irene preferred men of culture and refinement, even more so if she could order them around. Mac Alpin would never take that attitude of Irene's for long. He probably believed that women were for childbearing, child rearing, and cleaning swords. "Perhaps he would be a suitable protector for you, Irene," he said.

"Excellent," Irene purred. She closed her eyes in a somewhat seductive manner. "Well?"

"Well what?"

"Aren't you going to introduce us formally?" Irene asked.

"Very well, Empress, if you will accompany me." He began to pull her towards the group of performing blood-drinkers.

"Leave it to a Roman to flub up the lines," Mac Alpin chuckled.

"It's not flubbed up." Claudius appeared annoyed with such a correction. The Sugnwr Gwaed hated to be corrected in matters of singing.

"It's a common enough error. That tale is from before your time, young Claudius," the elder blood-drinker chided. He snatched a harp from a woman and began to sing. "This is the way my own mother sang it." Mac Alpin smirked for a moment. "As hard as it is to believe, Horatio, my mother was a bard. If she had her way, I would have been one as well. However, the Bards and Druids caught me wrestling when they came to call and determined that the Gods wished me to be in the battlefield." The Ekimmu Cruitne ceased talking and strummed the harp.

Mandubratius paused as they neared Mac Alpin and drew Irene to a stop.

The Ekimmu Cruitne does possess a pleasant singing voice.

Mac Alpin managed to sing a lovely tune in an old dialect that Mandubratius could vaguely remember from a glistening and faded past. He could recollect the last time he had heard that song. The bards came to sing it over his mother's grave. Mandubratius felt a brief shame as his eyes began to water. He gulped away the memories and swiped at his left eye, hoping everyone would assume his movements were to relieve an itch.

When the song came to an end, Mandubratius watched others sobbing into their hands and on the shoulders of companions. There were some mumbled appreciative compliments.

Claudius grunted and walked away, shaking his head.

"What's wrong?" Horatio looked around the circle.

Mac Alpin chuckled. "Lad, never ever tell a Sugnwr Gwaed that you can sing. Most of them can't accept the fact that an Ekimmu Cruitne can do it better than themselves. Take this harp back to Claudius. His ego is bruised. Ask him to teach you the song. It will heal his pride. He has an excellent voice, for a Roman. I cannot help but enjoy showing up Claudius once in awhile when it comes to singing." Mac Alpin chuckled as Horatio left the circle, clutching the harp.

Mandubratius cleared his throat before another song could begin. "Arwin Mac Alpin," he intoned formally, "may I present Her Imperial Majesty, Irene, Empress of the East."

"But we've met." Mac Alpin grinned.

Mandubratius rolled his eyes. "Her Imperial Majesty requested you for an important mission."

"Does Her Imperial Majesty know I don't follow her orders?" Mac Alpin asked. He started to laugh and shook his head.

"Her Imperial Majesty will reward you for your services," Irene answered. Her eyes twinkled of unspoken promises.

Mandubratius tried not to laugh at her brazen attempt to solicit free service.

"So, how much are you offering for my services?" Mac Alpin asked.

"I carry no coin with me," Irene purred. "I was rather hoping that my charming company might be enough to persuade you to protect me." She leaned up against an elm.

Mac Alpin laughed. "My apologies if I don't wish to sell my services so short."

Irene's face blanched, and she huffed a bit at the stinging remark. "How dare you not desire my companionship! I'm an excellent lover!"

The elder blood-drinker stopped laughing. "Oh, I did not know you meant that. Consider yourself protected, Basileus."

Mandubratius noticed Emperor Charles carrying Lucius towards his chair.

What insanity went on in that man's head? Then again, who could understand cats, especially Lucius, the cat of the Otherworld?

"I'll take my leave," he said.

"Of course," Irene said. "Thank you for suggesting a protector, sponsor." She returned her attention to Mac Alpin. "Tell me, what special talents do the Ekimmu Cruitne possess?"

Mandubratius grumbled under his breath and almost slapped his forehead with the back of his hand. How could he forget that particular talent of the Ekimmu Cruitne? Now he'd lose another confidant to one of the Celtic lines. Those damned lovable, beautiful, and blessed Celtic blood-drinkers.

chapter eight

eloise watched Charles rejoin the rest of his staff. She noticed Marcus pulling away and entering the queue to receive his serving of the wine and mushroom mixture. She approached the Emperor slowly, as he continued issuing orders.

His staff left to enter the line of mortals, and then Charles took a few steps to join them, flanked in procession by his guards.

"Charles, may I speak to you privately?" she asked.

He turned towards her and smiled. "Please procure a serving of the elixir for me," he said to his guards. The Emperor motioned her to join him in a quiet corner of the camp.

"You are hesitant to ask for volunteers for the feeding," she said. She met his eyes for a moment and then faced the growing moon. Heloise found it difficult to meet Charles' gaze. Far too many of her fond memories lived in his blue eyes.

"I told Marcus that I'd consider it after the men imbibed this concoction," he answered.

"The majority of the mortal soldiers have."

"Yes, my officers have reported a large amount of restlessness in the men. Some are fighting. No one has been seriously injured yet. I understand that's one of the side effects; others are composing poetry."

She noticed a slight smile on his face. Heloise turned back to him and felt her face pinched in a smile. "I meant to hint that now may be a good time to explain it."

"How can I ask my men to bare their necks and arms to allow someone to suckle at them as if they were nursing babies?" Charles whispered. "Have you experienced their feeding, Heloise?"

"Yes, I have."

"Did you enjoy it?" he queried in soft tones.

Heloise noticed Charles shuffle his feet a bit and stare down at the ground.

"It was somewhat frightening at first," Heloise admitted. "Then it became exhilarating. I knew what they were and once the experience was over, I requested for my memories to remain. It was a profound and spiritual moment for me."

The Emperor shook his head at the stars and grinned. "I cannot explain it, but I enjoyed it as well."

"So, you will speak with the soldiers?"

"How do you think other mortals will react to it?" The Emperor's eyes revealed his aversion to harming his men.

"If they are convinced that the blood-drinkers are angels, it shouldn't be hard," she whispered.

"It may be necessary for our associates to demonstrate their skills," Charles stated. "I heard whispered rumors, yet sometimes one must witness to believe. After the men are finished with drinking this wine mixture, I have asked Marcus to ask for volunteers and demonstrate the feeding technique."

"Thank you." Heloise touched Charles' hand. "I know this is not easy, but I suppose instead of paying them with gold, it will be done with blood."

"At least, they don't kill us," Charles sighed. "If that were the case, I'd offer to pay them in gold." He squeezed her hand, but continued to stare into the dark forests.

"Charles, if they did such things, they would not be welcome in my home."

Charles turned to her, studying her, with a pained face. "It just occurred to me that we're about to march to war, and you are accompanying us."

"Only this far," Heloise admitted. "Fianait will escort me home."

Charles squeezed her hand again with a gentle caress. "In a way, I'm sad you'll be leaving us… me." He smiled. "I was hoping to spend some time with you. We are fighting an evil far greater than many of us have experienced."

"I know." Heloise brought his hand to her lips and kissed his fingers. "Perhaps when you return from your battle, you could call on me."

The Emperor gave her a knowing smile. "Is that an invitation, Heloise?"

"I'd be honored to have you as a guest in my home." She watched his eyes spark with a fire.

Charles embraced her and pressed his lips firmly against hers.

After a moment of shared delight, Heloise pulled away, feeling giddy as the first time she'd seen Charles at her home. "I have to leave soon. I wish you all the best in your battle. I also know your daughter and granddaughter would like to get to know you," Heloise said.

At least, Lirienne would be excited to know of her true father.

"Thank you. I would like to spend time with them as well," Charles said.

Heloise bowed before heading for the line of mortals.

Julien sat down outside the perimeter, sensing the transformed Strigoi mill about him. He shook his head, trying to remove the strange weight in his mind from the mushrooms. He continued with training exercises involving several of the changed Strigoi. His efforts in instructing them with basic commands in Latin allowed for improvement. Yet, at the moment, their movements appeared to be as fettered as his mind.

Others stood a distance away and watched for any attacks against him from the other lines. Julien found their attachment to him to be endearing, yet Máire just seemed to deem their protection as annoying.

Father Xofer meandered towards him. His appearance revealed a concern. "May I speak with you for a moment, General?"

Julien considered correcting the priest once again for a rank that was not his, but Father Xofer never listened to his correction. Julien rose to respond.

"No, no, please don't get up." The priest held up his hands.

"Then take a seat, Father."

Father Xofer nodded his head. "Thank you." He lowered himself to the ground across from Julien.

"What's troubling you, Father?" Julien asked.

"Please don't call me that."

"What troubles you?" Julien repeated with a grin.

"I'm concerned about my people's future role in society after these horrors are over."

Julien almost felt a physical blow at his concerns.

"I'm not just concerned about the hundred plus here with us," the priest continued, "I worry for the thousands more we hope to free from the curse."

I am not sure what Father Xofer wishes me to say or how to respond.

"This is a great issue," he commented. "Would you not resettle in the Eastern Empire?"

"Not all of us are from the East, General. Some of us were changed in this empire. If it weren't for the gifts remaining after the change, we would not be able to communicate. Very few Franks know Greek, and very few Greeks know Frankish or Latin."

"I see." Julien nodded. "But why won't you go back to your homes?"

"Too many bad memories of friends, families, and in my case, parishioners that we killed," Father Xofer answered. "It would be too painful for families that may assume us dead or demon now. We've agreed it is best to leave them in peace."

"So, you need someplace new to relocate and new names. I can speak to the Emperor about your plight."

Father Xofer's eyes met his for a moment. His appearance revealed some amount of gratitude, but he appeared to still be hesitant.

"Perhaps you could join me in speaking to him," Julien added. "I think he would wish to meet with you."

The priest's compassionate face lit with relief and a sudden burst of appreciation radiated towards Julien like a beam.

Julien noticed the mortals drinking the wine mixture and rose. He motioned for Xofer to join him. They walked through the perimeter towards his father.

"There may be a bit of a language barrier," he said to Xofer. "The Emperor doesn't speak Greek very well. Do you speak any Latin?"

The other blood-drinker laughed. "Ge-Julien, I was not high enough in my order to learn the Latin language. I will be able to sense your emotions, but I cannot understand your words if you communicate with the Emperor."

"Then I shall translate." Julien walked over to where the Emperor stood drinking his cup of wine.

Ercanbald moved in front of him and belched. "Hello, Julien."

"Ercanbald," he replied. The secretary's breath reeked of mushrooms and wine. Ercanbald loved formality, so this greeting must have been an effect of the concoction. "May we speak with the Emperor?"

A booming voice interrupted him. "Is that Inspector General Julien de Divio, Count of Auxerre? Come here, my boy!"

Julien's voice faltered in an inopportune squeak. He glanced at Father Xofer, then back at his father.

"Just a moment, Imperial Majesty." Julien turned back to the priest. "The Emperor calls for us."

"Is that the tongue of the Greeks coming from your mouth?" The Emperor looked confused.

"My companion only speaks Greek, Your Im..." He watched the Emperor's face wrinkle in more befuddlement.

"I'm sorry, what did you say?" Emperor Charles asked.

"You asked if it was Greek. I assumed you knew it."

The Emperor started laughing. "I didn't say I spoke Greek! Now, who is your holy companion? I thought your friends were not of that persuasion."

Julien turned to Xofer. "Introduce yourself."

Xofer went to his knees and said his name.

"Why isn't that priest rising?" the Emperor whispered.

"I believe he waits for you to bid him to rise or kiss your ring," Julien answered. His father's eyes swam with the drink.

"Of course! Stand up, little father. What is it about priests always kneeling?" Emperor Charles chuckled. He grabbed Xofer and pulled him to his feet.

Xofer looked at Julien.

Julien grinned and shrugged.

"Now, I've met your holy companion from the east. What can I do for you, my son?" The Emperor stared at Julien.

Julien took in an unneeded breath and asked, "What do you know of the mirror that we acquired in Constantinople?"

"Irene said it was magical." His father laughed and slapped Xofer on the shoulder. "Your Empress is most amusing."

Xofer turned back to Julien. "Did I miss a joke?"

"No, sorry, we are discussing the mirror. Give me a moment to explain further." He returned his gaze to the Emperor. "I assure you the mirror is a powerful tool. I have witnessed it with my own eyes."

The Emperor's laughter died away. "What does it do?"

"The easiest way to explain it is that it drives the demon out of the Strigoi."

"It performs exorcisms?" His father's eyes grew large.

"I suppose that's one way to explain it," Julien answered. "It brings out the inner beauty of its viewer."

"So, what happens to the Strigoi whose inner beauty is brought forth? Does the poor soul fall dead? Does he receive eternal reward, or is he forever damned?"

Julien motioned his father in closer. "As you know the Strigoi are possessed, in a manner of speaking. When the inner beauty is brought forth, it overcomes the evil. Some become mortal; some die, and I believe they are forgiven for the transgressions that they could not control; others are more like the angels with us tonight."

"How many people have been saved by this miraculous looking glass?" the Emperor asked in a near whisper.

"They are accompanying us. They chose Father Xofer to represent them."

His father smiled, pulled back, and embraced the priest. "Then, tell him that we welcome him and his family to our encampment."

Julien repeated the explanations to Xofer. The priest simply nodded and hugged the Emperor in return. After a moment, the Emperor's eyes began to clear and he released the priest.

"Father Xofer and the others will assist us in battle," Julien added.

"Are they warriors?" Emperor Charles asked.

"Most are farmers, tradesmen, and there are some women."

"How do they expect to help us in battle if they have no training, my son?" The Emperor appeared to realize what he said and looked around the camp.

"They have learned a few skills, and they can aid the wounded," Julien answered.

Emperor Charles looked at Xofer. "What is it that you and your people wish in return for your service?"

Julien repeated the question in Greek.

"We wish to help others saved by the mirror," Xofer answered. "Those of us touched by the healing powers of the mirror would like a new home, names, and a new language."

Julien translated Xofer's words.

"I would be willing to provide them land in Auxerre," Julien added. "However, I don't believe there is sufficient housing, and they have the same feeding requirements as do the other angels." Julien noticed Ercanbald lingered nearby. "I can't allow the mortals of Auxerre to be fed on so much."

The Emperor remained silent for a moment. "Perhaps they can build a community outside of Paris. No, Orleans."

Xofer began nodding his head and smiling. "Orleans would suit us well, General. We did not wish to encroach on the homes of your kind."

Julien smiled. "Imperial Majesty, they are very grateful and humbly accept your gift."

"Excellent! Ercanbald," the Emperor called, looking for the secretary.

"I'm here behind your son!" Ercanbald answered.

"I wish you to give fifteen hundred hectares of forestlands to the southeast of Orleans to Father Xofer and his family. Give them any tools they may need. Also, see to it that the armory fits them. They may just be working with the wounded, but they must have some proper swords."

"I'll see to that," Ercanbald bowed and headed towards the armory.

The Emperor looked up at the night sky for a moment.

"Imperial Majesty?"

"Hmmmm?" Julien's father regarded him again before embracing him. "Thank you, my son, and thank your holy friend as well. I hope these gifts strengthen our bonds of friendship." He kissed Julien's left cheek and then began to wander towards the center of the camp.

"Is your father normally so familiar with his subjects?" Xofer asked.

"It would seem that the mushrooms have a greater effect on mortals than we first thought," Julien answered. "However, he does have a fondness for his friends and his subjects that is not usual in most monarchs, so I've been told. The only other monarch I've met is the Empress, and she is most unfriendly."

Julien's sentence ended as a crowd of the changed Strigoi rushed him and nearly knocked him off his feet.

"I forgot you all shared thoughts," he yelled to Xofer. "I hope they are pleased and don't plan on killing me."

The priest laughed and shook his head.

Mandubratius sat down on a large oak stump watching the procession of mortals sipping on their wine and making faces at the taste. He found himself agreeing with their assessment. This concoction tasted of vile, smelly herbs and mushrooms. The mortals grew loud as the wine mixture took effect. He heard steps and sensed Amata near. She set her foot on the opposite side of the stump and smiled down at him, as he stared up at her.

Amata's eyes turned to the mortals for a moment. "So, has Talia had her fill of you?" she asked him.

"What?" He decided to pretend ignorance.

"Your plaything, Talia," Amata queried, "is she tired of you? Is that the real reason you left our brothers from Constantinople?"

He could feel his impatience rise. "I told M—"

"Marcus told Edward, Edward told me," Amata interrupted him. "I know all about Seosaimhín and that she's the leader of the Strigoi. All that rubbish."

"If you know 'all that rubbish'," Mandubratius countered, "then why are you suggesting that there are other reasons for my rapid departure?"

"You are a complex man, Awvarwy," she said. Her blue eyes studied his.

"Stick to calling me Mandubratius, Amata," he hissed. "You've always had trouble pronouncing my name, and I'd rather hear that loathsome title that the Romans gave me than hear you slaughter the pronunciation of my real name. You Romans have no talent for the Briton tongue."

"Excuse me!" Amata replied in British. She smirked at him.

Mandubratius finished his wine and put down his cup. He covered his ears. "Enough with your attempts to speak my first language." He grumbled and lowered his hands. "The only Romans that come close to speaking British properly are Marcus and his lieutenant, and don't you dare tell either that I said such a thing."

I hope this will keep Amata from realizing I avoided answering her question. Usually, I can distract her by annoying her.

Amata grinned. "I didn't know that! Perhaps I sh—" Her eyes settle on him again, then she slapped him on the shoulder. "I hate it when you do this! I almost fell for it again!"

He hid his smile. "What, in the realm of fairies, are you going on about?"

"You haven't answered my question regarding the other reasons for leaving the Papal Army's camp besides Seosaimhín's visit."

"I was going to get to that, but you had to slaughter my name." Mandubratius smiled at her, revealing his teeth.

"Mandubratius—"

"Yes, that is the right name."

"MANDUBRATIUS!"

He stared up at Amata. "So, do you want me to tell you a polite lie or the harsh truth? Since I believe in neither, it doesn't matter to me."

"Tell me what you wish to tell me, and I will judge if it's a lie or the truth."

"Very well." Mandubratius turned back to staring at the mortals as they gathered near their emperor. His Imperial Majesty paced about, looking as if he were preparing to make a speech. He looked up at Amata again, noticing her fidget. "I found that I was tired of Talia," Mandubratius finally answered.

"Really? Do go on."

"I found Talia to be tedious in her submissive state," he added.

"You mean more so than when she was not submissive?" Amata chortled.

He knew that Amata and Talia vied for his attention soon after meeting. It had been somewhat amusing. Mandubratius sighed. "I admit that her small-mindedness has been rather disappointing. I'd hoped that, over the decades, she'd gain a better appreciation for broader and more long-term schemes."

Amata said nothing.

Mandubratius studied the gathering soldiers. He could see the few Lamia milling about and Julien attempting to be mortal. He continued. "While I have been fostering connections with the Church of Rome, a relationship that may benefit us and all Lamia for millennia, Talia has been squandering the gifts I gave her to re-acquire lands her family once possessed."

Mandubratius frowned and allowed his disappointment to reveal itself. As much as he hated to admit it, he trusted Amata with such information. In fact, he trusted Amata above all, except maybe Máire; though, he could not understand why he'd trust a Deargh Du so much. "I had higher hopes for Talia. It's not just the squandering of gifts. She got caught. If Felician were alive, he would have killed Talia for her failings, both her actions and personal shortcomings." He glanced at Amata. Her eyes seemed to darken.

"Were Felician alive, he would have killed you for your failure in Éire."

"You wound me with such barbs, Amata."

"I'm not attacking you," she stated. "It's the honest truth. Oh, wait. I forget you don't believe in truth or lies."

"Why must you harm me so with your words," he said, forcing his eyes downward, so that he might hide his grin.

"I was being candid with you. You know as well as I do that Felician would not have been happy with your activities in Éire." Lowering her foot, she sat on the stump next to him. "Felician probably would have told you to forget about the Phallus Maximus." Amata paused and stared at him. "Ugh! You've done it to me again!"

Mandubratius tried to keep in his laughter. "Whatever do you mean, my sweet Amata?"

Amata waggled a finger at him. "You know exactly what you've done! Talia's tedious behavior is not the only reason you left!"

"Other reasons?" Mandubratius stared at Amata in an attempt to appear innocent. Perhaps she would decide Gaius and His Holiness were reasons enough to leave. He could create reason for their influence in his leaving. Perhaps she had never realized that he left because of his own fear. He hated the dreams and horrific fantasies the Strigoi placed inside his brain.

"The true reason you fled is because you fear Seosaimhín, isn't it?" Amata said. She delivered her words with a gentle, loving tone.

Mandubratius turned back to face her.

Amata draped her arms around him, and he lowered his brow to her shoulder. Amata's black hair surrounded his face like a sweetly scented moonless night. He closed his eyes.

"There's no shame in being afraid of her," Amata whispered. "Máire told me about her." Amata hesitated for a moment. "I think she's been in my visions. Seosaimhín, not Máire."

"What visions?" He pulled away from her hair and studied her eyes.

"The visions I have had lately. First, from the mandrake before I began my journey to Bath with Patroclus, then later as I was under the influence of the Strigoi."

Mandubratius felt surprise at Amata's revelation.

Perhaps we share trust again.

"Please don't let it be known that Awvarwy, or Mandubratius, is a coward."

"You took a risk to give us information we needed. I don't see that as cowardice. Your actions may save the lives of our brothers and sisters regardless of your primary reason for joining us," Amata replied.

"Thank you, Amata." He heard the Emperor begin speaking to the gathered soldiers and fell silent. He wished to hear what Charles had to say. The elder mortal stepped onto a footstool and signaled for attention.

"Legions of the Empire, hear me," Emperor Charles called out. He held up his hands, and the milling mortals settled down.

"Many of you are wondering why we haven't set up camp. I have heard the rumors. I wish to push those rumors aside by telling you the truth. The Pope himself has requested our assistance through his emissary." He motioned to Mandubratius. "His Holiness asks for our protection from the demonic army we've chased. I've decided to answer his call for help. He and his army could be attacked any night. Therefore, we must begin marching night and day to reach our friends."

Voices rose in a strange mumble as soldiers muttered in their barbaric tongue.

"Silence!" the Emperor shouted, effectively squelching his men. "This demonic army has grown. I know what you're thinking. No one assailed by these demons has survived. You fear the demons and think that there is no way to kill them. But, I am here to tell you tonight that those beliefs are false."

Voices rose in confusion again.

"Some people who fought these demons survived. In fact, many demons have been sent back to hell."

The rough, chattering voices increased to a fevered pitch. The Emperor raised his hands for silence again.

"There has been a cadre of soldiers sent to help us from almighty God..."

Derisive laughs echoed in the camp. A few made the sign of the cross.

"You have, no doubt, seen these warriors around our camp. They are over three thousand strong, and they will help us defeat the demons plaguing our lands. They are the angelic hosts of God himself. They are called the Cothromaigh."

Laughter spread through the gathered forces.

The Emperor signaled for quiet again. "You doubt my words. I know how hollow they seem. Allow me, or rather them, to burn away the shadow of your skepticism. Let there be... light!"

The night sky became bright as noon. Over three thousand blood-drinkers flew overhead.

"Show-offs," Mandubratius whispered to Amata.

All the soldiers moved to their knees. Mandubratius could hear the reverent, whispered pleading of prayers. He noticed Julien joining the groveling soldiers. "Why isn't puppy flying about?" Mandubratius asked.

Amata shrugged.

One of the 'angels' descended towards the ground. A quick look revealed the truth of the angel's identity. Marcus approached the followers.

"Giving that man an audience is like setting Greek fire aflame," Mandubratius hissed. "His ego now lights up the sky."

Marcus landed next to the Emperor.

A throng of soldiers rushed towards him, but the guards held them back.

Marcus glanced around at his audience. "Calm down, everyone." He studied the soldiers, looking like the peaceful and holy paintings of the Christian saints and angels. "Please calm yourselves. I will walk amongst you shortly, but first I wish to address you. My name is Marcus. I'm the general that leads the Cothromaigh. I've spent the last few months roaming the countryside with a band of my officers, seeking our enemy and their weaknesses. We have fought against these adversaries and killed many of their number, but I must be honest with you and state that our victories were not easy. In fact, many of us succumbed to the mind-attacks of these demons and the humans they possessed."

"However, we've found a way to protect angels, mortals, and even livestock from the attacks. Each of you has already imbibed a ration of an elixir. This mixture will protect you and give you extra energy, so you can march with little rest. You'll be given a flagon of wine every night with the mixture that will protect you. We will drink this potion beside you."

Mandubratius watched the Deargh Du's eyes gleam with that greenish light as his glamoury increased. He turned away from Marcus' spectacle in annoyance. "It's so nice that the holy Deargh Du will lower themselves to join with us common blood-drinkers," he whispered to Amata.

"However," he heard Marcus say, "It is with great reluctance that I bring up this next subject. While we are angels, God did not give us ultimate powers. To balance our strengths, we cannot survive the sunlight. We must also consume blood each night."

The crowd's voices died. Then, a querulous voice queried, "Where is it written in the bible that angels must drink blood?"

"It's not addressed in the bible," Marcus explained, "then again, neither are angels to a great extent. Please believe me when I tell you that the process is painless, even pleasurable. The wounds will be healed, as well as many minor ailments you may have."

"I willingly offered my blood to several angels," the Emperor addressed his forces. "It is as Marcus says."

"Since I wish to make the point clear, we don't make any demands for sustenance; we will only take blood from the willing," Marcus added.

Whispers grew into loud chattering.

"I'm willing to receive the blessing of the angels," one soldier said. Others began to confirm the same feelings.

Mandubratius rubbed his forehead. "This rabble would suffer exsanguination, suck his cock, and still praise the angels and their God."

"Everyone who does not wish to serve us and..." Mandubratius watched Marcus frown for a moment. "...receive a blessing, please move to the western end of the camp."

"Well, time to make our selection," Amata said, rising from her seat.

Marcus motioned to the blood-drinkers in the sky, then the lights faded.

Mandubratius grabbed the shoulder of a standing soldier, fearful that otherwise he'd never find a donor. The darkness covered all but a few feet ahead. Mandubratius found others willing to give. A quarter of an hour passed, and then the darkness lifted. Stars gleamed in the sky again. The other blood-drinkers now stood outside the perimeter.

"Thank you for your gift." Marcus nodded to the soldiers.

"And thank you and God's hosts for your protection," Emperor Charles declared, while staring at the gathered forces. "We must be on the move. We'll depart in three quarters of an hour."

The soldiers began to collect their gear.

"Now, which horse shall I select for this journey?" Mandubratius mused.

"Riding?" Amata's face revealed her shock.

He chuckled. "Perhaps I should ask the Emperor if I can honor him by taking his horse."

Amata smirked and shook her head a little.

"I am the Papal Emissary," Mandubratius answered and met her eyes. "I deserve respect. I can make His Holiness kiss my ring."

"Of course, Mandubratius, what was I thinking," Amata purred. "The Jew's and Christian's God would kiss your ring Himself if asked. Still, I think you should run with us."

"I have to be seen as a mortal for now," he answered Amata as he began to look over the available horses.

"Angel? Sir Angel, please intercede with Jesus for me. My family's wine harvest failed last season," pleaded one soldier gently grabbing Marcus' tunic.

"My daughter is coughing and grows weaker by the day," another said.

"I fear I cannot control my compulsions, angel. What is to be done? I am married, but love another woman."

"I'm… not the right angel to intercede with God," Marcus said in reply, wondering what the Christian God thought of his antics.

Better yet, what does Morrigan think of this improper display?

He pulled away from the soldiers, lightly pushing them aside. He then wandered over to the gathered blood-drinkers, finding some annoyance that they were chatting as if they had all the time to prepare to leave.

"Ah, I must disagree with you, Patroclus, British women are much more feisty than their continental cousins in Gaul," Mac Alpin stated.

Marcus noticed Horatio trying to understand the conversation in Greek. Then he sniffed mushrooms in the wine and air surrounding them and felt his irritation grow. They had taken more than the needed dose. He kicked Mac Alpin. "I believe you'll discover that women of Éire are the most obstinate in the world, especially when Sáerlaith and Máire discover that you've taken extra doses of the special wine. You're supposed to make sure we have enough! Not drink it all the first night."

"I swear that I didn't know this was the special wine. The cooks were about to throw it out," Arwin answered.

"Alright, there's Sáerlaith now. I'm sure she'll understand how you've drained several days of rations in just one sitting. Perhaps the bloated corpse of your body will wash up in Dover, and you can tell the others in the Otherworld that your body made it back home."

"Honestly, general." Mac Alpin rolled his eyes. "We'll put the rest away. We all needed a way to rest. It's truly a misunderstanding. Don't send for Sáerlaith, she enjoys a disagreement a bit much. Sometimes, she reminds me of the ex-wife."

The others rose and wandered away, appearing a little drunk. Marcus looked down at Mac Alpin and offered a hand. "Arwin, I think you need to drink less wine," he grumbled, tugging the other blood-drinker to his feet.

"Perhaps you haven't fed enough, Marcus. I believe you to be weak."

The blood drinkers stared at each other for a moment. They both growled under their breath before they erupted in laughter.

"Arwin, I must borrow your nose," Marcus chuckled.

Mac Alpin covered his nose. "You may not have it. I rather like my nose, and you cannot take it." He began to chuckle again.

"Seriously, I need to find Máire," Marcus stated.

Mac Alpin sniffed the air. "Well, she's not around here."

"I know that. I can tell you that much, but where is she? I'm a little concerned about her wandering off alone and doing Goddess knows what. She's a little obsessed with those scrolls. I haven't seen her since the demonstration."

Mac Alpin met his eyes. "Your speech… brought tears to these eyes." He stifled his laughter and then gave in.

Marcus chuckled. "Arwin, concentrate, where is our Banbh Ceanúil?"

Mac Alpin sniffed for a moment and then blew his nose on his tunic sleeve. He sniffed the air again. "Ahhh, much better. She's to the southeast, about a mile away. Hurry back. We leave soon, and that bastard Roman general is a stickler for his marching orders."

"Then I suggest that you get everyone ready, so when I drag Máire back, we're ready to go."

"So, I get to order the men around," Arwin chuckled. "Alright, then." The blood-drinker turned away and headed for the milling mass of mushroom-drunk angels, shouting to get their attention.

The strange smell of lightning grew as Marcus neared the figure by the quiet stream, which fed northeast into the Kyll river. He noticed the scent begin to fade as Máire turned to face him.

"You are lucky, Marcus." She tipped her head to her left side. "If I had lost myself in the tools, I may have allowed the lightning to strike you."

"Why did you come out here?" Marcus asked.

"I'm practicing," Máire said, interrupting him.

"I can see that. What if someone sees you, Máire? Angels cannot perform such feats."

"But, I need to practice." She stepped towards him, and he could see a little obsession shine in her eyes. "Besides, Lucius is taking care of me."

"Where?" Marcus looked around her.

"Oh, come now, Marcus, I'm right behind you."

Marcus stared at him. "I should have been able to see you, Lugh."

The fairy cat stared at him with limpid green eyes. "You can only sense me if I wish it, Marcus. I wanted to hear you and Máire talk about these issues before I made my presence known. I love to watch humans and Deargh Du give in to their desires to bicker and be right."

Marcus picked up the cat and looked into his eyes for a moment. Grumbling as the cat grinned at him, he began scratching the top of Lucius' head.

"Oh yes, purr, purr." The cat paused for a moment. "My chin too, Marcus."

Marcus rubbed under the cat's chin before returning the discussion to his child-in-darkness. "I wish you would leave with me now."

"Nonsense," Máire chuckled. "I still need to practice. I will follow the army. I can fly faster than everyone walking. I can leave before sunrise. I'll get under cover with plenty of time to spare."

"The Strigoi are about, we have to stay together," he reminded Máire.

"Lucius will be my champion. He will protect me."

"Lucius may be a fairy cat, but he..." Marcus paused and tried to move past the absurdity of Máire's argument.

"Why do you stare at me and Máire with an open mouth? Are you a salmon, now?" Lucius grinned again before licking his lips.

He could hear Máire laughing and snorting behind him.

"Máire must stay with our group," Marcus informed them both. "Besides," he turned and addressed Máire. "I have a task for you."

"This is important," she said, looking stubborn. "I need to work on this."

"What if you accidently blow up Lugh and the Strigoi arrive," he asked.

"Fine! I'll go, you obstinate... errr!" Máire gathered the scrolls. "Now, what is this duty I need to do?"

Marcus tucked Lucius into his travelling bag. The cat peeked out the top of the bag. "Let's talk about it on the way back," he suggested. Máire would not be pleased, and he thought it would be safer to tell her what these duties involved as they travelled.

chapter nine

Valley South of Daun

Talia could sense a large number of blood-drinkers in the fields to the west of the river. She tried to keep herself from running as the screams of the combatants grew louder. After all, she needed these soldiers to lead her to wherever Mandubratius went. She turned to examine the forested hills to her right, across the river.

I could gain a safer vantage point from there.

The screams continued as she waded across the river and crawled partway up the hill on her hands and knees. Then the screams ceased, and a strange, eerie silence overwhelmed the entire area. Even the animals became quiet.

Talia found a vantage point where she could see through the trees at the battlefield across the river. As she looked over the battlefield, the moaning began. Whatever animals remained still kept counsel to themselves.

Thousands of bodies littered the field, like the scattered leaves of Autumn. Some lay still, while others writhed in pain. Standing figures moved between the soldiers.

Talia narrowed her eyes and studied the walking. She gasped a bit and covered her mouth as she realized they were Strigoi. She hoped they would not sense her.

The Strigoi picked up or dragged many of the soldiers to the forested glen to the northwest. Yet, many remaining bodies still writhed in pain.

The sky became purple as the stars began to fade. The sun would come soon in the east.

Talia fought her compulsion to dig a hole and hide. After all, there was a possibility that someone out there could help her rejoin civilization.

The Strigoi did not return from the forest.

She began to leap down the hill, swim back across the river, and run past the trees, towards the battlefield. The smell of spilled blood reviled and enlivened Talia. Despite her drive to feed, the scent of rot proved too strong for any of her other inclinations. Then, there was that incessant moaning. Talia sighed and began to walk amongst the fallen.

"It would seem that all remaining here are Lamia," she murmured, feeling some relief in talking to herself. She looked over the soldiers to her right. "You are all missing your heads, but the rest are trapped in the Strigoi's nightmares. Why did they stop killing you?" She knelt next to one young man. He was one of the many that believed in his angelic disposition now.

"Poor child," she murmured. "This must be so foreign to you. You believe the Strigoi to be demons. How misguided. Perhaps I should end your suffering now. It would be a mercy. Yet, your pain will end soon enough. So, why do the Strigoi kill these Lamia and spare you and the rest of your comrades?"

Talia sensed the dawn draw nearer. "I'm afraid that you won't do, young man," Talia whispered. "I need someone older who knows that they are Lamia." She stood up and began turning over the survivors until she finally reached the last soldier.

"Sextus? It's truly you?" Talia looked him over to verify her suspicions that this could be Sextus. "Yes, that is you. You can help me." She scanned the brightening skies and forests. A copse of trees stood not too far from Sextus. She dragged him towards the shade and began to dig a hole for the both of them. She pushed him into the hole and then rolled in, pulling the dirt over herself. She closed her eyes as sunlight warmed their grave.

"Don't worry," she muttered, after spitting out dirt. "Rest now, tomorrow we'll find that foolish Briton."

Cothromaigh and Imperial Camp East of Pelm

Gaius could hear the others talking quietly amongst themselves. Marcus and Mac Alpin attempted to engage him in conversation, yet Gaius could think of nothing else other than the humiliation on the battlefield and those who would suffer for it. He attempted to keep his shame within and not allow it to reflect on his face. He kept his chin level and shoulders back as he studied the tent. It seemed unremarkable, like all others here.

Perhaps the Emperor prefers simplicity.

Máire and Claudius were muttering in some other language, perhaps discussing his failings. Yet, that seemed unlikely. He wondered if the others would gently prod him out of leadership. After all, when Mandubratius showed up, he may not have a life to contribute.

A hand touched his shoulder and a chill ran down his spine. "Welcome, General Gaius."

Gaius wondered whether a dagger rested at his back.

Mandubratius turned around to face Gaius, leaving the hand on his shoulder.

"Thank you for welcoming me," he said to Mandubratius.

"I've spoken to some of the men who came back with you. They are all younglings," Mandubratius murmured. "The rest are gone."

"Yes sir, I lost the rest," Gaius admitted.

"And how many of the elder Lamia are lost?"

"One thousand, three hundred," Gaius answered.

"Thirteen hundred of our brothers are lying in the field of battle, waiting for the sun to claim them. When the first rays of sunlight touch their skin, they will cry in agony," Mandubratius deadpanned.

Gaius stared into Mandubratius' green eyes. They turned dark. "Yes sir, they will experience a most torturous death as the sun turns their flesh and bone to dust," Gaius added. He felt a few tears escape and hoped none would see them. Then, he realized Mandubratius' eyes looked watery as well.

"I grieve with you, Gaius. Your defeat was unavoidable. Your stature among other Lamia will not change. In fact, you should be pleased that you survived, rescued the survivors and the Pope. That will ensure our place in the Roman church hierarchy." Mandubratius slapped his shoulder in a hearty manner.

Gaius tried to hide his surprise, reasoning something must have happened during Mandubratius' travels to meet the Imperial forces.

The Emperor's secretary stepped out of the tent. "His Imperial Majesty calls on the entire staff of generals to assemble. Pass the word around."

"You heard Ercanbald," Mandubratius murmured. He patted Gaius' back.

"Don't look so glum, Gaius. I won't kill you."

The words themselves made Gaius feel ill. Mandubratius smiled at him as if all were right in the world. He resolved to be on guard at all times. There would be no telling when Mandubratius would attack.

"I suppose that means even popes can cry," Marcus muttered to the others. He, Claudius, Mac Alpin, and Máire continued waiting for the crowd of generals and their staffs to move into the tent.

"How many nights before the Strigoi attack?" Máire asked.

"One or possibly two," Marcus answered with a slight shrug. "At least, that is my best guess."

"What do you suggest we do during that time?" Mac Alpin queried.

"We need to find a defensible position, travel there, and fortify it," he replied.

"The surrounding areas are mostly wooded and hilly, with many rivers and valleys in between," Claudius stated.

"There's not much that we can do at this moment, the sun rises soon. I'll speak to the Emperor and see what the others think. Perhaps they can send out riders during the daytime, and they can make preparations to move. Besides that, I do not have the luxury of making decisions for all." Marcus noticed Gaius and Mandubratius walk into the tent. "I suppose it's time for me to join the others."

"Don't be too long," Máire said. She had that look in her eyes that informed him that she wished to have a long conversation with him again about the tools within the scrolls. Máire's eyes lit with mischief. "Perhaps I should begin calling myself General so that I can be invited to these gatherings."

The two other men chuckled.

"Maél Morrigan, I doubt they could handle a general such as you." Claudius smirked. "Let's get to the tents. I know Arwin must not keep Her Imperial Majesty waiting much longer."

Máire laughed and dragged an annoyed Mac Alpin away towards the center of the tents.

Marcus could hear Mac Alpin's outraged response to Claudius' joke and chuckled as he moved into the interior of the council tent. He looked over the generals and their staffs as they neared Emperor Charles. Mandubratius appeared calm, which probably really meant that he hid his bitterness and rage about the loss of the Papal army. Gaius looked as though he might be grieving. The pope appeared to be grieving as well.

"Gentlemen," the Emperor began. His words seemed soft. "I am certain that many of you already know that the Papal army has been annihilated. His Holiness, General Gaius, and a few angels are the only survivors." The Emperor turned to Gaius.

Gaius cleared his throat. "We were arrayed for battle. Our men faced every direction. When the enemy first appeared, our archers and swordsmen were successful. Then, the enemy swarmed and started to chant. Our men began to fall, even my Angelic forces. I lost my own lieutenant. We fled for our lives."

The Emperor added, "This was a tragic loss. However, I will remind everyone of our weapon that counteracts their mental attacks. This defeat will not happen to us. Now, I'd like to hear thoughts on how to avenge the destruction of the Papal forces." He scanned the generals.

One of the generals raised his voice. "I suggest we find their lair and attack them during the day."

"That is an excellent idea," the Emperor stated. "Were we dealing with beasts that cannot be saved, I would agree with that plan of action, but we are dealing with innocent beings that are possessed. We have saved many people from this with a holy relic from the Eastern Empire."

Marcus heard mumbles from the gathered soldiers.

"These are our countrymen," the Emperor added. "They have no control and recognize the evil they are forced to undertake. They wish to be free."

"Has anyone tried negotiating with these beings?" another general asked.

Marcus could hear Mandubratius laugh.

"Trusted Emissary, would you please respond to this suggestion?" Pope Leo nodded to Mandubratius.

"I shall refrain from commenting on the stupidity of this suggestion," Mandubratius replied. "This enemy would slit our throats long before we arrived at the negotiation table."

"As eloquent as always, Emissary," the Pope said.

The general looked a little angry at Mandubratius' comments, but it was indeed a stupid proposal.

"Are there any other suggestions that allow us to defend ourselves as well as save as many of these poor souls as possible?" Emperor Charles looked over the gathering of generals again.

"If you pardon my interruption," Marcus interjected. Heads turned to regard him. "I may have a suggestion."

"Go ahead General Marcus, please give us this suggestion," the Emperor said.

"I believe we should find high ground, fortify our position and wait them out," Marcus said.

He heard more grumbles.

"You wish us to wait instead of seeking our enemy?" another stranger asked him.

"Yes, I do. I'd rather defend a territory that I knew I had prepared for battle than seek out battle in an unknown terrain where the enemy can appear from nowhere and attack."

Marcus witnessed others begin nodding their heads and muttering in Frankish.

Emperor Charles turned to regard the Pope, who nodded once. "General Marcus, I think your plan is sound, but for one important aspect. How can you ensure that the demons track us down instead of continuing their rampage of the country?" Emperor Charles' blue eyes gleamed at him.

Marcus considered an answer before speaking. "They are led by an angel who turned away from the light," he explained. "We cast her out. She wishes for vengeance and will seek us out. She did not create these demons, but she has found a method to control them. We believe she uses a form of the elixir that we created."

"If she desires retribution from you, would she follow you and the rest of the Cothromaigh if you left our company?" another general queried.

"We will not divide our forces," the Emperor stated. "The demons may follow the angels, but it's more likely that they would possess us and then attack the Cothromaigh with a greater force." He turned to regard Marcus. "How do you propose we enact your plan?"

"First, I recommend that you send out riders to scout the east and west for defensible high ground. Second, I advise that we have the men clear the top, cut six-foot spikes that we can hammer into the ground, and fortify that position. Third, we make preparations as soon as the sun sets to move to our new encampment in that defensible position."

"That is a sound plan," Pope Leo murmured.

"I agree," the Emperor added. "We are, of course, surrounded by hills, but I think we are close to Ernstberg to the east. It is the highest hill around."

Marcus felt his internal sense of the position of the sun begin to warn him of an eminent sunrise.

"Good idea, but I beg your pardon, Imperial Majesty. I must retire to my tent."

"Yes, of course." Emperor Charles nodded his head. "Thank you for your suggestions."

Marcus headed for the exit and sensed Mandubratius and Gaius follow. He walked to the tent that exuded the scents of Máire and Claudius. He opened the flap and stepped inside. Both of them appeared to be asleep, and he saw Lucius curled up on Máire's legs, snoring. Marcus sat down in front of the bowl of water at one corner of the tent. He removed his boots and washed his hands, feet, and face.

"So, how did it go?" Claudius asked.

"The emperor liked my idea," Marcus said. He moved over to Máire's other side, sat on the woolen bedding, and laid down.

"I suppose now is not the time to continue our last conversation, is it, Marcus." Máire turned her face towards his.

Marcus tilted his head to regard her. He felt exhausted. "Some other time, chroí," he answered. Marcus closed his eyes and felt a thud on his chest. He raised his head and looked up at Lucius.

The fairy cat purred and stared into his eyes. The cat's eyes seemed to reflect a deep knowledge. Lucius closed his lids and shifted to curl up on his chest.

"Rest well," he said, patting Lucius.

"Do not roll over, Marcus," the fairy cat instructed him, "and sleep well."

Irene wiggled her bare toes and stared at them, wishing for a full bath. She felt that the odd Celtic notion of bathing hands, feet, and faces left too much dirty. Then, when they bathed, they preferred icy rivers and streams. Granted, there had not been much time for a long soak in hot, cleansing water or an icy body of water. "Where is that insufferable dolt?" Irene grumbled to herself.

"I'm on my way," she heard a voice echo in the distance.

Damn the excellent hearing of the Ekimmu Cruitne.

"It's about time you got back," she stated, "the sun rises soon."

"I'm outside and have an excellent vantage point for viewing the sunrise," Arwin stated. The tent flap rose and he walked in.

The brightness of the purple and blue skies startled Irene. "Close that flap!"

"I'm closing it right now," Mac Alpin's voice shouted in annoyance. He studied her and then seemed to examine the tent. "How is it that the rest of us have to stay cooped up without floor space and you get this tent to yourself?"

"I am Basileus Irene, the Empress of the East," she answered.

"And?" The infuriating smile on his face made her emotions boil.

"And nothing! That title gives me sufficient privilege over the rest of you commoners."

"Like you?" Arwin smirked. "At least, that's the rumor going around the taverns in Constantinople."

"Get over here and service me," Irene hissed.

Arwin sighed and grumbled something that sounded to be in Gaelic or that other language they spoke. He began to undress. Then he turned to the corner of the tent to wash his hands and feet.

"What was that?" she asked.

Arwin turned back toward Irene and said the same gibberish again.

"You know I despise it when you speak in languages that I don't understand!" Irene slapped her hands against the dirt floor.

Mac Alpin closed his eyes as his smile grew. "I said, Imperial Majesty, I hope pus and scabs seal your womanly parts shut!"

Irene growled and kicked Arwin's feet out from under him and straddled him before he had a chance to move. "That is very rude!" she snarled.

He punched her in the chin and rolled her over as Irene reeled in surprise.

She pincered Arwin's neck with her knees, and he elbowed her. She released him.

He forced his mouth on hers. His hands sought her breasts. They always began coitus with boiling blood. The fights raised both their spirits, and whatever wounds they gave each other disappeared with sleep.

Irene played with the hair over Arwin's arms. She discovered he was quite ticklish, and any soft caresses made him twitch. She felt exhaustion creep upon her, but she still felt annoyance that Arwin had left her alone for most of the evening. "The next time you decide to run off and leave me all alone, do not ask that boy to chaperone me," Irene said.

"What's wrong?" Arwin rolled her onto her back and stared into her eyes with surprising gentleness. "I thought Reginald did an admirable job."

"Reginald? I thought that was Julien. Whichever boy it was, he has no stamina and knows nothing about using his tongue." Irene attempted to keep her face serious. After all, following years of Leo's inadequacies, and Mandubratius leaving her, she considered certain pleasures to be quite important.

Arwin appeared to be confused. "But we were traveling most of night."

"A woman has urges and needs, and you were too busy trying to impress Marcus. I don't know what you see in that arrogant Roman! God, you and he aren't—"

"Aren't what?" Arwin started to laugh. "Irene, he is my friend but not a friend in that manner." He continued laughing as though it were the most hilarious thing he'd heard all night.

"So, why were you so late in coming to see me?" Irene queried. "As soon as the soldiers set up the tent, Reginald made some excuse about being there for muster. Then, I approached Patroclus for companionship, and he said the same thing. I was alone for so long. Are you seeing another woman at the same time as me?" Irene frowned.

"Well that would be more likely than a man." Arwin pulled up a blanket.

Irene slapped him, and he smiled at her. "I didn't say that you could cover up. I'm still looking at you. Who is it? Is it that tramp Amata?"

Arwin laughed. "No, I was joking, Empress. I have little time for women these nights. I am most flattered at your jealousy, though. In the Celtic lines, we seldom encounter envy within ourselves or others. I suppose it is not in our nature."

Irene grumbled at how the Celtic lines were so confusing. "So, why were you late?" she asked.

Arwin's smile faded. "The Strigoi attacked the Papal Army, and only a small number of Lamia and Pope Leo survived."

Irene stroked a hand over his hair, hoping he would continue talking. His voice was deep and pleasing to hear. Sometimes, she found herself asking him the same questions when they lay together like this, so she could enjoy it.

"We overheard the Pope crying when he was alone with Emperor Charles," Arwin added.

"Crying? Really?" Irene considered that information. "I wonder how I can use that to my advantage. Pompous bastard," she hissed.

"Is that in reference to me?" Mac Alpin chuckled. "I must say I rather like that as a nickname."

"Not you, you dolt." Irene tried to hide her smile. "I meant that pompous bastard, Pope Leo III."

"Well I, being a heathen, would agree with you, Irene. I'm curious, though, why would a Christian noble and Empress feel this way in regards to him?"

"Pope Leo," Irene hissed, "could not see past my lack of male genitals. He refused to see me as Basileus and protector of Christendom. He crowned that upstart Frankish barbarian emperor instead." The slight still stung. Irene's rage rose and heat infused her blood. She pushed Arwin onto his back and straddled him. "Now, service me again." Irene smiled down at him.

The smell of venison and pork roasting over fires woke Marcus, bringing forth strange memories of eating, yet he felt a little disgust over the somewhat offensive smell of cooking meat.

As he sat up, he noticed Lucius stretched across his feet, and Máire and Claudius still slept. Then, a shadow caught his eye, and he noticed a mortal soldier standing at attention, staring at the opposite wall of the tent. "Lieutenant," he said to the soldier.

"You promised me a promotion," he heard Claudius mumble in his sleep. "I've been a lieutenant to you for too long."

"Captain, actually," the officer answered.

"That sounds good… or major," Claudius muttered.

"Forgive me, captain, what brings you here this evening?" Marcus asked.

"He must be here to feed us," Máire stated sleepily. She turned a bit in her blankets to regard the soldier. "Is the sun still up?"

"No, the sun is down," Claudius yawned.

"The sun has been down for awhile, Banbh Ceanúil. What's this about food?" Mac Alpin shouted from another tent.

Marcus winced as he returned to studying the Imperial officer.

The officer looked back at him. "No sir, that would be my honor, of course… but I'm here for another reason."

"Then, I have two questions for you, captain," Marcus said. "The first is why are you here and the second is would you allow one of us to feed from you?" He noticed Claudius and Máire both looked pale and hungry.

"General, in answer to your first question, the scouts confirmed the proposed site, Ernstberg, should meet with your approval. They had consulted General Ebroin earlier. In answer to the second, I would be honored to serve." The captain's eyes shifted about a little, revealing his nervousness.

"Me first!" Máire called out.

"I call… damnit," Claudius chuckled. "Go on then, Maél Morrigan."

Marcus smirked. "Ladies first, then."

Máire pushed aside her blankets and rose to her feet, wearing a long tunic.

She carefully stepped over Lucius and smiled at the soldier. "Are you sure you don't mind this, captain?" she asked. "You seem hesitant, and I don't remember you volunteering to aid us before. If you do this, I promise I'll heal you and make you forget it, if you wish."

Marcus watched the captain blush.

"Would you be insulted?" the officer whispered.

"Not at all," Máire said. "We shall respect your wishes." She stepped away and lowered her eyes. "It is your decision."

He studied the officer, as the captain rolled up a sleeve and approached Máire. Marcus stood up and headed for the bowl of water.

"You may feed," the captain said.

"I wish we had time for a full bath," Claudius murmured. "If I must face death, I'd rather do so clean."

"I agree. Let's try to make time for that soon… major," Marcus chuckled. "You have your promotion... I will promise to do my best to remember it." He stepped into his breeches and tried not to smell the wafting scent of tantalizing blood.

"Thank you!" Claudius grinned. "Now, should we bother with shaving tonight?"

"I think not. We should examine this new location." Marcus rubbed a hand over the stubble on his cheek. He heard Máire whispering. He turned back and watched her kiss the officer's brow.

"Thank you," she said.

The officer seemed bewildered. He turned towards Marcus. "General, whenever you're ready, I'll be waiting outside." The officer then marched out.

"Prepare yourselves, in case we need to go to battle." Marcus tossed Máire her breeches and boots. He soon sensed someone else barge in.

"I am always prepared," Arwin said. He appeared to have freshly healing wounds on his face.

Marcus drew closer to get a better look at the scars. "The Empress?"

"That woman doesn't sleep!" Mac Alpin decried. He began pacing about. "She insisted on frolics all day. When does she rest?"

"When the rest of us are working," Claudius chortled. He pulled on his right boot.

"Yes, I can see that I need to speak with Reginald and ask him to keep her up all night," Arwin answered, smirking. "Irene hates him, though she seems to confuse him, Julien, and many of the Frankish nobles."

"Mac Alpin, since you're prepared, I need you to be my messenger."

"A mere messenger for a Roman?" Arwin's eyes widened and twinkled with merriment. "Such an insult!"

Marcus chuckled. "Be that as it may, it's an order."

"Fine, what is the message and who does it go to?" Mac Alpin asked.

"Inform the Cothromaigh to be prepared for battle as a precaution. After we receive our rations of elixir, I need twenty volunteers to accompany us to the proposed site. Everyone else needs to maintain defenses here. Ask the volunteers to congregate at the casks where they blend the wine with the mushroom mix."

"Should we get the army to begin moving in that direction?" Arwin asked.

"I don't wish to waste effort moving these men when this location's defenses are not yet verified. Besides, I'm reminded of an old proverb that my general once..." He could see Arwin's eyes wander to the ceiling. "'It matters not how hard the wind blows if one doesn't know to which port one is sailing'," Marcus concluded.

"Did all Roman generals go around spouting such things that should be common sense to anyone?" Arwin chuckled. "No, never mind. Don't answer that. Am I dismissed now?"

"You're impossible, Arwin," Marcus chuckled. "Yes, go, go!"

Mac Alpin left the tent.

Marcus heard whispers and laughter between Claudius and Máire. He turned and addressed them. "Now, can't you two get ready faster, or shall I send for a sergeant to motivate you? Major, your boots are deplorable. Máire, you missed some dirt on your face. Clean yourself." He watched Claudius and Máire smile and start to tidy each other, since they lacked mirrors.

"I'm ready," Lucius said. "I'm groomed and in perfect order, aren't I, General?"

"Lucius, you are my best soldier. Perhaps you deserve Claudius' old title of lieutenant." Marcus chuckled. He grabbed the pouch and held out his arms for Lucius.

The fairy cat propelled himself into Marcus' arms and began to purr.

"We know who the favorite is," Claudius chuckled. He came over and rubbed Lucius' brow. "General, perhaps you should speak to his Imperial Majesty and that high priest about keeping their troops here for now."

"An excellent suggestion," Marcus said, while helping Lucius into the pouch. "You two get in line for rations." He stepped out of the tent and noticed the captain snap to attention. "Captain, join my associates in the line for rations. I will go there after I speak with his Imperial Majesty."

"Yes, general." The officer followed Máire and Claudius towards the line.

"I have forgotten, Lucius, do you require the rations?" Marcus looked down into the pouch.

Lucius narrowed his green eyes. "As a fairy cat, I have no need for such revolting sustenance," he answered. "The Strigoi's mental attacks have no effect on me."

"I'm most relieved to hear that, Lieutenant," Marcus said. He walked towards the Emperor's tent and heard the buzzing within.

Ercanbald, the secretary waved him inside.

The Emperor and Pope Leo stared at a map on the Emperor's table.

The secretary returned to packing up the Emperor's bags.

Charles looked up from the map. "Marcus, good of you to come by, I've ordered the men to pack as if to move but to wait until we receive confirmation on this new site from you."

"Thank you, Imperial Majesty," Marcus replied. "I rather hoped you would do that. I will meet with my volunteers then and send you a messenger back with the news." Marcus walked towards the exit.

"Oh Marcus," Emperor Charles called.

Marcus stopped and turned back to face the mortals. "Imperial Majesty?"

"Please take the Papal Emissary with you on this mission."

"Why would his presence be necessary, Imperial Majesty?" Marcus asked. "I would think that the Pope," he motioned to Pope Leo, "needs the emissary's assistance."

The Pope grumbled a bit and rubbed his forehead. "I sent out the emissary to get my rations, General. He is constantly underfoot. Besides, I want the emissary to make sure that the defenses are properly blessed and that there are no heathen influences in the area." The Pope set his gaze on Marcus.

"Very well, I will invite him and tell him that we require his help tonight," Marcus answered. "However, I think that he'll see through that excuse... Holy Pope."

The Pope laughed. "Of course he will, but give the emissary that excuse anyway."

"Very well," Marcus nodded. He headed for the tent flap.

"General?"

Leo's eyes focused on Marcus again, then moved to the pouch at his side.

"Why do you carry that cat with you?" Pope Leo asked. "I did not think angels associated with baser animals."

Marcus lowered his head and caught the prominent smirk on the cat's face. "This cat belonged to a victim of the demons, my… Máire found him, and he was frightened and hungry," Marcus answered. "Lucius, or Lugh, survived the attack and became our mascot. God created all beings, Holy Pope, even black cats."

"That is so touching," Lucius purred. "Marcus, you should have never been a soldier. You would have been a most talented bard."

"Such generosity to lesser creations," the Pope replied. "You are truly an angel among mortals."

Lucius uttered a derisive hiss. "Lesser creations, indeed!"

Marcus patted Lucius for a moment. "Thank you for such a… compliment," he said to the Pope, while trying to mask his frown. "It is time for me to meet the volunteers." He turned away and trudged out of the tent, listening to Lucius utter various complaints about the rudeness of Pope Leo. He could hear the chatter of the blood-drinkers as he neared the casks, some still awaited their turn to drink their rations.

Mandubratius lingered in the line of mortals, still remaining silent despite all the discussion surrounding him.

"Good evening, Emissary," Marcus greeted him. The Lamia nearly dropped his goblet and his face turned gray.

"Marcus, I trust all is well," Mandubratius responded.

"Why yes, everything is well."

"Excellent," Mandubratius replied, becoming silent. He stepped to the front of the line and dipped his goblet in the cauldron. "Is there something you wish to discuss? I need to return this goblet with the elixir to the Holy Father," Mandubratius said.

"Actually, the Pope has changed his orders," Marcus began. "He wishes you to join us. I am leading a group of volunteers to scout and secure a potential defensive position against the demons."

"That sounds like a very important mission." Mandubratius uttered a weak chuckle. "Why am I needed to join such an august party?"

"Well, the Holy… whatever… has asked me to bring you along. He said something about you blessing the location and verifying that it is free of Pagan influence." Marcus tried to keep from laughing. A chuckle escaped and he covered his mouth.

"You'll forgive me if I verify these orders."

"You have no time, we're leaving now." Marcus grabbed Mandubratius' shoulder, when he felt a shudder moved through the Lamia.

Mandubratius dropped the goblet. The wine and mushroom mixture muddied the dirt below the cauldron. "But, I have no arms on my person."

"I am certain we have extra arms, Emissary."

"But, I have not had my rations yet, and I dropped the Pope's," Mandubratius replied.

Marcus revealed a full goblet from under his cloak and held it out to Mandubratius. "I added extra of the mixture to this blend for our long journey.

Well, not so long. It's just a few miles to the east." He winked at the other blood-drinker.

Mandubratius took the goblet and raised it with both of his hands. He tossed it back and handed the empty goblet to Marcus.

Marcus attached the goblet to his belt and motioned him to join the rest of the volunteers. "Thank you for volunteering," Marcus addressed the gathered twenty blood-drinkers. "I am certain Mac Alpin told you about the mission. The site is ten to twelve miles to the east. We have not seen the Strigoi, but they can still be out there. I believe that the best way to travel to this proposed site is to fly to a high altitude above the clouds, so we are too far away for any potential mental attacks. We will descend at the series of hills to the east, and if we witness any Strigoi, I'm confident a bow and arrow attack will distract them. Any questions?"

The blood-drinkers glanced around, looking to see if any questions would be raised.

"Who will carry me?" Mandubratius muttered.

"That honor will fall to the major and me." Marcus motioned to Claudius.

Mandubratius turned a sick green. "I am most honored to be carried by such high ranking angels," he uttered.

Marcus nodded. "We will take a lattice formation to the proposed site." He and Claudius approached Mandubratius.

"You aren't sick from that potion are you?" Claudius studied the Lamia.

"I'll be fine." Mandubratius shrugged as they prepared to take off.

In the Sky Between Pelm and Ernstberg

Despite the many times they carried Mandubratius, the exhilaration of rising towards the clouds thrilled him to no end. Perhaps this time seemed different because of the speed of the flight. The air seemed cold, exceptionally cold this night. He could swear that he felt ice crystals forming in his beard. He lowered his head and looked past his feet. The encampment merged with the rest of the ground and foliage. He then glanced over at Marcus, who appeared to be focused. After all, the Deargh Du seldom flew at this height.

Mandubratius looked down to find the camp again, but everything seemed to be dark, forested land below.

"We're at the limit for my nose," Mac Alpin shouted.

"Head due east!" Marcus yelled to the other blood-drinkers. "Ten miles, then we'll descend."

Their ascent stopped, and they began flying to the east. The Lamia caught himself considering what would happen if he fell from this height. "This must be a great shame for you," he said to Marcus.

"What?" Marcus shouted. The Deargh Du turned his head to the side.

"I said… this is a missed opportunity for you, and you must be ashamed to miss it," Mandubratius repeated.

The Deargh Du raised a brow. "Is what a shame, Emissary?"

"Oh drop the title, Marcus. Everyone here knows who and what I am."

"Well, is what a shame, Mandubratius?"

"That you and I are allies, now," Mandubratius chuckled. "You could eliminate me so easily by just letting go." He noticed Marcus exchange glances with Claudius and continued. "I would plummet, and I would be pulverized when I hit the ground. Not just pulverized, but my bones would become pulp. My blood would splatter over a wide distance. Mandubratius would be no more."

"Is he suffering effects of the potion?" Claudius asked.

"I don't think so," Marcus said. "Is this an invitation to drop you?"

"I don't wish for my life to end, but I'd feel so guilty that you missed an opportunity for vengeance," Mandubratius answered. "Isn't your mother known for Her acts of vengeance? She will be most disappointed if Her son does not continue with the family tradition."

Marcus ceased forward movement, pulling Claudius to a stop.

"Claudius, continue with the group, you are in charge."

The Sugnwr Gwaed stared at both of them for a moment and then took off to catch up with the rest of the volunteers.

"What do you know about my mother?" Marcus asked. His eyes revealed rage.

"I never said that I knew your mother," Mandubratius answered. "I doubt I've ever met Her, but if I had, I'm certain I would have bedded Her." He gave in to a swelling fit of laughter.

"If I did not know better, I would say you were drunk or out of your wits." The Deargh Du's rage appeared to fade.

"No, I'm not right now." Mandubratius leaned in closer towards Marcus' ear. "If I'm drunk, it's because I know things that make me fearful."

Marcus studied him over his shoulder. The starlight and his glamoury affected his eyes, turning them otherworldly silver. "What is it that you fear, Awvarwy?"

"Why is it that you toy with me, Marcus? Why don't you just end it?" The cold breezes made Mandubratius close his eyes.

"End what?"

Mandubratius opened his eyes again and found Marcus staring at him, as if he were something new and different.

"My life," Mandubratius answered, wondering about Marcus's daftness. *Were all children of deities touched in the head?*

"Awvarwy, I have no intention of ending your life," the Deargh Du replied.

"Máire almost ended my life. She had every intention of doing so," Mandubratius said. "I could see it in her eyes. She wanted to kill me." He uttered a mirthless chuckle. "I have given Máire every reason to kill me, Marcus, and now you toy with me. You should let me drop. Why are you toying with me?" His words became angry.

"I'm not toying with you. This sounds like an effect of paranoia and the mushrooms, Mandubratius."

"Come now, Marcus," Mandubratius leaned in again and began to whisper. "I know what's going through your mind. You will lull me into trusting you. Then you will let me fall to my death. You believe that I will bellow your name in an enraged scream as I fall until I impact the ground. It will give you perverse pleasure, won't it?"

"Were you to die, Awvarwy, it won't be at my hand. I will gain no pleasure in your death."

"But, I killed your mistress in Gaul. Don't you wish to kill me for that?" Mandubratius asked. His head ached now as he studied Marcus again.

An ember of anger rose in the silver and blue eyes. Then they became calm. "That was some time ago," the Deargh Du commented. "Much has happened since then." He fell silent for a moment. "What is this madness that you suffer? This isn't just the mushrooms."

"It is not the mushrooms that cause my madness," Mandubratius stated. "It is her and it is you."

Marcus uttered a strained laugh. "What kind of accusation is that?"

"Máire almost killed me when the lightning possessed her," Mandubratius answered. He stared into the dark skies. The moon seemed to glow brighter this night, despite the fact that she hid part of herself. "That skill with the lightning is not normal Druidic ability. Yes, Marcus, I've witnessed Druids do amazing feats, but I know that they can only harness the elements and energies. She bent that lightning to her will, Marcus, and allowed it to possess her." Mandubratius leaned in to whisper into Marcus' ear. "Máire can only do this because she is the grandchild of Morrigan, and you are Morrigan's son."

The Deargh Du became mute again.

"I had always believed that you and I were equals," Mandubratius continued. "Though, quite frankly, I didn't think you deserved to be Deargh Du. You should have been Lamia, and I should have been the Deargh Du. Now, thinking back on that it's quite amusing. You see, I was so content to think that we were equals, and that I would have an opportunity to get the upper hand. Now, I know the truth. You are the son of a Goddess, and I can never be greater than that." He grabbed one of Marcus' swords and tried to push himself away from the Deargh Du.

At last, he succeeded and began to tumble. The cold air rushed around him, and Mandubratius smiled. He watched himself hunting with the Chieftain he had believed to be his father, witnessed the horror of his gentle mother flayed on the altar, relived the passion of his first encounter with a beautiful blue-eyed brunette named Aelwyd, and the unending pleasure of killing the chieftain who had claimed him as his only son.

And then his momentum towards the ground ceased. Someone pulled back on his belt and tunic. Mandubratius turned his head to face whoever saved him.

"Why?!" he raged at Marcus.

"I don't desire your death," Marcus uttered in a grunt.

"But that is no reason. It's not a good reason!"

"I wouldn't forgive myself if she died," Marcus replied.

Mandubratius turned away and stared at the vast, dark earth below. Realizing what he'd almost accomplished, he focused on what Marcus said.

"Who is she?" he asked.

Marcus said nothing for a moment. "It's not important," the Deargh Du answered. He hefted Mandubratius to a standing position. "Grab my shoulder," he muttered.

Mandubratius wrapped an arm around his shoulders. "Tell me who she is," he demanded.

"No. Furthermore, you do not need to compete with me."

"No! Who in Hades is 'she?'" Mandubratius growled.

"Máire," Marcus answered.

"What does Máire have to do with my death?"

Marcus sighed as if annoyed. "Look, if you die, she dies soon afterward."

Mandubratius contemplated that answer and decided it made no sense. "How is that possible?"

Marcus turned away. "You and she are linked. You are each other's balance." The other blood-drinker's words became a hoarse whisper. "If you succeeded in your suicide, I would have lost her soon afterwards. I can't live without her in this realm, Awvarwy."

"So, Marcus, Son of Morrigan," Mandubratius began. "Had you not known of this link, would you have allowed me to die?"

"Over two centuries ago, I wanted you dead, but I don't right now," Marcus answered.

"That is not a convincing answer," Mandubratius stated, wondering why Marcus never exhibited God-like powers. If he had been the child of a God or Goddess, Mandubratius would have used whatever influences and might he could wield. In light of Marcus' revelation, his suicide attempt now seemed ridiculous. "Thank you for saving my life." He frowned at having to say such a thing.

"You were not yourself," Marcus replied.

"And you are not who I thought you were, Marcus, Son of Morrigan."

The Deargh Du's eyes revealed a quick flash of surprise.

"We should rejoin the others," Marcus stated. "We have a lot of work to complete before dawn. I trust that you will not reveal my lineage, or the lineage of my family, and you will say nothing of your connection with Máire."

"Of course, you have my word." Mandubratius stared at the ground as they began to fly towards the clouds again. He started to turn his head up towards the stars when he noticed Lucius peering at him from the pouch with that strange cat-grin.

chapter ten

Cothromaigh and Imperial Camp East of Pelm

áire glanced around the camp. Everyone seemed to be working and packing. They did everything but bring down the tents. She moved back into the tent she shared last night. Marcus tended to mumble in sleep during stressful events, and Claudius snored and kicked her.

Perhaps it would be best for me to find another tent for the next day.

Máire spread out a blanket and kicked off her boots. She pulled over another blanket and rested her head against it, sensing a nap would be in order. She closed her eyes. Perhaps Julien would join her. She drifted off.

A throat cleared. Máire opened her eyes, figuring another soldier must be looking for Marcus. She noticed no one entered her tent, yet the scent of a Deargh Du wafted from the tent flap. The large number of slightly unfamiliar scents kept her from identifying who waited outside the tent. "Come in." She tilted her head.

Sáerlaith walked into the tent and smiled at her. "Am I disturbing you?"

"No, not at all." Máire sat up quickly. "I was daydreaming."

"No, you were napping," Sáerlaith chuckled. She sat down across from Máire. "I hope you had pleasant dreams, free from the Strigoi."

"I don't remember if I dreamed," Máire admitted. "What can I do for you, Sáerlaith?"

The elder Deargh Du studied her for a moment. "You expressed an interest in teaching the rudiments of the tools from the scrolls."

"Oh, yes. I did offer my assistance."

"Well, I have some interested students who are curious about those tools."

Máire gulped away her reservations and grabbed her boots. "Wonderful."

Sáerlaith rose from her seat and offered Máire a hand after she finished pulling on her boots. The other Deargh Du's features were unreadable.

"Please take me to where the students are waiting," Máire said.

"The students are expecting me to teach them," Sáerlaith admitted.

"You didn't tell them that I would teach them?"

"Not as such," Sáerlaith admitted, meeting her eyes.

Máire tried to fight off her rising anger. "Why didn't you tell them?"

"You understand how a majority of elder Deargh Du think, do you not, Máire? Anyone who isn't five hundred years old is a babe in their eyes. The elders are somewhat set in their ways. Some may not wish to be taught by a youngling."

"But if I'm to be their teacher, what would keep them? Wouldn't they leave?" Máire asked.

"Part of being an effective instructor is learning to win over the students."

"What do you mean?" Máire stared into Sáerlaith's dark eyes, looking for answers.

"These students have gathered because they have an interest in the power the Druids wield," Sáerlaith answered.

"You mean, they aren't all druids?"

Sáerlaith shrugged. "Most of the Deargh Du druids are in Ard Mhacha. A few came with the warriors during the Strigoi attack on Britain to raise the mists and perform the feats they normally do, but we are primarily a force of warriors and druids that can wield swords. Then, I also invited the druids of the other Celtic lines. They are most curious about these tools. Still, there are several warriors here that took on a path that was forced on them but wished to be druids."

Máire tried to turn her thoughts away from Mandubratius, hating to feel pity for him again.

"It doesn't really matter who teaches them, Máire," Sáerlaith continued. "All you must do is win them over in the first few moments of your arrival. Then, they will be yours to instruct."

"Will you join me?" Máire met the other Deargh Du's honest stare.

"I shall not. There needs to only be one instructor. If I'm there, it will ruin your credibility. They would believe me to be the true teacher." Sáerlaith stepped in closer. "I know you have more knowledge and skill in these matters than I possess. This is why you will teach me the rudiments when we have an opportunity to do so." Sáerlaith squeezed Máire's arm gently. "Now, they are gathered in a clearing to the west across the river. It will be easy to find."

Máire nodded and headed for the exit to the tent.

Sáerlaith's voice stopped her. Máire turned back towards the elder.

"Remember you can win them over. After all, you wield what they seek." Sáerlaith beamed at her with a glowing radiance.

"I will do so," Máire answered. She pushed back the tent flap and flew into the star-filled sky, heading for the west.

Máire expected to see twenty or perhaps thirty waiting on her. Instead She witnessed about one hundred waiting on Sáerlaith's arrival. There appeared to be about forty Sugnwr Gwaed and Ekimmu Cruitne altogether, with sixty Deargh Du gathered in a semi-circle in the field. After she landed in the center of the group, all fell silent.

Máire met a few stares from the others and tried to smile.

An unfamiliar Deargh Du pushed her way through the gathered. Her dark eyes reflected annoyance. "We understood Sáerlaith would be teaching us, not someone so young."

Máire made no response to that. She found some solace in Caoimhín's blue eyes. "Most of you know me. I volunteered to instruct what I know about the tools."

"This youngling will teach us nothing," another Deargh Du muttered. "We have better things to do with our time. We should be gathering plants to prepare for the mist-raising in the upcoming battles."

Máire turned from their words and began to concentrate on opening the doors to the otherworld. She closed her eyes as she felt the veil breach. Energy flowed towards her when she whispered for the assistance of the Tuaths. Máire opened her eyes, sensing the curiosity of the others. They could smell the changes on the wind, she assumed. She stared down at her hand and started to spread it open.

Debris rose with the increasing winds in the distance. The center of the vortex bellowed a low rumble which began to grow in pitch and volume.

Máire caught sight of the others covering their eyes with their arms and balancing themselves in the mounting winds. The sound became deafening.

"Shed light on this manifestation!" she heard Caoimhín shout.

The Deargh Du allowed their glamoury to shine, and the vortex she manifested became visible to all.

Máire began to close her hand and felt as though she motioned the vortex towards her. The vortex shrunk in size and became no taller than her. She smiled and laughed a moment as the vortex seemed to voice a wish to grow again. Her thoughts returned to releasing the energy. She stared away from the vortex and studied her right palm. She closed her hand and whispered for the energy to return to its origin. The veil moved together again, and the vortex faded into dust.

Silence greeted her.

She met the stunned stares of the other druids and those who sought the path. "This is what one can do with the mastery of the tools. You must dedicate time to these studies, unless of course you wish to leave and forget this." Máire smiled.

"No, teach me. I wish to learn this from you."

She turned and found an aged Sugnwr Gwaed grinning back at her.

"As do I," another voice stated.

"We all wish to learn," Caoimhín said.

"Well then," Máire continued, "for everyone here to learn, you must do what I say, how I say it. If you deviate, you can injure yourselves and others. Now, I'll teach you a skill tonight that is not as spectacular as calling forth a vortex, but I believe that it can be used to stun the Strigoi."

She watched smiles widen at the thought of wielding such a tool.

"Now, I wish everyone to form a circle around me. Give each other at least ten feet of distance."

Máire allowed her glamoury to illuminate her face.

"Let's begin."

Ernstberg at the Summit

Claudius' feeling of satisfaction at earning a somewhat overdue and useless promotion still stayed in place as they neared the three mile mark.

Has it been three miles yet? Barely a blink.

"Claudius, wipe that shite-eating grin off your face," Arwin muttered at him. "Stop thinking whatever it is your thinking about and focus on the here and now."

Claudius snapped out of his reverie. "What?"

"I've been motioning for us to descend for several minutes, but you haven't been paying attention. We've overshot the hill, major. Have you forgotten what command means, youngling?"

Claudius chuckled. "Thanks for not shouting that out for all to hear, Mac Alpin. I was indeed lost in thought. Do you smell any Strigoi?"

"I can smell neither Strigoi nor blood-drinkers other than us. Though I do catch a faint stinky breeze of mortals and their horses below to the west amongst the trees," Mac Alpin replied.

"Maintain the perimeter when we land," Claudius shouted to the others. "I smell burning wood, they must have a fire." He flew towards the scouts. "Ho there!" he said, nearing their location, hoping they would not be surprised and send a volley of arrows to greet them.

"Who's there?" a mortal called out.

Claudius landed in front of them. "I'm Major Claudius of the Cothromaigh, and this is my scouting detachment."

The captain, or he believed the head mortal to be of that rank, and his men jumped to attention.

"I'm Captain Fulk. This is my scouting party. We're happy that you've arrived here safely."

"Yes, we're indeed fortunate that the Strigoi haven't attacked. Have you had an opportunity to fully examine the site?" Claudius asked.

"Yes, we've even mapped out the site and surrounding areas. We also mapped the larger hill about a mile to the southwest, Scharteberg, but we felt the slopes were too gentle to offer much of a defence. Oh, there is a cave just below the summit... over there," the captain said, pointing to the east. "We are indeed blessed to have a cartographer in our party," Fulk answered.

"That is quite fortunate." Claudius began to study the map near the glowing torches. He noticed Mac Alpin sniffing again. "Is there anything to report, Arwin?"

"No sign of the Strigoi, Claudius, but I smell our wayward friends. Marcus and the Papal Emissary will land shortly." Mac Alpin chuckled.

Claudius groaned at Arwin's lack of formality.

Better not risk allowing my new 'rank' to go to my head.

He had acted as one of the leaders of the Sugnwr Gwaed several times over the centuries and had not even expected them to grant him a title other than 'council chief' or leader of the Sugnwr Gwaed forces. "Thank you for the report, Arwin."

The captain and his men appeared to be a little confused at the strange chain of command. Yet, before they could ask any questions, Marcus and Mandubratius arrived.

Marcus set down Mandubratius. They both appeared to be sober.

"So, captain," Mandubratius, Michael, or whatever he called himself this night began. "Have you noticed any sites of Christian or Pagan origin on this hilltop?"

"No, my lord Emissary," the captain responded after bowing.

"Well then, my work is done," Mandubratius cheered. "Gentlemen, please proceed with your mission." The blood-drinker sat down in front of the fire and smiled.

"What happened to him?" Claudius asked Marcus in Gaelic.

"I suppose the cold air finally sobered him," Marcus replied. He walked around and leaned in to examine the work.

"Who did this?" Marcus asked. "It's excellent."

One of the soldiers saluted him.

Marcus nodded in recognition before turning his stare back to Claudius. "May I?" He motioned to the map.

Claudius handed over the map. Marcus strolled around the forested hill.

"Who's that?" the captain asked.

"Oh, that's our general, Marcus," Claudius answered. "Don't you recognize him?"

The mortal leaned in closer. "My sight is sometimes poor at night," he whispered. "I must admit I'm embarrassed for not realizing it was him. What is he doing?"

"He always liked to walk defensive positions," Claudius answered.

A few minutes later, Marcus returned, walking and looking over the surroundings and their corresponding locations on the scroll. "Yes, this is a good map," he murmured. "And I agree that Ernstberg is more suitable for defence than Scharteberg. I suggest we start clearing the top of the hill to allow for the placement of our tents in the middle, fortifications in a ring around the top, and a clear field of fire. We should also a path to the top from that ridge to the west so the Strigoi can get funneled in, and we can set up traps along that path." Marcus picked up the writing tools and began to mark areas for tents and spikes. After he finished, he handed the scroll back to Claudius.

"I will return to the camp and advise Emperor Charles that this site is acceptable. Edward will assist me in leading the armies here." Marcus smirked. "Major, you are left in charge. I am certain you and Arwin can start working on the plans for the construction of the battlements."

Claudius watched the Deargh Du grin at Mac Alpin and heard a soft utterance of stifled laughter.

Mandubratius stood up. "Since I'm not needed here, I wish to accompany you back to camp, unless that is a problem for you. I'm certain the Holy Father wishes my assistance during the move."

Marcus frowned for a moment, as he and the Lamia exchanged stares. "No, Emissary. That's not a problem at all."

Claudius saluted Marcus before returning to study the markings on the map. He heard the two blood-drinkers fly away and wondered if he could remember the process of building battlements in a short time.

"Perhaps we should start with gathering the timber," he said, while walking over to Mac Alpin.

"I agree. Let's begin in the center of the hill so we can set up the tents."

Valley South of Daun

Talia tried to open her eyes upon sensing the night skies overhead, but she had to squint, trying to keep the dirt from overwhelming her. She concentrated on discovering the presence of other blood-drinkers. Other than Sextus, she could not discern any others. Talia began to dig her way out of the shallow hole and climbed out. She reached back in and pulled out Sextus. He still appeared to be asleep.

Perhaps talking to him would rouse him.

"You seem to be well physically," she informed him. Talia glanced around the woods, certain that the dust of the dead Lamia would blow over them soon, yet the night remained still and quiet. "You've been attacked by the

Strigoi and are probably experiencing their nightmares." She could hear the sound of many heartbeats and hooves in the distance.

A deer studied them and judged the expanse between them.

"You are too weak now to fight off the nightmare," Talia whispered, "but I'll make you stronger. I shall return." She moved to her feet and sprinted after the deer. She chased the deer out of the forest and into the field of battle. The sight of the army's baggage train pleased her. They could sleep in the Pope's cart when the sun rose again.

Talia returned her attention to the deer and leapt into the air, bringing the deer down with her descent. The deer tried to squirm and kick its way free, but as soon as she began to feed, the deer quieted. In the process of feeling the rush of blood explode in her open mouth Talia realized that at any other time the blood of beasts would disgust her. Talia forgot that moment of worry and returned to feeding.

After releasing the weak deer, she stumbled towards Sextus and began feeding him. "I believe your troops may have left their baggage train behind," she informed Sextus. "I believe it would be best for you to recover there instead of under dirt."

Ernstberg Encampment and Fortifications

From the top of the hill, Marcus stared down at the expanse of wooded hills and valleys around, as well as the tributaries to the northeast, northwest, and southwest. The soldiers readied their defenses and planted great wooden stakes into the ground. Others set up tents on a plateau on top of the hill.

Máire and the rest of the druids remained in the distance to the northwest. Once in awhile he could hear gusts of wind, but all seemed calm and quiet. Other angels patrolled the borders, past the ring of wagons encircling their camp, which was almost as good as a palisade wall. Soon, Marcus could sense the Emperor approaching him.

"This is an excellent position, and the fortifications appear to be going well," stated Emperor Charles.

"Yes, your scouts did well, Imperial Majesty," Marcus replied. "I only know what defenses didn't work. I only took hilltop forts and never defended one." He smirked. "Since we don't have the time to build a protective wall, we put in spikes to deter an outright charge." Marcus scanned the grounds below again. "This could have been a hilltop fort once," he murmured. "We'll also collapse the tents if there's time, and we'll turn over the wagons to create another barrier. After hearing about the last attack from Gaius, I expect that the Strigoi will surround us again, so we'll have to use a perimeter of blood-drinkers as swordsmen surrounding your foot soldiers. Your archers and ours would be in the center of the camp."

"And where would the mirror be deployed?" Emperor Charles asked him.

"Máire will hold the mirror. She and the mirror will be on the south. I'll have some pit fires set on the plains opposite of the southern slope to reflect the light necessary for the mirror to work."

"Can't you use your own light?" The Emperor looked a little confused.

"We've tried that, but it doesn't work with the mirror," Marcus admitted. "I suppose glamoury is an effect of the beholder's perception."

"It is a small mirror. Does that mean it will only affect a small group of Strigoi at a time?"

"That's correct, and they also must see their reflection for the mirror to affect them. At least, that's what Máire and Julien told me," Marcus replied.

"Mmmmm, so what do you think needs to be done with the leader of the Strigoi?"

"If Seosaimhín makes an appearance, which seems unlikely, we'll kill her. I don't care who does it, but it has to be done." Marcus stared into the darkness again. "We will be ready for this, either way."

"So, were you present at the siege against Vercingetorix?" The Emperor's question broke his train of thought and worries about preparation. His last sentence was to settle his own thoughts.

"That was after my time," Marcus chuckled. "I wish I could have seen it. Doubtful it would have helped us in our strategy, though, as the defenders at that hill fort surrendered. I don't believe the Strigoi will accept that from us. But they can't fly, and they won't bring battlements." He smirked.

"There are many times I believed my next battle would be my last," the Emperor replied. "This elixir should allow us to prevail, but what will happen if it does not?"

Marcus leaned up against one of the tall trees. "My kind will die and become dust, and the Strigoi army will increase in size again. No... It will work. It has to."

The Emperor smiled. "Yes, it will. I'm going to go down to the camp and find the rest of my staff. Are you going to stay up here?"

"For a little while longer," Marcus answered. "I rather like having this view of the camp."

Máire looked over the series of small vortexes hovering in front of her students. Their satisfaction infiltrated the grove, and she felt herself smile, pleased that they learned their lesson. "Now, send the energy back home to the Otherworld," she said. The concentrated wind storms faded into the gentle night breeze and the invisible path to their home faded into the mists. "I think that's enough for tonight. We should head for our new camp."

An Ekimmu Cruitne waved to her to gain her attention, and in response Máire nodded her head.

"You taught us to summon small vortexes," the blood-drinker began, shaking her blonde plaits over her shoulder. "Will you teach us to harness larger ones or other elements next?"

"You all did excellent tonight, but more practice is required before you summon something requiring more energy," Máire replied.

"How large is the vortex you can summon?" another student asked.

"I can summon larger ones, but that's not important. What is important is control and not allowing the forces to dominate you. The camp is about ten miles from here, you should go," Máire suggested.

The majority of her students nodded and took to the air, but a few remained to pack their supplies.

"You aren't coming with us?" Caoimhín met her eyes. He raised silvery brows in some confusion.

"There's something that I must do," she informed him.

"Don't take too long." Caoimhín waved an elegant finger at her. "You may know how to do this, but I'm still older than you."

Máire smirked. "I'll be fine. I shall see you soon, Caoimhín. Thank you for being patient with my teaching methods."

Caoimhín chuckled. "Join us soon, or else Julien will send us to track you down." He turned and flew away.

Máire watched him become a glowing speck in the black skies. She examined where the others created their vortexes and focused her mind. The time arrived for new knowledge. She read about it again earlier. Her eyes closed as she readied herself to part the mists.

She sent for the energy to start a fire, and then a small sphere of burning light began to grow above her. "Thank you, Lugh," she whispered, addressing the God of light and wisdom. Then she wondered if she should be thanking Brigid. The fire began to sputter, and so she willed herself to concentrate on it. The yellow flame glowed, and she willed the ball of light to move.

A tiny voice whispered of rewards if she allowed the fire to strengthen. She pushed the fire away and allowed it to increase in size.

Máire couldn't believe the ease of moving the flame. She smiled at the contained inferno and closed her eyes for a moment, willing it to grow in diameter. She slowly opened her eyes and watched the blazing orb expand. It became six inches in diameter, then a foot.

Máire considered changing the intensity of the heat. The scrolls mentioned the process. The fireball, sensing her wishes, turned blue. Starlight became visible and the ball grew again. She pushed the fire away from her, remaining convinced that an increase in the heat of the fire would allow further opportunity to work with the element gathered from the Otherworld.

The gleaming starlight around the fire began to shimmer as the flame blazed white and blue. Máire allowed more energy to flow past the mists.

An explosion of light blinded her, and Máire squinted. A whisper told her to allow the fire to encompass her and embrace her as the lightning did before.

A warmth gathered as Máire allowed the energy to join her. The warmth soothed her but then turned wrathful. The strange smell of burning flesh and hair filled her with revulsion. She concentrated on focusing the energy away from her, but the flames moved closer. Growing fear tugged at her stomach, and Máire realized that she no longer controlled the fire. She cried in agony.

The fire grew, wishing to consume all.

She imagined the fire fading through the mists. A pulse of energy pushed Máire to the ground, and the barrier between the two worlds closed shut. She opened her eyes, and the fire was nothing more than a puff of smoke. Exhaustion consumed her. Máire closed her eyes and wondered where she would wake.

The muffled sound of voices woke Máire and the overwhelming smell of various blood-drinkers flooded her senses. She tried to move her mouth and speak, but she could say nothing.

"So, she's aware of us now?" Arwin asked.

"Máire's mouth is moving, so I believe so," Claudius answered.

"Who found me?" she squeaked.

"I watched you." Caoimhín's visage grew clearer, and his silver hair reflected the candlelight. "You summoned a fireball, and then you pulled it towards you. The heat... I could feel it myself, despite our distance."

"What were you thinking?" Sáerlaith's voice rang over Máire's left shoulder. "You know that you're not supposed to let energy control you."

"I'm sorry." Her voice revealed her pain.

"I believed you were mature enough to teach other druids who wielded the arts centuries before your birth," Sáerlaith continued. Fury raged in the other woman's voice.

"Sáerlaith, calm yourself," she heard Marcus intone. "Sometimes, instructors need to fail."

Sáerlaith's face grew clear as she seemed to reflect on his words.

"The students will benefit from her mistake," he added.

Máire closed her eyes, feeling his hand caress her hair.

"They can see the consequences of her error," Marcus continued.

"I will tell them the consequences of allowing the energy to take control," Máire answered. She opened her eyes and stared up at Sáerlaith.

Sáerlaith met Marcus' eyes and then stared down at her. The elder Deargh Du's eyes turned dark. "Very well, youngling. The next time you feel like pulling such a stunt, Caoimhín may not be there."

Máire nodded her head. "I know I shouldn't focus on my appearance, but how badly burned am I?"

Caoimhín returned to her sight. "I healed you after the doors to the Otherworld closed, but your arms, chest, abdomen, and face are still blistered. You're lucky that you didn't lose your hair."

"Thank you." She reached for his hand and patted his wrist.

Caoimhín smiled at her.

"Sun nears, let's try to get some sleep," she heard Arwin mutter. "Sleep well, Banbh Ceanúil."

Activity bustled around her as several began to leave the tent. She felt Marcus' eyes on her. He kissed her brow and pulled away without a word.

Máire closed her eyes and sensed Julien move in closer. She could not think of what to say to him and kept her eyes shut. Then, a solid weight landed on her feet, and she opened her eyes to see Lucius peering at her with half-closed lids.

"Why did you do such a thing?" Julien interrupted her thoughts about why Lucius appeared to be so pleased with the current situation. "Many of us count on you and your participation in this battle," he whispered. "You cannot participate if you're dead."

"The energy," she said, wondering how to explain it. "It beguiled me. It begged me to allow it within myself and to know me. I did so with the lightning, and I overestimated my talents." Máire reached for his arm, feeling a strange need to know someone would be nearby.

"Why would you allow the lightning to possess you? You could have been immolated." Julien's voice rose a little, and the shushes from the other blood-drinkers made her feel like a small child interrupting an important ceremony.

"I believed that I could possess the lightning instead of it possessing me," Máire admitted. "I know it makes no sense. It worked then, and... that's why I tried with the fire."

"And you failed." Julien lay down next to her. Disappointment reflected from the dark regions of his eyes.

"I wanted to explore the limits," she whispered.

Lucius walked across her stomach, and she moaned a little at the pain.

"Please don't explore the limits again," Julien said.

She watched him roll onto his back and turn away. The smoke from the extinguished candles brought back memories of the demanding fire. She felt a hand on her opposite side slide around her fingers and squeeze them with gentle pressure. She closed her eyes, grasping Marcus' hand. She hoped Julien would forgive her for trying to press her limits.

Buchenlochhöhle

The sun's bright light heated even the coldest corners of the cave.

Seosaimhín paced through the passages of the cave, looking over Nagirrom's newest warriors, praising what a blessing these soldiers were, carrying weapons with them and possessing the stunning traits of ferocity and devotion. Their strength surpassed that of the normal Strigoi. Seosaimhín's feet caressed the cold floor as she approached the altar and effigy.

Nagirrom perched on the statue, regarding His world with avian clarity. "It is past sunrise. Why are you not asleep?" the crow asked. His words whispered a gentle lullaby to her soul.

"You say the sun has risen, ivory crow. Yet the sun sets on our time in this place," Seosaimhín answered.

The winged form tilted His head. "You do not intend to return?"

Seosaimhín smirked. "Like rabbits in spring, our numbers will double again once we face this emperor's forces. We would love to see this Imperious Majesty beg for his life." She focused again on the rabbits. "With so many rabbits, Nagirrom, a new warren is needed."

"Why not have two warrens or more?"

"How does one control the horde from a distance?" Seosaimhín asked with an expansive shrug of her shoulders. She found these questions grating and began to pace the cave.

"It is not your destiny to always rule the Strigoi, my child. You are their mother, and chicks must leave the nest and fly." Nagirrom raised His wings to demonstrate.

"Our destiny was to bring about death and chaos through the Strigoi," Seosaimhín stated. "Was it not?" She stared at the arresting white crow.

"You were not created for that purpose, Seosaimhín."

"Created? We were not created!"

"Ha!" the God uttered in mirth. He extended a wing towards the walls of the cave. "Everything around you was created... the moss, the lichen, the stone, and even you."

"You imply that someone created us for a purpose?" She stared into the dark eyes. "Who created us?"

"Who created you is not important, Seosaimhín. What truly matters is that you fulfill your purpose."

Seosaimhín clasped her elbows. "We shall not take any more actions until you tell us who created us."

"You don't sound convinced that someone created you, Druid of Dementia," the crow croaked.

Seosaimhín laughed and shook off her tears of amusement with dirty fingers. "We are our own genesis, mighty Nagirrom. We captured a soulless one, drained ourselves of blood, and feasted on the poor wretch's virtue. Then we had its power. It changed us. It shaped us." Seosaimhín tried to concentrate on the bird again. "No one but I created us... I mean me."

"Do you know the identity of the Deargh Du you fed from?" The crow turned to groom His snowy feathers.

"No, we do not. Nor did we care. It was a fly in our web."

"What do you remember of the transformation?" Black eyes stared into her soul again.

"Our body wracked with pain." Seosaimhín turned to study the paintings smeared on the cave walls. "We convulsed, spat out our teeth, and gained strength. We received the beauty. We received the gifts."

"Did you see anyone?"

"What?" Seosaimhín placed her hand over a circle, watching it smear with the deliberate movement of her fingers.

"Did you see someone? Did you travel to a world outside of this one?"

"We remember darkness—"

"And then?" Nagirrom prompted.

Seosaimhín closed her eyes, remembering the bright sun dappling the green valleys, the walk through the field of the judged. A woman approached her with hair the color of dried blood and sporting blue tattoos. A blood-red ribbon waved in the wind. The woman's eyes revealed a moment of harsh anger and then discernment. A caw broke through the distant music. A flutter of white caught her eyes. The bird landed on the woman's bare shoulder and nuzzled her crimson hair.

"You!"

"Ah, you remember now," the crow murmured.

"Yes! We witnessed you... you with her."

The crow chortled in radiant joy. "I am named for She who created me, Seosaimhín, but I am Her opposite. So, my name is opposite to Hers. I am Nagirrom. N-a-g-i-r-r-o-m. In reversing these letters, Her identity is revealed."

Bile rose to Seosaimhín's throat. "Morrigan."

"Your true creator, for it was not some poor, wayward Deargh Du that you tricked and fed upon, but the Goddess Herself. You are Her daughter."

Seosaimhín roared, rushing towards the false God. A tingle of energy rose within her body, and she released it at Nagirrom. A bright burst of light and sound echoed in the cave, and a loud crash greeted her ears. The smell of burnt poultry infused the air. Seosaimhín exhaled and stepped away from her altar. Disgust at the sight of the shrine and the figure of Nagirrom filled her. She closed her eyes, willing the altar to disappear under the earth. The sound of collapsing walls greeted her ears, and sheer elation elevated her soul upon seeing the effigy turn to powder.

"We will grow our army! It will only go where we will it to go. It no longer serves you!" Seosaimhín spat on the remains of the altar and the statue of Nagirrom.

Tír na nÓg

Adhamdh walked through the green waves of grass. The blades tickled his legs, but he could not enjoy the gentle caresses of the fae that played in the leaves of grass. He approached the stone table. "She killed me!"

Faces turned to regard him with amusement and somewhat condescending smiles.

"What did you expect, Adhamdh?" Lugh chuckled.

"Her very nature is chaotic," uttered Manannán Mac Lir. "More so than any—"

Morrigan interrupted Him by clearing Her throat.

Manannán smirked. "That is to say any person bound to the realm of earth."

Brigid flicked a golden curl away from Her pale neck. "I honestly don't see why You must go to such trouble to raise your brood, Morrigan. After all, innocent lives are at stake."

"People die every day from a variety of causes. Pestilence, famine, disease, war, and yet from all that death more and more come back to the world. My trials are such a small shadow on the vitality of man," Morrigan replied.

"Come now, isn't there an easier way to allow Marcus to come into his own?"

"This is the best way," Adhamdh answered. He felt himself redden again. "I'm sorry, I spoke out of turn."

"No, Adhamdh, you are right. If Marcus didn't have a great challenge facing him, he would not find his path," Morrigan answered.

"True, there is no greater challenge than to face his sister," Lugh agreed.

"It just seems so destructive," Brigid responded. "I agree but I just take more joy in creation than destruction."

Morrigan chuckled. "I shall tell you that the next time you let the waters rise."

"Yes, yes," Brigid answered. "I know that this must be done. Your brood may still call forth my energies."

"And mine as well," Manannán added.

"I'm curious as to why one of my brood had such difficulties mastering fire."

Morrigan studied Lugh.

Lugh opened His mouth to reply when mists rose to the east. Soon, a beautiful figure exited the haze. The Goddess Dana, bejeweled in graceful and timeless flowers and greenery, joined the party.

Adhamdh quickly bowed his head, noticing the Gods and Goddesses lower their eyes to the ground in a show of deference to the Great Mother.

"A person in the world has successfully called forth my energies. Do any of you know anything about it?" Dana ran Her fingers along the cool stone of the table. Her adolescent features belied Her true nature.

The Deities turned Their eyes towards the Phantom Queen.

"Yes, Great Mother," Morrigan began. "She is one of my brood. Do you wish me to intervene?"

Dana met the other Goddess's eyes. "No." She grinned. "It has been far too long since someone called for my energies and assistance. I relish being needed. I trust all is well in that plane of existence. It feels well," the Goddess added. "Everything seems to be in perfect balance."

"Adhamdh," Morrigan called as she turned to him. Endless love reflected in Her dark eyes. "Why don't you watch the activity in the world? I need your assistance in watching the Celtic lines learn the gifts that We and the other pantheons gave them."

The rest of the Gods and Goddesses turned to look at him. He was but a child in their eyes.

"I will do so, Goddess," he answered. Adhamdh walked away from the table and separated the layers between his world and the world of man.

chapter eleven

Encampment on Top of Ernstberg

arcus took another step forward, and a familiar scent caressed him. He turned towards Máire and smiled, although she didn't seem to notice him. Her red brows appeared somewhat sparse, but otherwise she looked to be well. Yet, a prominent frown marred her features and guilt invaded her eyes. "How are you feeling tonight, Banbh Ceanúil?"

"I'm… better." Máire struggled with her words. She lowered her eyes.

"Liar." He slid a gentle finger under her chin, raised it, and met her eyes. He hoped his words belied playfulness.

"Do you really want to know how I feel?" she asked. The steady frown remained on her face.

Marcus heard a throat clear from behind them, a polite reminder that they were queued in a line and that many expected some movement towards the cauldron. He pulled back, removing his finger from her chin enabling Máire to step forward. "Of course I do. Whatever concerns you, concerns me." Marcus advanced another step forward towards the cauldron after Máire.

"I am embarrassed and confused," she admitted. "I'm embarrassed because I allowed fire to control me. I'm confused… in general."

"I thought we resolved this matter early this morning," Marcus replied. He took another step.

Máire leaned in. "Julien's words were most upsetting. He seemed very disappointed with me. He usually…" She paused. "He loves and forgives without reservation, but he turned away last night, and I have no idea why."

"You know why this bothers you, I think." Marcus followed her. "You just don't want to admit it."

"You sound more and more like Mandubratius every night," Máire hissed.

"Fine, perhaps I do, but you must admit to what is bothering you."

"Alright!" She revealed her impatience. "I think it's because I'm a poor mother-in-darkness to Julien. He needs my attention, but I have little time to give it to him now."

"Personally, I think it has little to do with that," Marcus posited. "He's just disappointed that you can be hurt and make the same foolish mistakes that the rest of us do."

"I can't help that." Máire took another step towards the cauldron.

"Máire, all children go through this. They find out their parents are not as perfect, omniscient, or as godlike as they thought they were."

"How do you know this?" she asked.

"Well, I was a mortal father once, and I know I disappointed my son." He frowned. "Not to mention, both of my parents disappointed me immensely, except for Lucilla. She did her best to know me before..." He fumbled for words. "I'm sure that your own father made a mistake or two, and I know I've made more."

Máire waved a hand. "Yes, I know there were mistakes and disappointment."

"You need to allow Julien the same courtesy. He will move past this small disappointment," he said. "You should grant him the opportunity to watch the training and perhaps join in." He allowed Máire to dip her cup into the brew before he did the same. They exited the line and began to drink.

While the wine masked the taste, he still abhorred imbibing the sludgy mixture. Soon the effects would take over, and he'd have to remind himself that the sky wasn't normally a dizzy pattern of bouncing moons and stars. Once the immediate effects faded, he would find himself somewhat absentminded or quite amorous. The sky stabilized and became static again.

Máire looked around the camp. "But, he's pretending to be a mortal still," she whispered in Gaelic. Her attention turned to the dark skies. The firelight's illumination brought forth her features, and he found himself staring at her.

"Hmmmm?" He looked at her eyes and noticed her dilated pupils.

"We were speaking of Julien," she groaned in annoyance.

She always seems to weather the consequences of the mushroom mixture with greater ease.

Marcus nodded and attempted to clear his head. "I can ask the Emperor to excuse his son. Eventually in battle, however, Julien's nature will give him away. We can tell anyone who asks that he received angelic gifts. Besides that, everyone's heads swim with this." Marcus made a face and finished the mixture quickly. He wondered how so many of the blood-drinkers seemed to love drinking the elixir. Máire guzzled the drink and seemed to ignore the effects. Perhaps all the sponnc she used in rituals prepared her for the result of hallucinations and distractions.

"I will ask him to join us, then." Máire wiped her mouth with her sleeve. She looked up at him, her eyes sparkling with intensity. "Will you join us?"

"No. I intend to run the mortals and blood-drinkers through drills. I thought at first that Latin would be the primary spoken language, but there seem to be many Frankish dialects," Marcus answered. "I think we will utilize whistles for this battle." He paused in his speaking and watched Máire lower her eyes, as if disappointed. "After this battle, we will decide if I need lessons, though I'd prefer they be private," he added.

Máire's eyes and mouth turned bright as she smiled. "Excellent," she answered. "It's a rare occasion when I get to instruct you on… anything."

Marcus caught himself smiling back at her. Her lips twisted a moment, turning her smile sly and seductive. The sudden urge to have her pushed away the thoughts of any immediate training. The elixir brought forth strange dreams, fantasies, and hallucinations he could disregard. However, he couldn't ignore the other effects. All his efforts to behave or run drills faded into the background with other unimportant issues. He picked up Máire and headed back to the tent. He could no longer ignore his cravings.

She began kissing him as he parted the doors of the tent with his boot.

Valley South of Daun

Talia stirred amid the dirty and stench-filled blankets. Hunger embraced her as a passionate lover might. She extended her senses towards anything, rather any being that danced with life. She soon detected a small herd of some animals. Talia opened her eyes and turned her face towards Sextus, who remained a sleeping slug. She sat up with a grunt and studied the covered windows, confirming night ruled the sky once more.

Time to feed.

Talia found her feet. She could smell the deer grazing in the distance. She crept from the papal cart, relying on her stealth and speed, and leapt onto the unsuspecting animal, biting into its dirty fur. She ignored her revulsion, as power warmed her body, and she happily gorged herself. A few minutes later, Talia pulled away from the filthy beast, feeling a little queasy. The red-tinged memories of her Strigoi-influenced nightmares settled in her brain. Her husband again arrived and whispered of his suffering as a Lamia. That nightmare faded after a few moments of confusion.

Talia closed her eyes, feeling a cold hand caress her hair.

"Keep it as a remembrance of tonight," she heard Mandubratius urge.

She opened her eyes and saw Mac Turrlough insert a gleaming, golden torc in his pouch and then pull out several sharpened bear's claws. He pushed back her blankets.

Mandubratius grinned and waved at her.

The pain and smell of blood grew too much to bear.

A noise interrupted Talia's reverie.

She stared at the carriage upon hearing a sad moan. She left the deer, which joined its brothers and sisters in the grass at the distant edge of the forest. Talia pulled back the door flap and crouched down next to Sextus, who opened his eyes and stared at her. "Sextus, it's me, Talia."

There was another sound from the other Lamia. "Then, I survived."

Talia raised her wrist to her mouth and bit down. The smell and taste of her blood filled the wooden enclosure. She pulled Sextus towards her and placed her hand at his mouth.

He began to feed. After a few minutes, his mouth moved away, and she pulled back her arm.

"I fed from a deer, if you need more," she informed Sextus.

"The others," Sextus said, meeting her stare. "What happened to them?"

"I could only save you," Talia admitted. "However, I did not see all the Lamia soldiers amongst the fallen. Perhaps some survived. At least, I hope our brothers would not all suffer… such a painful demise."

His firm grip latched onto her arm. "Tell me what happened," he growled.

"I did not see the battle, just the aftermath," Talia replied. "The Strigoi started to carry out the wounded mortals. The sun was almost upon us, and I only had enough time to save and secure one person. You. I carried you from the battlefield. Two nights ago, we slept in the forest."

"I must see it."

"See what?" She stared into his dark eyes.

"The battlefield." His eyes flickered and then glowed red.

"I can show you the field," Talia replied. "However, after that, we must leave and find my sponsor."

Sextus looked confused.

"What's wrong?"

"You still want to follow him?"

"If we find him, we find safety. He is with the other lines. Perchance even Emperor Charles has joined them," Talia answered. "Besides, I have seen too much in my nightmares to not."

Sextus shuddered. "Nothing frightens me more than their horrific visions. How do they always know these things?"

Talia shrugged. "Who's to understand how the Strigoi think?"

"Why haven't they come back?" Sextus jerked his head around to study the walls. "The Strigoi, I mean."

"They are busy with their younglings," Talia answered. "I predict that they'll leave for the north, soon. We need to leave and stay ahead of them. Thank merciful God that they are slow."

Sextus nodded and sat up. He climbed onto shaky feet and began to dress. He seemed to force himself to look soldierly. "We must pack what we need and leave," he said with calm determination. "We will stop at the battlefield on the way. I wish to see if my sponsor's belongings rest there. If so, I must give them a proper burial. Gaius would wish it that way." Sextus stooped to pick up a weapon, his hand shook, while Talia picked up the blade and held the pommel out towards him. "I owe you my life," he said.

She stared into his dark eyes again and gave a curt nod.

Sextus turned and exited.

She sensed him moving and heard him grunt, perhaps pausing to pick up other weapons. Talia parted the cart door flaps and stepped out into the chilled air. She found Sextus nearby.

He took a deep breath and exhaled. "I hate the Strigoi's induced nightmares. My apologies for repeating myself, but I do hate them." Sextus stared at her. "I am ready now. Where is the battlefield?"

"Follow me." She said nothing more and led him towards the field that still smelled of spilled gore. Talia pointed towards a tree in the distance. "That is where we slept the first day."

Sextus began walking the expanse and breadth of the now-empty field.

"Do you see anything belonging to Gaius?"

Sextus shook his head. "If he is gone, I will say my farewells to him after we find the other blood-drinkers. We need to leave." He stared at the night sky, as if scanning for a familiar star pattern. He turned to Talia and pointed towards a set of bright stars. "That constellation will lead us north and to our friends," Sextus stated.

Talia nodded, wondering if she had anyone she could call a friend left.

Encampment on Top of Ernstberg

Máire dipped her hands in the bowl of water and began to splash herself. She turned and extended the somewhat clouded water to Marcus.

He chuckled and waved it away as he continued getting dressed.

"You don't mind stinking of... us?" She felt her face twist a bit.

He pulled his tunic overhead. "No, I have no such problem. In fact, I'm quite certain I still smell better than the majority of soldiers."

"Fine, go ahead and smell." She retracted the bowl, ignoring the sudden compulsion to throw the water at him. "So, what do you plan to do tonight, other than stink?"

"I plan on a session of drills tonight after meeting with the Emperor, my staff as it were, the Lamia leadership, and the rest of generals. We must figure out a method to work together. I have no idea what to do if the whistles don't work." His blue eyes settled on her. "Don't you have a class to instruct as well, Banbh Ceanúil?"

Máire grinned at him while donning her breeches. "Yes, we will work with Brigid and Her water today. There is a small river to the southwest, right?"

Marcus closed his eyes briefly. "Yes, to the southwest. I remember."

"And do I look healed?"

Marcus leaned in and tapped her brow with a fingertip. "Your eyebrows are somewhat sparse, but you look fine. Just make sure they know the truth about what happened." He pulled her in for another kiss. His lips rested on hers for a moment, before he turned and marched out of the tent.

She could hear him calling for Claudius and a few of the others regarding preparations. Máire ran a finger over her eyebrows and felt a bristled set of fuzz. She stepped outside and flew towards the gathering near the lake, landing outside of the loose circle, and meandered to the center.

"Sorry I'm late." Máire stared into the faces. She heard chuckling and mumbled jokes. She smirked, realizing she couldn't lie when, apparently, she and Marcus weren't quiet. "I'll teach you a little about the aspect of water tonight, specifically…" She paused, having trouble talking over the chatter. Máire concentrated on making her tone neutral and light. "Is there a question that anyone wishes to voice?"

"Your eyebrows?" A Sugnwr Gwaed in the distance squinted at her. "I take it Marcus didn't burn them?"

She had begun to hear muttering about her accident before sunrise.

"That," she said loudly, "is a good question." She lowered her voice. "Remember that I said that you had to maintain control over the energy until you released it back through the mists to the Otherworld? Well, I lost control over fire energy. I falsely believed myself to be the master, and I allowed it to grow beyond what I could influence." Máire paused and looked over the blood-drinkers. "It almost took a life of its own," she admitted. "The fire felt like a sentient being and told me to release it, that it would allow me to control it, but I knew the truth. Still, I let it dominate me." The fields yielded nothing to her but the chirrups of crickets. She heard a throat clear.

"How did you prevent the fire from taking you back with it to the Otherworld?" Caoimhín's blue eyes gleamed in the darkness.

"At the last moment, I found enough control to send the energy back through the parted mists. I'm not entirely sure where the control came from," Máire added. "Then, you found me. The lesson is that all of you should not try to control more energy than what you are capable of, or it will turn on you." She looked at the gathered faces. "Are there any other questions?"

Silence met her ears.

Máire nodded. "Let's begin, then."

Marcus walked through the tent with Claudius, Mac Alpin, and Gaius a few steps behind. His feelings of ebullience continued as he found the mortal generals, the Pope, and the Emperor looking up at him from a map. He sensed Mandubratius in the shadows of the tent. The Lamia's green eyes settled on him. The weight of their stares reminded him of his duties and his joviality began to fade.

"Were you waiting on me?" he asked.

"Aye, they were. I asked them to wait until you were finished with your... prayers." He heard Arwin start to chuckle.

"I do trust those prayers were finished without interruption?" The Pope smirked for a moment as he returned his attention to the map.

"Absolutely," Marcus answered.

"Excellent, now we were discussing plans to defend the hill." The Emperor's glassy blue eyes met his. "Why not meet them on a flat open field," Pope Leo asked, "if you don't mind my queries into battle strategy?"

"The hill will slow them down. The Strigoi are not fast... demons," he informed the Pope. "Also, we fortified the hill."

"Why not use hit and run attacks?" Mandubratius asked.

"We could attack from the air and inflict causalities," Marcus replied. "However, I do believe we are trying to injure them and not kill as many as possible. Many are the Pope's men. We should not delay this attack. Our supplies of the elixir wane every night."

Whispers echoed in the small tent, and Marcus watched heads nod in comprehension.

"Is it in their nature to delay?" the Emperor asked.

"They do not have the minds for advanced tactics, nor does their commander," Claudius answered.

"They would immediately lay siege after surrounding the hill," Marcus added.

"What happens if the siege lasts over the course of the night," the Pope queried.

"The mortals will leave the camp at daylight then, with all due haste," Marcus replied.

"And your people?" the Pope asked.

"We would fly and carry our friends as necessary," Marcus answered.

"This plan is as sound as any that might work against the Strigoi," the Emperor commented.

The Pope nodded. "Then, I ask permission to train your soldiers, Imperial Majesty. They need instruction on how to fight alongside our warriors."

The Emperor looked over his staff.

"I see much benefit to this training," one of the mortal generals commented.

"As do I," the Emperor replied. "I'd like you to include the coordination of my generals under your command during this exercise and upcoming battle.

I always find it best to have one person in control of the battlefield. Wouldn't you agree, Marcus?"

"Yes, Imperial Majesty. The honor is to serve." Marcus caught himself saluting the Emperor. He stopped and lowered his arm.

The Emperor smiled at the ancient tribute. "Indeed. Well then, proceed at your discretion."

"I trust then that I may send the Inspector General to join a special group of our warriors?" Marcus asked.

"Yes, I think Julien would prefer that," Emperor Charles answered.

Marcus nodded. "Generals, bring your staff to my tent in half an hour. Have their subordinates bring the soldiers to the field at the top of the hill in parade formation. Dismissed."

The generals left. Mandubratius even exited the tent in silence.

"I wish my subordinate was here," grumbled Gaius.

Marcus turned towards Gaius, offering comfort. "Sextus died with honor. However, you have another child-in-darkness that can assist us in the drills."

Gaius smiled, nodding his head. "Yes, sir." He saluted Marcus and left.

"Claudius, Arwin, my tent looks like shite," he informed the last two remaining members of his staff in Gaelic. "Ask some of the mortals to clean and set up the map on my table."

"You mean our tent looks like shite," Claudius replied. "But, I never minded having someone else clean."

Mac Alpin grumbled under his breath. "I'll wager the Basileus' tent isn't even as messy, and she's much louder than you and Máire. By the Gods, what did you and Banbh Ceanúil do to it?"

Marcus grinned. "Just... on your way." He followed them out, nodding in the direction of the Pope and Emperor.

"Leo? You are making faces." Charles handed the maps over to Ercanbald. "What is the source of these misgivings?"

"I know the Strigoi are not demons, but I still cannot help being fearful of them. They..." Leo lowered his head as he struggled to come up with words. "They... possessed my men and changed them into ravenous monsters." The Pope stared at him. "Doesn't this instill some fear into you?"

"I do have my concerns, Leo," Charles said, pulling over a chair for Leo and sitting down across from him. "I fear that the elixir may not be as effective as the Cothromaigh believe it can be. I also worry that the mirror from Constantinople may not assist us as much as they believe it will. I also am concerned that the angels may be forced to kill more of your soldiers and my people than we expect."

"How many do you expect to die?" Leo queried while shifting in his chair.

"Twenty five to thirty percent, but our defenses will minimize how many of them can attack us at once. Our friends can attack with a precision arrow strike from the air to disable as many Strigoi as possible."

Pope Leo leaned forward in his chair. "Tell me, what does this mirror do, exactly? How will it save these poor, cursed beings?"

Charles mused for a moment on how the Strigoi were now the poor and cursed. "I am told that the mirror brings out the inner beauty of the viewer. Those who have been possessed by the madness of the Strigoi turn into something… less dangerous."

"How do you know this, Charles?"

"I've met some of them," Charles answered. "I can assure you that they are not ravenous beasts. They are here with us, in this compound."

"They are here in this encampment?" Leo rose to his feet and began to pace over the threadbare rug that covered the dirt. "Do they pose a threat?"

"I believe that they do not," Charles answered. "I met with their leader, Father Xofer. He's a priest of the Eastern Church."

"How did—"

"Marcus and the rest," Charles interjected. "They found them after acquiring the mirror from Constantinople. After they escaped this curse, they decided to help those who wielded the mirror. They wish to save as many of the Strigoi as possible."

"So, what have they become? Are they human or something else?" The Pope's face twitched a little. His dark eyes focused on Charles.

Charles felt himself staring back at Leo. "What else would they be? There are beasts, us mortals, and angels and demons, Holy Father. Are you saying there are other things in existence?"

"I'm inquiring whether those who were once Strigoi are now more… angel than human," Leo replied, "or perhaps something else entirely."

"That is a most interesting conclusion for the Pope to derive. So, this new creation is not one of the other four?" The Emperor tried not to smile.

"If the mirror has driven out the evil within the Strigoi, then they are not demon," the Pope replied with a serious frown.

"So, how does your conclusion fit in with church doctrine?"

Leo's face turned dark, realizing his game. "You know damn well what the doctrine is, Charles. If something is not wholly classified, then it's demonic, and the scriptures reveal that angels are not born of man."

"Forgive my confusion, Leo. My education has been lacking. You and I both know I'm a simple man." Charles could not help but smile. "But, you just said that you believe the changed were a separate group between angel and human and were not demonic."

"Yes, then you asked about church doctrine. That's different." The Pope's features remained austere.

"And what about church doctrine?" Charles studied his nails.

"I'm above church doctrine, remember?"

Charles gave no response.

The Pope relaxed into his chair and stretched his arms overhead. "I imagine controlling such a vast empire must be difficult. People must be fed, have a trade, and have amusements and order. I also know you live in two worlds... one that the public sees, and the other that resides behind the curtain. I live in three."

"Three?"

"Like you, I have the public and private lives. Unlike you, I'm exposed to secrets beyond belief."

Charles leaned forward in his seat. "What kind of secrets, Holy Father?"

"Honestly! The kind of secrets that are secret, Charles." The Pope stood and paced on the carpet again. "So secret, in fact, that to speak of such things openly could result in my excommunication and execution."

He could sense Leo wished to speak. "This is hardly an open conversation."

"What are you implying?" Pope Leo challenged.

"You are intimating that you know of secrets that could get you excommunicated in regards to the changed Strigoi."

"Not to them specifically. When I asked you about the changed Strigoi being human, I considered the possibility that they could be from one of the hidden races."

Charles leaned back and stared at Leo, who stopped pacing and placed his hands on the top of his chair. "Other than the races of beast, human, angel, and demon?" Charles ascertained.

"Yes." The Pope glared at him.

"By 'hidden', the church doesn't know they exist, but you know the truth."

"If people knew that there were other types of beings with angelic powers, born of man, they would become distraught with fear. It would rip apart the fragile fabric that is our church. Not just the church, but Christianity itself." Leo's face grew gray.

"Do these hidden races have names?" Charles tried not to grin.

"Yes, they do, but I don't know all the names... just a few. I know a few other than the Strigoi and the changed Strigoi. They are called the Lamia, the Sugnwr Gwaed, Ekimmu Cruitne, and the Deargh Du." The Pope began walking again and wringing his hands.

"Leo, sit. Calm yourself," Charles suggested. He felt honest shock that Leo revealed the truth. "I know Marcus is Deargh Du. The rest of the Cothromaigh is composed of those groups and the changed Strigoi."

"You knew?" Leo sat down and put his hands to his face.

"Yes, as did you, my friend. Does this change anything?"

"For now, I do not think so, but we must be prepared if our people see them do things an angel would not do."

"I agree," Charles answered.

"I suppose we should go watch these drills. What duties does the Inspector General have with this special group?" The Pope raised his brows.

"I'm not certain. We can ask him later."

"No, I think it will be best for me to send someone else to ascertain what these people do," Pope Leo answered.

Charles caught his arm. "Tell him to be careful." He smiled, deciding to say nothing more of Julien. He considered revealing that secret to Leo. However, sometimes he needed secrets. "Ercanbald," Charles yelled, calling for his secretary.

Stream Southwest of Ernstberg

Máire motioned for the others to continue their work on their own. They decided that the most efficient use of water in a battle would be simply the element of surprise, or annoyance. Her students practiced creating orbs of water and dropping them on fixed targets. She hoped it would assist with something in the battle. She had doubts, but hoped the annoyance of stinging water might distract the Strigoi from attacking so many at once.

After a spending a few minutes watching her class, Máire sensed Julien and one of the changed Strigoi land a short distance away from her class. From her vantage point, she could tell her child-in-darkness sported a nervous smile. Despite his avoiding her, she could see the apology in his eyes. She realized Julien's eyes told all. It could be a weakness for him, but in some ways it proved him so much more endearing than herself or her own father-in-darkness.

"May we have a word with you?" Julien asked.

"Of course, Julien."

"Marcus told me that I should participate in these training classes with you. I really do want to learn about these tools."

"Oh did he?" Máire felt her face reveal joy. "Then, I suppose you better hurry and join the others. Go ask Caoimhín to explain to you the basics, and I will join you and the others in a moment." She watched him grin and walk towards the others. "Father Xofer," she greeted while facing the priest. "What can I do for you?" She noticed the priest's somber eyes brightened, and he reddened a bit.

"I… rather we'd like to witness how the Deargh Du and the other Celtic races touch the fabric of your creation and pull forth its energies."

Máire looked for the other transformed Strigoi but saw none. "We?"

"The other changed will experience what I experience," the priest explained. "We did not want to intrude with a large number of prying eyes."

"Ah!" Máire nodded her head. "So, why does your line wish to see this? It is an ability you do not possess, though I may be wrong in my assessment."

Father Xofer smiled. "Your assessment is correct. However, we admire your intimacy with the deities who created you." He lowered his head for a moment. "In fact, we are a little jealous." Father Xofer looked at her with a nervous little smile. "We feel as though we have never been so closely embraced by a deity. We yearn to understand the bond. Perhaps we can throw aside the doctrines that divide us and focus more on our relationship with our patron or matron.... to seek that bond."

Máire examined his face, searching for Lamia cunning within its characteristics. She then realized his face, like Julien's eyes, could bear little but his truth. She then heard her name called in the distance. "It may take some time for me to explain your presence, but I would be honored for you, and the others through you, to join us and witness our bond with the Tuaths and the Tylwyth Teg." She offered him her hand. "Come and join us in our communion."

His fingers gripped hers with gentle strength. "Thank you."

Ridge West of Ernstberg

Marcus judged that the drills continued to be going better than expected, and the Pope and Emperor appeared to be pleased. He soon caught sight of Edward in the distance, as a party of the Ekimmu Cruitne left to patrol the outreaches of the surrounding territory. Turning to face Edward, Marcus motioned for him to approach. "Did you find any of the Strigoi?"

Edward nodded his head. "Yes, we did. The main group of Strigoi camped within a four hour march from this location. At least, we estimated four hours. You understand how they move. We all had different opinions on how long it would take them to reach us, but four hours is what the majority's consensus is. None of us witnessed Seosaimhín."

Marcus scratched his chin. "So, they can attack mid-evening tonight if they wish. Thank you, Edward." He mulled over his thoughts.

"What position does Arwin recommend for tracking their progress?"

"He arranged the scouts in a line to the Southeast. We plan on falling back as the Strigoi approach, before they can concentrate an attack on us. He also suggested that there are flankers when they fan out and surround the encampment," Edward answered. "He mentioned it seemed to him a very sensible plan that you would approve of." Edward's face creased in a half-smile. "Or something in that line of thinking."

"Yes, it's a sound plan," Marcus replied. "Please tell everyone to be wary of Seosaimhín. Fianait arrived from Vézelay. She has an excellent nose for a Deargh Du. Take her with you. She's due west with the training soldiers. I believe you can find her."

Edward smirked. "I know." He pointed to his nose and then flew off.

Edward's scent faded, leaving behind the varied essences of the mortals. Another series of strong smells grew on the wind. He could hear Mandubratius cursing under his breath. Marcus glanced over and saw Máire follow from the same direction. He then spied a soaking wet Mandubratius.

"I caught him watching our training exercise," Máire shouted to Marcus. She looked quite pleased with herself, as if she'd caught a master spy.

"Mandubratius, spying on you? I'm so disappointed, Awvarwy."

Mandubratius shook his hair out, and Marcus backed away, avoiding drops of water that landed mostly on the ground and Máire, whose countenance turned from pleased to rather sour. "I was representing the interests of His Holiness in this matter," Mandubratius replied. "He personally requested that I witness any Pagan rituals to make sure the practices did not influence the children of the Church."

Marcus bit his lower lip at seeing Máire stifle her laughter. The Lamia appeared to struggle with his indignation.

"Now tell me, General of Generals, who answers to heaven above..." Mandubratius raised his palms towards the sky. "What do you propose to do to settle this great injustice?"

"I am most contrite that I have no dry clothing to offer you," he informed Mandubratius. "Perhaps you can convince a camp girl to help you dry off."

Mandubratius squinted, then started to laugh. "That was quite witty, Marcus. Most impressive." He stopped laughing and became serious. "Unfortunately, I was there as an official representative of Pope Leo, and he might see this as a slight."

Marcus closed his eyes and sighed. "Can't the two of you behave like civilized children for a single evening?"

"I'm sorry," he heard Máire utter. She sounded somewhat penitent. "However, the Emissary was not invited, nor did he ask to join us."

Marcus opened his eyes and gave her a quick nod.

"But Father Xofer was there," Mandubratius replied.

"He asked for an invitation. You could have asked, but decided instead to spy on us—" Máire tried to explain before Mandubratius interrupted her.

"I'm the Papal Emissary! I don't need a fucking invitation!"

Marcus noticed the two of them fall silent and stare at him. "Such language, coming from a Papal Emissary, and I'm to play judge here?"

"No," Máire answered with a defeated sigh.

"Yes," Mandubratius rallied. "She told her students to drench the Lamia spy. It was most rude!"

"Fine," Marcus muttered. "Máire, apologize to Mandubratius for soaking him and for urging your students to do the same. Emissary, in the future, request Máire's permission to watch training, and lay off the swearing in front of mortals. Máire, go find the Emissary dry clothes and assist him."

Mandubratius tipped his head to the side. "Your judgment is acceptable."

"It is most certainly not!" Máire answered in a terse hiss.

Marcus smirked. "I'm so glad we're all in agreement. Stop acting like children. It reflects badly on all of us, and the mortal soldiers may be encouraged to behave in such an undignified manner. Now, the sun is almost up. I need to tell Emperor Charles and the Holy Pope that the Strigoi are about four hours away from the camp." He looked over at Máire, who still managed to look perturbed. He leaned in closer to her. "Good night. Just remember, you need to behave in a manner befitting an angel."

Máire glared at him. She then turned on her heel and grabbed Mandubratius' arm, dragging him away.

Marcus chuckled at the thought that this would do them both a world of good. They needed to remember the temporary alliance between their races and themselves. He then brushed away that thought and walked toward Emperor Charles and Pope Leo.

Buchenlochhöhle

"We all know you are in pain, but there will be a grand feast tonight for all of us," Seosaimhín promised to the large crowd of Strigoi. A strange scent wafted from the distance... not the scent of delicious death and droning madness from the Strigoi, but something else… clean and full of vigor.

A blood-drinker watched them, hidden in its cloak of shadows.

Seosaimhín eyes wandered over the dirty lunacy of her children. "We shall make short work of these scouts," she whispered to the grand force. She focused on the spy closest to her.

To catch it, one would have to move faster than it could react.

Before thinking further, she found its neck in her shaking hand.

As the Ekimmu Cruitne opened her mouth to call attention to her friends, Seosaimhín ripped her throat out and tossed the body aside. She flexed her fingers, annoyed that she needed to keep at least one alive.

Seosaimhín laughed. Then, she sensed movement. She dodged the aerial attack of a swordsman. His glancing blow brought forth stars.

Her sudden rage offered new energy, and she felt a bolt of lightning obey her will and dash out of the dark clouds. It arced through the warrior and dropped him from the sky to the earth.

She whistled to her hordes, and they responded eagerly to the promise of a meal. Seosaimhín's hatred rose. She brought forth energy to smite the rest of the scouts.

Perhaps Nagirrom's magical gifts belong to us now.

She dispatched the lighting towards the others, and they plummeted to the cold, harsh dirt.

The Strigoi caught them and nearly tore them to pieces.

She felt a strange essence hum in the sky, but soon the hum faded into silence. She contemplated discovering what caused the strange noise, but her hunger surged after the attacks. The desire for sweet blood dwarfed what the defiled Strigoi could offer her. Perhaps she could find sustenance elsewhere.

The morning skies began to turn light.

She ran for the caves, trusting that the others would follow soon.

chapter twelve

Encampment on Top of Ernstberg

andubratius couldn't help musing on the fact that this could be his last day in this realm. However, his headstrong companion seemed to have no such worries, as Máire continued to pull him towards the large group of tents, but then she stopped. He noticed confusion settle over her face.

"It's that one," Mandubratius said, pointing to the smaller pavilion in the distance. He decided that the Emperor's idea of a humble tent might not be such a bad idea, after his last encounter with Seosaimhín. A feeling of darkness and doubt advanced on him again at the memories of the experience. That and the increasing dreams about his mother.

Damn the Strigoi for dredging up such horrible remembrances.

Máire pulled up the flap and walked into the tent. She turned to face him, reaching for his tunic.

"You don't need to do this," he said. He sat down in a chair in the corner and began to pull off his wet boots.

"What?"

Mandubratius emptied out the water from his boot onto the dirt and stuck it on the right arm of his chair. "You heard me."

"But Marcus said—"

"What he said is immaterial." He pulled off his other boot, emptied it, and stuck it on the other arm. "I mean, right now, it really doesn't matter, does it?"

Máire remained silent.

Mandubratius stood up to finish undressing, but then he stopped and met her eyes. "I apologize for spying on you and your class. The Pope asked if I would, and I wanted to watch you again." He unfastened his tunic and heard the soft pattering of paws against the dirt outside.

Lucius ducked his way into the tent and then hopped onto the chair.

Mandubratius chuckled and patted him. He turned towards Máire again and noticed how bewildered she still looked. He gave her a half smile, pulled his tunic overhead, stuck it over the back of the chair, hoping it would dry. After nudging Lucius out of the chair, Mandubratius sat down. He began to peel off his wet breeches.

Máire studied the cat for a moment and then returned her gaze to him. "Apology accepted," Máire replied. "I'm sorry for soaking you and goading my class to do the same." She walked over to a bag and pulled out a small blanket and an extra tunic, before tossing the blanket in his general direction.

Mandubratius chuckled as he caught it. He finished undressing, stood up, and began patting himself dry. "I accept your apology," he said. He extended his hand for the tunic, which Máire handed it to him. He pulled the tunic over his head and then stared back at her. "The sun will rise soon. You better hurry back to your tent while there is still shadow. However, if you wish to stay, there is an extra cot, and I do have a spare blanket."

"I'm not sure about this." Her forehead wrinkled.

"If you're worried about impropriety, many of us will be dead tomorrow evening anyway." He sensed the heat of the sun rising.

"I don't care about propriety," she uttered. "I don't wish to be burned. I will accept your offer of the spare cot." Máire looked around. "Where is it?"

"I lied. There isn't another cot," he answered.

She laughed and shook a finger at him.

He realized how much he'd missed her laughter. "I do have blankets and padding, enough for two people and one fairy cat." Mandubratius glanced at Lucius and heard a contented purr.

"That should be fine then, you trickster. Not you, Lucius." Máire sat down on the chair and began to pull off her boots and breeches.

Mandubratius pulled the extra blankets out of another bag and crouched down to roll out the padded bedding, settling the blankets over top, then Lucius jumped on the bedding and began to knead it into place. Mandubratius found himself watching the cat with much amusement.

"One of these nights, your tricks will get you in trouble, Awvarwy," he heard Máire say. She crouched down in her tunic and pulled back the blankets, wrapping herself and Lucius, who curled up with her, in the warmth.

Mandubratius smirked. "But Máire, I enjoy my tricks, especially when they get me in trouble. That's what keeps life interesting. That is the spice of my life." He rolled under the blankets and turned to face Máire, who looked perplexed. He winked at her. "Sleep well," he said, while staring into her large eyes, before lying back against the padding.

He sensed her lean in, and then Máire kissed his brow. She pulled back. "You sleep well, too." He continued staring at her as she began petting Lucius.

The cat stretched and purred in feline contentment.

He watched Máire lie back down before closing his eyes.

Buchenlochhöhle

Seosaimhín ducked into the cave and moved through the stooped Strigoi, their eyes lowered at her demanding gaze. She passed into the cavern where she slept. She then noticed a pair of bright green lights glowing from within.

"Deargh Du?" She smiled. "You need not fear Seosaimhín."

A loud sound of annoyance echoed in the cave.

She allowed herself to illuminate the shadows and found a large, black cat staring at her. Seosaimhín licked her lips, thinking cat blood would do.

"Hello, little moggie," she greeted the cat. "We need a tasty snack, and you look scrumptious."

"I must insist that you do not try to feed from me," the cat sneered. He stared at her with an arrogant glare. "It would be your last experience in this existence."

"Nagirrom?" Seosaimhín scanned the cavern for a sight of the white crow.

"I assure you that I am not Nagirrom. He and his kind are beneath me," the cat stated.

Seosaimhín ducked to the ground to stare at the invader of her quarters. "Then, who are you?" she asked the cat.

"You may call me Lucius. Though, I have many other names. I could spend all day telling you them, if you wish."

"What are you doing here?" Seosaimhín met his ready stare. "Do you wish to stop us?"

The cat's face and mouth turned up in a feline smirk. "I have been observing you for the last half hour." The cat flicked his tail about. "You exhibit talents beyond that of a mere Deargh Du."

"We… I killed Nagirrom, and now I possess his gifts," Seosaimhín replied, feeling much pleasure at that memory.

"Is that what you believe? Most fascinating." The cat flicked his ears forward, giving him the appearance of being interested in her words. "So, you had no capabilities or talents of calling forth energies from the Otherworld directly before killing Nagirrom?"

"That's correct," Seosaimhín answered.

"Mmmmm," the cat trilled in a purr and narrowed his eyes. "That's most interesting."

"You still have yet to answer the question. Are you here to stop us? Are you a threat?"

"I could be, if I choose to be." The cat stopped purring and opened his eyes fully. His green gaze lit the dank cavern. "However, I'm not here to thwart you, Seosaimhín. Though I am curious, why do you wish to kill all these people and further increase your army of Strigoi, when the population here cannot sustain the number you have already?" The cat lifted a dark paw and licked his foot.

"They are the force that opposes me, therefore I must defeat them," Seosaimhín replied.

The cat stopped his grooming. "What made you oppose them in the first place?"

"Nagirrom convinced me to take over the Strigoi and lead them into battle. He said it was necessary."

"So..." The cat looked over the cave ceiling. "... where is Nagirrom?"

"His desiccated flesh, broken bones, and blood grace his shattered effigy," Seosaimhín hissed.

"Yet you still proceed with his wishes, Druid of Dementia. Why is that?" The cat tilted his head to one side.

"I attack because that's my desire. I wish to bring death and misery to this world. Nagirrom may have advised me to use the Strigoi to this end, but I trained them, I increased their number, and I wield them against those who would stop me."

The cat's smirk reappeared. "Are you sure there aren't other reasons for doing this?"

"Are you trying to delay me?" Seosaimhín stared into the cat's eyes, trying to identify his motives.

"Not at all. I just wish to understand you."

"Are you Nagirrom?" Seosaimhín asked the cat.

Why is it always so difficult to communicate with animals?

The cat sighed, revealing a dark impatience in his eyes. "I already said I was not. He's a white crow. Do I, in any way, resemble a white crow? Do I even sound like him?"

"No, you don't." Seosaimhín sat back on her legs.

"Well, I'm glad that we've established that. Now, where were we? So, why else are you attacking them?" The cat picked up his other paw and began grooming it with a long, pink tongue.

"There are no other reasons," Seosaimhín answered.

"Isn't that a tad contradictory?" Lucius lowered his other paw.

"It is not. You are confusing me." Seosaimhín felt her rage rise.

"I think you're lying," Lucius answered with a loud purr. "There are other reasons."

"There are none."

"Was your ego bruised?" The cat's words turned mocking.

"No!"

"Did someone hurt those you loved?" His eyes gleamed like the fire of dragons.

"No!"

"Did your father beat you when you were a child?" The cat almost snorted in laughter.

"How dare you mock us?" Seosaimhín snarled at the cat. "One more insult from you and we shall call blue fire from the sky and turn your flesh to soot, as we plan to do to Marcus and Máire... especially Máire."

"I see. Carry on. Please don't let me keep you from this eminent battle." The cat looked at something over her right shoulder, revealing little more than disdain for the current conversation.

"Give us one good reason why we shouldn't drain you and leave your carcass for the night creatures," Seosaimhín hissed at Lucius.

"Were you to attempt such an ill-conceived act, the Strigoi would no longer have a leader," the cat replied. The bright twin beacons of his green eyes lit the cavern again, exposing a profound storm within his placid features.

Seosaimhín experienced fear and dread, which she did not expect. The power revealed in his feline eyes disclosed his true nature. Her thoughts on the matter faded as she noticed his tail whip about as if he were quite irritated.

"I would appreciate it if you would refrain from staring. We cats interpret a stare as a direct challenge." Lucius stared at her and crouched down, exhibiting hostility. His ears lay flat against the sides of his head.

Seosaimhín stopped staring. "Do you wish to stop us, cat?"

Lucius pulled out of his aggressive posture. His eyes became wide and sweet. "As I said before, I'm not here to stop you. I have the answers I sought. I shall take my leave of you and I bid you good hunting." The cat leapt into the air and flew away with such speed that Seosaimhín had to wonder if she imagined the entire episode.

"Too much potion," she muttered. She sat on her bedding and found a large amount of black hair littering the tattered blankets. "Filthy cat."

Encampment on Top of Ernstberg

Máire opened her eyes and sat up. She turned towards Awvarwy and noticed he still slept. Part of her mused on why she thought of him now as Awvarwy and not Mandubratius. It could be the sight of a rather peaceful and uncharacteristic smile on his face or the fact that he didn't harass her once during the day. It allowed her to see past Mandubratius and to the mortal Briton beneath the Lamia. She searched for Lucius but did not see him.

Awvarwy stirred and opened his eyes. He beamed at her, and she forgot her suspicions of him for a moment. Now, he seemed little more than a mortal chieftain, waking from a long nap. "Good evening," he uttered mid-stretch. His hands went behind his head. "Did you sleep well, Maél... Máire?"

She extended her arms and yawned. "It was very nice to sleep without the constant interruption of snoring, farting, and belching."

Awvarwy chuckled. "I am glad I assisted you in acquiring a restful sleep. I do hope you will inform me later who makes such a racket." He stood up and offered Máire his hands. She took them, and he pulled her up with ease.

"They all do. I'm certain you must as well, on very rare occasions," she said, to which Mandubratius smirked and said nothing else. "For a man who loves the sound of his own voice, you're being very quiet," she said, surprised he had little else to declare.

"I'm merely being contemplative," Mandubratius replied as he pulled on his breeches.

She began dressing as well.

"No, that's not the whole truth," he muttered. He turned to meet her eyes, and it seemed as though Awvarwy re-appeared. "I have a feeling that some of our group will die, including me."

"Everyone thinks that before battle. I feel that way every time, too," she assured him, then she admitted, "I feel more anxiety for this one, though. Perhaps it is because I will allow myself to experience the possibility of loss during this battle."

"Yes," he stated, "but this is a very strong feeling that I, or someone else I know, will die. I fear if it's not me, it will be you. I've developed a… fondness for you, and I don't want you to die, now."

She noticed his pale features become red for a moment, despite the fact he had not fed in some time.

He lowered his eyes as if to avoid seeing her response.

Máire mused over his sentiments. This did not seem to be an act, but he had tricked her before. "Awvarwy, I'd love to return your fondness, but given our history, I feel I cannot. I have forgiven you for your transgressions, but I'm afraid that if I allow myself to reciprocate on the feelings you say you have for me, you will laugh at me later for falling for your ploy."

Mandubratius looked hurt. She considered embracing him and telling him she had lied, yet Máire resisted her compulsion. She still worried that he manipulated her in some way.

"I'm truly sorry that I have not regained your trust. I cannot blame you. I hope one night soon, I will earn your trust again."

"Perhaps you may yet." Máire patted his back and then ducked around him to get to her boots.

Máire left Awvarwy's tent feeling somewhat confused about the last day but decided to let it pass. She headed towards the line of gathered mortal soldiers sipping at their elixir and hoped for a dinner donation from a few.

"Máire?"

"Father Xofer." She shifted her eyes in a nervous fashion, feeling somewhat self-conscious. "How are you this evening? Did you sleep well?"

"I did. Thank you. I wanted to thank you again for allowing us to view your workings." The priest beamed at her, and her discomfort faded.

"It was my pleasure," she replied, sensing that he must have noticed her embarrassment and wished to alleviate it.

"The others and I believe that we may have some gifts that may be somewhat similar to powers gracing the Celtic lines," the priest said before taking a sip of the potion. He made a strange face, rather like a child tasting an unpleasant food. "My family and I have decided to leave the encampment, for a short time, to learn these tools and how we may be of service to the defenders of these lands. We are not content to serve as mere medics in this battle, Máire."

Máire tried to keep from frowning. She wanted to keep these changed Strigoi safe, but she knew forcing them to stay would never work. She tried to think over how to react to Father Xofer's news.

"The Strigoi are not far," she warned him. "You may not have much time to practice."

"All the more reason for us to leave now." The priest patted her hand.

She felt a calm settle around her. While she knew he had brought forth the feeling, Máire decided she should not stop him or the others. "Be safe then," she replied. "I hope our workings are successful, Father Xofer. Return here if anything seems to worry you or the others, please."

The priest nodded and turned away.

Her hunger raged in her head. Máire returned her intentions to the group of soldiers finishing their elixir.

Julien snorted himself awake and rubbed his eyes. Sitting up, he studied his surroundings. Máire's bedroll and blanket remained folded between Claudius and Marcus, who were both snoring happily. Though, he knew most blood-drinkers didn't exactly need to snore, perhaps it remained as a strange habit from days of mortality. Either way, he wished to know where Máire was. Julien stood up and walked over to Marcus' left side. He contemplated for a moment on how best to wake him and decided to shake him.

"WHAT!"

A dagger pointed at him. Marcus' eyes blazed bright green.

Julien vowed to allow others to wake Marcus from now on. "It's me, sorry. I'm just concerned," he said.

"Oh, by Morrigan's strength, you and Máire are most annoying sometimes. Is it sunset already?" Marcus sat up and blinked his eyes. They faded into blue. "Concerned about what?"

"Have you seen Máire?"

Marcus closed his eyes for a moment and then squinted. He finally opened his eyes and stared at her bedroll.

"Oh," he muttered. "No, I haven't seen her since before sunrise. Claudius?"

Claudius continued to snore.

Marcus grabbed one of Claudius' boots and threw it at him, hitting him squarely between his shoulder blades.

Claudius sat up and snarled. "Did you throw a stinky boot at me, General?" he asked.

"Calm yourself, Major," Marcus said. "Yes, I thought it best to get your attention that way. Have you seen Máire?"

"She probably went to get us breakfast," Claudius answered. "At least, that is my fervent wish."

"Máire usually doesn't roll up her bed so nicely," Marcus commented.

"True, she'd never make it as a soldier," Claudius muttered. The two blood-drinkers got out of bed and began to dress.

"She's fine, I'm sure," Marcus assured Julien. "She may have decided to bunk closer to food."

"Fine, I'll find her," Julien muttered. He began dressing. A few moments later, he ducked out of the tent and dodged his way through the lines of soldiers and activity at the center of camp. He saw six soldiers put together a large table, while others rolled up tents and other supplies. He witnessed a changing of the guards and then noticed the line of blood-drinkers queuing for their nightly rations. He saw a familiar figure join the line and ducked in behind her.

Máire turned and grinned. "Good evening." She dipped her cup into the cauldron and pulled out a serving of the elixir. She passed it to him and grabbed his mug off his belt, filling it for herself. "You did feed first?"

Julien took a sip. "No, I did not. Where were you? I was worried." The fact that she slept elsewhere needled at him.

"Oh, I thought Marcus would have informed you." She took a sip and exited the line. They joined the rest of the gathered forces.

"Informed me of what?"

"Oh, he punished me for dousing Awvarwy last night, though I seem to remember that it was your idea to have a live target." She smirked at him. "Anyway, Marcus thought it would be amusing for me to assist him in finding dry clothing."

He frowned. "So, where did you sleep?"

"By that time, the sun was up, so I slept there."

"You spent the day alone, with Mandubratius, in his tent?" He felt a tight rage burn within.

Máire gave him a most playful grin and guzzled the rest of her drink. "Yes, Julien, the two of us were all alone in his tent! Though, we did have a cat chaperone us. He even shared his bedding with me." She laughed.

"Did he harm you at all? If he did—"

"Julien, I'm flattered that you wish to defend me, but you don't have to be my protector."

Julien stared at her. He felt so confused at that moment that he could not help himself. "He killed your father and was responsible for the deaths of many others you loved. He also tried to kill you!"

The utter absurdity of this almost makes me laugh.

"Yes, and I've tried to kill him, too," Máire answered. Her smile faded. "We may not survive tonight, Julien. He and I decided it would be best that we prepare for the Otherworld by closing our debts to each other, in a manner of speaking. It's a tradition of my... our people." She shrugged. "I don't know how to explain it, really."

Julien's urge to laugh passed, and he sighed, feeling disgust that she would forgive Mandubratius. "I just... worry about you," he said, "especially when that viper is near."

Máire attached the empty cup to her belt and placed her hands on his cheeks. She stared into his face for a moment, her eyes a vast expanse of green. "I'm older than you, Julien. I don't need your guardianship. I just wish you to be you, my love."

"Someone might see us," he murmured.

"Then, you will inform them I am giving you my blessing." She gave him a quick kiss and pulled back. "Don't worry about Awvarwy. Let me deal with him. You worry about helping your father and my father-in-darkness in this battle." She turned towards the west. "I think I hear Ercanbald calling for you. You'd better go to the feast."

"Alright," he said, pulling her in close. He inhaled deeply. "I will join you later when you deploy the mirror." He released Máire and headed towards his father's secretary. He glanced back over his shoulder, but Máire had disappeared into the crowd.

"Inspector General?"

Julien turned back towards Ercanbald. "Yes?"

The secretary pulled out a chair for him a few seats down from his father.

The Emperor was drumming his fingernails against the table and looked up as Julien sat down. His father gave him a brief nod and returned to staring at the opposite end of the table where the Pope and his staff sat. Candles lit the table, adding to the illumination of the torches.

Servers placed bowls of stew on the table. His father's staff of generals took their seats. He noticed Mandubratius sit down at the Pope's right hand. The Lamia stared at the dish of stew with ill-concealed distaste. Someone poured wine into his cup, and Julien began drinking.

"Now, lower your heads for the Holy Father's blessing," he heard the Emperor say.

Julien put down his cup.

"Oh, Holy Father, protect us in our time of greatest need," the Pope intoned. "Bless those who fight in Your name this night. Bless…"

The Pope's oddly soothing voice began to drone, and Julien tried to keep his eyes from closing. He started to study the rest of the mortals and then noticed that Mandubratius was looking them over as well.

The Papal Emissary turned towards Julien and winked at him.

Julien frowned, slumping back in his chair. He heard the footsteps of a racing mortal and turned towards the Emperor. The soldier stopped at the head of the table as the Pope continued his prayer.

The Emperor motioned the guard forward.

"Imperial Majesty, there is a woman and soldier at the gate. They both ask to speak to the Papal Emissary," the soldier whispered.

"Who are they?"

The Pope paused in his prayer.

"The man claims himself to be Sextus, one of the last surviving angels of the Papal Army. The woman claims to be Lady Talia of Époisses."

Talia paced from one side of the dirt path to the other as Sextus remained standing at the gate. His tranquil peace at rejoining the rest of the soldiers did little to settle her anxiety.

If only I could speak to my sponsor in private. The nightmares of events from the past seem to increase every hour. Perhaps a tonic would cure this continuing torture.

The scent of a familiar mortal disrupted her fears. She could see Emperor Charles move past his soldiers. His face revealed revulsion upon recognizing her. She could sense and smell others behind him. An entourage of Deargh Du followed the Emperor. She watched Sextus push his way past the guards and run towards his sponsor and the other Lamia like a lost child, joyful at the long-awaited reunion of his family.

She saw Mandubratius appear from the throng of gathered forces. His eyes revealed nothing. She wished again to have him tell her that the Strigoi were nothing to be feared, only an annoyance in their eternal lives and that the nightmares would fade. She lowered her gaze and studied the other blood-drinkers from under her eyelashes.

"You are dismissed," the Emperor said to the guards at the gate. "Return when the captain gives his orders for you to do so."

Talia raised her eyes, stared into the sea of faces, and witnessed her own child in a distant corner, but Reginald avoided her gaze. She looked back at Mandubratius, feeling safer already with him watching her. She heard muttering in Frankish and decided to make herself humble. Talia moved to her knees and lowered her face to the dirt.

"How is it that you walk amongst the living, Lady Talia? I witnessed your death at Máire's sword." The Emperor's dry voice revealed no mercy.

"Lady Talia is a Lamia, father," she heard a voice whisper. She looked up and saw Julien de Divio at the Emperor's right side.

The Emperor spun to face the other blood-drinkers. "No one saw fit to inform me of this?"

Talia shivered at hearing his voice. She had nowhere else to go. The Strigoi would surround them all soon. They already blocked off any escape, barring the western route after their attack against the Papal Forces. Yet, she heard no words from her sponsor to alleviate her terror.

"It seemed unimportant, Imperial Majesty," she heard Marcus reply. "Julien and Lady Heloise were vindicated. It seemed best to move on."

"We believed she would not cross our paths again," she heard Máire say.

Talia stared at her niece for a moment and ducked her eyes out of embarrassment and confusion.

"I did leave," she answered. "I went to find solace with he who knows me best." She glanced up to look for her sponsor again. "Through a series of events, I find myself here with Sextus, wishing to escape the onslaught of the Strigoi's nightmares. Mandubratius, I will do whatever you wish, just offer me your protection!"

Her sponsor met her eyes.

"Marcus, I want you to draw your sword and decapitate this... woman," the Emperor hissed. "She endangered my family and me."

Talia lowered her head and heard the sound of a sword being pulled from a sheath. She thought that perhaps death would bring her release.

"Wait."

She heard an annoyed huff.

"What is it, Papal Emissary?" The Emperor's voice revealed his dark mood.

"Imperial Majesty, it may be wise to have an additional angel defending us," she heard Mandubratius say. His words implied facts and not begging.

"After all this woman did to my family?" the Emperor roared.

"Please, Imperial Majesty, allow her to defend us."

She raised her head and witnessed Reginald kneel in front of Charles.

"Reginald, I know now what she did to you, because she played the same game with me," Charles whispered. "Are you saying you wish me to forgive this traitor for what she did to your family and me?"

He pulled Reginald to his feet.

"Imperial Majesty, we witnessed that she can handle a blade," Reginald explained. "I suggest that you allow her to fight the Strigoi after giving her the elixir. If she survives, you can pass judgment on her. Perhaps, she can earn your mercy in battle."

She witnessed Reginald's dark eyes rest on her. Talia lowered her head again. His kindness embarrassed her. "I live or die at your whim," she said, finding words. "Command me to fight, Imperial Majesty, and I'll stand with my peers and fight. The Strigoi hold strands of my mind now. I wish to join in this struggle to free it from their madness."

"I will vouch that Talia will not escape," Mandubratius said.

"If I agree to this," Charles said, "it would appear to some that she has risen from the grave. How do I explain this to the few who witnessed the battle between her and Máire in Aachen?"

"After tonight's battle, your soldiers will tell tales of men and women who rose from mortal wounds. They will witness the Inspector General of the Gendarmes and the Papal Emissary exhibit angelic traits. They will know that we may be something resembling angels, but they might harbor suspicions that we are not what we claim," she heard Marcus state.

"I know," Charles answered. "I figured the Holy Father could come up with some explanation of strange miracles and equally strange angels."

"If the battle is won," she heard Máire say. Talia looked up at her niece.

She watched the Emperor study Máire. "Do not say such things," he said. "You are the closest thing to an angel in this realm, and I need hope from angels."

Máire nodded. "I am sorry, Imperial Majesty. You are right. We offered hope to those in Éire, Scotland, and Britain. Now, we offer hope to the Emperor of the Western Empire."

She noticed Máire smile at the Emperor, radiating a warming beauty, and the Emperor's face turned serene.

"Thank you," he said. He turned back to Talia, and she lowered her face again. "I have made my decision," she heard the Emperor say. "Talia may live to fight. If she proves herself worthy in battle, she will be free to leave with her family."

"Thank you," she said. She heard the Emperor turn and walk away. Talia looked up to see him snap his fingers.

Reginald and Julien turned away, following him with the retinue of blood-drinkers.

Talia glanced to her left and witnessed her niece staring at her as if torn.

Marcus wrapped an arm around Máire. "Come, there are preparations to make, Banbh Ceanúil. I need you to assist me," Marcus said in Gaelic.

Máire allowed him to propel her away, but her eyes remained on Talia.

Talia lowered her face to the ground. She sensed her sponsor move in closer and wondered what humiliating act she would have to do now, not that she cared. She would do almost anything to be safe. Talia felt a hand pull her to her feet.

Mandubratius stared at her for a moment. "You need elixir," he said, pulling her toward the camp. "I... we must prepare for the worst in this battle, Talia." He led her through battlements, spikes, and a wall of collapsed carriages to a large cauldron. "It is a most bitter-tasting brew," he explained along the way, "but it's not so bad after the first few sips."

She met his eyes and felt calm. Talia took the offered cup from her sponsor and began to drink the sludgy wine.

Marcus' mind wandered as he polished his armor. In his day, the generals always suited in their best for battle. It seemed appropriate to meet Seosaimhín and her forces in such a fashion. But after a moment, he returned to his thoughts on Morrigan's words. He glanced down at his nails and wished for a page to assist in this duty. He picked up his armor and began to dress himself, but the straps began to tangle. At that moment, he heard the tent flap billow.

"I told you I'd help you with that," Claudius grumbled. "I said give me a few minutes to feed."

"One would assume that you'd find food closer."

"The Lord of Hosts said mortal man was too easy tonight. I wished to chase down a stag." Claudius pulled off the armor and straightened the straps of leather.

"Why not just feed on a horse?"

Claudius finished setting the armor on Marcus and began fastening it in place. "Cernunnos told me, during the Night of Trials, that the most satisfactory meals are the ones that require chasing," Claudius answered. "Besides, I did really want to see how foolish you'd look when you attempted dressing yourself."

Marcus chuckled. Picking up Claudius' armor, he returned the favor. After he finished buckling the straps, he stood back up.

"So, how do I look?" he asked Claudius.

"Very much like a mortal I knew. He was a fearsome bastard, but my best commander," Claudius replied. "Truthfully, you look like a proper Roman general. All that is missing is the helm. How do I look?"

"Like that snotty senator's son who weaseled his way onto my staff," Marcus replied. "However, I loved him as if he were my own son. I have something to show you." He went into one of the bags and pulled out two blankets. He tossed one to Claudius. "I had a blacksmith craft these for you and me."

Claudius unwrapped his gift and held up a helm. "Why didn't you tell me? I'm speechless," he said, looking it over. He chuckled a moment. "My only complaint is that this helm is not a major's helm."

Marcus shook his head and laughed. "Sorry. I had it made before your promotion."

"Do you think this armor will dispel the illusion that we are angels?" Claudius pulled on the helm and began tying and buckling.

"For all they know, angels may have an affinity for Roman armor," Marcus answered. "I'm certain that the events tonight will dispel many illusions about angels."

After they both walked outside, Marcus pulled on his helm. "Can you smell it?" Marcus asked.

Claudius closed his eyes and inhaled. "Yes. The party of scouts returns, and one is bloody."

"Summon the Emperor and the High Priest," Marcus said. "Have them meet me here."

Claudius nodded, turned on his heel, and headed to the Emperor's tent.

"Máire, to me," Marcus yelled, knowing that she would assist him with the healing. He felt a rush of air surround him as she arrived at his side.

She examined him and chuckled. "You cannot leave your Roman roots, can you?"

"Now is not the time for amusement," he replied, eliciting a serious expression on her face. "Arwin and his group return soon, and Claudius and I smell blood."

She turned towards the west and sniffed. "There aren't as many of them returning." She looked back at him. "Are they returning to report to you?"

Marcus shook his head. "The plan was only for Edward to keep in contact with us. That means…" He trailed off.

"Something is very wrong?" she whispered.

He heard the footfall of elder mortals and looked over to see the Pope and Emperor attempting to keep up with Claudius.

They stopped as they reached him. The two mortals looked quite winded.

"What is so important that your man insisted on us running to meet with you?" the Pope asked.

Marcus pointed upwards, and then Edward and the majority of the scouts landed, carrying Mac Alpin.

Edward crouched to help his father-in-darkness to the ground.

"Arwin!" Máire squatted and began healing him.

"Edward, a report please," Marcus said, turning as Edward stood up.

"It was Seosaimhín," Edward answered. "At least, I think it was. She attacked us one by one. Some she fed to her hungered masses. The rest of us escaped."

Arwin coughed and uttered a strange half-growl. "That's not the worst of it," he said, looking up at Marcus. "She pummeled us with stones. They appeared out of thin air."

"She knows the gifts, then." Máire patted Mac Alpin's arm and glanced up at Marcus.

"How was one woman able to kill so many?" The Emperor stared down at Arwin.

"Imperial Majesty, we were separated to maximize our perception. She just seemed to know," Edward answered.

"How close are they?" the Pope asked Edward.

"An hour, give or take a few minutes," Edward admitted.

The Pope shuddered a bit.

"What do you recommend we do?" the Emperor asked while raising his eyes away from Mac Alpin, addressing Marcus.

"Calm yourself, Holy Pope," Marcus said. "Charles, I recommend assembling the men, with the exception of the post guards. Have them assemble for inspection." He paused. "Forgive my familiarity, Imperial Majesty. The elixir fogs my brain a little sometimes."

The Emperor shrugged. "I'm just Charles right now."

Marcus nodded and then faced Claudius. "Major, you know what to do."

Claudius saluted him.

Marcus returned the salute and watched his old friend walk into the distance. The Pope and Emperor followed him, as did a majority of the scouts.

Marcus faced Mac Alpin but caught Máire's eyes. "How is he?"

"Nothing a flagon of mead won't fix, you Roman bastard," Arwin replied with a smirk.

Marcus crouched down. "We've been out of mead for a long time, my friend. Will you be able to fight?"

"I'll not let a woman wielding stones keep me from fighting this battle," Mac Alpin roared.

"Those weren't stones, they were boulders," Edward replied. He sat down and smiled at his father-in-darkness.

"Eadwina, shut it! Now help me up!"

"You can't levitate yourself, Arwin?" Máire asked. "If that is the case, you will rest and not participate."

"Woman, you are impossible!" Mac Alpin countered. He rose off the ground but wobbled mid-flight.

"Are you sure you can fight?" Máire asked.

"I'm not only sure I can fight, but I can fuck too. Let's leave these boys and meet in that tent over there, one of the last still up," drawled Mac Alpin.

Marcus sensed others begin to approach.

"I think that there are others better suited to that, Arwin," Máire chuckled.

The elder Ekimmu Cruitne inhaled. "Ah, yes... the Basileus approaches." He found his footing on the ground. "Just know you'll be missing a great deal more fun than either of these two could give you." He slapped Máire's backside and began to call for the Empress as he trod off.

Edward shook his head. "When he gets like this, I worry how much he's in pain, but I need to find Amata before the assembly." He stood up and brushed off the dirt.

Máire smirked and stood up. "I hope that show was not just a show and that he will make it through this battle with little more than scratches."

"Frankly, I'm grateful for the levity before swords are drawn." Marcus stood up and helped her to her feet, eliciting a smile from her. "Máire," he said, pulling off his helm. He smoothed a hand over his hair.

"Yes, General?"

"It should take them some time to assemble. I feel some anxiety. Perhaps you and I could do something to ease my concerns?" He leaned in and gently played with a plait of her hair. He watched her smile widen.

"I see." She stared at him for a moment. "You need to relax. Is this what you said to camp girls before taking them to bed?"

"No," he chuckled. "I usually just grabbed whichever one was closest."

"Well, I'm pleased I get to have a say in this." She smirked. "Put your helm back on, and we can address these anxieties of yours in that tent."

The soldiers stood in inspection array. Claudius took his place amongst the angels and noticed eyes examining his new helm. He returned their stares, and the soldiers looked elsewhere.

He inhaled and noticed a few latecomers. Mandubratius arrived and took a spot next to Gaius. He turned his sight to the seated monarch and high priest. The Emperor appeared in gleaming armor. The Pope looked most uncomfortable.

"What are we waiting for?" the Pope whispered to the Emperor.

Claudius turned his head, sensing Marcus approaching the soldiers in a rush. Máire followed behind. Claudius nodded at the captains to issue the order to stand at attention, first in Latin, then Frankish, then Greek.

The Emperor and Pope rose from their seats, and Marcus paused as if considering saluting them or bowing, then changed his mind.

"Shall we review them?" Marcus asked.

"Yes," the Emperor said.

"Claudius, Gaius, Ma …Papal Emissary, generals," Marcus called out while glancing at them over his shoulder, "please join us."

The assembled officers began looking over the ranks, lead by Marcus. He paused in his inspection to stand in front of a soldier. "State your name."

The soldier turned his head to meet Marcus' piercing glare. "Bero, sir"

"What is the signal to release arrows, Bero?"

"Two whistle blasts, sir!"

"Correct. Well done."

The soldier relaxed a little.

Marcus walked toward the ranks of blood-drinkers and paused in front of one of the few remaining Lamia. "State your name."

"Verso, sir."

"What is the command to attack the enemy with swords?" Marcus asked.

"Three whistle bursts, sir," the Lamia answered.

Marcus looked over the rows of soldiers for a moment. He backed away and headed to the center of the field where the others waited.

"Stand easy," he instructed the army.

The officers repeated the order to the ranks in Frankish and Greek.

"The enemy will begin to surround us," Marcus stated to the forces. His voice carried through the night air without yelling. "Shortly after, they will begin their attack. We must be vigilant, in case they change their tactics and decide to attack us without surrounding us." The officers translated for those who only spoke Frankish or Greek.

Marcus paused and seemed to think over his words. "I will not lie. The enemy before us is frightening, and even I have succumbed to their mental attacks." His features became hard and determined. "However, we have a defense that will put us on even ground, the elixir you have all imbibed for the last five nights. If you did not take it tonight, you will be amongst the ranks of the enemy or the dead."

Claudius looked up at the stars, hoping Marcus would not be too long-winded.

"We have trained together," Marcus added. "We have a battle plan that maximizes our capabilities. In addition, we have assistance from above and our sacred mirror to deploy. We hope this will mean freedom for as many of our enemy as possible. We are united in our cause, and we shall prevail over the evil possessing our brothers and sisters." Marcus turned and faced the blood-drinker ranks. "Now, my brothers and sisters in darkness," he roared in Gaelic. "Know that the Gods and Goddesses watch us tonight. Victory awaits us!"

Claudius found himself yelling an old war cry in response. He looked around, shocked to see his own sentiments echoed.

Marcus smirked at him. "Dismissed, go to your defensive positions," the general barked.

The officers began repeating the order to the other soldiers. He then noticed Máire depart for the wagon where the mirror lay protected in a nondescript box.

Claudius walked up to Marcus. "Your speech was short this time," he commented to the resplendent Roman Deargh Du general. "That's good."

"Are you suggesting that I'm tedious and dull, Claudius? That is most hurtful," Marcus chuckled.

"Not in the slightest, General." Claudius chuckled as well.

"General, where should the Holy Po... Father and I go?" the Emperor asked, interrupting their chat.

Marcus turned back towards the mortals. "That depends. Will you fight with us?"

"I believe that I face the same danger as the foot soldiers," the Emperor answered. "I will join the ranks wherever I am needed."

"And you, Pope?" Marcus asked.

Pope Leo nodded his head. "I am not a warrior, but I cannot hide in the back. I will go where I am needed."

Marcus nodded. "Claudius, take the Emperor and the Pope to the command circle. I am certain their expertise in battle strategy will be necessary. I will be there shortly. It looks as though Máire needs assistance."

Claudius saluted him. "Yes, she appears to be most confused with the bindings for the mirror."

Marcus returned the salute and walked towards the western edge of the encampment.

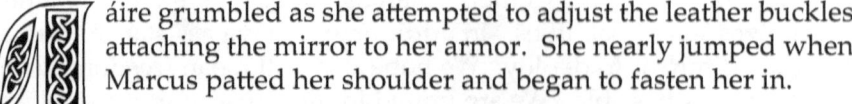

chapter thirteen

áire grumbled as she attempted to adjust the leather buckles attaching the mirror to her armor. She nearly jumped when Marcus patted her shoulder and began to fasten her in.

He finished and looked her up and down. "Be safe, Maél Muire," he murmured. "I don't know what I'd do if I lost you."

"If you were lost, I'm not sure what I'd do either," Máire admitted. She stretched out her arm and took his hand.

"I would hope that you would thrive and find happiness and the balance," he replied.

"Why are you speaking like this," she asked. "You have never said such things to me before a battle."

Marcus squeezed her hand. "The enemy is different than the Lamia or any of the other lines we fought in the past. We may fail, and if that is the case, the world as we know it will end soon thereafter."

She moved into his arms, despite the mirror between them. "Then, we would meet again in the Otherworld. Even if one of us dies, we will still meet there. So, do not worry over how this battle will end. If Morrigan calls, then you, I, or the both of us will go."

"You are right," he whispered, but he managed to look uncertain and worried. "Did I tell you what my nightmares were about?"

Máire shook her head.

"I killed…" He paused and fell silent for a moment. "It makes no sense, really. I shall have to tell you about it some night when we are back in Bath or Vézelay."

She patted him and pulled back. "I am to meet Julien and Edward at the western border, and you are to go to Command."

"Take good care of both of them tonight, especially my grandson-in-darkness," Marcus said. "I had no need to tell him or Edward to watch for you. They will make sure you are safe."

Máire blinked back her tears and heard a throat clear. She looked in the direction of the sound.

"Down here," Lucius said.

"Lucius!" Máire smiled, crouching to pet the fairy cat. "Where have you been? I looked for you when I woke this evening."

Lucius rubbed himself against her hand. "If you must know, Máire, I went to relieve myself, then I found a stag that needed teasing. He chased me through the forest and ran into a tree that he did not see." The fairy cat chuckled.

Marcus leaned over and scratched the cat's head. "Do you wish to fly with me, Champion of fairy cats?"

"I was hoping you would ask," Lucius replied. "Is there room in your... oh, you're wearing armor."

"I had not considered that, Lucius. I am sorry." Marcus straightened up. "That's not a problem."

Lucius levitated to Marcus' eye level. "As you can see, I will have no trouble accompanying you."

"Lucius!" Máire laughed. "Why did you not tell us you could fly? I caught you several times when you fell from the bag and you thanked me!"

The cat purred. "I am a trickster, Máire. I enjoyed having you and the others carry me. Besides, you are a good conversationalist, and I wanted to be nearby."

"Is there anything else about you that we do not know?" Marcus chuckled.

Lucius looked at Marcus, and his eyes twinkled. "The things you do not know about me could fill the oceans, General. The things you do know about me would not fill a single tear." The cat smiled, revealing gleaming teeth.

"The enemy's in sight!" a soldier yelled.

"Deploy the mirror," Marcus told her. "Lucius, I am concerned that the Pope might be a little frightened of a flying cat."

"May I curl around your neck until you reach Command?" Lucius asked. He flew behind Marcus and settled in. "I'll wager that you won't even realize I'm here. Once we arrive, I will hide in plain sight and watch the battle." The cat purred. "I love battles."

Marcus pulled Máire in for a quick kiss and then departed.

Máire watched him leave and then flew to the western perimeter, near the ridge. She landed next to Edward and Julien and gave them a cautious smile. "I guess this is it." She stared into the forests surrounding them and then at the path cut into the ridge. "I guess you both already know the plan, but here it is again. We're going to try to change as many Strigoi as we can. Edward will create the light source. Julien serves as my protection. Seosaimhín lurks somewhere in the forests, and I'm certain that the idea of us transforming her army of slaves probably will infuriate her. So, be careful and we can retreat or change our tactics if necessary." She met Julien's eyes. "Are you ready?" She looked over to Edward.

Edward nodded his head. "I'm ready. Let me know if I need to defend the mirror as well."

Julien nodded and patted her shoulder. "Tell me if this mirror becomes too much of a burden, and we will switch places."

She smiled. "Thank you, but only I may wear this stylish garment." She leaned in and embraced him, deciding it would be best that they not speak of death and destruction. She pulled back. "I am very proud of you."

Julien smiled and took her hand. "And you will..." he paused and chuckled. "Let's go find a good vantage point so that you may shine."

Patroclus leapt, shooting three arrows at various targets. With another bound, he took his next shot at a target but hit Claudius instead.

"Watch out, I'm not your enemy! I'm attempting to act as distraction."

"Sorry." Patroclus plummeted towards earth and leapt again, after having a chance to look over the other archers. "Claudius, more are falling, and the Lamia are starting to look as though they are affected." He could feel the strains of the Strigoi magic try to unsettle him. "Get out of here, major. They are starting to affect me. Warn the others that we may have to switch tactics."

He fired another series of arrows at three more Strigoi and then began to plunge back towards the earth. He looked up in time to see Claudius fly towards Command in the center. He prepared himself to jump again but struggled to focus on his duties.

Patroclus hit two more Strigoi in their legs, and they roared in pain. He could barely register himself falling towards the ground. He felt himself hit the ground, but he felt no pain. Then, the garbled and frightening nightmares from his days of mortal soldiering returned. Patroclus clutched his head with his hands and could tell that he was screaming. The rest faded into gray.

Claudius felt disgust at leaving Patroclus to the Strigoi, but his duty to inform Command of the Strigoi's progress overcame his dread. Marcus appeared to be watching the team with the mirror.

"General," he called as he landed.

Marcus faced him. "Yes, major?"

"Our advantage of archers has been neutralized. While the Strigoi are not able to bring down the numbers they normally do, they are still bringing down the archers," Claudius summarized.

Marcus rubbed his chin in thought. "Lead those who remain into the air. We will rally the ground forces to attack. It appears that we can no longer win this war by wounding the Strigoi."

"I know," Claudius answered. "I'll gather the troops that can fly and do so." He whistled for the blood-drinkers that remained in the field. He heard the whistle repeat while landing amid the remaining blood-drinkers. "While the elixir is helping us stand, many of our archers have fallen to their attacks.

We need to stop wounding them and begin killing them. We must rally the ground troops and take out the Strigoi or, at least, distract them enough to allow the ground troops to overwhelm them."

Marcus tried to keep his temper in check. Now there would be fewer changed Strigoi than planned because the elixir did not have the strength necessary to prevent the full force of their attacks. He turned towards the Emperor and Gaius. "Our archers are falling. The elixir does not offer complete relief from the Strigoi attack." He figured they heard some of his and Claudius' conversation.

"So, now it's come to a ground attack?" Gaius asked.

"I'm afraid so," Marcus answered. He noticed the Pope wander over to him while muttering a prayer.

The remainder of the Imperial staff joined them.

"We shall concentrate our efforts on the west, north, and south. The height on the eastern edge will prove some difficulty for them, I think. Maintain a perimeter to the other sides, but keep watch on the east just in case."

Marcus noticed generals repeat his orders to their underlings in Frankish and Greek, and then whistles pierced the air. He sensed a large number of blood-drinkers fly towards the north. He turned back towards the west and could see Strigoi falling to the mirror along the path cut into the ridge there.

Máire, Julien, and Edward looked to be in fine spirits. Lucius appeared near them. The cat's eyes glowed, revealing a strange logic and insight.

Marcus pushed aside the thoughts of flying cats and scanned the skies for Seosaimhín.

Talia tried to keep from pacing. Her thoughts had cleared not long after the elixir. However, a deluge of emotions raged within and varied every few moments. She turned as she sensed another blood-drinker land near her.

"Are you ready?" Sextus asked.

Talia nodded.

He picked up his whistle and blew the signal for a sword attack.

She began to run with the others down the northern side of the hill.

Their advancement seemed to surprise the attacking Strigoi. The slackened-mouth stares revealed little other than mindlessness. Before she could strike, Talia watched Sextus leap into the throng of Strigoi.

The Strigoi began to scream as blood flew and splattered.

Talia licked at the putrid blood but gagged a little at the taste.

Sextus knocked down and beheaded the Strigoi surrounding him and kicked his way out of the falling bodies, as he backed towards the line of the enemy. Others began hacking at the Strigoi.

She felt her own bloodlust begin to rise. Talia yelled and rushed into the wave of malformed bodies. Screams assaulted her eardrums, and she watched mortals and some blood-drinkers fall.

"Fall back to the next defensive position!" Sextus ordered before blowing into his whistle.

The cries of the fallen pierced her with guilt as she left them to their uncertain future. She just started to run, unsure of the direction she took.

Mac Alpin's urge to rush into the surging Strigoi grew. Small groups would turn to stare at an individual, and soon the mortal would fall. Then he remembered his duty to watch for Seosaimhín. He soon smelled Edward approach. His son-in-darkness prepared to report.

"How are they?" he demanded before Edward could speak. He could see Julien and Máire in the distance. The fire lit their figures.

"As well as any of us." Edward paused and stared down at the battle. "It appears our forces are falling back to defensive positions."

Arwin scanned the grounds below and watched the Lamia fight, looking for the Empress. He caught sight of her brawling with the rest of the Lamia and some of the mortal forces. "There she is."

"What? Irene?" he asked Edward, revealing his distraction.

"No, Seosaimhín," Edward answered.

"Drop the flare," he told Edward.

His son-in-darkness lit the light and waved it at the Command. He could see Marcus turn towards them.

"Edward, go back to Máire and Julien," Mac Alpin ordered. "We will stop her." He signaled to his troops to follow him towards the Strigoi's mistress. They flew towards the north.

"General, the Strigoi have breached the line at the west," a young mortal lieutenant informed Marcus. "We have lost contact with Sextus' cohort. They are presumed dead or unconscious."

Marcus nodded. "They did their duty, return to your general."

The mortal saluted him and left.

Explosions rocked the land. Mandubratius winced at the bright light and covered his eyes for a moment.

"I'm in awe of Edward's work," he muttered.

"What?" The Holy Father faced him.

"They are throwing clay firepots in the south," Mandubratius relayed.

"Does that mean we're in danger?" The Pope turned to look over at the Emperor and Marcus talking.

"It means you better start praying hard to your Jewish God because it looks like you may be joining him soon. Me, I'm going to the Otherworld. Heaven sounds far too dull to suit me." He tossed out the words to see if he could get any reaction from Leo.

Instead, the High Priest went to his knees and began to pray.

Mandubratius decided to let him keep praying. "Gaius!" he bellowed.

The general ran over to his side. "Yes, sir!"

"Ready whatever men we have left and grab whichever mortals that are willing to follow me," he ordered Gaius.

"Where to, sir?"

"We will reinforce the west."

Gaius saluted him and started issuing orders.

"Reinforcing the west?" He turned and found Amata and Irene standing side by side. They appeared dirty and disheveled, but he found great comfort in their arrival.

Irene flicked dirt and blood off her tunic

Amata rested a hand against her sword and smirked. "Do you have room in the company for two women?"

He chuckled and grinned at them. "I couldn't imagine any other women I'd rather die with than you two."

"I'm not planning on dying," Irene informed him. "Especially with someone who isn't of noble blood."

"If we survive this massacre, I'm going to retire from the Lamia leadership for a few centuries. Irene can take my place," Amata chortled.

"If we survive this, Amata, I'll give you the best going-away feast you've ever seen, and I'll toss you out of the temple of Mars myself," Mandubratius answered. He watched Gaius race back towards them. A gathered force trailed behind him. He frowned, feeling an odd shiver crawl up his spine. Mandubratius looked for a nearby Strigoi, but found nothing. He looked up into the skies and noticed a familiar figure in the west.

"Seosaimhín has arrived," he murmured, trying to keep his fear at bay.

Mac Alpin flew straight towards the crazy hag.

Her face lit up in a beaming smile, the kind of smile that revealed fang, immense pleasure, and insanity all at once.

"Hold back," Arwin yelled at the others. He could not miss this opportunity.

Seosaimhín made a strange gesture and shut her eyes.

Arwin continued towards her but hit a dense, immovable object. Mac Alpin began to fall, but he managed to catch himself. He opened his eyes and witnessed his friends falling back to earth, with strange spears protruding from their bodies. Arwin peeked around the object and noticed Seosaimhín start to watch him again, with the same placid smile lighting her dark features.

His rage grew as did his strength. He flew away from the earthen spike towards Seosaimhín as quickly as he could. He heard a crushing sound and then watched stars dance. Arwin felt himself begin to fall. Everything began to turn gray.

Seosaimhín's laughter darted over the wind, and he witnessed her fly towards Edward, Máire, and Julien.

Then his vision grew black, and Mac Alpin slipped into oblivion.

"Julien, how many have we saved?" Máire's shaky voice revealed too much about her state.

"I have lost count," he admitted. "I can do nothing more than protect you."

"I cannot think of numbers either," she replied.

"Then, let me take the mirror," Julien urged. He nearly cut Edward when the Ekimmu Cruitne arrived.

"I'm back," Edward informed him. "Were you not focused?"

"I have no choice but to place all my attention on them," Julien said while motioning to the Strigoi.

"Always be aware of your surr—"

"Máire, forgive the interruption," Edward stated. He wiped his brow with his arm. "I spotted Seosaimhín. Arwin left to intercept her with his escort."

Julien tried to distinguish Seosaimhín from the Deargh Du flying with Mac Alpin. "Can you see her now, or rather smell her?"

"Yes," Edward answered. "In fact, I've been watching her. She is injuring many blood-drinkers."

He sensed Máire point the beam of reflected light towards another group of Strigoi.

"How far away is Seosaimhín?" Julien asked.

"I suggest you prepare," Edward said before drawing his blade. "She's heading directly for us." He felt his jaw slack as Mac Alpin fell. "By Morrigan's strength…" he squeaked. He sheathed his sword. "Forget fighting her. Take that mirror to the center of camp. Guard it."

Edward turned away from Julien and Máire and reached behind his back, pulling out two firepots.

Seosaimhín remained out of range, but he decided to close in.

He flew towards her.

Her eyes stayed fixed on something else in the distance. Her mouth opened and her lips moved.

Edward launched the firepots in her direction as the distance between them decreased. He counted to three and pulled forth his blade, preparing to meet Seosaimhín.

"Another has fallen," Caoimhín stated.

Claudius watched the vortexes and balls of water continue to pummel the Strigoi. While it slowed their progress, they still gained ground, and they still managed to focus their energies on the other blood-drinkers.

"Let's spread out," Claudius said, shouting the orders in Gaelic. "Can you create larger vortexes and water balls…" he shrugged, "whatever you call them?"

"We were only taught to bring forth a small amount of energy," a Deargh Du replied.

"Make them larger, or they will bring us all down."

"Understood, we will do our best." Caoimhín closed his eyes, then a larger vortex appeared in the distance and cascaded towards the Strigoi.

A strain grew in the blood-drinkers under his command, but no one fell.

Perhaps the Strigoi could not focus their attack.

However, more Strigoi arrived to replace their wearied associates.

Claudius closed his eyes for a moment, refusing to voice the sarcasm that lodged in his brain about this being the easiest of tasks. The night already seemed an eternity.

"West, defend the west!" Marcus yelled to the ground force consisting of Lamia and mortals. He witnessed Mandubratius and Amata face him. They whistled to their cohorts, turned from the north, and headed towards the west.

"Fianait!" He motioned to the final member of his staff not actively involved in the battle. "I need to join the others. Defend the Emperor and the Pope. Charles, I'm going to the west. Fianait will see to your defense."

Máire paused mid-flight and turned back to see Edward charge Seosaimhín.

"Mandubratius is right. She looks different," she murmured.

Julien tugged at her arm. "We need to get the mirror back to the ground."

Máire shook her head a little. "She must be stopped."

"Máire," Julien urged.

"I'm going to help Edward. You do what you feel is right," she said.

"I'm coming, too," a voice informed her.

She noticed Lucius' luminescent eyes studying her. She flew after Edward, but then explosions lit the sky, blinding her.

Mandubratius stabbed one of the Strigoi and grabbed Horatio, shaking him out of the Strigoi-influenced reverie. "Wake up. Your hated sponsor commands you to fight." He punched Horatio, and the other Lamia fell to the ground, shaking his head as he came out of the trance. Mandubratius heard the others slash through the first wave of Strigoi.

A sudden burst of explosions shook the battlefield. Body parts and dead Strigoi fell onto the grounds surrounding their party.

"What in Hades was that?" Amata called out.

"Someone's falling," Horatio called out, pointing towards the sky.

"I see two," Mandubratius added.

Máire began to plummet. She expected to feel the hard ground break her fall. Instead, something stopped her before she reached the ground. She turned and looked down at Julien.

"This wasn't a well-thought plan of yours, now was it?" He gave her a sardonic smile.

"Hush," she muttered. "I had to look out for Edward." He placed her on the ground.

Máire gasped at the sight of Edward's body in the distance. She forgot to hand over the mirror. Instead, she flew towards Edward. She paused, hearing insane, mocking laughter echo in her ears.

The laughter became a mere cacophonous cackle. "All your friends have fallen, Maél Muire. Now it's your turn to fall."

Máire turned towards the voice. A rain of rocks began to pummel her. It would do no good to attack Seosaimhín. She decided to breach the gate between worlds instead and draw forth energy from the Otherworld. Before she could call forth energy, the mirror on her chest exploded into fragments. The shards tore into her flesh. The painful and fresh cuts burned. She started to tumble towards the earth again.

Words to call forth the energy finally came from her mouth, and she landed on a cushion of water. She willed the water to remain in place. Máire sank to the bottom of the water. Her feet found solid ground, and the water receded into the earth. As she shook out her wet hair, she noticed Seosaimhín land. Even though Seosaimhín's features blended into the night sky, Máire could see astonishment revealed in the other Deargh Du's face.

Máire lifted away the remains of the fasteners and buckles on the harness for the mirror. A few remaining shards broke as she tossed it to the ground. She looked up and witnessed Seosaimhín's eyes glow green. Her fanged smile reflected the fire from the explosions.

Marcus flew towards the south, when a strange scent of burning flesh overwhelmed his nose. For a moment, he wondered whether the defenders had sacrificed themselves. He landed outside of a large, smoldering crater. Several stunned Strigoi crawled out of a mass of bodies littering the crater. He prepared himself to charge against whatever remained. Sensing other blood-drinkers in the distance, he decided to advance before inflicted fear and their nightmares ruined his opportunity.

But then a sudden calm overwhelmed him. He heard a whisper purr in his ear.

"Let me steer you through this rabble, my brood." Morrigan's words caressed him with a blood-filled desire.

Marcus relaxed and could feel his body move as She controlled him. A yearning for battle and bloodlust welled up from within. The thirst that he always curbed and kept hidden, for fear that such destruction would engulf him, demanded release. He heard screams as vitae splashed over him like water.

More than half of the spell casters lay on the ground beneath them. Hardly anyone remained in the sky. The loud explosion had distracted them and the Strigoi. However, the Strigoi recovered from the shockwave and concentrated their efforts, bringing down more of the airborne warriors.

"This situation doesn't look good," Claudius muttered, taking aim at a Strigoi. The arrow met its mark, and the Strigoi squealed and fell. He drew back the bowstring and targeted another. The numbers of Strigoi stumbling towards them seemed staggering.

"There's a surprise," Caoimhín hissed. The Deargh Du created a large ball of water and succeeded in distracting six Strigoi. "Claudius once again overstates the obvious." The Deargh Du chuckled.

"Well, if you have a suggestion to make, Caoimhín, I am more than willing to listen to it." He hit another two Strigoi and nocked another arrow.

"You are almost out of arrows," Caoimhín informed him. "I suggest we fall back to the east or south. You can restock your weapons on the way. Or you could pillage the dead or immobilized."

"We were ordered to keep the Strigoi at bay."

Another of the druids fell.

"Look around you, lieutenant. We are nearly outflanked."

Claudius paused in the middle of drawing back the bow. He could hear Marcus again rallying the others to join him in the west.

"It would seem your observations are correct," Claudius released the arrow into a Strigoi's chest. He whistled to the remaining Druids. "Let's fight our way towards the south and when we pass the Strigoi, we shall head west. Also, I received a promotion, Caoimhín. It's major now. Move out to a higher altitude," he ordered the remaining blood-drinkers.

The Deargh Du pulled down the darkness, and Claudius found himself cloaked within it as they flew towards the stars.

Máire pulled forth the energies of the Otherworld. A ball of lighting emerged from the mists, and she cast it at Seosaimhín. Halfway towards the intended target, a large spike rose from the ground, and the ball of lightning exploded on impact with a loud crack.

Máire closed her eyes and called forth a vortex of wind and sent it towards Seosaimhín, but a boulder appeared in her line of sight, and she dove towards the ground to avoid it. She shuddered as the boulder crashed against the ground in the distance. Máire willed the water to form into shards over the crazed Deargh Du and fall. A few hit Seosaimhín, but the majority landed on an earthen roof hovering over her.

The laughter grew.

Máire closed her ears to the annoying distraction, collected a ball of fire, and threw it towards her target.

The roof moved downwards, protecting Seosaimhín from the onslaught of flames.

Máire own rage at this grew. She began an onslaught of water at the structure. She heard a crack and continued lobbing fire and water at Seosaimhín. Soon, the edifice collapsed. At that moment, she felt a strange tingling at her feet and dodged out of the way of a growing stalagmite. Another sprouted from the ground, and she took to the air.

A series of large boulders flew towards her, but she sent forth another vortex, which pushed aside the huge stones and continued towards Seosaimhín.

The other Deargh Du tried to escape the vortex, but it engulfed her.

Máire noticed the boulders ceased hurtling towards her and took a few moments to decide how to destroy Seosaimhín.

Julien rushed over to Edward, smelling burned flesh. He stopped at Edward's head and witnessed that Edward's legs were missing, as well as his right arm. Shards of clay covered him, and Julien almost didn't recognize him. He kneeled down. "Edward?" He observed an almost imperceptible nod. "Don't try to talk, Edward. I will heal you as much as I can." He placed an arm on Edward's left shoulder.

Edward attempted another nod.

"Stay still," Julien ordered. He closed his eyes.

"How is he?"

Julien opened his eyes and noticed Lucius lying on top of Edward. He didn't want to say the truth about his condition.

"There is nothing that can't be healed," he said to the cat.

The fairy cat leaned in and sniffed Edward's chin. "What did this?"

"Shhhh, I need silence to do this." Julien closed his eyes again. After a few moments of healing, he looked at Edward and noticed his friend appeared to be more at peace. The wounds no longer bled. Julien pulled up his tunic and cut his wrist with Edward's knife.

The Ekimmu Cruitne grabbed the offered wrist with his left arm.

After a few moments of feeding, Julien pulled his arm back. "Sorry, Edward, but I do require some for myself."

"May I speak now?" Lucius asked with a huff. He waved his tail as if irritated with Julien.

"Yes, I'm sorry for interrupting you," Julien answered.

"Who's here?" Edward touched Lucius with his remaining hand. "Oh, it's Marcus' favorite. Hello, Lucius."

Lucius nuzzled Edward.

"What was it that exploded, Julien? I have never seen a mortal wield fire in such a way before." Lucius closed his eyes and purred for a moment.

"Edward makes clay pots with different elements, Lucius. They explode on contact."

Lucius rubbed Edward with his nose again. "Interesting," the cat purred.

"Someone is coming," Edward whispered. "I can't tell who because of the smells."

Julien drew his sword and whirled around. He prepared to attack whatever drew near.

"It's me." Mandubratius held up his hands.

"Sorry," Julien said as he pulled back. "We could not tell if you were friend or foe. The smell of the burned flesh and Edward's clay pots are overpowering."

"It is most fortunate for you that the Strigoi swarm lies further west. Horatio, Amata, and Irene lead the attack against them. I believe Reginald is with them. I think I even saw Talia join them."

"Máire? Where's Máire?" Edward whispered.

Julien realized he forgot about her and the mirror after smelling Edward.

"Would you look after Edward?" he said to Mandubratius.

A wavering maelstrom of energy thrummed through the skies and distracted Julien. He noticed Máire and Seosaimhín's battle in the west.

"I'm not sure if you'd be much help to Máire now," Mandubratius replied.

"I could slip in behind Seosaimhín," Julien replied.

"You may be harmed by the energies those two wield," Lucius warned.

"That's a risk I will take," Julien answered.

"Perhaps a distraction will assist you," Mandubratius stated. He scratched his chin.

"Perhaps," Julien murmured. "Edward, did all of your firepots explode?"

"Mmmmm," Edward muttered. "Roll me onto my left side, Julien."

Julien crouched again.

Lucius leapt off Edward as Julien gently rolled the other blood-drinker onto his side.

"Do you see any?" Edward asked.

"I see three pots," Julien answered. He pulled them out of Edward's belt and put them aside. He lowered Edward onto his back and noticed the stubs appeared to have new flesh.

"If you're going to do this, youngling, do it now," Mandubratius suggested.

"Those three will only distract her," Edward reminded Julien. "She seemed… impervious to fire. I don't know how to explain it. I don't think they'll do more than annoy Seosaimhín."

"I understand," Julien acknowledged before flying away.

The explosions and screams of his worried generals further increased Leo's fears. The battle seemed hopeless. He considered praying again, but he decided he had little rational thought left to pray. Then he overheard a report from Fianait to Charles.

"I'm not sure if we can hold this position much longer, Imperial Majesty."

"Do you suggest we leave, Fianait?" Leo said, interrupting them.

"I think if we tried to flee, they'd follow us and run us down, Holy Pope," the blonde warrior replied, meeting his eyes. She returned her steady gaze to

Charles. "What I suggest is that we move the rest of the way up the hill. The Strigoi are poor climbers."

"The summit seems a small place for us," the Emperor replied.

"I don't wish to be morbid, Imperial Majesty, but look around. How many do you see standing to guard you and the Pope?"

"I'm ready to fight if that is a challenge to join the others." Charles' eyes gleamed with pleasure at the promise of fighting.

"Imperial Majesty, we need you and your mortal associates to survive," Fianait replied. "Look." She turned and faced the battlefront.

"Shadow obscures my view," the Emperor admitted. "I will take your word that many are incapacitated."

"Very few of my kind and the Celtic lines remain aloft. The Lamia are gone, and I cannot smell them. Almost a thousand have fallen."

"Is it futile to change our position?" Leo asked Fianait. "Perhaps I should return to prayer."

"Leo, you can pray all you want, but you will do so from the top of the hill," Charles stated.

"Everyone who can hear my voice," Charles shouted. "Move to the top of the hill." He turned to his staff. "Repeat the orders."

The cacophony of men shouting orders echoed around them. Explosions in the distance made the hill shake again.

Fianait stared into the west.

"Imperial Majesty, perhaps we should dismiss our escort, so she may join her family," Leo said.

Fianait shook her head. Her golden plaits swung. "Forgive me, Holy Pope, but my place is here to give you, the Emperor, and his staff protection. Marcus charged me with that duty, and I will not leave." She turned to the gathering soldiers. "Let's move." She motioned them to begin marching and took a position behind him.

The hilltop came into view, in the middle of their barricades, littered with collapsed tents, gear, and the wounded who could be pulled from the battlefield.

Perhaps that will be a better place to pray.

chapter fourteen

arcus wiped at blood on his forehead as he looked at the bodies littering the field. He sensed a new threat from behind approaching, several threats, in fact. He leapt into the air on instinct and drew his blade to attack the first intruder.

Something deflected his attack, and Marcus fell on his back. He could sense Morrigan leave his body. He felt a soft kiss caress his brow. He could almost feel Her tongue lick at his forehead as She faded away. Then a caw echoed in his mind. The entire sensation left him a little confused.

"General Marcus, it's Horatio," a voice said.

The smell seemed familiar. He remembered there were Lamia here, and one of them was named Horatio. He studied the young man for a moment. "I'm sorry, Horatio. I didn't realize it was you. I…" He tried to reason an explanation that made sense.

"What happened here?" Horatio uttered, looking around at the battlefield. "Did you do all this? No wonder you attacked us…" Horatio trailed off. "We're here now, General, to help you in defending the west."

Marcus sat up, staring at the scattered, dead Strigoi. "It would seem that is not necessary right now, Horatio." He stood up. "It appears that the Strigoi are circling to the north at the bottom of the hill."

"Then, that is where we must go," Horatio replied. He whistled, and the rest of the troops who were with him rejoined him.

Marcus noticed Lamia interspersed with mortal soldiers. Then he turned, noticing the battle between Máire and Seosaimhín. "Máire," he murmured. He looked back at the young soldier. "I need to go assist her."

Horatio nodded his head. "Then, we'll meet again at our victory feast, General, and I will out-drink you."

Marcus looked down at his boots for a moment. "That is what Claudius would say," Marcus informed Horatio. "Well done. We will drink to your promotion, Lieutenant." He patted Horatio's shoulder before flying towards the battle in the sky.

Fianait turned to stare down the hill as the Strigoi advanced towards the fortified top. She unsheathed her blade and headed towards the remaining soldiers. "Remain here. Defend your Emperor and Pope. I will return."

The Pope and Emperor continued up the hill, dodging mud and treacherous slopes.

Fianait thought over what Marcus would do in this situation. Her brain yielded little to answer that question, and she turned back towards the mortal soldiers awaiting her orders. But first, she needed words with the emperor. She flew towards the top of the hill and landed next to him. "The Strigoi approach us from the west. Our only path leads us east, Imperial Majesty. My apologies for bringing you here."

"God help us," she heard the Pope mumble.

The Emperor turned and studied the east for a moment, with its steeper slope. "We bought ourselves some time, Fianait. Thank you."

She nodded. "I will go lead the rest of your staff and soldiers in defense of the summit." Fianait trudged down the hilltop and joined the mortal warriors.

The Strigoi continued to plod towards them.

"Hold your position!" she ordered, drawing her sword.

The Strigoi line broke into an uneven run.

She prepared herself for the madness.

Within ten yards of reaching her and the rest of the soldiers, the Strigoi stopped, all in unison. They seemed little more than flesh-bound statues.

"What are they waiting for?" a young soldier to her right asked.

She heard a strange and wordless chant begin. A tickle in her head revealed that the Strigoi probed her mind.

"Charge them!" she shouted. She hoped reinforcements would arrive soon. Fianait leapt into the sky, bringing down her sword in a wide arc. She sliced through one of the Strigoi. She heard the other soldiers engaging their attackers in earnest. She hoped the mirror would arrive soon.

Fianait sliced off the legs of several Strigoi before the tickling returned. It grew difficult to swing her sword. Her head raged at the intrusion, and she wailed in pain. Fianait closed her eyes, and her grip on the sword began to slip. She stumbled and fell to her knees. Suddenly the sensation disappeared. No pain or tickling remained in her head. No nightmares of battlefields and murdering friends came to haunt her. Fianait opened her eyes and rose to her feet. She looked around at the fallen Strigoi, who appeared insensate.

A few of her soldiers scrambled to their feet.

The Emperor, the Pope, and their guard ambled towards her. They appeared to share the same shock that she knew could be seen on her face.

She sensed other blood-drinkers arrive and whirled around, sword in hand, but she found herself facing Father Xofer and many of the altered Strigoi. They all stared at her and she felt a little nervous. "Father Xofer, did you do this?"

"We incapacitated the Strigoi." The words seemed to come from all the changed at once.

"All of you?" Fianait verified.

"We watched the Druids and found gifts within ourselves." They answered in unison again.

"But... how..."

The changed Strigoi seemed to look inward all at the same time.

Fianait found it somewhat unsettling.

"We are needed elsewhere," Father Xofer informed her. They turned and began to run towards the southwest. As Fianait watched them leave, she found she could not understand their actions. She gently kicked a fallen Strigoi, whose eyes remained still and glassy. She then whistled to one of the emperor's staff. "Tell the Emperor I'm going to the southwest," she informed him. She waved to the Emperor and took to the skies, following the pack of changed Strigoi.

"Young one weakens and grows tired!" Seosaimhín shouted to Maél Muire as they landed. She lobbed another boulder at the other woman. "Little Maél Muire wishes to sleep. We will not sleep!" Sensing a huge reserve of energy ebbing through the Otherworld, she felt she only controlled a miniscule fraction.

Maél Muire threw another ball of lightning in her direction.

Seosaimhín pushed an iron stalagmite through the ground in the path of the lightning. The lightning passed into the iron and then the earth with a gentle crack.

Maél Muire stood in the distance, panting. She looked overwhelmed by her exhaustion.

"Too tired to channel more, my sweet?" Seosaimhín shouted in the wind.

Controlling earthen metals gives us so much glee!

Maél Muire straightened herself.

"What's this?" Seosaimhín smiled. "Young Soulless One pulls out more energy."

A white, blazing, heated sphere appeared in front of Maél Muire and blinded Seosaimhín for a moment. As the huge ball of lightning careened towards her, she created another small wall of metal from the earth a few inches from her feet.

Seosaimhín beamed as the blistering orb hit her wall, turning the metal gold and bright blue in spots. A loud boom echoed in her ears, and the metal grew hot. Seosaimhín looked behind her and the earth appeared scorched. After exiting the safety of her wall, she could see Maél Muire on one knee in the dirt. Seosaimhín laughed again and shook her head. "The young one needs to surrender."

"The young one will never do that," she heard Maél Muire shout in reply.

Seosaimhín gasped as a bolt of lightning struck Maél Muire, but she did not fall or burn to ash. Instead, the youngling Deargh Du appeared to be absorbing the energy. Her red hair stood out in all directions as Maél Muire's face glowed with a newfound light. She stood and continued absorbing more power from the Otherworld and the deities.

Seosaimhín looked back at her wall, thinking that if she didn't do something, she would become scattered ash on the winds. While staring at the wall, she imagined the presence of that metal invading her body. Seosaimhín closed her eyes and allowed a spike of that same metal to pierce the earth under her feet.

It moved through her with the sting of a knife.

She heard herself wail in pain for a moment before she could take control of the agony. The aching pressure became joyful pleasure as the metal infused her body. A small prick of pain swam through her back, but the negligible pain seemed more of an annoyance than anything else.

Two more explosions occurred in rapid succession. Her irritation at this interruption multiplied. Seosaimhín turned and looked at the source of the explosions. She sniffed the air, sensing the cause. It was not the Soulless One of Rome, but another that smelled a lot like Maél Muire.

Seosaimhín stared at the stranger with large eyes the color of the sea. He looked German or Frankish, perhaps, and appeared to be shorter than the Soulless One of Rome. However, he still exuded that exasperatingly sweet glamoury. She considered killing him outright for a moment, but decided it would be fun to watch him and Maél Muire squirm.

Maél Muire still appeared to be absorbing energy from the Otherworld.

Seosaimhín stared back at the whelp that now approached her.

Oh, he wishes to play the distraction!

She decided to allow him the privilege of watching his mother-in-darkness succumb to a most painful death. Seosaimhín paused in the final agonizing steps of imbibing metal to send an elongated orb of gold out of the earth and into his stomach.

His sweet yelp of distress pleased her. The child tried to back off the spike, but Seosaimhín watched with gleeful satisfaction as she barbed the gold on the end, preventing him from removing it. His distress turned to a wail of pain. "That must be very painful, my sweet!" she called out to the stranger.

He stared up at her and struggled again.

"Don't leave just yet," she said to him.

"Let us finish this," Maél Muire shouted at her.

Seosaimhín turned and examined the fully-radiant Deargh Du that walked towards her, resplendent with blue energy. "Of course!" Seosaimhín smiled and began to walk towards her. "Do not worry, young one. I'll allow your whelp to live long enough to see you die."

The other blood-drinker said nothing but revealed that grating smile that divulged she believed otherwise.

Seosaimhín grabbed Maél Muire, and the youngling's smile faded into neutrality, her stare resolute. The thrum of energy wearied Seosaimhín, so she increased her effort to maintain her own energy.

Lightning pulsed about them, and her pain level increased, making it difficult to concentrate on defeating Maél Muire. Her mind flexed between clarity and confusion on how to end this stalemate. She vaguely remembered how the iron stalagmite seemed to channel the lightning into the ground. Seosaimhín pointed her foot at the ground and willed iron to move from her toes into the soil. She grimaced at the pain, but she found a large store of pleasure at this latest feat.

She grinned at Maél Muire. "It is time for you to die," Seosaimhín hissed. She thrust iron rods into the Deargh Du's flesh.

The other woman's eyes widened in a momentary lapse of pain, and energy flowed from Maél Muire into the ground.

Tremendous pain arced through Seosaimhín. However, the pleasure from seeing surprise and then panic in her enemy's eyes made any pain worthwhile.

Maél Muire's energy is diminished with each pulse! The Soulless One's eyes are rolling back into her head! We have won! Only one thing remains...

She pulled the iron back into her body and stared at Maél Muire in bliss. Seosaimhín looked down at her hand, wondering how it would feel to have a sword attached to her arm. One formed during her consideration. Shiny, sharp, and keen for blood. As she kneeled at Maél Muire's side, she heard the Frankish twat blathering in the distance. "Soon enough," she purred and then pushed the distraction aside. Seosaimhín examined Maél Muire and discovered that all the grace of the Deargh Du had faded, and she looked very much like a mortal, or perhaps even a child.

Maél Muire's head lolled forward.

A strange moment of longing tugged at Seosaimhín's heart. The daughter she always had hoped for, a daughter-in-darkness that she could have raised and taught. "And treasured," she whispered. "Go to sleep, daughter that should have been mine." Seosaimhín raised Maél Muire's chin and kissed her forehead. She raised the sword to strike, but then everything turned black.

Reginald slashed through another of the Strigoi's arms and sides, incapacitating it, and heard a scream of pain in the distance. The scream became shouting and babbling. The shouting and babbling he recognized. "Julien?" Reginald turned away from the Strigoi and the battle and ran off up the hill to the east, deciding that the rest of the Lamia could wait. He could see lightning bolts striking a strange metal object, but Reginald gave that no more thought. He reached his brother and stared at the strange golden skewer piercing Julien's stomach and back.

"Julien?" He touched his brother's shoulders and watched Julien's eyes open. Julien's face turned a sickly, pale gray, and his lips opened for a moment as if trying to say something. Reginald heard nothing but decided to slice through the gold.

Julien collapsed to the ground and shivered, but the spike remained embedded in his back.

"Deargh Du react badly to gold," Reginald murmured, remembering the others speaking about it. "Forgive me, little brother." He placed a boot on Julien's back for leverage and yanked out the spike, tossing it aside.

Julien uttered a soft cry.

"I'm so sorry," Reginald whispered as he kneeled next to him. Reginald rolled Julien onto his side. He ripped the sleeve of his tunic before biting his wrist. Reginald brought up Julien's head and began to feed him.

Julien met his eyes and then pulled away from his wrist. His eyes darted towards the metal and lightning.

Reginald looked in that direction and saw the lightning stop, and then a hazy figure appeared. He pulled back his arm and stared at Julien again.

"Máire," he heard Julien squeak.

Reginald looked back over at Máire. Her eyes had rolled up, and she slumped forward. A triumphant Strigoi stood over her, at least, he assumed it to be a Strigoi. Or perhaps it was their infamous leader, Seosaimhín.

A blade gleamed in the darkness above Máire's head, and Reginald almost turned away. He prepared himself to carry Julien, but then he watched, stunned, as the strange and cruel figure fell away, leaving Máire to collapse.

A throat cleared behind him. Reginald cursed himself for not realizing someone watched him. He turned and met Father Xofer's eyes. Behind him stood a large group of the transformed Strigoi, clasping hands with each other.

Father Xofer moved in closer and touched Julien's arm. "You will recover, Inspector General," the priest intoned.

Julien nodded and closed his eyes.

"Where have you all been?" Reginald demanded.

"Forgive us," the gray-bearded priest replied. "We were working on the attack along the northern approaches. We came to aid and assist, but we witnessed the Strigoi attack the Emperor and Pope. After disabling the Strigoi at the peak of the hill, we saw Máire fight that strange Deargh Du."

Reginald looked again at the Strigoi and then back to the Changed.

"Are you doing all this?" He motioned to the insensate Strigoi.

"Yes. We learned to combine our powers and fight our family," Father Xofer answered.

Reginald stared at Seosaimhín's body again. "Is she dead?"

"No, she is not," the priest replied. He closed his eyes and became silent. After a few moments of this silence, Father Xofer opened his eyes. "Her mind is trapped... for now."

Reginald stood. "I'll take her head." He turned away from the transformed Strigoi and crouched his body to sprint away, but a hand grasped his arm with an almost unbearable strength.

"I don't think you can," Father Xofer said. "Do nothing to her. It's not for us to do." The priest's eyes and voice filled him with the strangest of fears.

He heard Julien mutter something, then he witnessed one of the redeemed Strigoi collapse. "What happened?" he whispered.

"If you wish to save your brother, get him out of here, now." Father Xofer released him.

Another of the Changed fell, but Father Xofer took his place.

Tossing Julien over a shoulder, Reginald ran for the summit of the hill.

After finding a safe place for Julien, I will go back for Máire.

Mandubratius stared at the figures in the distance and saw Reginald pick up his brother, leaving Máire, the changed Strigoi, and Seosaimhín. He heard footsteps and found Horatio staring at him.

Edward remained on the ground with Lucius lying on his stomach.

"Edward's well enough to move now," Lucius informed him. "Tell that young man to take him to safety."

"Horatio," Mandubratius called out upon finding his tongue. He decided first to ask about his family. "How are Amata and Irene?"

"They fought bravely, even Talia fought well," Horatio answered. "I went to see the general. He seems somewhat out of sorts."

Mandubratius nodded. "I am certain that it is an effect of being around the Strigoi. Horatio, take Edward and retreat to the hill."

After Lucius hopped off, Horatio picked up Edward, who uttered a soft moan. "Aren't you coming?" Horatio asked.

"Your place is there with Máire and Marcus," Lucius told Mandubratius. His voice now sounded human, and not so catlike.

"My place is there with Máire and Marcus," Mandubratius repeated. He stared at Lucius, wondering if the fairy cat manipulated him. Though, he couldn't deny the worry that his prediction would come true, that they would all die together and travel on the ship for the Otherworld.

"Are you insane?" Horatio stared at him and appeared much confused.

He heard a soft chuckle from Lucius. "That may not be far from the truth, Awvarwy," the cat commented.

Mandubratius smirked. "Probably, but I am needed. At least, I believe I am." He stared at the red-hued, fire-lit skies.

"Go then," Lucius said. "Seosaimhín has been subdued. Or, at least, my eyes tell me that."

Mandubratius concurred. "Please tell Amata that Edward needs her," he told Horatio before turning away.

"We must make haste," the fairy cat said as he jumped into the air and flew towards Máire and Seosaimhín.

As he raced after the cat on the ground, Mandubratius witnessed Marcus land a few feet away from Seosaimhín. He decided Marcus meant to take her head. Mandubratius reached Máire's side and crouched down next to her. He saw that her eyes were open, but they rolled to the back of her head.

When Mandubratius touched her, she felt as limp as a corpse, but there appeared to be no visible wounds. "Máire, wake up. Seosaimhín is down." He looked up at Marcus, who continued to stare at Seosaimhín, and then over to the changed Strigoi, who held hands in a circle. Mandubratius returned his attention to Máire and took her hand. "Please wake up, Maél Muire," he bade.

Mandubratius looked over at Marcus again. Rage grew within, as the fool just stood there with his back towards them. He stared now, not at Seosaimhín, but at something Mandubratius couldn't see. "Marcus, wake up! Either kill Seosaimhín or heal Máire!" Mandubratius shouted. "Do something, you Roman bastard!"

He let his fangs extend, and bit into his wrist, preparing to feed Máire. Looking up, he saw a pair of glowing green eyes on the opposite side of Marcus. Lucius stared at the Deargh Du, and neither appeared to move at all. He could hear unintelligible whispers between the two of them. He rubbed Máire's throat, hoping some of his blood would be able to revive her.

Mandubratius decided to take Máire to the camp. One of the other Celtic blood-drinkers would heal her. He slid his arms under her and heard a moan. He looked down to see if she woke up, but her face remained slack. Mandubratius heard another moan. He looked over at Marcus and Seosaimhín. This time, he could see Seosaimhín stir ever so slightly on the ground.

Marcus heard something about healing Máire, but it seemed to be rather odd that he did not heal her earlier. He soon realized he could not move at all. Even his mouth remained closed, despite his will to say something. He began to panic.

Did a Strigoi find me? Could it be the one that originally gave me the nightmares about the Helvetians and poor Lucilla?

"Do not trouble yourself with such inconsequential trivialities, General. Cease your struggles," a resonating voice informed him.

Marcus witnessed green glowing orbs in front of him.

"Yes, it's me, your new lieutenant. Remember?" Lucius queried. "And it resonates in here because there is nothing in here." A gentle chuckle echoed in Marcus' head as the trickster continued. "No, that was most rude of me. I consider you quite smart for a mere Deargh Du."

Have you done this to me, Lucius? Marcus queried in his head.

"Of course I did!" Lucius answered.

Why?

The fairy cat's mouth widened into a strange, almost human-like smile. "There are many answers, Marcus," Lucius began, "I'll start with the simpler ones." The smile faded away. "Awvarwy is tending to Máire, so she's no longer in immediate danger."

Marcus could smell Mandubratius now.

"Ah, you sense him, excellent," Lucius added. "Now, I'll allow you to talk, but we must speak quietly."

Marcus felt the ability to move his lips again.

"If Máire is no longer in danger, allow me to kill Seosaimhín," he requested in a whisper.

"Marcus, sometimes I don't know why I bother. The answer seems so obvious to me!" Lucius looked up at the sky. "You can't kill Seosaimhín, because Seosaimhín is your balance!"

"My balance?"

"I am quite surprised that your mother didn't tell you about your sister. I must tell Morrigan that once again she's left me to deliver good tidings."

"Shut up and tell me about this," Marcus hissed.

Lucius' eyes widened, and he laughed a most un-catlike laugh. "Seosaimhín is your sister-in-darkness! If you kill her, you'll die soon after. That's the balance, remember?"

Marcus felt utter revulsion at the revelation.

How could Seosaimhín and I share common blood?

Lucius stopped chortling. The levity disappeared from the fairy cat's eyes. "I must apologize for my outburst. I know this is difficult for you."

"Sister or not, balance or not, she must be stopped."

"But Seosaimhín has been stopped, at least for now, but not by you or Máire. Though, I must admit she gave her all," Lucius answered.

His confusion grew through the silence.

"The transformed Strigoi are attacking her mind. You have a window of time in which you can act," the fairy cat informed him.

"What?"

The cat's features turned irritated, and his voice belied impatience. "What are your concerns, young one? Saving Máire, killing Seosaimhín, and stopping the Strigoi, yes?" The cat sighed. "I said scant moments ago that Máire is safe and Seosaimhín is temporarily incapacitated." Lucius waved his tail, revealing his annoyance. "You must stop the Strigoi, Marcus."

"I have been trying to stop the Strigoi, Lucius. Morrigan Herself took me over to aid in this battle!" His words still remained at a whisper.

"Don't you see what She did? She's trying to encourage you to embrace what you are!"

Marcus could think of nothing to say at that.

"Marcus, don't you see? This is what Morrigan wanted you to accept. You are a God. Act like one!"

"But… that's impossible and a lie! I'm Deargh Du."

"Look, I don't know how Gods and Goddesses procreate. Whether They fornicate in the clouds or simply will Their children into existence. I know not the answer to that fascinating question, but I digress. Suffice it to say, you are a God and your Ma is disappointed that you haven't come into your own. That's why I'm helping you achieve your potential. Then, you will no longer be tied to the balance and Seosaimhín, because you will be beyond those trivialities." The cat's face turned benevolent. "Believe in what you are, Marcus."

"But… I'm afraid," Marcus admitted. He would consider this another one of Lucius' jokes, but the fairy cat seemed so serious.

"Gods do not know fear! They act. Now, it's time for you to act."

"What must I do?" Marcus whispered.

"First, show some enthusiasm," Lucius purred. "You're a god after all, not a whiny mortal. Listen closely, Young God, this is what you must do."

Awareness came to Seosaimhín like the touch of a feather on her nose. It tickled her. Her hearing and sense of smell awoke, nearly overwhelming her mind with sharp intensity. Soon, the force of these sensations faded. Her dry throat itched for moisture, but she lacked the strength to close her mouth. She tried to open her eyes, and when she did, stars beamed above and dirt lay beneath. She allowed her eyes to close in exhaustion.

Those who conspired against her remained in her head. She could sense others nearby. The child disappeared, however the scent of Lamia drifted with the wind. She sensed her prey, Maél Muire, nearby, who smelled of near death. Then she discerned the Soulless One of Rome in close proximity, but something unknown also lingered.

My Strigoi… where are they? Ah, there they are. Scattered, but still attacking.

Seosaimhín took in a deep breath, drawing in a variety of aromas. Upon exhaling, she heard herself moan. As she inhaled again, more strength returned, but not enough to rise yet. Seosaimhín opened her eyes again, but the presence in her head still rallied against her.

We will defeat it. Soon, our strength will come, and we will shatter their control. Then I will shatter their bodies!

Yet before that beautiful realization, she needed to regain her strength.

Mandubratius looked away from Seosaimhín, deciding it was time to leave, although Lucius and Marcus were still oblivious to everything. Mandubratius hefted Máire over his shoulder. She seemed light, and part of him wondered if a good strong wind would pull her out of his grasp. He could see the remaining Strigoi meandering about the foot of the hill.

They seem to be slowed. Perhaps Seosaimhín's leadership motivates them into attacking.

After searching the route to up the hill, he finally found a path clear of Strigoi beneath the ridge to the south and up the southern slop. He took a few strides up along his chosen path, when a low vibration pulsed through the air. It grew louder. Mandubratius stopped. He could see the Strigoi stop and sniff the air like rodents sensing a predator. He turned towards the sound.

Marcus rose into the air. Energy, smoke, and luminescence swirled about him, but this was not the typical glamoury of the Deargh Du. The energy and sound pulsed.

Before he knew it, he moved in closer to see whatever trick Marcus planned.

Wisps of smoldering smoke started to coalesce over Marcus' head. Stars began to disappear from the sky.

"What a strange illusion," Mandubratius whispered, entranced by this show. Now he stood, having returned to the place he had found Máire. He laid her down and crouched next to her. He noticed that she blinked and, opening her eyes fully, she uttered a soft, strange noise.

"Máire?"

He watched her stare up into the sky. She moved her lips, but he heard no sound from her.

"You're safe for the moment," he told her, pushing a plait of hair away from her eyes. "I had to see this. You should see it as well. It's quite remarkable, and I have seen many marvels, but not this. I felt drawn back here. I cannot explain it." He scooted around her and lifted her head up to rest it against his legs. Mandubratius pointed up at Marcus. "What is he doing, Máire?"

Her lips moved again. "M… m… mirror."

Maniacal laughter interrupted them, and he realized that he had forgotten about Seosaimhín during this impressive show. The crazed blood-drinker rolled onto her hands and knees, struggling to get to her feet.

Awareness of the changed Strigoi came into his mind. He noticed that only three remained in the circle, holding hands. Their faces revealed tight masks of intense concentration.

"Imperial Majesty, the Strigoi have ceased their attack."

The Emperor stepped closer to the northern edge of the summit.

"They appear to be meandering aimlessly," the Pope commented, joining them. "What happened?"

"I don't care," Charles murmured. He turned back to his staff. "Tell the men to fortify their position on the hilltop. Reinforce the the defenses." After issuing his orders, Charles watched Fianait approach closer.

"Sir, I mean Imperial Maj   "

"Confound it, Fianait, forget the formalities for now. What do your eyes see?"

"Friends are returning, sir. I see Reginald de Divio carrying your son, and I see Horatio carrying something."

"Carrying? How is my son, Fianait?" Charles demanded.

"He will live, Imperial Majesty."

Charles pushed aside his fears. "And the general and Máire?"

"Máire has fallen, but I see someone tending to her," Fianait replied. "Marcus is…"

He turned away from Fianait, hearing loud footsteps. He witnessed Reginald and Julien's arrival, with Horatio carrying what first appeared to be a torso. Then he realized with growing horror that the torso possessed an arm and head. "Edward?" he whispered upon recognizing the mangled body. He turned back to his son as Reginald lowered Julien.

Julien uttered a cry as his brother placed him on the dirt. He seemed worse off than Edward, even though he could only see one wound on him. Yet, his son appeared to be turning gray.

"Edward has only one arm and appears to be in better health than Julien," Charles said. "What happened?"

Fianait landed and crouched next to Julien. "I've seen this before. It is gold poisoning. Gold is an anathema to the Deargh Du," she explained. "Bring

Edward in closer, Horatio, so I can try to heal them both."

Horatio followed the orders, and the blonde warrior placed her hands on both Edward and Julien.

She closed her eyes.

Charles took a step closer, trying not to gape in awe as his son regained color and Edward's leg and arm grew buds.

"I will be walking in no time," Edward commented with a weak chuckle.

Fianait pulled away. "I must feed." She paused. "We must all feed, especially your son, Imperial Majesty."

Charles crouched next to Julien. He considered ordering the others to feed them. Instead, he witnessed the Pope get up from his prayers and roll up his sleeve. The Holy Father extended an arm towards Fianait.

Charles pulled out a small knife from his pack and cut a shallow wound at his wrist. He lowered his hand towards Julien.

His son latched onto his hand with a feral sound.

Charles felt momentary fear lapsed into a strange blend of pleasure and giddiness. He studied Julien during the feeding, watching his son flush. As he pulled back his hand, a strange thrumming resonated through the air. "What is that noise?" he asked.

chapter fifteen

"This is an excellent beginning," Lucius purred. "Brigid Herself would be impressed with this, and manipulation of water is one of Her many talents. Now, think over how there is moisture in the air. You can temper this moisture and turn it into an icy dome, covering all of us, Marcus. This dome must encompass the entire hill and the surrounding valleys and ridges. Just remember that it must be strong enough to support its own weight."

Marcus frowned in concentration as the fairy cat continued speaking. "This undertaking is not easy," he hissed.

"I apologize. I forget how hard this might be the first time. Do not forget, I am here to help you, Marcus."

The dome grew larger in his mind's eye, past the outlying parts of the hill and its western ridge. Soon, however, he sensed a shortage of water in the air, and the need for more water became tantamount. Marcus called forth water from the river sources to the northwest and southwest to aid in the creation of the dome.

This seems so much easier than the work of the Druids. Perhaps this meant that I am indeed a God.

Marcus ceased that distracting thought and returned to forming the dome.

"Do not worry about the interior texture," Lucius informed him. "When it's time, you will imbue it with the properties of the mirror."

Marcus nodded his head but couldn't remember if he made the movement at all. Awareness of his own body faded as the energy he wielded overtook all his senses. He pushed his doubts away.

Doubting myself will lead to failure.

Again, this process had seemed such a struggle for Máire, yet for him, it was so simple and instinctual.

All thanks to Lucius.

"You are most welcome," Lucius murmured.

Marcus found himself beaming with joy at his mastery of this task. He could feel the dome nearing completion.

The pain faded into a dull ache, and Julien finally found the strength to look around. His wound appeared to be healing. "Excuse me," he called out, but no one spoke a word. He gave up on waiting and slammed a fist against a nearby foot.

His father looked down at him and then returned his awestruck face to the sky as if entranced.

"Am I missing something?" Julien shouted, surprised he mustered enough strength for that.

"An angel has arrived," Pope Leo replied.

"Here, little brother," Reginald whispered, while propping him up.

Julien glanced up and stood in awe, staring at the shimmering dome that almost obscured the entire sky. He fell silent and continued to stare up at the dome. After a few moments of heartfelt wonder, he started to look for familiar faces. He could see Fianait propping up Edward, but no one else from his family appeared to be around. "Where's Máire?" he asked Reginald.

"She..." Reginald paused. "She's not dead. I picked you up and sensed another blood-drinker arriving. It was not a Strigoi, so I figured they came to rescue her."

"And Seosaimhín?"

"Father Xofer and the Changed attacked her... with some sort of mental attack... thing." Reginald continued to stare into the sky. "My God, that is the most beautiful thing I've ever..." Reginald stopped talking again.

"Why is Marcus in the sky?" Julien asked.

"I don't know," Edward muttered. "However, I smell the Strigoi gathering again, as well as many other blood-drinkers."

A reverberation interrupted their conversation.

Julien looked up, and the dome wobbled as it landed on the ground. The completed structure refracted starlight and dimmed the objects in the heavens, until those lights disappeared. Only the torches and fires remained lit.

The dome settled around the circumference of the hill, or at least he sensed it come to rest, with the edges neatly filling in the valleys and ridges.

Marcus could feel his brow wrinkle.

"Now, you are ready to charge the properties of this mirror," Lucius informed him.

He felt the cat land on his left shoulder and curl around his neck. The fairy cat leaned in next to his ear.

"How?" he asked the fairy cat.

Lucius' whiskers tickled his neck and right ear. "Think of Aphrodite's mirror," the fairy cat whispered.

"I am doing so. I remember looking into it," Marcus said.

"Will it into existence in your mind's eye so that we both may see it," Lucius replied.

Marcus squeezed his eyes shut as he concentrated on the mirror.

"Yes, I can see it now," Lucius stated, "but you don't seem to see it as I do."

"I don't understand," Marcus replied. "What else is there to see?" He could feel the cat purr again and heard a chuckle.

"You're a God. Look for things that the mere mortal or Deargh Du cannot see."

Marcus began to seek those differences and shook his head. An image began to clear, and a strange light radiated from the mirror. The light expanded and shattered the small frame. He could see the Otherworld in the light. Snow-laden mountain peaks overwhelmed the landscape. He could almost feel the bracing air.

"Yes, Marcus. This mirror channeled energy from the Otherworld, though it's a realm I have little familiarity with. Focus on the energy from the realm. This is the energy your dome must release."

Marcus stared past the mountains and into the waves of energy. Clarity bloomed. "You mean—"

"Precisely. You must create a mirrored surface on the dome. Then you must bring forth that energy from the Otherworld."

"I don't understand how the mirror works," Marcus said. "I just see it and its properties."

"You don't have to understand how the mirror works. You just need to will it to do what you wish it to do," Lucius purred in his ear.

Mandubratius saw another of the changed Strigoi fall as Seosaimhín wedged a foot under herself. The mad woman's strained laughter cut through his awe and reminded him that they were in danger.

"Flee," he heard someone whisper. "Flee and hide."

Máire's pleas brought him further out of his reverie.

"We'll leave together," Mandubratius assured Máire. As he picked her up, he stared at the dome, becoming transfixed by its beauty again. Then, a gentle vibration settled over the land, and he stumbled a little. He started to run for the slope. As he ran, he glanced down at Máire, who struggled in his grasp.

"No, let me stay," she whispered. "I can help."

"You're not in any shape to help Marcus," he replied. But then a stone wall pushed its way out of the earth in his path. Mandubratius tried to stop, but he and Máire slammed into the wall. He fell over backwards and witnessed bright stars light up his field of vision.

"One more to go," he heard Seosaimhín promise. "Your load is not light, is it, Awvarwy?"

Someone started shaking him. "Mandubratius, I can take her legs."

"What?" He looked up at Talia and could barely focus.

"I'll take her legs. I had to follow you," she muttered as she picked up Máire's feet. "I lost you in the crowds for some time."

"Why?" he asked Talia. He shook off his bewilderment as he gathered Máire's arms.

"I don't want to leave Marcus! Leave me!" Máire sounded frantic.

Talia met his eyes. "Later," she promised. "The Strigoi revealed too much in my dreams, and I will fight here beside you."

Mandubratius nodded. With his and Talia's grips on Máire secured, they started to carry her away. He didn't pay much attention to where they went, as long as they moved away from Seosaimhín.

Before they could get very far, he heard a loud, agonizing scream in the distance. Such a cry of fear intrigued him, but it also excited him in ways he didn't want to admit. Mandubratius looked up to see the priest fall to the ground, and then his eyes darted to the one who menaced them all.

Seosaimhín's eyes settled on his, and then stone walls began to rise again in all directions.

He heard a strange crack and felt a burning wetness against his right temple. He dropped Máire and fell to the ground, stunned.

Talia dropped Máire's feet. "I'll help him... I must," she whispered. Talia unsheathed her blade and stepped between Mandubratius and her niece.

What am I doing?

She looked at her sponsor, and all became clear.

"Don't take another step," she said to Seosaimhín as the Deargh Du strode towards them triumphantly.

Seosaimhín smiled. "We don't need to step in order to kill you, Talia." Seosaimhín's hand moved, and Talia saw it glimmer in the refracting fires.

How could a hand shine like a blade?

Talia attempted to dodge Seosaimhín's hand, but something hard and cold hit her in the right temple. Lightning shot through her, and the sword fell from her limp hand. She stared up into the sky and beheld the mirror reflecting the glowing fires in the distance. Talia mused on the radiance in the sky, until Seosaimhín blocked her view and smiled at her.

"I must feed. Your blood smells of sweetness and dark deeds. Dark, like mine. Pity." Seosaimhín's visage revealed fangs and glowing green eyes, but she possessed none of the Deargh Du's serene beauty.

The pain in Talia's throat radiated through the rest of her body, and she screamed when the attack began. Visions of torture and fear pounded in her head. She opened her eyes, sensing a strange brightness surround her. A soft noise made Talia turn her face. Mandubratius still appeared to be unconscious. However, she could see Máire staring at her, confusion apparent in the Deargh Du's somber green eyes.

Máire extended a pale hand towards her.

"Aunt Teá?"

Talia smiled at her niece.

Her vision faded to black.

"Very good, the transformation is complete and perfect." Lucius' words echoed in Marcus' mind as whiskers wiggled against his neck.

He forced his mind back to the mirror, instead of the abrasive tickling. "Now it will work?" he asked Lucius.

"Of course not, my pet," the fairy cat replied.

"Why not?" Marcus tried to keep his impatience in check.

"Do you remember how the original mirror worked?"

"I never used it," he answered.

Lucius tsked. "It needs an external light source, but not one created by the Deargh Du, remember?"

"That I remember," Marcus answered, "but the fires Edward started are too small. How do I create a light source?"

"Well, Máire knows how, but she could never master the amount of energy needed. You saw what happened when she called for Lugh's light." He could almost sense the fairy cat purr.

"It nearly incinerated her."

"But, you don't have to worry about that. You're a God," Lucius informed him.

"Yes, I understand now. All I need to do is part the mists and bring forth Lugh's light into myself. I can create enough of a light source to reflect the properties of the mirror to everyone below." Marcus paused. "That would be like sunlight. Wouldn't that kill all the blood-drinkers?"

"Have you been to the Otherworld?"

"Yes, Lucius."

"Have you been on the surface of the Otherworld in the daylight?"

"Yes," Marcus repeated.

"Did you die?"

"No."

"The light of the Otherworld is the light that you will channel. It will harm none, but you must make the light brighter than the sun you remember as a mortal for this plan to work."

"Why is that?" Marcus asked the voice in his head.

"So the light can penetrate the eyelids of the unconscious. Let's hope it will reflect into the eyes of those laying facedown," Lucius replied.

"I understand," Marcus answered. He wished to say more, but he didn't want to further distract himself.

"Excellent," Lucius whispered. "Then, let there be light."

Horatio pointed at a figure hovering in the sky. A misty figure shrouded in radiance. The brilliance spread throughout the sky. "I don't understand what I'm seeing," he muttered.

"It's Marcus," Fianait whispered, as if in awe.

The Emperor squinted at the glaring brightness. "I can see that, Fianait, but what is it that he's doing?"

Leo stared overhead, watching the glow reflect off the sky. He would swear that he could see faces in the radiating light. Such clarity seemed baffling.

Maybe the Deargh Du are more than mere angels or demons. Those labels seem not so much incorrect as just inapplicable.

Then night became day.

Leo heard a collective gasp of fear from the blood-drinkers surrounding him. He fell to his knees in apprehension, adoration, and reverence. He heard Charles collapse and begin to cry out for blessings from God and his saints.

The other mortals nearby fell to their knees in veneration.

"I know what you are," Leo called out to the distant brilliance in the sky. "You are one of the Seraphim, bringing us the pure love and light of God!"

He lowered his face to the ground and prayed for redemption. His eyes were not holy enough for this vision of beauty and fire.

Mandubratius shook his head at the bright light.

Seosaimhín stopped and turned to stare. She became still and silent as an ancient statue.

He heard a loud thud, followed by shouting in the distance.

"The Strigoi have fallen!"

He could hear queries on the wind in many languages about the sunrise in the middle of the night. Mandubratius turned away from the luminous cosmic display when he heard Seosaimhín muttering.

"My army! This cannot be!" She began to move in a manner seemingly like the flapping of a wounded bird. "My army... destroyed!" Her head rolled from side to side. "This light is not natural! Who brought forth this light and mirror! She who wielded the mirror lies here!" The Deargh Du then sniffed the air, before letting out a blood-curdling scream.

Mandubratius covered his ears at the shriek.

"Marcus!" Seosaimhín raged. Her screams continued. The earth beneath her shook, and boiling stone began to ooze out of the ground at her feet.

Steam blurred his vision, but he could see her midnight skin turn a dark red. Yet, Seosaimhín remained intact. With an exaggerated effort, Seosaimhín leapt into the sky.

The steam dissipated, allowing his vision to clear enough to witness her flight. Drops of fiery lava fell to the earth as Seosaimhín flew, scorching the ground when they landed.

"Marcus, please see her," he heard Máire whimper to the skies.

All Marcus felt now was surging power and invincibility. Every moment spent bathing in the light of the Otherworld increased his strength.

I am a God!

That seemed no longer ridiculous or impossible. The cares, worries, and fears of the mortal and Deargh Du personas of Marcus faded into oblivion. Even the Strigoi's nightmares seemed but a silly memory. Marcus looked down and witnessed the Strigoi arise from their ugly forms. Many had been transformed into the Changed. Others appeared to be mortal!

Friends and family stared at him in awe.

His former lieutenant's mouth moved, and he could hear Claudius ask, "Marcus, what are you doing?"

God Marcus could not help but laugh. He scanned the fields and found Mac Alpin, shading his eyes from the light.

Fianait, Edward, and Julien stared at him from the summit of the hill.

He turned his eyes towards the ground and observed Máire and Mandubratius returning his gaze. They both gaped at him in shock.

Máire's lips moved, but he couldn't make out what she said. He did recognize her fear, though.

"Lucius, go comfort Máire." He glanced back at the cat on his shoulder.

Lucius' face turned up in a smile, and the fairy cat leapt off, flying towards the ground.

He noticed Máire's lips quiver again, but this time he heard one word of the warning. 'Seosaimhín'.

A dark red lump, what appeared to be Seosaimhín, came into his view and closed in on him, yet her movements were sluggish.

"Lucius, she's about to attack me. What do I need to do?" He wondered why he uttered that to a distant speck.

The speck turned and faced Marcus. "What would a God do?" he heard the cat's voice in his head.

Marcus did not answer. The time to answer Morrigan's call drew near. He could feel a force begin to build in his right arm. Strength continued to gather as Seosaimhín drew closer. He understood that waiting would be necessary.

Energy, steam, and power surrounded Seosaimhín.

He felt a strange thrill of confusion at her terrible visage.

No matter. No balance remained between them anymore. I am a God. She is just Deargh Du.

Her smoking form continued its advance.

He called forth water from the Otherworld. It appeared with nothing more than his suggestion. The water dispelled the heat of Seosaimhín's arrival.

One foot more.

Her smiling countenance grew frightening to behold. The momentum of her movements surprised him. For a wavering moment, he felt a trickle of fear.

Gods do not know fear.

He stared into her colorless eyes and launched a strike, pushing all of his weight and will into the hit. The energy of the Otherworld joined him.

Her fist shot towards his face.

He decided to not bother with blocking any oncoming blows.

At the moment of impact, he met her gaze, and the ferocity of her smile grew.

His blow met the left side of Seosaimhín's face, and his elation multiplied.

But then her fist collided against his face, and his elation transformed to pain.

Máire felt Lucius tuck himself into her lap and purr. She adjusted herself to see Seosaimhín and Marcus better. She stroked Lucius for comfort as she stared into the sky. She felt Mandubratius shift behind her. He said nothing, and for that, she felt a great deal of relief.

A strange clarity allowed her eyes to fix on Marcus and Seosaimhín. She knew she would never see such precise detail any other time, yet she pushed aside that disheartening realization and concentrated.

She felt her mouth drop as Seosaimhín and Marcus pummeled at each other. The blows seemed to move through skin, blood, and bones.

"No, no, no, no," she murmured at them both, frightened beyond belief. Marcus' head, neck, and chest seemed to cave in. Yet, the same thing appeared to happen to Seosaimhín. They became nothing more than pulp after a few moments of battle with each other. Then a dense cloud of energy began to expand. "No, no, no," she muttered again as ripples played across the mirrored dome. Mists clouded the pulp that remained. She began gasping quickly. "Don't allow this to happen," she petitioned all the Gods and Goddesses in an unsteady and weak voice.

A voice in her mind informed her that both Seosaimhín and Marcus tapped into the energies between the two worlds.

Anything could happen.

The skies weakened and then breached. The pulverized remains of her beloved and Seosaimhín disappeared into the Otherworld.

Even if one of us dies, we will still meet there.

Remembering her earnest words, as if time without him would be easy, she began to sob.

The mirrored dome shattered, and an explosion of light and sound thundered through the skies. Then heavy rain began to fall. A harsh wind hit Máire, and she collapsed backwards against Mandubratius. Darkness swallowed her whole.

Lucius stopped purring and looked up at the tear in the sky. The breach into the Otherworld started to grow larger.

He shut his eyes and willed the rip to mend. Soon he sensed the magic fade away. The world became mundane and normal again, as the rift disappeared into the star-laden sky.

It is done.

He felt a sadness and regret that he tried to ignore. After all, this was all part of the game that he did not start. He blinked back tears. He allowed his voice to travel to the Otherworld, and it found his intended target. "Satisfaction is mine, Phantom Queen," he said, though he felt little satisfaction in his voice.

The sky turned dark again after the dome shattered.

Arwin looked up upon hearing whistling. Not from people, but from above. Starlight reflected from a metal sword. Then he realized its sister fell towards earth as well. Mac Alpin remained still as they landed in the dirt, point first. He knelt in front of the closest one and grabbed it by its warm hilt.

These are Marcus' swords and not some Lamia's cheap gladii.

Arwin stared into the stars and stood up on unsteady feet. His head still ached. He extended his senses and could discern other blood-drinkers running towards him.

But where is Marcus?

"You Roman bastard, this isn't funny! Show yourself!" he raged at Marcus. "This is a very poor joke!"

He could perceive Claudius, Caoimhín, and Sáerlaith racing towards him.

"Damn it all, you smelly, ragged-nailed, half-Gaul piece of cac, get back here now! This is not amusing at all!" He choked back his sobs. He felt hands on his shoulders.

"Arwin, he's gone," Claudius informed him in gentle tones better suited to soothe a fussy child. "Marcus is gone."

Mac Alpin dropped to his knees and began sobbing into his hands. He knew Claudius told the truth, but he wanted to hit him all the same.

He could hear the Emperor and Pope shouting in the distance about setting up what tents survived the attack to shelter the angels, while others called attention to the cave near the summit. Sunrise would come upon them all soon, but he couldn't care less about that now.

Mandubratius grumbled as he awoke. A pulsing pain in his head made him wonder if a Strigoi remained. He placed a hand on his head as he sat up and rubbed at his eyes. He then noticed that a weight rested against his legs, and a strange noise brought him further from the dream world. He stopped rubbing his eyes and blinked a few times.

A keening figure leaned her back against his thigh. Máire rocked back and forth, sobbing into a hand and into Lucius' black fur.

Why does she make such hideous noises?

He then remembered witnessing a battle between Seosaimhín and Marcus. Mandubratius looked up in the sky, but the heavens were now dark, and the combatants were gone.

Has there been an explosion?

He turned his attention to Máire, who continued wailing.

"...so sorry, Marcus. I'm so sorry," she called out in Gaelic. "I didn't stop her," she continued. "I couldn't stop Seosaimhín. I'm too weak and too stupid. This is all my fault! I should have challenged her with you." She continued to cry into Lucius' back.

The fairy cat turned and nuzzled her, saying nothing.

A strange realization came into his head.

Marcus has died. My arch rival is dead!

But instead of elation at that realization, he just felt drained.

Máire returned to her keening.

I wish to say something, but what could I say that would not sound like a patronizing lie?

He scooted in closer and embraced her.

She turned a little and began sobbing into his shoulder. A wet spot grew as she wrapped her free arm around him.

He started rocking her, remembering a strange moment when his mother did the same for him. He tried to remember what she said to him during those times when he was only a child.

Then, Mandubratius noticed Lucius stop rubbing his nose against Máire and stare at him. The cat's features revealed a strange contentment. He could not guess at what other emotions appeared in Lucius' eyes. After what appeared to be an eternity staring, as the cat's eyes became somewhat human for a brief lapse of time, he heard two words in his mind.

For you.

chapter sixteen

Hinterweiler, at the Northwest Foot of Ernstberg

harles walked to the Pope's side, as the sun streamed down upon them. The entire world seemed… refreshed. "Did we not fight a battle here last night, Leo?" he asked his friend. "Did we not scorch the earth upon which we stand?"

Fresh flowers, new saplings, and green grass waved at them as a gentle wind blew through the valleys surrounding Ernstberg.

Sweet smells caught at his nose, and the Emperor smiled.

"Why yes, I believe we did, Charles." Leo chuckled and smiled.

"Nothing was alive, Leo. No plants, no animals. We burned, trampled, or frightened everything away. All that remained last night was soot, blood, and sulfur. But this morning, after the dust of the dead disappeared into the sun's rays, these flowers appeared."

A butterfly landed on the Pope. The man simply smiled at it.

"Where did these wildflowers, saplings, grass, birds, and butterflies come from, Leo?" Charles turned and motioned towards the top of the hill. "Is that not our campsite? Did we not fell all these trees to fortify our defenses and clear a path for fighting? What could change this hill from the wasteland we created to this most beautiful sight?"

The Pope smiled at him. "The love of God, his merciful son, Jesus, and the Holy Spirit did this, Charles. Also, I believe that Marcus is an angel of the highest order. There is no other explanation for what I saw last night. He is of the Seraphim. This is God's will and God's most gracious bounty."

Charles watched the Pope's eyes swell with unshed tears.

"I have never felt such love from God before, Charles. I have lived in the holiest of places and seen the glories within, but it cannot compare with this."

"But they are Deargh Du, Ekimmu Cruitne, Sugnwr Gwaed, and Lamia, not Angels, Leo," argued Charles.

"Perhaps the rest of them are mere blood-drinkers, Charles, but Marcus is something more. I am going to erect a monastery here in his name on this very spot."

Charles experienced a strange sensation.

It matters little that the Holy Father believes Marcus to be something he was not. What matters instead is the memory of the battle, the beauty of this place, and its effects on the people present.

He mused for a moment on the beauty of God's newest creation. Whatever deity brought forth such beauty mattered little. What mattered most was to enjoy it and appreciate it. "I would like to come to the opening of this monastery, Leo," he stated.

"Of course, Charles, I would never dream of not inviting the Emperor of Christendom."

A sudden series of worries nagged at him. "Will anyone believe what happened, Leo? I don't know if I can believe what I remember, and I experienced it."

"Perhaps it is best to leave this event unrecorded, Charles. The masses would not understand this, and it would frighten them. It may be said that I am hiding the truth, but I would rather that my flock be happy and not look for the Strigoi under every rock."

"How do we explain the death and... the demons?" Charles met the Pope's eyes again.

"An illness that caused visions," Leo suggested. "It proved fatal to some. That is a partial truth, at least."

"I think the masses can live with that version of history," Charles replied.

"Indeed." Leo smiled.

The smell of a mortal entering Claudius' tent woke him fully. He rolled onto his side and stared at the Emperor's man. "What do you want?" he grumbled.

The soldier cleared his throat. "General, I have the evening status reports. It seems that some of the former demons are from other regiments. A detail has been established to re-integrate them. Another detachment has formed, committed to leaving with the Greek priest for Orleans." He stopped speaking and stood at attention.

Claudius chuckled and shook his head. "Who are you, and why are you telling me this?" he asked the soldier.

"I'm Dagobert from the Emperor's staff." The soldier appeared somewhat slighted by Claudius' forgetfulness. "I'm General Cassyon's adjunct. I am here to assist the General of the Cothromaigh, and you are him."

"I'm not the general. Marcus is the general."

"Forgive my bluntness, sir. General Marcus perished in the battle last night," Dagobert replied.

"Well... go find someone else. I have no desire to be a general." Claudius rolled onto his back.

"You are the most qualified for the position, according to the Emperor." Dagobert took a few steps closer to Claudius' prone form.

"What about General Gaius?"

"He perished as well."

Claudius closed his eyes, making a face. He wanted to sleep and forget the last night. "And his lieutenant, Sextus?"

"Insufficient experience, sir."

It appeared Dagobert planned on spoiling his plans.

Claudius gave in and sat up. "Mac Alpin? Oh yes." Claudius paused and smirked. "He hates military officials and finds them tedious. He would never want to be one."

"He expressed those very opinions and rewarded me with the flat of his sword for my troubles, sir," Dagobert stated.

"Hmmmm, why not the Legate Patroclus?" Claudius mused.

"He is inexperienced as well." Dagobert began to pace. "Sir, we do have a lot of work to do."

Claudius waved his hand about impatiently. "No, you have someone else to see. What about… Mandubratius." Yes, that ambitious fool would jump at this opportunity.

"Who?"

Claudius sputtered in annoyance. "General Michael Tolomei!"

"He does have the skills and experience, but he's not one of you. The Emperor specified that he would rather deal with you."

Claudius closed his eyes again, trying to ignore his growing impatience. "Ah ha, Julien de Divio, the Inspector General of the Gendarme. Dagobert, go speak with your emperor and suggest Julien de Divio."

Dagobert chuckled. "Julien de Divio suggested that you be granted this appointment."

Claudius grumbled and stood up. "Fine, then… I'll be sure to thank him for this. Tell your emperor that I will be at his tent as soon as I'm dressed and I've fed."

"You may feed from me if you wish, sir."

"Do you wish to reconsider, seeing the mood that I'm in?" Claudius started to look for his boots.

"My offer will stand."

Claudius sighed. "My hunger gets the better of me, Dagobert. I will accept the offer as a matter of convenience." He grabbed Dagobert's arm and bit into the underside, still annoyed with this entire situation. He wished for time to think, not work. The matter of Marcus' will needed to be addressed, and he and the Sugnwr Gwaed needed to consider their plans. He released Dagobert after realizing he took too much.

The soldier swooned for a moment before steadying himself.

"My apologies." Claudius put a hand under Dagobert's arm. "I forget how it feels to be the messenger." He closed his eyes and began to heal him. After a few moments of quiet concentration, Claudius pulled back his hand.

"Sir, I'll take my leave and tell the Emperor that you will join him soon," said Dagobert, who then trudged out of the tent.

While gathering his shaving supplies, Claudius realized his shaving partner had died. He sat down. "You did this deliberately, Marcus, so that I would have to take your place. I will curse you for that." He laughed. "And you also know Mac Alpin is not to be trusted with a razor." He rubbed his eyes and decided it would be best to throw himself into his duties.

Julien exited the Emperor's tent and walked towards the pavilions that served as recuperative facilities. He stopped, upon hearing Father Xofer speak to the changed Strigoi.

"So you see, this is not divine punishment, my children. God wishes you, and all of us, to be his eternal warriors on this earth," Father Xofer said.

Julien leaned against a tree to listen to the priest's words. At least, Father Xofer never put him to sleep.

"I understand, Father, but the feeding seems to be the work of the devil," one of the newly transformed stated.

Father Xofer raised a hand. "But we do not kill, my friends. We even have the opportunity to allow animals to survive our feeding."

Another stood up. "Gracious Father, I remember doing horrible things," the member of the Papal forces stated with a nervous twitch. "I also recall my friends here doing the same."

Father Xofer nodded his head. "Yes, we all have these memories, my son. That is the very nature of the Strigoi, but that was a demon that controlled us. The sacrifice and miracle last night broke the demonic bonds that controlled you, and us all, in the past."

"What does it mean?" another soldier asked. "Does this mean that we will all go to hell?"

Father Xofer smiled. "No, no, no. As before, if we live honest, righteous lives, we go to heaven. If we choose to do evil, then we will need to worry about the consequences."

Many looked relieved with that news.

"But Father," a woman whispered. "I am so conflicted. I... feel that there is more out there than simply the Holy Trinity and the Saints. Will I go to hell for this?"

Julien noticed many nod their heads a little.

"If there is more, all we need to know is that we are beloved by someone greater than us," Father Xofer answered. "We are loved, and they wish us to do kindnesses to others, no matter in whose name we do it. We can discuss this later when we are at our new home in Orleans."

The priest smiled at Julien.

"I thought you all communicated without words," Julien stated.

Father Xofer chuckled. "But, Inspector General, I'm a priest. I like to talk. I do not wish to be silent now, as many of us here feel comfort in speaking to each other. If we fall silent, we may lose our beautiful voices."

Julien watched the others gathered giggle and laugh.

"So, Father, how is it we are now something different? Why are there others who became mortal?"

Father Xofer frowned. "The longer you are Strigoi, the more gifts you receive. We can view this as a blessing. I think that many would see it as a greater opportunity to do good works in our lives. We cannot undo what happened, but we can surely do things now that bring a balance to what we did when we had no control over the impulses that horrible woman set loose in us."

The gathered Strigoi nodded.

Julien stepped back, allowing them to return speaking amongst themselves, but Father Xofer stopped and took Julien's arm.

"You're planning on visiting your mother-in-darkness, Julien. Tell her that we know the sacrifices she and Marcus made for us," Father Xofer said. "We honor them and you for your aid and selfless acts."

Julien shook his head. "I am hardly selfless, Father Xofer," he admitted. "I know we are all flattered by this, but I'm not sure if any of us wish to be honored. I know Máire will be happy to hear that you remember the sacrifice Marcus made for us."

The priest and his flock nodded in unison and then continued their discussion.

Julian began walking towards the healing tents. He smiled as her scent grew stronger, even through the overwhelming smell of mortals and various races of blood-drinkers. Part of him worried about what would happen to the Changed Strigoi, but it would be best for all that they should be allowed to discover themselves.

After arriving at the first healing tent, Julien pulled back the tent flap and saw Máire lying down in a cot, with Lucius sprawled across her and Mandubratius seated next to her on the ground, holding her right hand. Máire had slept through it all, while Mandubratius looked to be quite drowsy and somewhat malnourished and gray, though he did manage to look up, and he appeared to recognize Julien.

"Julien," the Lamia acknowledged while nodding a little, with no condescension lacing the word.

"Hello, Awvarwy," Julien said, wondering if it was right to call him that name. He sat down a foot away from him.

The Lamia smiled. "You say my name very well, thank you. I do not feel quite like Mandubratius right now."

"Are you well?" Julien asked.

Awvarwy's eyes revealed a spark of amusement, perhaps Mandubratius still lurked there. "Julien, your query to my well-being is so endearing, but I hardly believe that you are trying to ascertain my wellness, correct?" He smiled. "She's doing well enough. I wish she would wake up again to greet you."

Julien noticed Awvarwy squeeze Máire's hand. "Wake up, chroí. Your child-in-darkness is here."

Máire stirred. "Julien?" She opened her eyes. "Hello, my love, I am so glad you are here to visit me." She exhaled and stretched a little. "Did you bring Marcus with you? He has not come to see me."

Julien met Mandubratius' eyes. The other blood-drinker shook his head vigorously.

"I have not seen him tonight, Máire." Julien stood up and leaned in to stroke her hair.

She offered him a weak smile. "No matter. I'll find him later," she murmured. Máire turned a bit and appeared to notice Mandubratius. "Awvarwy, you look… gray. Go feed. You gave me too much." Máire began to sit up. "I suppose the General is busy doing his duty." She made a face before sliding back down to rest on the cot.

"You should continue resting," Mandubratius said in a soothing voice.

"I know I should continue resting," Máire answered, "you don't have to manipulate me into resting, you know. I'm tired."

"I will do whatever is required to keep you in this cot," Mandubratius answered. "If you are so stubborn that it requires a little mind-bending, so be it."

"Mmmmm," Máire closed her eyes. "Good night to you both, then."

"Did you?" Julien inquired.

"A little," Mandubratius admitted. "It was merely a nudge for her own good. She does need to rest."

"How long has she been like this?" he asked.

"You mean talking about Marcus?" Mandubratius sighed, and the humor left his eyes again. "Since sunset," he answered. "She wakes up." He waved an arm. "Tells me that I look bad, and to go find Marcus after I feed. Then she gets tired, and I tell her to go back to sleep. She seems to believe that nothing happened, and I don't have the heart to tell her the truth."

"And you expect me to be able to tell her?" Julien asked.

The Lamia tilted his head a little. "I am not her child-in-darkness, but you are. I had to tell your brother that Talia is dead, and that she died in a most unselfish manner, because he and I are tied by bonds of blood. You should do this, Julien. I… held her after she saw them die, and her tears were hard to bear. I refuse to give her more bad news."

Julien sighed. "Alright, but I wish for Sáerlaith to help me with this. Perhaps she'll tell Máire the truth. I am not a good messenger of bad news either." He closed his eyes and extended his senses to find Sáerlaith. "I shall return." He raced out of the tent and towards the hilltop to the southeast.

He soon found her, dangling her legs over the side of a boulder east of Ernstberg's summit. He slowed a few feet before reaching her and walked.

"Hello, Julien. How is Máire? You smell of her." Sáerlaith turned to look up at him.

Julien sat down next to her. "She doesn't remember Marcus' demise, Sáerlaith. She believes that he's alive and taking care of camp business."

"Was what we witnessed death?" Sáerlaith asked.

Julien swung his feet over the edge of the boulder and felt a strange fear at the how far down and far away the valley below was from the summit. He considered her question as a cool breeze moved past them. "I don't know," he admitted.

"Marcus may have seemed flesh and blood to us, Julien, but he is much more. His mother-in-darkness, your great-grandmother-in-darkness is a Goddess, a very powerful Goddess. I believe that the person who interacted with us was not the entire being." Sáerlaith paused. "When the body disappeared, the rest of Marcus continued to exist, and I believe Máire knows that on an instinctual level. She could be more sensitive to his non-corporeal self than we." Sáerlaith met his eyes.

"But," Julien countered, "Awvarwy… Mandubratius… whoever he is, said that she witnessed Marcus' and Seosaimhín's disappearance, and she was crying over it."

"Then, you should assure her that Marcus is in the Otherworld, but he remains with her in some form. When he chooses to rejoin us, he will walk the earth again."

Feeling the conversation was over, Julien shifted his weight to get up, but Sáerlaith reached out with her left hand and gently touched Julien's leg.

"Don't go just yet. I need to speak to you about the wake for all that passed on. Beltane will be upon us soon, and I don't see the Pope listening to me. Many of the blood-drinkers wish for a celebration."

"I am sure the Pope will do something involving rosaries and a funeral mass," Julien replied.

Sáerlaith chuckled. "I do not see many of our kind going to a rosary or mass, Julien. Marcus told me that he, Claudius, and Mac Alpin celebrated a wake before you became Deargh Du. You know well that our traditions of remembrance are older than the Church's. Our people want to remember those who died with those traditions. I know many would consider it an insult to Marcus' memory if there were no wake."

Julien smirked. "I will inform the Pope that there will be another celebration of remembrance and that he can tell his flock about it if he wishes to do so, but you have to assist me by telling Máire the truth."

Sáerlaith gave him a pained smile. "I will do my best to do so." She stood up. "Will you come along, or are you trying to avoid a confrontation?"

"I think it is best for a woman..." He paused and looked at Sáerlaith. "Mandubratius probably handled her reaction better than I could, Sáerlaith. I just don't want her to associate me with bad news."

Sáerlaith sighed. "You know that sad-eyed stare of yours will only work with me a few dozen times, Julien. Just know that this means you are as much of a coward as Awvarwy."

Julien stood up. "I am sorry I am such a disappointment, but I'm certain that you would rather have me deal with His Holiness, correct?"

Sáerlaith smirked. "Yes, Julien, but you must make sure he doesn't interfere with our 'unholy' celebration."

"Agreed," he acknowledged, before heading back towards the Pope's tent.

"Adhamdh, you are as stubborn now as you were before," Sáerlaith muttered. She had tried to part the mists earlier to ask about Marcus, but her father-in-darkness ignored her call.

Now that Julien asks for advice about Máire, I have no idea what to do to assist in this situation.

She stepped into the first medical tent and found Mandubratius sitting in the dirt, holding Máire's hand and watching her.

Despite all they have done to each other, there must be some rather confusing feelings there.

"Awvarwy," she said as she sat down next to him, prompting him to face her. She allowed her glamoury to shine. "You look malnourished." She patted his leg. "You need to feed. You have done so much. You should look after yourself for a little while, Awvarwy."

The worry lining his face made him appear older.

"I'll watch over her," Sáerlaith assured him. "She's safe. I promise."

Awvarwy nodded. Rising, he ambled out of the tent.

She wondered why she thought of him as Awvarwy, instead of Mandubratius.

It could simply be that he looks so mortal, tired, and sad.

She looked over at Lucius, who said nothing to her. He merely stretched his legs and then tucked his feet under himself.

Máire shifted a little in the cot. "Sáerlaith," she whispered. She opened her eyes, revealing their beauty. "Did you make Awvarwy leave?"

"Yes, my sweet. I thought it best. However, I'm really here because many of us are worried about you."

Lucius began to purr loudly.

"I know," Máire whispered. She cleared her throat and spoke louder. "Thank you for sending him out. I have no idea why he feels the need to watch over me. It's a little nerve-wracking."

Sáerlaith bit her lip and decided to stop avoiding the truth.

Máire needs to know what happened.

"It may be because he was with you when Marcus and Seosaimhín disappeared," Sáerlaith admitted. "When we found you, he was holding you, and he almost didn't let you go."

"Marcus didn't disappear," Máire answered. "I think I understand what happened, I just didn't want to admit it." She started to sob into her hands.

Sáerlaith leaned forward and patted her shoulder.

Máire inhaled and made a strange hiccupping sound. "They both possessed elemental energies when they struck each other," she explained. "Then their bodies began to disintegrate with each ensuing blow..."

Sáerlaith could tell she held back the descriptive details.

Sobs wracked the other woman again. "And it's my fault because I wasn't there when he needed me," Máire concluded.

Sáerlaith rubbed her back. "No, chroí, this is not your fault. You were incapacitated. Many of us were, but I heard from Julien and others about what you did. You did your best, Máire. It's just that you are not Seosaimhín's equal."

"But it wasn't enough!" Máire's hands rubbed Lucius as her tears dripped on him.

"Listen to me," Sáerlaith whispered. She forced Máire's head up and stared into her eyes. "With your participation and Marcus' sacrifice, the balance has been maintained." She wiped away Máire's tears. "Many Strigoi are now human, the others are the Changed, and I know they are so glad that Seosaimhín no longer controls their minds and their bodies. Many had to die, but it had to be done."

"Of course." Máire sniffed and wiped her face on her sleeve. She still looked upset, but it appeared that her tears had stopped for now.

"I thought this news would have brought you more comfort than it has," Sáerlaith admitted. She found a stool and pulled it over to the cot. She sat down next to Máire again.

"It does, but it's just…" Máire looked around the tent, and then scooted closer to Sáerlaith. "I still sense him. My eyes witnessed his death, but my heart feels his presence." Máire's movements became animated. "I know he still exists, Sáerlaith. I know that makes no sense, but I feel it." Máire shifted around so much that Sáerlaith wondered whether the cot would collapse.

Lucius leapt off the bedding and stalked off as if annoyed with all the movement. The fairy cat remained silent as he exited the tent.

Sáerlaith turned back to Máire. "I know how you feel," Sáerlaith admitted.

"How?"

"When I lost Adhamdh, it was the same. To this night, I feel his presence now and again. It seemed very strange and unsettling at first, but now it gives me comfort." Sáerlaith took Máire's hands in hers. "I don't like to speak of it because I think it would make the others worry."

"How is that possible?" Máire asked. She swiped at her face again.

"They are the sons of Morrigan," Sáerlaith answered. "You and I cannot understand the mysteries that surround them."

"Then how do I live with that?" Máire pulled up her knees a little. "There is such a conflict of perception."

"One night at a time, the same way I do. We can be thankful together that we know they still reside with us in one form or another."

"How did Adhamdh go?" Máire asked.

Sáerlaith wrapped an arm around Máire and embraced her. "I will tell you one night, when the memory of Marcus doesn't immediately make us cry," she said.

After a few minutes of listening to the women from the outside of the tent, Lucius trotted through the camp, wrapping himself in shadow. He could smell Awvarwy to the east of the summit of Ernstberg. The Lamia remained somewhat hidden, but still in public view. Lucius contemplated revealing his upright form for a moment.

Bah, too much trouble. The others could see me. Besides that, I enjoy the feel of grass and dirt on my pads. The gentle breeze plays with my fur.

The sight and smell of a field mouse distracted him for a moment. He shook away the baser instincts of his form and continued to the boulder where Awvarwy sat, swinging his feet over the edge.

At least he no longer appears to be gray.

Lucius flew into the air and closed his eyes to keep his presence a secret. He hovered in front of the Lamia but kept his eyes closed. "Good evening, Awvarwy." He struggled to keep from purring or laughing as the Lamia scooted back a little.

"Lucius?"

Lucius opened his eyes, revealing his presence, and drifted closer to Awvarwy. "Yes," he drawled.

The Lamia inhaled. "You startled me, fairy cat. I had no idea that you were in front of me."

"I prefer to sneak up on my prey," Lucius purred. He watched a slow smile spread over Awvarwy's face.

"So, I am your prey now?"

Lucius flew to the boulder and landed next to Awvarwy. "Is that what you think?" he asked.

"You are Máire's champion," Awvarwy answered. "I believe you are here to tell me to leave her alone and that you will keep her out of trouble's way."

Lucius laughed. "On the contrary, I wish to foster your relationship with her."

"You do?" Awvarwy sounded surprised. "I thought you preferred her to stay with her own kind. After all, I know you love Marcus."

"I do love Marcus," Lucius replied, hearing sadness creep into his voice. He tried to retain control and keep his voice neutral. "He and I share common blood, and he is one of Morrigan's best." Lucius fell silent for a moment and stared into the star-filled night. The smells of the revived life on the hill thrilled him. "Awvarwy, what I did, I had to do... for you."

"What you did?" Lucius watched the Lamia's eyes reveal confusion, then remembrance. "Oh... yes. I thought that was a dream... or something from the Strigoi. That was you?"

"Yes, that was me."

Awvarwy looks flummoxed.

"You mortals can be so dense, sometimes," Lucius added.

"I'm not mortal. Remember, I'm Lamia, Lucius."

"You never should have been Lamia," Lucius grunted. "You were supposed to be something better." He looked back over at Awvarwy and noticed his mouth open and close like a salmon's.

"I always thought that this was not how my life was supposed to be," Awvarwy whispered. "How did you know?"

"Because I was there when you were conceived, and I was there when your life was set into motion. I watched your first steps," Lucius replied, "your first hunt, your first game of hurling, your first kill."

The Lamia's mouth fell open again.

"Everything was going well, until that dark night when the Lamia took you. If only..." Lucius trailed off. "You may not know this, but we are not always 'all-hearing' and 'all-seeing'. If that were the case, mortals would have no real choices. Felician caught me by surprise. He found you before I did. And here we are, Awvarwy, my son, the Lamia and I."

"Son?"

Lucius decided that seeing would ease all doubts, yet this place was too conspicuous. He nudged Awvarwy off the boulder and hovered above it. He then drew a glyph of transportation on the boulder so the two of them could travel to his corner of the Otherworld. "Come with me, Awvarwy," he said.

"Come with you? Where? Why is that section of the boulder glowing?"

"You and Marcus both have a strange habit of repeating what I say. Yes, please come with me."

The Lamia stared at the boulder. "But why is that glowing?"

"Look... it is a gateway, just trust me."

"But I don't understand," Awvarwy whispered.

Idiot child.

Lucius glared at him. "Just touch it with me."

Awvarwy nodded sheepishly then touched the boulder.

At the same time, Lucius touched the glyph with an outstretched paw, then the mists surrounded them.

Soon, the mists faded, and sunlight lit their view.

Awvarwy blinked at the sun and surveyed their surroundings. "What magic is this? Where are we?"

Lucius turned away for a moment and decided to assume his human form. He stood upright and felt the fur disappear. His clothing, weapons, and jewelry appeared on his body and became solid.

Once he completed the transformation, the man ran a hand over his hair and beard. Lugh, no longer Lucius, turned towards his son. "This is my home, Awvarwy." He smiled. "I'm not really a fairy cat or one of the fae at all. I'm a God, Lugh Lamfada."

Lugh's Realm in Tír na nÓg

A man stood in front of Awvarwy and met his gaze steadily. The figure's green eyes reflected fire, but then he could see his own eyes in this man's... this God's... gaze. His doubts faded.

Yes, this is my father.

Awvarwy felt his breath catch in his throat as the glamoury melted away and the figure gleamed glorious radiance. It was almost blinding.

The brilliance faded a little, and he saw the smiling face. It seemed so familiar.

His father shook back long, dark hair and a braided plait. He wore a simple tunic and trews, but the bold and intricate design on the tunic took Awvarwy's breath away.

He and Lugh resembled each other a great deal. Granted, his father appeared very much a resplendent and well-built man. However, that knowing smile and eyes reminded him of his own face when he had looked into Aphrodite's mirror.

"Yes, there is a bit of a resemblance." Lugh chuckled.

"I..." Awvarwy stammered, attempting to find his voice. "I have no memory of you, but I know you are my father. I have... so many questions." His words faded into shy whispers.

"Patience, my son. There will always be time for questions later. Let's spar!" A sword and spear appeared, and Lugh tossed him the sword.

For once, his taste for battle seemed to fade even as he caught the sword by the hilt. "I don't feel much like fighting," he admitted. "After the battle with the Strigoi, I need time..."

He witnessed some disappointment in his father's eyes, but then a smile reappeared.

"Yes, I am sorry. Sometimes I forget that you and Cu Chulainn are quite different. You are right, we must speak. There will be time for sparring later. After all, what is time in this place?"

Lugh wrapped an arm around him, and together they walked towards a great stone dun. "Your brother has earned his place in the order of things, Awvarwy. What have you earned?" His father studied him, waiting on an answer.

"I have a place as one of the leaders of the Lamia. Surely, that deserves some respect."

"I suppose that is true." Lugh chuckled. "I have little respect for the Romans and Greeks, but at least you rule over them. Now, come with me. I have a wonderful story to tell you." Joviality shone in his father's eyes.

"A story?" Awvarwy grinned. "What is this story about?"

"How your mother and I met," Lugh answered, "but let's eat and drink together first."

chapter seventeen

Encampment Outside of Hinterweiler, at the Northwest Foot of Ernstberg

áire awoke again and felt unsteady. Hours had passed, but she could still sense the quiet night outside. Lamps and a few candles lit the tent. She stretched her legs, feeling a purring weight on her feet.

Lucius peered at her, but remained silent. His eyes lowered as he prepared himself for sleep.

She rubbed at her dried tears and felt some embarrassment for them. However, the tears had been necessary. Máire looked around the tent and spotted Sáerlaith sleeping in a small cot on the opposite side of the tent. She also noticed a dark figure to her right. "Awvarwy, why are you still here? Did you feed yet?"

He appeared pale, but he no longer looked gray. His green eyes met hers and gleamed with the typical, naughty merriment. "Why Máire, I'm hurt that you didn't expect for me to return," he purred.

She blinked a few times, trying to remember their last conversation.

He reached over and patted her hand with a gentle touch. "I am your dearest friend. Where else would I be?"

She studied him, wondering how he could play the jokester so well. Máire cleared her throat, deciding to try the game herself. "I considered that you would be with one of your other dearest friends, though I'm not sure who, since your list fluctuates night by night," she commented.

Mandubratius chuckled. "Such cruelty from my old friend. I have been by your bedside throughout most of the day and night."

"I know," she admitted. "I was playing your usual game, Awvarwy... or is it Mandubratius, now?" She watched him smile.

His eyes seemed to gleam again. "I know," he murmured, "and I enjoyed it most thoroughly. I am Awvarwy, right now. At least, that is what I wish for you to call me. I just hope no one else attempts to say it, as they usually make it sound so horrible. Yet, I rather enjoy hearing you say it." His playfulness faded. "How are you feeling?"

She realized she felt well. She pulled her legs away from Lucius and sat up, resulting in the fairy cat giving her a vexed stare and an annoyed sniff. She turned to face Awvarwy, meeting his eyes. "Thank you for watching over me." Máire tried to stand and then felt him pull her to her feet.

He wrapped his arms around her in a somewhat awkward embrace.

She rested her chin on his shoulder for a moment and felt a little less confused. Then, they both pulled back.

"I need to stretch my legs," she commented. "Care to join me?"

"Of course," he answered. He walked towards the exit and waited for her.

"I remember the destruction of the landscape," she recalled. "I'm not sure if I'll enjoy this walk. I will concentrate instead on seeing my family."

"Your family is fine," Awvarwy said. "Julien and Edward have completely recovered. Mac Alpin's hard head protected him. Claudius now has taken Marcus' position. They have been asking after you, but they had duties and wished for you to recover more before they demanded your time. They will not be insulted if you take some time for yourself. I am certain that they know it's necessary." Awvarwy motioned her towards the exit.

"I suppose you are right," Máire replied. "I just hope the battlefield will not make me too melancholy."

"But, Máire, the outside is not as you remember it." He pulled back the flap for her to stepped out.

Upon leaving the tent, a wealth of green and vibrant flowers met her sight, and soft grass cushioned her bare feet. Animals whispered and birds sang of their lives. A sweet smell wafted through the camp on a gentle breeze. Areas of the forested hill to the south and southeast that had been cleared for the battle or devastated during the battle now sported new saplings. If the sunlight had been visible, she would swear she had walked through the mists to arrive in the Otherworld.

Awvarwy joined her outside of the tent. "Everything started blooming the morning after the battle, or so I was told. It is quite breathtaking, isn't it?"

She found no words.

"Perhaps, this is Morrigan's way to restore the balance," he added.

Máire stared down at the wildflowers, thinking that such an outcome did not exactly sound like the workings of her grandmother-in-darkness. "I'm not sure if this was Her doing," she said, "but I'm thankful nonetheless." She headed up the hillside and sensed Awvarwy following her.

Mortals and the newly changed bowed, backing away from her.

She wished to ask them to stop, but she felt compelled to continue.

The hair on the back of her neck rose. Something different rested here amid the flowers and new trees. Máire stopped.

"I believe this is where you stood when you fought Seosaimhín," Awvarwy informed her. He shuffled his feet as if anxious.

"Yes. The energy we set forth on each other still resides here. It will return to its home soon." The memory of the battle seared through her mind, but she tried to brush it away with pleasant thoughts. Then a shiny object caught her eye. "What's that?" she inquired as she darted towards it, forgetting to wait for an answer. Máire knelt down in the grass in front of it.

"'In memory of Marcus of Bath, who perished on this spot serving God and the people of two empires'," Awvarwy read. "I am glad Leo wrote nothing here about the Seraphim. He's convinced Marcus is one of their number. He seemed so pleased with that false belief. I figure Leo deserves his delusion."

"He's not dead, you know," Máire blurted out.

"Of course he's not." Awvarwy sat down. "That will be our secret, Maél Muire. However, he is gone from this place." Awvarwy stared into the stars.

She watched him lean back a little against his open palms and stretch out his bare feet in front of him.

"It's odd, but I will miss Marcus," Awvarwy admitted.

Máire felt her brows rise in surprise and confusion.

"He was an enemy, of course, but in a strange way, we became brothers that night we were transformed."

Máire examined him to see what trick this could be. His eyes revealed honesty and nothing else. Awvarwy remained, for now, while Mandubratius faded into shadow. He stood abruptly up and asked, "Do you need to be alone?"

Máire shook her head. "I had an opportunity to say goodbye to him before the battle, and it was exactly what we needed to say to each other. I wish to go see my family, now. You may join me if you wish."

He extended an arm to her again.

She took it, and Awvarwy helped her up. They started for the tents. To her surprise, she realized she still grasped Awvarwy's hand and did not mind it at all.

Arwin blamed himself for Marcus and Edward. No amount of pretty words from the others, even from Edward himself, could allow his guilt to fade. He shifted a bit as he continued to stare at the stars, but his reverie was cut short by the sound of snapping twigs. Arwin grumbled at himself for focusing on the skies, not his surroundings. He sensed a Lamia approach. After a few moments of judging smells, he realized the Empress stalked through the surrounding forest.

She muttered curses under her breath, as she flicked away bugs. "Arwin!" she shouted, stepping out of the copse of trees. "I know you're out here!"

He ducked behind a boulder, hoping she'd return to the hill encampment.

She sidestepped around the rock as he considered his options, but then he jumped a little, upon realizing she had found him.

"So, this is where you've been hiding?"

He grunted in assent.

"I've been looking for you all night." The Empress crossed her arms over her chest.

"Why?"

"I need coitus," she said. "I am bored, and everyone else is in a stupor. Half of the time, they whine about the dead, and the rest of the time, they stare at the heavens and talk about how beautiful everything is now."

"I'm not in the mood," he admitted.

"How can you not be in the mood?" Irene shrugged her shoulders. "I am in a bit of a stupor myself, now! It's so beautiful here." She motioned to the expanse of nature. "Afterwards, I'll even join you in that dreadfully cold stream."

"That's not what I meant," he answered.

"Then, what do you mean?" Empress Irene drawled. "You may think you want to be alone, but if you really wished it, you wouldn't have allowed me to join you here."

He looked at her.

She frowned at him, yet she still managed to look rather regal and lovely.

"I can't help but blame myself for Edward's pain and Marcus' death," he admitted.

"Are you a God?" she asked, arching a brow.

He stared back at her, trying to understand the question.

"Yes or no," Irene pressed. "Does Arwin Mac Alpin wield powers well beyond that of an Ekimmu Cruitne? Does he manipulate nature to suit his needs?" She smiled at him. "Does he travel through time to right all wrongs?"

"No."

"Are you a soothsayer that can divine fortunes? An Alchemist crafting gold from other metals, or an astrologer with an innate knowledge of the stars to guide us through times such as these?"

"No!" he yelled. "I know where you're going with this, Basileus."

"Then shut up and let me speak," she challenged. Her eyes remained the color of the calm seas.

He shut his mouth.

"First off, I visited Edward earlier, and he's recovering well. Unlike my spoiled son, yours did you proud." She smiled. "As for your friend Marcus, you weren't there, you couldn't have been there, and if you had been there, there would have been nothing you could have done. Seosaimhín almost killed Máire, and Máire knows those Druidic magics. Arwin, you would have ended up dead or dreadfully wounded like Julien." Irene wrung her hands, but she met his eyes again and asked, "What makes you think that you should punish yourself for not being able to help?"

Arwin shrugged and pouted, not wanting to admit the truth.

"I think Edward would like to see you," she said. She stretched a hand towards him.

Mac Alpin nodded his head. "Alright, Basileus."

"Coitus afterwards, you brutal Briton," she purred, squeezing his hand as they walked towards the camp.

"By the Gods, woman, you don't give up, do you? And I'm Scots and Pictish, not a Briton!"

Irene smiled and pushed him over, straddling him before he could say anything else. "Whatever."

Julien remained seated on the grass. The well-lit hill loomed in the distance. He had finished his few duties, such as writing recommendations to his father about who might be able to take over his position in Aachen. He planned to lean back and allow the grass to hide him, but he sensed Máire approaching. His senses also alerted him that a Lamia lingered in the distance.

The Lamia faded into the forest as Máire drew closer.

He remembered a night, a few months ago, when he witnessed her bathing and believed her to be a Goddess. Tonight, Máire seemed earthbound.

"I missed your visit," she said. "Is there anything you need, Julien?" She sat down beside him.

"I'm sorry," he replied. "I wanted to find something to do. I'm starting to realize what we lost with Marcus' death."

"It will be difficult for us," Máire admitted. "However, you and I must accept that Morrigan called him home. We will meet him again, one night."

"That is exactly what the priests say in church. Do you remember them saying that?"

She nodded a little.

"They say that when we die, we'll meet our loved ones in the afterlife. Sometimes it's amusing how a Christian belief reflects older ones."

"Indeed," she murmured. She inhaled as a new scent grew.

Father Xofer stepped through the grass and stopped a few feet away from them.

"Máire and Inspector... Julien," he greeted them. His smile faded into what seemed to be pain.

Máire arose and met the priest, taking his left hand.

"Father, what ails you? Are you in need of healing?"

"We are all…" he stammered. "All of the Changed need to be healed. Sadly, this is not the kind of wound that a Deargh Du's healing could cure."

"How is that?" Julien asked. He stood and joined them.

"When the few of us that were left standing fought against Seosaimhín, she shared her darkness. We tried to shield it from the others, as it made us ill." The priest's eyes turned inward. "We tried to sequester it, within ourselves. However, it slipped out during our sleep earlier today. Now, everyone has shared Seosaimhín's darkness. We are trying to decide who we should ask for guidance. If we do not receive guidance soon, we fear we may become as Seosaimhín."

"That would be the Holy Trinity and the Saints," Julien stated.

The priest revealed a nervous smile. "Julien, you have witnessed that the dogma is ridiculous at times, and the scriptures can be fictitious. Wisdom is contained therein, but much has been fabricated by man to advance their greed. I have seen living proof that Deities outside the view of Christianity exist and may actively participate in our existence. The mirror that transformed us is a sterling example. Aphrodite, or some other Olympian, created it in Her honor. Look at yourself, Claudius, Mac Alpin, and even Mandubratius. You are all creations of a different deity or supernatural being. I will always love and honor Jesus and His father. I believe Jesus was an attempt by a God to connect with us. However, I believe that the greed of the Church taints our concept of God and His son. We have created a God in our image. In order to cure our disease of the spirit, we need to re-assess what we believe and who we will honor." The priest then fell silent.

Julien nodded. "My apologies, Father. I should have known your position. I have seen a Goddess in Her realm. I know part of Her resides in me. I can understand how you must feel, as I am finding my way as well."

"Father." Máire regained his attention. "I know you plan to leave for Orleans soon. When? I do hope you and yours will visit us soon in Vézelay."

"We leave at sunset," Father Xofer answered.

"No farewells?" Julien asked.

"It takes all my strength to stand here and speak with the two of you. My people are in hiding, feeling shame at the darkness that engulfs our minds." He turned to Máire. "Please know that we are sorry that we cannot be at Marcus' wake. I'm sure Julien told you that we honor Marcus for his sacrifice. We know who he was." The priest's dark eyes moved to Julien again. "I know you wish to keep in touch, Julien." The priest embraced him. "However, until we are cleansed, it would be best to not seek us out." He turned to embrace Máire. "When the time is right, we will find you and renew our friendship."

Máire nodded. "Keep you and yours safe, Father." She kissed his cheeks and pulled back.

The priest nodded and returned to the forest without another word.

Julien took Máire's hand, upon seeing the tears in her eyes, and held her close.

As they embraced, she leaned into him.

Julien rested his chin and cheek beside her curls.

Patroclus stretched as weary, rather motley group of warriors trudged into the tent early. He could see Fianait teaching Horatio one of the Celtic board games. The Druid Caoimhín with a few of the other Deargh Du and Sugnwr Gwaed played dice, after sending some of the Ekimmu Cruitne off to another corner in order to stop them from influencing the games. However, one bedroll remained unrolled. "Where's Sextus?" he asked.

Horatio looked up from his game. "I haven't seen him. Perhaps he's feeding before sunrise." He moved one of his chieftains on the Fidchell board.

"Mmmmm," Fianait murmured while studying the board. "I saw him earlier at Marcus' Point."

"Marcus has a point now?" Patroclus tried not to laugh, concentrating instead on the missing soldier.

"It's our running joke," Caoimhín added. "Mac Alpin named it a few hours ago. It's the boulder on top of Ernstberg that we all seem to enjoy sitting on. It's a lovely spot to watch the sky. Perhaps he is enjoying the view."

"I hope it's just that." Patroclus stood up. He had a strange feeling. "I'll go see if he's still there." He exited the tent and strode up the hill. Once he reached the hilltop, Patroclus and headed east for the boulder. He could see a form in the distance. "Sextus!"

The figure didn't move, so Patroclus continued to the precipice. Sextus stared into the darkness before turning towards him for a brief moment, and then he lowered his face to stare at his boots. "Are you here to redeem your honor as well?" Sextus asked.

Patroclus stared at the eastern skies. "But honor was not lost," he said. "We were victorious."

"It was a pyrrhic victory, Patroclus. Many Lamia lost their lives, including our sponsor."

"Even so, you did not fail our Patron or our line. There is no reason to wait for the sun."

"Gaius is dead!" Sextus shouted. "My honor is gone, and only the sacrifice of my life will redeem my honor." Sextus pivoted his torso to stare eastward.

Patroclus backed a few steps away from the irrational Lamia. He drew his sword and hit Sextus in the back of the head, knocking him out. Patroclus caught him and hefted him up, wondering who could best talk him out of this. He headed down the hill northwest towards the new encampment and Mandubratius' tent, but then he remembered the co-consul had spent the last day sleeping in one of the medical tents. He continued his jaunt, with his burden slung over his shoulder, preparing for Mandubratius to deal with this.

Sextus awoke with a strange pounding in his head. He felt a great deal of confusion at the sharp pain. However, a staccato shout gained his attention.

"On your feet, lieutenant!"

Sextus shook his head.

"I said… on your feet, lieutenant!"

A sharp kick to his backside accentuated the order.

His senses began to return, and he leapt to attention. He stared past Mandubratius' scowling visage to the tent wall behind the co-consul's head.

Then, Mandubratius began to walk in a slow circle around Sextus.

Sextus could smell others, including something that did not fit into the realms of a mortal being. The sound of a purring cat distracted him. The cat's ceaseless stare frightened him.

That cat finds the strangest occurrences to purr.

Mandubratius turned to face him again and stared into his eyes.

Sextus stared at the same spot behind Mandubratius, feeling rage because of Patroclus' intervention and wanting to shout out, but he remained quiet.

Mandubratius' eyes remained on him. "I am told by a reliable source that you were about to fall on your sword, or step into the sun."

"It is my right," Sextus replied in an angry whisper.

"Yes or no will do, lieutenant!"

Sextus took in an unsteady breath and calmed himself. "Yes, Consul."

"Please explain why you felt honor bound to take your own life," Mandubratius continued.

"Gaius is dead!" Sextus repeated. "I feel that my honor is gone, and only the sacrifice of my life will redeem it."

"Your arrogance knows no bounds, Sextus." Mandubratius' eyes moved away. "You think you are the only person who grieves for Gaius? You think you're the only one who called him friend or mentor? Look around you."

Sextus lowered his eyes.

"Turn, damn you! Look!"

Sextus felt spittle land on his face. He turned his head and recognized many that fought alongside Gaius. Their faces remained blank.

"Sextus, I wish you to tell everyone here the appropriate conditions for falling on ones' sword," Mandubratius urged.

"Defeat when success is assured." Sextus paused and thought over other reasons. "Sometimes, it's necessary when you bring shame to your family and to Rome. You will do it when your commander tells you to do so." He looked over the gathered soldiers.

"Very true," Mandubratius answered. "Now, let's analyze your situation. Let's see if your circumstances call for one to commit suicide out of shame. Was victory assured?"

"No," Sextus admitted.

"Were we defeated?" Mandubratius began to pace again.

"No, Consul, but the victory was pyrrhic."

"Yes, I will accept that answer. Now, are these the reasons you feel justify your suicide?"

"Those factors weigh heavily on me," Sextus replied. "Many Lamia lost their lives in this battle."

Mandubratius faced him. The other Lamia's features calmed, and his rage seemed to subside. "Many, many more lost their lives in the Papal forces. You were but a handful that survived, Sextus. Most of those who survived that attack and this one now stand before us." The Consul and general inclined his head towards them. "Your duty is not to end your life, Sextus. Your duty is to lead. If you feel that you should walk into the sun, do so now, and I will not stop you. Otherwise, accept your promotion to general. You will be the co-consuls' eyes and ears in Rome, as your sponsor was in Constantinople."

Sextus felt an inkling of pride interspersed with guilt. He willed the guilt away. "I choose to serve the Consuls of the Lamia."

"The honor is to serve," the assembled Lamia yelled and then saluted him.

Mandubratius smiled. "Good. Then get some sleep." The Consul and general turned away.

After being dismissed, Sextus found an empty spot with blankets and proceeded to lie down. He closed his eyes in prayer to thank the Gods and Goddesses for his new duties and an opportunity to redeem himself. He sensed Patroclus lie down a few feet away. He would thank him tomorrow for saving his life. He had to wonder whether the co-consuls decided to re-locate to Constantinople for now, and whether Patroclus would have new orders as well. Sextus yawned and closed his eyes. Sleep overwhelmed him.

Charles walked amongst the soldiers, smiling and shaking his head at the honorifics to an emperor. He felt too much joy to be hearing 'Imperial Majesty' over and over. He sent Ercanbald to dispatch letters to Aachen and Rome, as well as a messenger to Lady Heloise to inform her of their victory and that they would be returning to Vézelay soon. Charles paused, upon hearing Julien issue orders to low-ranking soldiers about the storage of the leftover wine. He moved in closer and cleared his throat.

"Inspector General, a word…" He motioned Julien forward.

"Carry on," Julien said to the soldiers.

They returned to rolling a barrel towards a cart.

Julien walked over and appeared to be reticent to meet his eyes. "Yes, Imperial Majesty?" His voice seemed subdued.

"You know these are not your duties, my son," Charles said.

"I know, but since the battle, my duties haven't required much. There is nothing for me to do. I'm a man without a purpose," Julien answered.

"Nonsense," Charles replied. "Isn't your purpose to maintain the balance?"

"I know, but other than that…" Julien dusted off his hands. "The balance has been maintained, or re-established, for now. I'm sure once I travel back to Aachen with you, I'll find new duties at court. Though, I can no longer hold the title of Inspector General. A gendarme needs to be able to march, day or night."

"That is true, but you have already informed me of these changes," Charles said. "I am most pleased that you wish to join me, Julien, but you're a Deargh Du, now. That is a higher calling. Surely, you would rather do that than stay in Aachen. I know there is building that will commence in Vézelay, and both of your families need you."

My son needs to grow into his new role.

Charles found a steady rock and sat down.

"Yes, that is so. It is a higher calling, but you're my father, and I've only recently been told this. I wish to get to know you better," Julien stated.

"Yes, well I am so happy to hear that," Charles commented. "However, my duties and yours are different. You would find the court tiresome. We both hate the pomp of court."

"That may be so, but—"

"Julien," Charles interjected, waving away his son's excuses, "you are my blood, but I'm not a close family member to you. Your mother is, and Máire is. Even Mac Alpin, Claudius, and the others are more of a family to you than I am." Charles bit his lip. "It pains me to say this, but part of me feels that Marcus seemed more a father to you than I am."

Perhaps Julien misses, and needs, that support.

Charles rose from the uncomfortable rock and began to pace.

He will be better off with his own kind, now. They understand his needs.

He turned to meet Julien's eyes. "The help I'm giving you is this… I'm telling you that you need to find comfort with the Deargh Du and the other blood-drinkers. Only then will you find purpose, again."

Julien blinked back tears, and Charles quickly embraced his son.

"I'll make it a point to visit Vézelay often," he promised Julien. "Besides, I'll be traveling there ahead of you. I made a promise to your mother to visit her, and I'd like to meet my daughter and granddaughter."

When Julien pulled back, he looked a little surprised.

"Now, go find Máire. She was looking for you earlier. Stop bothering the lower orders. They don't need you to tell them their jobs."

"Thank you, father." His son smiled and then headed towards the tents.

Charles watched Julien walk away and found himself at the brink of tears.

Why is it so hard to let my children walk away?

"I wanted you to stay with me in Aachen with the rest of my family," Charles whispered to the wind. "I still wish you could succeed me." He glanced around and, reassured that no one witnessed his tears, Charles wiped them away on his sleeve. He then looked up at the stars. "That was very difficult, and one of the most unselfish things I've ever had to do."

Reginald stopped at the spot and crouched down, running a hand over the grass. He backed away a few steps and sat down on a boulder. He wished that he had pulled Talia's body and head into a tent.

She deserved a true burial, but I forgot that Talia would turn to dust at sunrise. She disappeared, melding with the strange and renewed beauty of the landscape.

He shifted and wondered at the confusion of feelings. The sound of footsteps and the scent a blood-drinker broke him from his thoughts.

The interloper clear his throat.

"Hello, Julien, you found me," greeted Reginald without looking at him.

His brother walked around him and sat down on the grass beside the boulder. "I was concerned," Julien began. "I couldn't find you in camp, and I wished to bend your ear."

"I wished to be alone." Reginald's eyes turned towards the horizon.

"Well, do you wish to speak now?"

Reginald heard himself utter a humorless, dry chuckle. He decided to speak anyway, despite his wishes to remain silent. "Does anything seem different about this place?"

Julien looked down at the grass for a moment. "Strange and beautiful magic dwells within," his brother replied. "At least, that's what my senses inform me."

"But, do you feel anything?" Reginald asked.

His brother shrugged a little. "As I said, there is a magical energy, but other than that, I sense nothing. I suppose that my senses are lacking in some ways."

Reginald tried to keep from rolling his eyes at Julien. "This is where she died," Reginald stated, gesturing to the field.

"Oh… Reginald, I am sorry. I forgot." Julien began to stare at Reginald.

As his brother stared at him, Reginald realized that Julien did somewhat resemble a puppy at that moment. Reginald smiled at Julien. "You had a golden spike inside you, Julien. I think you had other concerns besides the whereabouts of my sponsor."

"Are you in mourning?" Julien asked.

"To be honest, part of me is rejoicing that Talia is dead," Reginald whispered. "It's Justice tipping her scales for you and our mother. However," he paused and turned away, staring into the vast expanse of darkness, "part of me sees her death as some selfless act. I don't know or understand her motivations."

"From what I understand, she was not the type of woman who put others before herself," Julien stated. "I remember her manipulations."

"Of that, I'm distinctly aware." Reginald slid off the boulder and sat on the grass. "Still, she gave her life to save two people."

"Part of me thinks that she truly desired to protect her sponsor. Máire was just… there," Julien said.

"Perhaps," Reginald replied.

"If you wish to mourn her, I will leave you." Julien rose up. "Please find me when I am needed."

Reginald felt a pat on his shoulder, and then his brother turned and walked away. After several minutes in quiet contemplation, more footsteps approached, interrupting his thoughts. "I'm not ready to return to camp, Julien," he called out, assuming his brother had returned.

"I'm not entirely sure she wished to save me," a familiar voice over Reginald's right shoulder murmured.

The interruption, and the speaker, annoyed him. "How is that true?" he demanded while looking over at Mandubratius. "You made her."

"I sponsored her," the other Lamia said in a soothing tone, offering a gentle correction that one might give a child. Mandubratius walked past the boulder and Reginald, keeping his back to him.

"I didn't realize her ruthlessness when I sponsored her," Mandubratius admitted. "No, wait… it's been some time since then. Yes, I remember now, she had always been hardhearted. I thought it would be no problem to control Talia. I mean, I control myself, after all. I suppose you can easily see my arrogance now," the Lamia added.

"And why would she not desire to protect her sponsor?"

Mandubratius turned around and faced him. His green eyes glowed a little in a manner that reminded Reginald of the Deargh Du. "Perhaps she would," Mandubratius answered. "Despite her thirst for independence and power, Talia always returned to me. Now, she has eternal independence." Mandubratius scratched his bearded chin and then sat down in the grass across from Reginald. "This sight is spellbinding," Mandubratius uttered in a half-whisper. "I hope you do not mind another mourner for a while. I will miss Talia's determination and single-mindeness sometimes, though I will not miss her selfish actions."

"You feel her final act was selfish?"

Mandubratius confuses me more than any of the other blood-drinkers.

The other Lamia shrugged. "I'm not one that can understand female thoughts and motives. I could live for an eternity, yet they would still perplex me."

They both fell silent as the wind picked up, allowing the grass and leaves from the new saplings to whisper remembrances of Talia's deeds.

Claudius stooped over and picked up the small mirror. He ran a finger over the stubble, trying to remember the last time he grew a beard. However, without a shaving partner, there seemed little point to continuing the practice. He didn't quite look like himself, yet perhaps a beard would work. After all, everyone else had one. Even Horatio appeared to be attempting one.

He sensed movement outside of the tent and sniffed. Máire approached, alone. He turned towards the tent flap as it rose and smiled at her.

She walked in, wearing a dress instead of her usual traveling gear. Máire strolled over to him and took his hand. She raised the mirror and examined them both side by side. Her earlier sorrows appeared to have faded, although he felt that a greater depression may overwhelm her after the festivities passed.

Claudius wrapped an arm around her, wishing he could think of the right thing to say.

Máire reached out and traced her thumb over his stubble. "You've decided to grow it out," she said with a smile. "It suits you, Claudius." She leaned in and kissed his cheek.

"It's not exactly my choice," he admitted. "I'm sure it will look better later, but for now, it's itchy."

"What? Mac Alpin didn't offer to shave you?" Her eyes belied her amusement.

"Arwin says shaving one's chin is an affront to all the Gods, and to shave another man's…" He chuckled. "He would only consider doing such a thing as a joke to a man passed out from drink. Speaking of changing appearances, it's been a long time since I've seen you in a dress, and you appear to be missing some plaits."

"Thanks." Máire pulled back and twirled a bit. "Julien bought it in Hinterweiler. It's not exactly my taste, but I realized he hasn't seen me without muddy clothing and plaits in quite some time. Perhaps Warrior Máire decided it was time to feel pretty again."

Claudius smirked. "Warrior Máire is and has always has been pretty." He scratched his chin. "Hmmmm, perhaps Arwin has forgotten my shaving jokes."

"Doubtful," Máire replied. "He didn't take your last joke too well, did he?" She smirked, and her eyes twinkled in merriment.

"Indeed, he looked horrible without the beard." He chuckled. "Rather like a plucked bird."

"Yes, and then he chased you when he discovered you holding the razor."

Claudius touched the top of his head on impulse. "Yes, I remember you, Marcus, and Edward, laughing at me while Arwin shaved me bald. He has no sense of humor, sometimes."

"Marcus provoked him more, though," Máire commented. "Of course, I think they both relished their disagreements."

"Yes." Claudius frowned, feeling melancholy for a moment. He fell silent, and then realized it was not time to be sad. He walked back over to Máire and took her hand. "Did Marcus ever tell you that I would have his will?"

"Will?" She looked a little confused.

"Yes. Wills are legal documents that people write in order to… stop that! Ouch!"

Máire released his ear and smiled. "Sorry, but you know very well that I know what a will is. You are teasing me to keep my spirits up."

"Yes," he admitted, "but we digress. Marcus and I would dictate our wills together before battles, just in case."

"Is there some formality you planned on for reading this will?" she asked.

"I'm Roman, aren't I?" Claudius answered. "Of course, there's a solemn and dignified formality involved in the reading of a will. First, we'll all need to gather in one place."

"Well, who is in it?" she asked. "I assumed it would be you, me, Arwin, and possibly Edward and Julien."

"I suppose he wished to be generous to several of us," Claudius answered. He sat down and began to pull on his boots. "Now, would you do me the honor of finding Arwin, Edward, Julien, Sáerlaith, and Mandubratius and have them meet me here in half an hour?" He stood up.

She shrugged. "Alright. I can do that." She leaned in and kissed him before turning on her heel. "Don't feel as if you have to keep me entertained, Claudius." She met his eyes, but the spark faded a little.

"I liked sending you on missions to find mystic artifacts," he admitted. "It became a challenge for all of us, but our duties have changed. Apparently, I'm a general, now."

"Wonders will never cease," she said. "It's about time."

"Do you think that will impress the elders of my line?" he asked Máire.

She laughed and shook her head. "Claudius, I doubt Cernunnos Himself could impress that lot!"

He smiled a little as she walked out. "Like it or not, I can still make you laugh, Banbh Ceanúil," he murmured. He began to prepare for the reading, pleased that she didn't seem to dwell in despair.

Perhaps dealing with the creation of the new Deargh Du stronghold in Vézelay will keep her mind busy and away from the loss.

Awvarwy remained silent. For once, the silence did not annoy him or make him nervous.

Reginald's eyes remained closed, and his lips moved in a nearly silent prayer.

Awvarwy considered praying for Talia to Lugh, but then he reconsidered that. As a Christian, she would probably prefer prayers be said to the Jewish God and His son. He tried to think of an appropriate and humble way to begin a prayer, when footsteps and an undeniable presence interrupted him.

"Ah, there you are," Máire said. "Hello, Reginald."

Reginald inclined his head towards her.

"Awvarwy, your presence is requested." Máire crouched, lowering herself so they would not have to stare up at her.

"And your beauty is blinding." He smirked. Upon seeing Máire turn pink, he felt his smirk turn into a true smile. "Also, I'm so glad you didn't call me 'Mandubratius'."

"Thank you." Her eyes darted away from his, and she stood up. "Claudius is… he requests your presence, I mean. Apparently, Marcus mentioned you in his will."

"That's rather intriguing," he said, feeling astounded at the news. "I have no notion of why he'd deem me worthy of any of his possessions." He paused and chuckled. "By the Gods, Marcus hasn't left me dung, has he, Máire?"

"I know not what he's bequeathed to you, Awvarwy, but if you don't follow me, you'll never know. Let's go, or we'll be late."

"Fine. My curiosity compels me to follow, even though I think this may be nothing more than a final opportunity to insult me." He stood up and looked over at Reginald. "There is a wake, Reginald. You should consider going. Talia loved a good celebration. Besides, we orphans must stick together."

"I'll think on it," Reginald muttered.

Awvarwy turned to follow Máire, who was several paces ahead. "I'll allow Marcus a final insult," he shouted, before catching up with her. "You seem to be in good spirits."

"I have an opportunity to help my line with their new home," Máire commented. "I am looking to the future with a happy heart."

"I am glad to hear that. I feared you would be in mourning for a long time."

"I am certain I will mourn him," Máire admitted. "However, I should move on, and he waits in a better place. Morrigan wished him to join Her, and I have to remain here as one of Her balances in this realm."

"Of course. You handle this trial with an impressive amount of grace and dignity." He realized she faked her stoicism, but he couldn't fault her for trying to look strong.

When they arrived at Claudius' tent, everyone gathered appeared rather uncomfortable on the floor. Claudius paced in front of the portable desk and managed to look his new role.

Máire sat down next to Julien, and Awvarwy took a seat a few feet away.

"Well, it appears that everyone is here," Claudius said. He pulled out a scroll and unrolled it. "Excellent. Let's begin, shall we?" He cleared his throat. "I, General Claudius Metrius Sertorius of the Sugnwr Gwaed line, read this will to the beneficiaries of General Marcus Galerius Primus Helvetticus of Bath of the Deargh Du line."

"Roman bureaucracy," Awvarwy muttered.

"Honestly, Claudius," Mac Alpin grumbled. "Get on with it. I don't want to miss the wake."

"Now, show some respect, you two. I will read this as Marcus dictated, without inappropriate interruptions," Claudius chided.

Mac Alpin sighed and fell silent.

"Thank you both." Claudius cleared his throat again. "'I, Marcus Galerius Primus Helvetticus, having fallen in battle, do bequeath my family, friends, and others my earthly possessions to be dispensed in the following manner. To Claudius Metrius Sertorius, who will make an excellent successor to my duties, though he will complain about them, I bequeath my home in Bath on the condition that my family and friends can visit and reside there unless they drink all the bloodmead or attempt to set it afire.'"

"It doesn't say that," Edward uttered.

"I swear on Sulis that these were his words exact," Claudius said with a smile. "'Also, Claudius must care for my extended mortal family, the descendants of Berti and Sitara, and Leandros Galerius. To Arwin Mac Alpin, I bequeath my swords, arms, and armor here and in Bath. Claudius will guide you to their location.'"

"I deserve the house," Máire muttered. She looked a little bewildered.

"Maél Morrigan, you hate the house in Bath." Claudius chuckled. "Marcus knew that. You thought the baths were too hot. May I continue?"

Máire shrugged.

"'To Edward, I leave ten thousand livres or current equivalent, not to spend on mead, but to improve your methods of not blowing up my home,'" Claudius continued. He cleared his throat again and grabbed a cup of wine. After a few swallows, he returned to the papers.

"'To Julien de Divio, I leave you also ten thousand livres and my brass horn, which is to be sent to you from my home in Bath. Please learn to play it better than I could. I believe Banbh Ceanúil says that I sound like a pair of rutting mules when I play it.'" Claudius chuckled. "You must tell Julien about the horn."

Máire grinned. "We all know Marcus played the horn horribly. The people of Bath thought the noises were farts from a hideous and unspeakable monster." She patted Julien's leg.

"I have never played a musical instrument in my life," Julien lamented. "I am almost certain I will scare the people of Vézelay with this horn." The youngling appeared pleased.

Claudius laughed. "Now, he says that he is certain that Máire relayed the tale of the Beast of Bath. I shall continue. 'To my beautiful Banbh Ceanúil, who has my heart, I leave the remainder of my monetary fortune, stored in the locations that Claudius knows about. I believe it is valued at two million livres in silver.' So, Maél Morrigan, do you still wish to trade for the house?"

"No," she replied. "I think I'll let you enjoy it. You will appreciate it more than I could."

"Yes, very true," Claudius answered. "Now, I begin again. 'To Sáerlaith, who accepted me and loved me, aside from my unending love for you, there is only one thing of mine that interests us both, the set of ancient artifacts from civilizations past. Claudius will deliver these treasures for safekeeping in the new stronghold when you feel the time is right. Please keep an eye on my new family in Vézelay.'"

Awvarwy watched Sáerlaith nod and close her eyes.

"'To Mandubratius or Awvarwy ap Manaywdan, Co-Consul of the Lamia and former Chieftain of the Trinovantes,'" Claudius paused. Awvarwy noticed the others in the tent turn to study him for a reaction. "'I bequeath to my dear friend a treasure of untold value that has enriched my own life and shall enhance yours.'"

Awvarwy couldn't help but feel some excitement. He heard the others mutter and murmur amongst themselves.

Claudius allowed for tension to rise. "'My Fidchell set.'"

"Fidchell set?" Awvarwy asked. "Edward and Julien get ten thousand livres, but all I get a Fidchell set?" He looked at Julien. "Well, I suppose it's better than a horn."

"Please allow me to finish, Mandubratius," Claudius urged. "'I leave you my Fidchell set because you'll need the practice for the next time we meet. You are the worst Fidchell player I've ever competed against.'"

"It's only because he hides the chieftain and cowers when confronted." Awvarwy chortled. "Never once did he present a challenging attack."

"'I am certain Awvarwy states that I'm a horrible player of Fidchell as well, but now is the time for celebration and not arguments. Do not cry at my wake. I wish to see you all enjoying yourselves. If any beneficiaries did not survive, it is up to Claudius and Máire to decide who receives my bequeathal.' Now I'm finished," Claudius rolled up the scroll.

The general passed weapons to Mac Alpin and presented the Fidchell set to Awvarwy.

Awvarwy thanked Claudius and began to head to the exit of the tent. Before he exited, he looked over his shoulder and caught a glimpse of a small scroll passing between Claudius and Máire, who then kissed and parted. "Do I get a scroll too, general?" he asked.

"No. It is a private message from Marcus to his daughter-in-darkness," Claudius answered. "Now, move along. There is a celebration to attend."

Awvarwy left the tent, holding the Fidchell board. "I think I understand the challenge, Marcus," he murmured with a smile. "I shall prepare for our Fidchell tournament in the Otherworld." He then tucked the board and the bag of pieces under his arm and headed towards the wake.

chapter eighteen

harles settled back on his cot, planning for a peaceful night of sleep. Tomorrow, he would leave for Vézelay. He believed that the Deargh Du and his son would arrive before him. As he closed his eyes, he suddenly heard voices rise as one, calling for women, wine, and song in Latin. Loud pipes and drums overwhelmed the sounds of animals, as loud feral shouts were called and repeated by revelers.

He jumped to his feet and witnessed a staggering bonfire come to life. The call and refrain of a song echoed through the forest like an ancient call to life and all its pleasures. However, his displeasure rose at another sleepless night. The Pope's funeral rites had lasted too long.

The foreign noises brought the mortal soldiers out of their beds.

Loud laughter and the racket of celebration set Charles' teeth on edge. "Ercanbald?!" he shouted into the growing din. "What is that infernal noise?" He had heard talk of a wake from Julien and assumed it would be a mournful remembrance, not this bacchanalia.

"Yes, Imperial Majesty," Ercanbald yelled back in response. "I know this celebration is dreadfully loud. The angels are toasting their victory, I think."

"Or would this be how they mourn?" Charles shouted back.

His secretary shrugged. "They are foreign angels with strange customs, Imperial Majesty. I've noticed that they cry during joy, so perhaps festivals during mourning would not be so outlandish for them."

"Foreign or not, and angels or not, they are disturbing my sleep. What are you going to do about it, Ercanbald?"

"I will speak to them, Imperial Majesty." Ercanbald ducked away.

Charles crossed his arms over his chest, waiting for his secretary to return and for the rejoicing to settle down. If anything, the shouting and music grew louder.

A few moments later, a very pale and trembling Ercanbald returned.

"Well?"

"I spoke to them."

"And?" Charles stared impatiently at his secretary.

"The big brute with the unkempt beard told me to leave and stop dishonoring his dearest friend's wake, or he'd turn me into dinner," Ercanbald replied with a shiver.

"You didn't stand your ground? You are an old woman! That Mac Alpin was testing you. I'll go speak to him myself."

"But, Imperial Majesty, your robe!"

Charles held up a hand and simply walked away from Ercanbald into the swelling music. The heat of the bonfire warmed the air, and the idea of wearing a robe now seemed quite ridiculous. He heard noise overhead and shuffled back as figures leapt over the bonfire and cheered. Obscene sounds and giggles now grew louder as the musicians stopped and began playing a new song. This time, the words seemed like the braying of animals. Then he saw naked men and women wearing makeshift animal masks darting around him. He turned and felt a young woman back into him.

The young woman stood, revealing herself to be mostly disrobed. "I'm so sorry," she cooed. The stranger pulled up her mask enough to reveal a rather seductive smile. She pulled him in for a kiss, and he tasted honey, flowers, blood, and wine. Yet, a strange smell of something like incense or burnt herbs seemed to surround the woman.

Charles felt a moment of light-headed shock as he returned the kiss.

The sound of a slap from the other side of the woman jarred his attention.

He noticed a masked figure slap her backside again, then a sharp sensation woke him as the woman bit down. He felt her fangs caress his tongue, but then she pulled away, uttering a little gasp of pleasure at the next slap. Charles felt a lingering moment of disappointment as the woman darted away from him, into the writhing throng of naked and nearly naked blood-drinkers dancing to the music.

He realized a cup of wine had been pressed into his hand. He raised the cup to his lips and smelled the scent of honey and flowers mixed in. Charles paused a moment, wondering whether this wine contained extra ingredients besides honey and flowers. He pushed aside his mild disgust drank it anyway. It was sweet and thick, but he found no taste of blood. After gulping down the rest of the sweet beverage, he wiped at his mouth with his hand. The smell of the herbal incense grew as he left in search of more of the delightful beverage, but laughter distracted him. He looked over to the source of the laughter and witnessed another masked woman run towards him.

The woman raised her mask, revealing her to be the Empress, and smiled at him before, ducking around a tent.

Mac Alpin chased after her.

Charles turned back, heading towards the barrels of wine, and faced the original masked woman, who pushed back her mask, revealing herself to be Máire, who smiled.

Her green eyes darted from side to side, as if she were drunk or experiencing the effects of some other intoxicant. She opened her mouth to say something. Perhaps she did say something, but whatever she meant to say halted as the Papal Emissary, who appeared to be naked as well, grabbed her by the waist and said something in a guttural tongue Charles couldn't understand.

Máire burst out laughing and turned towards the Emissary. She slapped his left cheek in a playful manner before saying something in reply, prompting the Emissary to laugh.

Charles watched as the pink handprint faded away.

Mandubratius raised his hand to return the strike, but Claudius shoved the Lamia aside, picked up Máire, tossed her over his shoulder, and ran off.

Máire and Claudius laughed as if it were the greatest joke ever played.

The Papal Emissary stood up, shook his head, and chuckled at whatever they had said. He then turned and raced towards Basileus Irene.

Charles felt a hand reach under his tunic and grab his groin in a playful manner, as a pale face with hair of moonlight and spun gold eased into his view, smiling at him. "Fianait?"

She met his gaze, and her eyes glowed green.

He closed his eyes and slid a hand over those silken tresses, as she began to pleasure him. His objections to the raucous party faded, as his desire and joy grew.

Julien lay under a blanket of stars, with one leg crossed over the other, watching the billowing smoke plum around the celebrants like a strange, gray snake. Among the revelers, he spied his father and the Pope chatting over wine. He witnessed many blood-drinkers, including Claudius and Máire, leaping over the bonfire.

He remembered the joyful pleasures of the first wake he had attended. However, Julien felt little bliss or enjoyment tonight.

Marcus left me a horn and money. Everything will be different with him gone.

In the midst of his contemplation, he saw Sáerlaith sit down next to him.

"Julien, I hope you do not mind me joining you." She appeared to be one of the few still clothed. "Are you not enjoying the wake?"

"I have trouble understanding the celebration," he admitted. "I should be happy, but I'm worried about the future."

"Ahhh." Sáerlaith stretched her legs out. "I am not worried, because you will be with us in Vézelay. You will tie us to these foreign lands. You should join our council." She smiled. "Marcus would have wished for that. Of course, he would have liked to see Máire take her place amongst us, but something within me says that she enjoys her time outside of the group. She finds governance to be dull. However, I think you will help your line immensely."

Julien found no words.

"Enough about duties. Let's go enjoy this celebration of our friend. You do know our merry-making and love-making is to honor Marcus, right?" Sáerlaith extended her arm. "This is a commemoration of his life. I see him gaming," she pointed towards Mandubratius and Amata playing Fidchell, "and drinking," she motioned towards his father, the Basileus, Pope Leo, Mac Alpin, and many others imbibing. She gestured towards a playful fight between many blood-drinkers. "And there is Marcus carousing. This is all for him, Julien. Well, him and the rest of our fallen allies. He wanted this... no tears, remember? None will leave this celebration unsatisfied." She chuckled. "Even though he was Roman, Marcus was truly one of us," Sáerlaith added. "He hated being thought of as an ungracious host. So, will you bed me now, or continue mourning someone that has gone home in glory with the Phantom Queen?" Sáerlaith tossed aside her clothing, and the winds shifted, dispersing the sponnc over them.

Julien grinned and pulled Sáerlaith towards him, as the sponnc set his mind adrift. His worries escaped. Elation whispered in his ear as Sáerlaith began to feed from him.

Her mouth and tongue teased over the wound as she tugged at his clothing.

Some time had passed since the last time He had taken mortal form in this world. He embraced the wind, loved the feel of the blades of grass between His toes, and the anticipation of catching that female blood-drinker. He tackled her and laughed as they rolled into the valley.

Pleasure distracts me from my duty, but what does one delight matter?

After melding with her, He arose and faded into the darkness.

The Sugnwr Gwaed female snoozed on the grass, oblivious to His movements, or His identity.

He could sense Awvarwy in the distance. His foster son's whereabouts remained outside of this plane of existence. He found shadow and changed His form into that of a familiar, furry, black cat. He began to trot towards the Lamia.

He passed numerous blood-drinkers, who cooed and patted Him. He attempted to mimic Lucius and did well enough.

No one seems suspicious.

He noticed Awvarwy speaking to a woman with a noble bearing. Their conversation seemed to be nothing more than flirtation. Another figure appeared in the distance, and the woman he spied scampered off towards the Ekimmu Cruitne.

He slinked in front of Awvarwy and flicked His tail back and forth. Impatient with the wait, He began to groom his front paws.

"Lugh, I thought—"

"Do not refer to me by that name in this form. It may raise suspicions."

Awvarwy looked stunned and somewhat embarrassed at his tone. He decided to curb his tongue.

"Forgive me, Lucius," the Lamia said, before tilting his head to the side. "Weren't we just talking a few minutes ago?"

"Yes," the cat purred. "You saw me, and we spoke about families."

"Yes." The Lamia closed his eyes. "The sponnc, wine, and mushrooms do strange things to my brain, Lucius."

"It is indeed a delightful substance, Awvarwy. Follow me, so we can talk without too many ears." He scampered off to the southwest, while Lugh's slightly drunk son followed him. Once they were out of earshot, He stopped and stared up at the mortal. "Well now, here we are, Awvarwy. Tell me, what are your designs on Máire?"

Awvarwy laughed. "Oh father, you know very well my designs on Máire," he whispered. "We spoke about it, remember?" He coughed a little as smoke trailed from the fires. His eyes went to the skies. "I want to marry her, Lucius," he stated, beginning to chuckle. "I want to marry her and retire to a home in the country, and we will raise sheep." The mortal dropped to his knees and continued laughing.

I have heard stranger wishes. Oh well.

"So, that is your intention? To marry her?"

"Yes," Awvarwy acknowledged, raising a finger. "I'm not so sure about the sheep, but I really do think she and I would make each other happy."

"I'm not sure if that's a wise idea, anymore… in the short term, at least."

"Why is that? I really do want to make her happy," Awvarwy whispered. His eyes became green and sad.

He almost wept for the Lamia. He crawled over and placed a paw on Awvarwy's left leg. "It appears that Morrigan is not happy that Her cherished son does not walk this realm. She's also upset that his removal was done in your name. Granted, you aren't responsible for it, but I have it on good authority that should you engage in any kind of romantic overtures to Máire, Morrigan would intervene and banish you to the Field of the Judged. I wouldn't be able to help you, then."

Awvarwy became silent for a moment, before speaking further. "What do I need to do to redeem this situation, then? You said this was for me. I didn't ask for Marcus' death. I wished to end it myself, once, but that is entirely different."

"This is for you, but there are things about the Tuaths that are beyond your understanding, Awvarwy. Imagine having to match wits with someone while playing one thousand games of Fidchell at the same time. Word has it that you cannot even win one game at a time. At least, Marcus says so."

Awvarwy's eyes turned dark for a moment. "I never had much time to play Fidchell as a mortal, Lucius, because of my so-called father's treachery. I thought I was going to escape these insults. What's next? Will Marcus or his Matron call me 'Ragged Nails'?"

"You can redeem yourself, son." He met Awvarwy's eyes.

"How?"

"You must give up the leadership of the Lamia to someone less controversial." He groomed a paw for a moment. "Tour the world. Get to know the people, not as a conqueror, but as a visitor and a diplomat. Besides, I believe Máire would appreciate that as well."

"That is a hard price," the Lamia swallowed. He looked up, staring at a copse of trees in the distance. "However, for her love and Morrigan's blessing, I will do that."

He felt himself purr, sensing the Lamia did not lie. He wondered how long Awvarwy could keep paying the price. He had to admire this lad for being willing to give up power for love and blessings.

If only I had done this sooner. Ah, well.

"Dare I ask if there are further requirements?" Awvarwy met his eyes.

"There are."

"Name them, assuming it is more than one." The Lamia sat down.

He leaned up against Awvarwy.

This Lamia seems most perceptive, and not as addled as most mortals or other blood-drinkers.

He purred and nuzzled against him, finding it easier to act as a fairy cat. "First, I advise you to select high-ranking Lamia as ambassadors to the Celtic lines. They must be honest."

"And what else, Lucius?"

He purred. "Do not pursue the Phallus Maximus."

Fires of desire burned in Awvarwy's green eyes at that condition, but the Lamia soon sighed and shook his head. His eyes grew calm. "I will do as you recommend, Lucius," he said. "How will I know if I have gained Morrigan's favor?"

"Not favor, so much as less revulsion. Her temperament changes too much, Awvarwy. Máire will let you know when the time is right." He attempted to hold back His smile.

"You realize this redemption could take a long time," Awvarwy stated. "Máire pretends to be fine, but misery holds her."

"True, but that is Máire. Time?" He chuckled. "What is time to the Tuaths, or the Lamia? We exist in infinite planes. We have no time, Awvarwy."

"Are we talking months, years, decades?"

He bounded onto Awvarwy's shoulder and leaned in towards an ear.

"Morrigan is a Tuath and chooses to be a Goddess. Like women, Her mood can be tempered, especially if you help Her children recover from their loss. If that is the path that you pursue, you will find that redemption can be earned in years... or a decade or two... instead of centuries."

He noticed his whiskers tickled the mortal and found pleasure in watching him smile.

"I am pleased that you told me this before I made a fool of myself, or found myself condemned to the Field of the Judged."

"Then go, my son, and find redemption." He nuzzled Awvarwy's ear before hopping down. He then raced into shadow again. Upon reaching a hiding place, He looked back at Awvarwy and whispered, "You are much better than I gave you credit for, Awvarwy ap Lugh." He then changed into His true form and parted the gates of the Otherworld. He joined the winds as a vortex and flew through the mists.

He stopped after reaching the other side, landed, and closed the passage.

Lugh stared at Him with a grimace. His foster son's eyes became wet. "What have you undone, Manannán?" Lugh asked.

"I have undone nothing, Lugh." Manannán chuckled. "He had it too easy, son. He needed challenges. That is what we do for those we love." As Manannán headed towards the waters of the Otherworld, he heard nothing else from His foster son. Lugh would forgive Him soon.

Better My challenges than the Phantom Queen's.

Claudius stretched out, while everyone else rested against the cushions, sated and staring at the early morning stars. He raised a brow upon hearing Máire utter a snort. "What's so amusing?"

"Would you send me that silly jade tiger, Claudius?"

He grinned. "Certainly."

"Jade tiger?" asked Julien before sitting up.

"Inside joke," Claudius explained. "We used to have contests to entertain ourselves and keep Máire busy." He chuckled. "We had to come up with some artifacts, and we would hide them. One of us would make up a crazy story to convince Máire to find the artifact, and the jade tiger was our last contest." He paused before admitting, "I will miss that game."

"Hmmmm, that does sound like fun," Horatio chuckled. "I wish we had wakes in Italy. My father's funeral was two years ago, and all we did was weep for days. I think he would have enjoyed a celebration like this."

"I hate funerals," a familiar voice stated.

Claudius looked up and noticed the Pope had joined them and sat down.

"Indeed," the Emperor chuckled. "I hope you will remember this when there is a wake in my honor."

Claudius raised his cup. "Let's give one last toast to the victors who gave their all." He watched cups raised and various honors were spoken in different languages.

"So," Edward asked, "when do we go home?"

Claudius realized he hadn't considered his traveling plans. "The mortals will leave at daybreak, I'm sure," he said.

Emperor Charles grumbled a bit. "Yes, it will be a long day."

"I'm sure a few mortals and draft horses will remain to take our supplies to Vézelay," Caoimhín said.

"Aye, but some of us are heading north," Arwin stated. "We'll be fine. A good hole in the ground is all any of us need. We've gotten soft, sleeping in tents." He smirked.

"Well, then call me soft," Amata replied. "I plan on enjoying a tent until I can get a real bed."

Arwin chuckled. "Amata, I heard about your victories in battle. You are not soft."

Amata stroke a hand over Edward's newly formed legs. As the two lovers shared a smile, Claudius wondered whether he would be entertaining an extra house guest.

"So, where are you going tomorrow night," asked Patroclus as he looked around the circle of recovering blood-drinkers and mortals.

"I don't know about the rest of you, but I have a wonderful house in Bath to make my own," Claudius answered.

"I will go back to Aachen, after Vézelay," the Emperor answered, "where I will go to my hunts, my numerous children, and many beautiful women."

"Please refrain from chasing the women in Vézelay," Julien advised. "That is, if you wish to chase my mother. She may not be pleased if you do not behave." He chuckled.

"For your mother, I'll consider behaving," the Emperor answered.

"Mmmmm," Arwin looked serious for a moment. "I think I'd like to stay in Bath for awhile, Claudius, if that is possible."

"Possible?" Claudius tried not to laugh. "You heard the general's orders. You and all his friends are invited to stay with me as long as you wish. Even if there were no such orders, I would love permanent guests. Besides, I assume some of the Deargh Du will stay with us in Bath until their stronghold is complete. I will need you, Edward, and Horatio there to keep them in line." He noticed Sáerlaith grin. "However, there will be no explosions, Edward."

"I have money to pay for new equipment and safety measures," Edward replied. "The home will be safe, Claudius."

"May I stay in Bath, too?" Amata asked. Her arm rested on Edward's leg.

Claudius had to wonder how long their relationship could last, but Gods knew Edward needed Amata.

Mandubratius laughed loudly, interrupting his chance to invite Amata.

"Amata, you hate the cold. You remember the cold and the rain, don't you? Besides, I plan on going to Bath to be the ambassador of the Lamia to the Ekimmu Cruitne and Sugnwr Gwaed. I miss Britain."

Claudius witnessed the light of truth in Mandubratius' eyes, though it summarily faded, to be replaced by cunning. "When was this decided, Mandubratius?" he queried. "I thought you loved being the co-consul of the Lamia."

"Just now." The Lamia smiled. "I tire of the responsibility, to be honest. It's not fun, anymore."

Claudius thought over that comment, reasoning that Mandubratius wished to find the treasure. He opened his mouth, hoping his statement would not be too boorish and offensive, but Sáerlaith interjected.

"I realize this is not the Deargh Du's concern," Sáerlaith began, "but I think it would be inappropriate for you to personally take an official residence in the Anglo-Saxon kingdoms or Scotland."

Claudius knew his eyes reflected gratitude to her.

The head of the Council winked at him.

"Oh, Sáerlaith, is this because of our little squabble in Éire? That is rather small, after our alliance and all we've been through in the last few months," Mandubratius drawled.

"I would welcome our alliance to continue, and would enjoy having a Lamia ambassador, Awvarwy." Sáerlaith offered a most lovely smile to Mandubratius, along with some of her glamoury. "I also believe that the other Celtic lines would appreciate ambassadors from the Lamia line."

"Yet, you would prefer me to not serve my line in such a manner." Mandubratius' eyes reflected a tiny shred of manipulation.

"Yes, that is correct," Sáerlaith affirmed. "I cannot speak for the great councils of the Sugnwr Gwaed or Ekimmu Cruitne, but I feel that they might feel the same."

"But, I'm not so bad," Mandubratius purred.

"I am certain that both lines would welcome ambassadors," Claudius responded. "I will even send a letter of introduction, though part of me doubts that they would listen to me." He chuckled. "I left that realm of politics some time ago."

Mandubratius looked at the faces around him. "Very well, then. Could Amata serve as the ambassador to either line, since she will be in Bath anyway?"

"I will speak to the Council of Ekimmu Cruitne on her behalf," Mac Alpin offered. "I am certain they will appreciate her wisdom."

"I will send letters of introduction to both councils," Sáerlaith added.

"I had hoped to escape politics, but I suppose being an ambassador would not be so bad," Amata replied. "Thank you both."

Mandubratius turned his gaze towards Máire. "And where are you going? Back to Bath, with your family?"

Máire shifted a little. "Some of my family is going to Vézelay to begin work on our new home," she answered. "Vézelay is where I will go."

Mandubratius nodded. His eyes revealed a rare gravity. A moment of disappointment appeared and then faded. "That is a good idea, Máire. Your family needs your assistance." The Lamia moved his eyes away from Máire and looked amused again. "Well, then. Getting back to the topic of ambassadors, Sáerlaith, how would you feel about Patroclus acting as ambassador to the Deargh Du in Vézelay?"

Sáerlaith turned to Caoimhín. "You have always been an excellent judge on these matters. What do you think?"

Caoimhín closed his eyes, and everyone fell silent. "I think he'd serve all parties with dignity and fairness," he said.

"You've been drafted," Amata chuckled. "Welcome to politics, Patroclus."

"The honor is to serve," Patroclus replied and then belched.

"Horatio, perhaps you would serve as the Lamia's ambassador to the Sugnwr Gwaed, since I assume you will be in Bath," Mandubratius stated.

Horatio hiccupped. "Yes, I wanted to return there."

"Can you aid him in becoming the ambassador?" Mandubratius asked Claudius.

"I will do my best," he replied.

At the least, Horatio will have a home in Bath.

"Excellent." Mandubratius rested his hands on his knees. "Perhaps Reginald would be willing to act as our ambassador to the Emperor. Do you think he would be interested?" His keen gaze settled on Julien.

Julien shrugged. "It will give him something to do, which would suit him, I think, but I have no idea if he'd be interested. Ask him, don't ask me." Julien scooted over and rested his head against Máire's left shoulder.

She grinned and wrapped an arm around him.

"Now that that's settled, I'm pleased that you have accepted our ambassadors as much as you could," Mandubratius stated as he looked over the gathered blood-drinkers. "I was wondering if you would extend to us the same honor."

Mac Alpin laughed. "Why are you looking in my direction, Awvarwy? I hate Rome, and while I can speak for Amata to the Council, I cannot speak for my Council. I doubt I will be recommended for any diplomatic work."

Mandubratius took a long draught on his wine. "I was asking for an appointment or suggestions from you. I know you would rather go anywhere but Rome, Arwin."

Claudius chuckled. "Arwin's ex-wife will go with a suggestion of his, and she holds much sway on the Council. They are still somewhat friendly."

"You had a wife?" Julien sat up. "That answers many questions." His face revealed a wide smile.

"Youngling, what are you speaking of... what questions?" Arwin's eyes turned dark.

"Your short temper, the desire to couple with anything, including that wolverine with a crown, as well as any animal," Julien continued, goading Mac Alpin.

"Excuse me?!" The Basileus rose up, enraged. "I am not a wolverine!"

"I'll show you what it's like to be an animal!" Arwin leapt to his feet, even though he still appeared to be unsteady with drink.

Julien sprinted away, looking a little fearful. They both disappeared into the surrounding forests.

The Basileus shrugged and sat, looking as if she forgot about the insult, or simply didn't care anymore.

"I hope they'll return before sunrise," Máire commented.

"Arwin will return in an hour or so," Edward informed her. "Julien may be limping to you for comfort soon after."

Claudius leaned over and patted her hand. "They'll be fine."

They fell silent again, staring at the stars.

"Why are there so few mortals here?" Fianait muttered.

"Perhaps because I told them that if they came to this celebration, they would go to hell," Pope Leo replied with a shrug.

"And you are risking your soul for this unholy gathering, Leo?" Mandubratius smirked. He then set up the gifted Fidchell board.

The Pope shrugged. "Most mortals wouldn't be able to understand this. They would be fearful of experiencing this kind of celebration." Leo leaned back against a rock. "I am their spiritual leader, so I am required to understand these gatherings and put them in a context that the children of God will understand."

"Mmmmm," the Emperor muttered. "Well, I'm here because I can do whatever I wish. I believe that God wouldn't give us appetites if He, She, or They didn't wish us to enjoy them."

"Charles, please don't speak that belief too loudly," Pope Leo murmured. "We need the Church to maintain order. Besides, the Church keeps our people honest and forthright. You can't disagree that the Church does some good."

"Of course," the Emperor answered. "I am certain the people will always have faith in the institutions in Rome." His voice revealed something of a contradiction to his words.

Claudius stretched his arms overhead. "I know there's something I must do, but I can't remember. I'm not even sure if I can move," he yawned.

"Perhaps you're thinking about who should be your line's ambassador to the Lamia," Mandubratius mused.

"No, I'm sure that's not it, because I hold less sway with the great council of my line than Mac Alpin does with his. I plan on spending at least a decade in Bath before returning to London."

"I am sure that I can suggest a few," Sáerlaith offered. "Fianait, would you like the honor?"

"Even though it is not the Deargh Du's slogan, I will echo Patroclus' sentiment. The honor is to serve," Fianait said before grabbing another cup.

Claudius noticed a moment of disappointment in Mandubratius' eyes.

Perhaps he wishes Máire will volunteer.

Máire crossed her arms over her chest and looked sleepy.

"Fianait will be welcomed in Rome, but not by me. Sextus will have that honor," Mandubratius replied. "I promoted him to general and told him that he would be in Rome, now." He nodded towards the semi-conscious new general.

Sextus nodded his head. "I am the co-consul's eyes and ears," he drawled, grinning, before belching into his hand.

Claudius raised a brow at Mandubratius' decision.

Mac Alpin fell down next to Máire, looking winded.

"That was quick," the Deargh Du muttered to Arwin.

"No need to do more than was done," Arwin replied to her. He turned his attention to Mandubratius. "And where are you planning on going, Awvarwy?" he asked.

"Arwin, I'm pleased at your interest in Lamia politics," Mandubratius replied with a smile.

Claudius caught Máire's gaze and rolled his eyes.

That Briton dominates any conversation.

"I will be helping install the ambassador and future consul, your beloved, the Basileus Irene," Mandubratius answered between sips of wine. "For now, we shall be co-consuls, though."

The Basileus dropped her wine cup. "I... what?" she stammered.

"I thought you wanted to be consul," Mandubratius stated.

It seems a bit too convenient to be believed. I wonder why?

"Well, yes, I did. I just didn't know it would happen so quickly." The Basileus' blue eyes sparkled with pleasure.

"So, I assume you accept." Mandubratius poured himself more wine.

"Of course!"

Claudius noticed Arwin looking down at the ground for a moment, before returning his gaze elsewhere, wondering where Julien hid.

"Excellent. Then, you are ambassador and co-consul." Mandubratius shrugged. "Once you are comfortable with your new role, I will step back and tour the allies of the Lamia to boost our relations. In fact," the Lamia turned his eyes to Claudius, "I'm hoping I'll be welcome at your new home in Bath. I did love the view from the western bedroom on the top floor."

"So did Marcus," Máire blurted out. She sighed and looked at her feet.

Claudius thought over Marcus' instructions, thinking Mandubratius didn't truly count as a friend, but then again, he had left him a favorite game.

"I'd be honored to accept you as a guest to further relations between the Celtic lines and the Lamia," he said.

I will need to find a safe place for the treasures, in short order.

"Thank you for that most gracious invitation, Claudius. I'll send word when I intend to visit." Awvarwy then glanced at Sáerlaith. "Will I be allowed to visit the Deargh Du?"

Sáerlaith's eyes lowered for a moment. "You have an invitation to visit us in Vézelay, Awvarwy. However, I'm afraid that neither we nor you will be invited to Ard Mhacha, anytime soon."

Claudius sensed a strange moment of fleeting sadness and pity on the Lamia's face, yet it passed.

"I sincerely hope that one day you may all return to Ard Mhacha," Awvarwy said.

"Until that day comes, we will be most content in our new stronghold in Vézelay," Sáerlaith replied, "thanks to Julien's family and the Emperor. Where did you chase him to, Arwin?"

"He got away with nary a scratch," Mac Alpin answered.

"I wouldn't say it was nary a scratch," Julien called out from the trees.

The Deargh Du appeared from the forest with an arrow in his left shoulder.

"Arwin! You shot him with an arrow!" Máire shoved Arwin, stood up, and rushed to Julien.

Mac Alpin smirked. "What did you think I'd do?"

"It's not that bad," Julien muttered. He appeared to be a little embarrassed with her fuss.

Máire grumbled, grabbed the shaft of the arrow near the wound, and yanked it out.

Julien winced a little, muttering something to himself.

Claudius flinched as Máire removed the arrow from Julien's shoulder, but the other Deargh Du fell silent.

Marcus should be here, partaking in the festivities.

"I'm tired now," Claudius admitted to the celebrants. "I think I'll go to my tent." He forced a smile, hoping they wouldn't think he was mourning his old friend. As he trudged towards his tent, he heard the remaining revelers say their good-nights and begin to leave for their own beds.

chapter nineteen

By ones and twos, Máire looked on as the wake celebrants weaved towards their tents. However, she found herself desiring solitude. She decided to trudge up to the top of Ernstberg and peer at the vast expanse of forest, one last time, from the boulder east of the summit, which seemed so popular with everyone. She pulled her cloak in tighter around her body to try to stay warm, since the rest of her clothing remained in her tent. She started her walk, when someone called her name.

"Máire."

She stopped and turned on her heel, knowing that husky voice anywhere. "Awvarwy." She met his stare. "You look…"

"Dressed? Clean?" He chuckled.

"You've done better than me." She gave him what she felt was a limp smile. "I probably stink of wine and festivities."

"Nonsense," he purred. While walking forward, he moistened his lips. "I've been meaning to talk to you."

She had avoided anything more than coy playfulness with him, and now she felt nervous at his approach.

Awvarwy tilted his head a little and smiled. "There's something we need to discuss."

"Yes… we do… don't we?" She couldn't find sufficient words.

"I made something for you. I planned on bequeathing it to you, if you survived and I did not. I still want you to have it." He pulled out a bundle of cloth and extended it to her.

She recognized it as one of his old and dirty tunics. Máire suppressed her initial suspicion that perhaps this was a joke. After all, it would be just like Awvarwy to present her with dirty laundry. Curiosity grew and took hold of her. Máire held out her hands. "What is it?"

He chuckled and placed it in her palms. "Open it, chroí. It's not just a tunic." His fingers slid over hers for a moment.

She pulled away the fabric layers, and a mottled figure appeared. A fine dusting of black soot seeped onto her fingers for a moment. Máire flicked the dust away. She smiled as she held a small raven carving. She almost began to cry. Its beauty radiated in the firelight. Morrigan Herself loved to take this form. Coherent words still proved impossible to find. She finally swallowed her speechlessness. "Thank you," she whispered.

A flash of shame overwhelmed her, as she realized she had nothing to give him in return. Then she remembered her Lucius carving she had created. She had intended to present it to Marcus or Lucius himself, but under the circumstances, it seemed appropriate that it should go to Awvarwy.

"I have something for you, as well." She stroked a finger over her raven. "I planned on leaving it for you if I passed to the Otherworld." Her words were a lie, but she couldn't hurt his feelings. She glanced up at him, and he looked like a pleased child.

"What is it?" he asked. His smile made Máire forget her earlier misgivings.

She placed a finger on his lips, ran to the tent with her supplies, and fished the miniature figure of Lucius out of her bags. She wrapped in his tunic and ran back out to where Awvarwy stood. Máire presented the package. "Here."

He smiled and opened it. A chuckle rang out as he held aloft the miniature Lucius.

"I think of you as being very catlike," she admitted. "You purr, you preen." She shrugged a little. "I really see this when you and Lucius are chatting."

She witnessed a misting in Awvarwy's eyes. Then she found herself wrapped in his embrace.

"Words cannot describe how this gift makes me feel," he murmured in her ear. Shifting the carving to one hand, he brushed away her hair and turned her face to him with a fingertip. His lips settled on hers.

Her uncertainty grew, but she forgot her bewilderment as his mouth caressed hers. Máire vaguely remembered that she did not wish to do this, but her arms slid around him anyway.

Will I be able to say 'no' if things go any further? Part of me wants him. Perhaps it is the drink, sponnc, and other herbs in my system. Yes, that must be it. That would definitely explain my strange desire.

When Awvarwy pulled away, she felt peculiar disappointment well within her. Reminding herself of the lives Mandubratius had destroyed in order to gain the Phallus Maximus, she tried to convince herself to be relieved that he pursued no further.

"Thank you, Máire." He backed a step away. "I regret that I won't be able to live in Vézelay. However, I will visit when I have an opportunity."

Her conflict grew, along with disgust for herself. Mandubratius had killed her family and loved ones, like a cat destroying birds or mice when it wasn't even hungry.

What am I thinking?

"Sunrise is soon. I'm exhausted," she stated finally, giving up on the idea of walking to that boulder with a wonderful view of the eastern slope. The situation now seemed awkward. His feelings for her were obvious. However, this was against her disposition. She hated him, or at least she thought she did, once.

"I am tired as well," Awvarwy admitted. "I will see you in the evening before we leave. Rest well."

She watched him turn and walk towards his tent. Following his departure, Máire trudged towards the tent she shared with Claudius and Julien. She pushed up the flap and walked in.

Her son-in-darkness slept, while Claudius looked up at her from his bedroll and blankets.

She lay down between Claudius and Julien. Saying nothing, still considering the events of the last few minutes, she ran her finger over the figure of the carved raven again.

Claudius watched Máire as she stared up at the ceiling of the tent. She held a small, wooden raven in her hand. "If you want to talk about it, you can," he advised her.

She shook her head a little. "It's not a subject that I want to utter to myself, Claudius. Thank you for your concern, though." She placed the raven above her head roll on a stack of bedding. "Sleep well."

"You too," he said, wishing he could say something that would make her feel safe and secure, but he felt certain that it wouldn't work. Before he could close his eyes, he sensed a mortal approach the tent. He looked up and saw Máire rolling onto her side, obviously sensing the same, familiar person. Claudius arose as the Emperor pulled back the tent flap. "I see you recovered well, Imperial Majesty," Claudius greeted.

"I must look better than I feel, then," the Emperor replied, smiling. "General, may I take a moment more of your time?"

Claudius nodded. "Yes, Imperial Majesty."

"Please call me Charles in private, general."

"Then, please call me, Claudius." He motioned to a folding chair, and the mortal sat down.

"I know the burdens of leadership are heavy," the Emperor began.

Claudius chuckled. "Very soon, my burdens will disappear. I plan on returning to Bath. Not much to do there but watch the growing town and act as host to many celebrations."

"You are Marcus' second," the Emperor replied. "That means you commanded many of the races, and mortals as well. That sounds like leadership to me. Why give that up?"

Claudius shook his head. "I am a very small figure in the world of the Sugnwr Gwaed. True, I led them, once. Then things changed, and I just didn't want to deal with the infighting anymore. I'm an outsider again, as more and more of my line are Saxon. The politics between bickering Saxons, Romans, and Britons will make anyone want to escape. Granted, the Saxons have become less barbaric, but they are uncultured and strange, sometimes."

"And that's when you returned to Bath," Máire interrupted with a yawn, before returning to her feigned sleep act.

"Yes," he answered. "Many centuries ago, I had enough. I moved from a leader down to a senator, and I decided that it was time to stop being a politician and just enjoy an extended life."

"Still, you were a leader, once, and Julien told me that Marcus was in exile for some time. You may find yourself as the leader of your line again, or more." Charles crossed one leg over the other. "The blood-drinkers as a whole need centralized leadership. After all," he leaned forward, his blue eyes became keen, "this will happen again. Someone must bring the blood-drinker lines together. Divide and conquer, unify and overcome." The mortal smirked and sat back, yet his eyes still revealed a lust for land and glory.

Claudius leaned in and stared into those blue eyes. Then he moved to the Emperor's ear and allowed his voice to take flight, to make sure this supreme mortal leader understood.

"Charles," he began in honeyed tones, "if you go to Britain, with your armies, you will not survive the journey. I will make sure of that myself, if necessary. You have no desire to add anymore to your empire, do you?" He pulled back and smiled as if he finished telling Emperor Charles a dirty, but nevertheless amusing joke.

The Emperor stood up and clasped his arm. "I have no designs to add the Anglo-Saxon kingdoms to my empire, Claudius. Dealing with the Saxons on their own was bad enough, and people still curse me for destroying their sacred forests."

"I'm very glad to hear that, Charles. Now, the sun is about to rise," Claudius replied.

"I hope you do not mind if I ask one more question."

"Not at all, Charles."

"If a man desired to become a champion of the balance, whose favor would he need to ask?" The Emperor's eyes revealed a deep need.

"Hmmmm." Claudius pursed his lips. "By champion of the balance, I assume you wish to be Deargh Du. If I were you, I would speak with Máire or Sáerlaith."

"Máire, that would be quite odd," Charles admitted, rubbing his chin. "Sáerlaith saved me from Talia. I think I will approach her... later."

"Well, you could always ask Julien."

"Would that not make me my own grandfather?" Charles uttered a dry laugh.

"I suppose so," Claudius chuckled. "However, if you wish to join us, you should consider joining The Hunt. You are well known for your skills, and the Lord of the Wild has many ancient leaders in His hunt, or there is always the Ekimmu Cruitne. They would appreciate your skill in battle."

"That is a lot to think about," Charles admitted. "I should get a few hours of sleep before I leave for Vézelay. Sleep well, and best of luck to you and yours in Bath," the Emperor told him. He then exited the tent.

"The Emperor as a blood-drinker," Máire commented, turning back towards him. "That is an interesting thought, is it not?"

Claudius nodded his head. "He could be a boon to any of the Celtic lines. Let's hope the Lamia don't decide he should join them."

Máire shrugged. "I don't think their leadership wants another leader in their ranks. Better to manipulate a mortal leader than transform him." Her green eyes smiled a little.

"Yes, that does sound much like Mandubratius' thinking," he said.

"Claudius, you hardly ever use your Sugnwr Gwaed vocal skills. Why is that? Is it because of the similarity to manipulation?"

"It seems a bit like mind-bending sometimes, but in order to make it work, I have to speak it as opposed to simply placing the thoughts in the mortal's mind." He shrugged. "Isn't that what the Lamia do? I cannot understand it fully. Besides, Charles really is quite busy with his duties. I just wanted to make sure he remembered them." He yawned.

"It's not him I'm concerned about, it's you. Are you thinking about that unity of all the blood-drinking lines? You aren't thinking of becoming Claudius Metrius Sertorius, Emperor of the Isles, are you?"

"Part of me likes the idea of the three Celtic lines in unity, Máire, but I fear I'm not emperor material. It's a lot of work. It will be hard enough to get all the blood-drinkers to put aside their differences," he chuckled. "However, you should be concerned with Emperor Charles' aspirations. I've seen one other man exhibit that same desire for conquest, gold, and power."

"Caesar? I mean the first one."

Claudius nodded a little. "It's thrilling to be in front of someone with such aspirations, but I remember what it was like." He sat down on the bedding next to her. "To go back to the topic of manipulating Charles the Emperor, I had half a thought to encourage him to take over Ard Mhacha, but I thought it would be a bit much. I know little of the balance, but part of me says it would be wrong. That is why I suggested Sáerlaith if he wanted to become Deargh Du. She would teach him about the balance. He could be almost as good as you or Julien."

She smiled. "Thank you."

"You're welcome. Anyway, Emperor Charles would have to give up a lot of power to become a blood-drinker." He shifted. "Returning to the idea of a unified group of the Celtic lines, while part of me knows we cannot get all the blood-drinkers to cooperate, the rest of me thinks that we should consider working together. At the very least, the leaders of the Celtic lines should meet once in awhile. After all, Marcus and you will not be in Bath anymore to serve as a contact point to the rest of the Deargh Du."

Máire nodded. "If you were one of the ones on this... grand council, would you ask the Deargh Du that remain in Ard Mhacha to join?" Máire lowered her eyes.

Claudius wondered how she could ask such a question. He knew his own feelings toward them. "If those... people," he spat through gritted teeth, "approached me with open hands, I would have no words with them. It's an illegal government, as far as all of us here are concerned. The true Deargh Du will reside in Vézelay, except for those who join me in Bath. I think Marcus would like that. Also, it may be necessary to split numbers until the stronghold is complete to keep from arousing too much suspicion."

Máire smiled. "Yes, I think Marcus would like that. I will support you in a grand unified council of the Celtic lines, Claudius. However, if you start sounding like Mandubratius or Gaius Julius Caesar, I will leave you behind."

Claudius shook his head and chuckled. "So, the last I'd see of you is your pretty backside?"

She smirked. "Perhaps I'd hit you first. However, I am serious. There should be talks between the lines, so the next time this happens, things can go more smoothly."

"Perhaps you should be on this council, Máire."

Máire looked over her shoulder at Julien, who slept like a baby. "Politics are not for me. It's best to leave them to my son-in-darkness. He needs duties, and I'm certain taking care of the Deargh Du will suit him. I believe that you, Mac Alpin, and Sáerlaith can argue the points for this council very well. Mac Alpin will be able to do so very loudly. I am certain they will accept it just to get him to shut up."

"Perhaps," Claudius yawned. "Let's save the rest of this conversation for another night." He curled back into his blankets. "Good night, Maél Morrigan."

She slid back down next to him. "Good night, general of the Cothromaigh."

Máire could feel herself nearing the unsuspecting rat. Her whiskers tingled in anticipation, in tandem with her twitching tail. She sensed her prey sitting nearby. She sprang and batted the rat with a ginger-colored paw. The game became cruel fun, but nature seemed to encourage her instincts. Them, she sensed another animal approach.

"Are you enjoying this as much as I?" it asked her.

Máire looked up from the rat at a black cat staring at her. His eyes narrowed, and his smile became feral.

The rat scampered off, attempting to flee, but Lucius pounced on it.

"So, are you enjoying my dream?" asked Lucius.

"Your dream? This is my dream, I think."

"I sensed you were asleep. I wanted to talk, so I invited you into my dream, Máire."

"I didn't know fairy cats could do this." Máire watched Lucius playfully bat the rat without much menace.

"I didn't know a Deargh Du could draw forth raw energy from the Otherworld and wrap themselves in it," he replied. He stopped hitting the rodent. "I'll catch you again later," he promised, before releasing it. He met her eyes again. "Even if I kill it, it comes back the next time I dream. Sometimes, I'll allow myself to enjoy the sensation of sleep." He stalked closer to her and crouched down, tucking his feet under himself. Lucius lowered his eyelids, leaving them half-closed.

Máire copied him. "This is most relaxing," she commented.

"Indeed," Lucius answered.

"So, why did you invite me to your dream, Lucius?" She vaguely remembered him saying something about what they didn't know about him could fill an ocean.

"You have such a good memory, Máire," he purred. "I brought you here to say goodbye, for now." He licked a paw and smoothed an errant hair.

"You're going?" She felt sadness overwhelm her again. "Why can't you stay, Lucius?"

"I already left, chroí. I'm not even on your plane of existence, now. Don't worry, we'll meet again soon.

I didn't know he was gone.

Of course you didn't know... I didn't want you to. I left because I have duties in the Otherworld, and I accomplished what I set out to do in your realm."

Máire stared at the fairy cat. "You had your fun, you mean. You came to our realm because you wanted fun." She watched his tail wave back and forth. Something about his body language and tone worried her. He wasn't a soft and furry cat anymore. "You didn't come here for fun, did you?" Máire whispered. "You had a singular purpose in mind."

"You are so very smart, Máire." Lucius smiled. "That is why I love you. I love all the Deargh Du, but sometimes I cannot help but love you and Marcus more." His mouth moved into a strange, almost human-like, grin.

"So, who or what are you really?" Máire asked.

"Why, I'm Lucius the fairy cat, and I'll see you again soon," he purred. "I hope *you enjoyed this dream as much as I have."*

Máire awoke and sat up. She shook herself and stared at her hands.

No paws.

Julien snorted and awoke. "What's wrong, Máire?"

"Nothing." She ran a hand over his hair and slid back down next to him. "Go back to sleep, Julien."

He muttered an assent and closed his eyes.

She tried to entice sleep again, but nothing came. The birds chatted to each other in the quiet camp, as the majority of the mortals had left with their leaders.

Horatio looked on as the remaining allies and livestock departed after one last feeding, carting away supplies and tents. He noticed many of the allies speaking in different languages and embracing each other. He wished again that he could understand their languages. He tugged at Máire's sleeve. "I don't understand their words," he murmured.

"We are parting ways, and many of us may not see each other for decades. I am saying that I wish them all a safe journey and a long life, and that is what most of the others are stating."

"Decades?" Julien asked.

"Centuries even, for some." Máire grinned. "Who can say how events will play out."

"I'm still not accustomed to the idea of living for centuries," Horatio added, looking at Julien.

"I think it will be a most entertaining adventure," Julien answered.

"It's not always easy. You'll witness mortals you know grow old and die, governments change, names of countries change, even the landscape may change, yet you are constant." Her green eyes settled on Horatio. "Keep yourself busy and keep in touch with the world around you. You cannot be an eddy in the current of life. You'll love Bath, Horatio, and I know Claudius will be an excellent patron to you, even if you and he are not in the same line."

Her smile made him feel a little dizzy.

Reginald de Divio approached his brother. "Julien, can I borrow your lodgings in Aachen? For some reason, Mandubratius wishes me to reside there." Reginald seemed relaxed after the evening of frivolity last night.

"So, like me, you're one of the ambassadors of the Lamia," Horatio said to Reginald.

"Yes, though I'm not exactly sure what I'm supposed to do," Reginald replied.

"From my experience, foreign ambassadors attended social functions and did nothing more than ate, drank, and went after every woman in court," Julien murmured.

"Sounds like a fine duty to me." Reginald smirked. "I can live with that."

"So can I," Horatio added. He turned to Máire as talk grew louder and asked, "What are they saying now?"

"Something in Gaelic," Máire answered.

"And, what does it mean?" Julien placed an arm around her.

"Long life and prosperity to all here," she answered.

Claudius walked to the center of the circle. He said something in two languages and then switched to Latin. "Until we all meet again."

Everyone repeated his words. Then an explosion of chatter began anew. Horatio found himself being hugged by many. After the strangers released him, Mandubratius walked over and embraced him.

"We will meet again soon," his sponsor whispered in his ear.

Awvarwy pulled away from Horatio, hoping that he had frightened the youngling.

No such luck. Have I lost my touch? Then again, perhaps he needs to accept that he has changed.

Awvarwy even found the parting ceremony touching. He used to make light of these ceremonies and their seriousness, but he didn't wish to do so now. Looking around, he saw a lot of familiar faces. Too his right, Máire stood a few feet away. He approached her, wishing to practice his flowery platitudes of departure on her. As he approached her, Máire's eyes seemed to brighten. Awvarwy wondered how she'd managed to forgive him. He found himself a little suspicious of her motives, as he did not even attempt to manipulate her.

Of course, this could be part of the testing from his father and Morrigan.

Máire walked toward him and kissed his cheeks. She embraced him after the kisses. "Try to stay out of trouble, Awvarwy," she whispered in his ear.

"You know 'Trouble' is my dearest friend, after you," he murmured. "She and I walk hand in hand."

"I know." Her face twisted in an amused grin. "When will you visit Vézelay?"

"When you tire of boredom, I'll be there." He kissed her and turned away, walking towards the Basileus. On his way to her, he blew a kiss to Amata, and she returned it.

Irene finished her good-byes to Mac Alpin as Awvarwy joined them. Together, they witnessed other groups of blood-drinkers begin to leave, walking in different directions. Each cluster began to fly or run. All became still and silent again. The lands seemed pristine beyond belief.

Perhaps my father has done this, or was this a final wish from Marcus?

Irene wrapped an arm around him. "We should leave, Awvarwy."

He smiled. "Arwin taught you to say my real name, didn't he?"

Irene said nothing. Her large blue eyes sparkled with magic and timeless beauty. She began to run towards the east.

He followed her.

Constantinople and the precious beginnings of a unified Lamia line awaited them.

Tír na nÓg

Morrigan sat in Her chair, cleaning Her fingernails with a sharp dagger. Her annoyance grew with every passing moment. Part of Morrigan desired greatly to overturn the table and upset the beautiful meal. She glanced across the table at Manannán, who played with a small vortex in His left hand. Otherwise, He appeared calm as the lake in the distance.

Brigid twined Her golden locks in Her fingers. She licked a finger to gently tame an unruly curl.

The matured and matronly Dana, covered in green and floral bounty, sat down at the head of the table. Many seats remained empty for this meeting. The other Tuaths had Their own duties to attend to at this time.

Morrigan could sense Ruarí and Adhamdh shift in their chairs behind Her. She was the only deity that brought Her family with Her today, yet they remained silent. She drummed Her clean nails against the stone table, feeling Her bile rise.

Where is Lugh?

"Morrigan, please stop that," Dana requested.

She nodded and went back to toying with Her blade.

A change in the atmosphere signified Lugh's arrival. He trotted towards the table in the form of Lucius. The feline hopped on the table and purred.

"Get off the table, Lugh." Dana frowned. "That's not funny at all."

Lucius plopped into a chair and turned around. He sat down and rested His chin against the stone table, studying the food.

"Turn into your human form, Lugh." Dana continued to frown at Him. "You look so —"

"Cute? Fluffy? Adorable?" A large grin settled on His features.

"Change and be silent, Lugh. I didn't summon you here for entertainment. Now, change into a more suitable form and behave," Dana stated, sounding like a firm, yet loving mother.

Lugh acquiesced, becoming a familiar form. He smiled at Dana.

"Now," Dana began. "I understand all of You have been up to some manner of mischief that has been causing a disruption between this world and the world of the mortals. I want to know what's going on. Morrigan, You begin."

Morrigan pointed a sharpened fingernail at Lugh. "You influenced My son to break the Balance, Lugh. You, who claim to love all, influenced him to advance Your son in the mortal realm. You encouraged wild and outlandish thoughts and beliefs within Marcus."

Lugh smiled.

"I asked for an explanation, not an accusation," Dana remarked. Her eyes, which reflected the beauty of Their surroundings, became as ice.

Morrigan turned Her glare on the table. "I wanted to test My son to see if he was ready to take his place by My side," She replied.

"And that test was Your daughter Seosaimhín?" Dana asked.

"She was part of My test, yes. Marcus needed a balance."

"I don't know why you feel the need to surround Yourself with chi—" Dana stopped Herself and grinned.

Morrigan noticed the remainder of Dana's family gaze upon the Mother of Tuaths.

"I am sorry for the interruption." Dana nodded to Morrigan. "Please continue."

"I asked Adhamdh to influence Seosaimhín in her dominance of the Strigoi and to steer them in a destructive conquest," Morrigan continued.

"For what reason?" Dana inquired.

"Aside from testing Marcus?"

"Yes," Dana drawled. Her eyes settled on Morrigan.

"To be honest," Morrigan added, lowering Her gaze, "I was a little bored. Besides, with what the Deargh Du will face, they need friends. The chaos brought them close and their enemies closer as well. Of course, it went as planned, until Lugh spoiled My test!"

"That's enough, Sister!" Dana informed Her. "Lugh, is this true that You spoiled Morrigan's test of Marcus?"

Lugh's smile faded. "I was only doing to Her son what She did to Mine, Great Mother. She corrupted My tests for Cu Chulainn so he would fail."

"And now your Lamia son covets My granddaughter-in-darkness!"

Lugh slammed His fist against the table. The Otherworld shook, but the table remained steady. "Covets, yes, but he himself was led astray by My own Foster-Father."

The vortex in Manannán's hand grew in size until it popped out of existence. "What?" Manannán looked at Lugh, visibly upset with the accusation.

"It would seem, Manannán, that Lugh is accusing You of duplicity in His affairs *with Morrigan."*

Manannán Mac Lir stared at Lugh. *"I simply felt Awvarwy had it too easy. He needs a challenge."* He met Morrigan's eyes. *"This will also help solidify the Deargh Du."*

Morrigan ducked Her eyes, trying to remain calm.

Dana turned Her gaze upon Brigid. *"What part do you have in this, Sister? You look such the pleased cat, Brigid."*

Brigid gave a little shrug. *"Unbiased observer?"*

"Then in that case, I will leave it to You to punish and instruct Morrigan's children," Dana replied.

"Punish?" Morrigan arose from Her seat. *"Why is Brigid given free rein to punish My beloved children?"*

"You care too much, Sister," Dana explained. *"Yes, we love all Our mortals, especially those who embrace Our teachings in one way or another. However, both Marcus and Seosaimhín violated the veil. One of them believed himself to be a deity, and if I had not intervened, they would have broken the bounds between Our world and theirs."*

Morrigan sank into Her chair. *"Aren't you going to punish Lugh's Lamia son?"*

"I am certain Awvarwy will receive ample punishment, Morrigan, in due time," Dana answered.

"Do any of Us get punished?" Morrigan asked.

"No," Dana replied.

"I think Manannán should be punished," Lugh pouted.

"He won't, because I asked Him to interfere. Somebody has to be the Balance," Dana chuckled.

Morrigan sighed. She noticed Lugh meet His Foster-Father's eyes and smile a little. *"That seems appropriate, Dana,"* She said.

"I'm so glad you approve," Dana's smile grew in beauty. *"As for Marcus and Seosaimhín's punishment, it's one of which You will approve, Morrigan. I know of Your love for tests and redemption through trial. Brigid and I have discussed it, and I am certain We will all see that it is fair for all Our children."*

Dana grabbed an apple and bit into the meat of the fruit.

Morrigan nodded. *"I will accept Brigid's punishment, as long as Lugh and Manannán do not interfere."*

Manannán created another vortex in His hand. He looked over at Morrigan. *"Sister, I will not interfere,"* He stated.

She nodded in gratitude.

Lugh smiled at Her. *"I won't interfere."* He transformed into Lucius and rested His chin against the table again, purring, *"Neither will I."*

The Tuaths turned to study Her.

"Well, I won't interfere!" Morrigan answered.

Dana scanned the table. "Good, then it's settled. Now, do not cause Me to bring You together on this issue again. I love You all, and I will see You at My home for Beltane." Dana's body became light and flowers. The glorious light faded, and the flowers danced on the wind.

Brigid beamed Her own radiance. "I will see you at the festivities." She became a golden-eyed cat and bounded away, leaping into wildflowers with unrestrained joy.

"Farewell, My Foster-Son and Sister," Manannán bade as He rose from His seat. Wind encompassed Him until He disappeared into the vortex, and it moved towards the gate between worlds.

After the other Tuaths had departed. Lugh left His cat form and then stretched, before walking over to Morrigan.

Knowing He wanted to talk in private, and Her not wanting an audience, She motioned for Her children to return to Her dun.

Without any complaints, Ruarí and Adhamdh departed.

Morrigan ignored Her urge to plunge Her dagger into Lugh, but She knew He'd only laugh. She waited patiently for His next move.

His mischievous face grew somber. "I apologize for what I did to Your son, Morrigan. I hope that You will understand that I did this because of Cu Chulainn. I love Marcus with all of My being, as much as I love Your other children, Sister. I am so sorry. I cannot help it, but Your granddaughter makes My son a better person."

Morrigan sighed and closed Her eyes, feeling He spoke with honest sincerity. "Awvarwy has done much to make Máire hate him. I don't know if they will be reconciled in this life, but I accept Your apology, Brother. Now, please forgive Me for My role in Cu Chulainn's demise in the mortal realm. Dana and I decided that I had to maintain the Balance during that battle."

"I know," Lugh whispered.

Morrigan dropped Her dagger on the table and embraced Lugh.

He rested His cheek against Hers. "Until next time, My Sister," He said. Lugh then backed away and became bright flame, disappearing to His realms in Their world.

As She took the form of a raven, Morrigan wondered as to what Brigid's plans would be. She flew past the Field of the Judged and spied Her home on the horizon, where Her family awaited Her.

epilogue

The singing of birds brought him out of the gray void. Winds rushed past him, but for some reason the plunging sensation gave him little concern.

Birds? Where did they come from?

He tried to remember why the song of birds seemed to surprise him, but the answers spiraled out of his reach.

Warmth began to surround him, casting out the cold.

Images began to cascade through his mind, demanding attention, but he couldn't associate any meaning to the random, violent visions.

The sights became more frightening when he grasped that he couldn't remember his name. His entire life lingered in the distance, tantalizing him with recollections of his past.

His plummet soon ended, and he cried out in pain as he landed on what felt to be earth.

A growing glow distracted him. He opened one eye, keeping the other shut in case of danger. The bright luminescence blinded him, and he screamed, while covering his face with an arm, forgetting the agony from his fall.

Sunlight offered no pleasure, only death. That much he could remember. He waited for death, still moaning in pain.

However, death never arrived, yet the distress remained. He could feel grass, sand, and stones under his skin, and his body ached.

He stopped his fearful cries and moved his arm. Opening the same eye, he felt the stinging reward of throbbing anguish begin anew.

Why did the sun fill him with such a demanding and ceaseless fear?

He became still, realizing he wore no clothes.

The aching soon faded, and he attempted to open his other eye. At that moment, a feminine shadow covered him, and the delicate smell of a woman filled his nostrils.

"Where am I?" the Roman croaked in one of the many languages in his mind, *while trying to look up at her face.*

The shadow shook her head, unable to comprehend his foreign words.

He tried different sounds and words. Finally, she seemed to understand him.

"You are in my garden in Nippon-koku," *she said, her voice mirrored the music and beauty of the song birds.*

---

continue the journey with...

Dynasties of night
Morrigan's Brood Book VI

about the authors

Heather Poinsett Dunbar

Born in Houston, Texas, Heather began writing her first book at age eight. While her grammatical structure left much to be desired, she continued to hone her writing and storytelling skills. During a college internship in London, England, her curiosity about ancient cultures and mythology intensified. She backpacked through Europe, fell in love with Scotland, cried at the retelling of part of the Ulster cycle, garnered ghost stories from the Beefeaters at the Tower, wandered the Roman ruins in Bath, and danced around the stones in Avebury.

After spending all her spare time studying these new interests in many libraries and on the road, she began working on her masters' in Library science at the University of North Texas. She now resides in the Houston area with her husband and three cats. She loves exploring the local culture as well as the many Celtic festivals and events in Texas. She also works as a librarian for a local college and at a corporate library in downtown Houston.

Christopher Dunbar

Chris Dunbar was born in Greenport, Long Island, New York and then moved to Texas as soon as he could, at least that is the story he tells to native Texans, such as his wife. Chris keeps searching for ways to leave Houston, like moving to Auburn, Alabama, Dallas, and even San Antonio, but Houston just keeps reeling him back. Chris' day job is performing Business Continuity and Disaster Recovery, but his night job is coming up with creative ways to wound and maim the characters he and his wife Heather created. For fun, Chris enjoys the occasional novel and video game, but he also likes to delve into his Scottish ancestry and tool leather. When he can find the time, Chris pretends to play the Bodhran and the didgeridoo, much to the chagrin of his cats, Clyde, Brigid, and Maeve, not to mention his wife Heather. Chris is also an avid wearer of the kilt.

look for these morrigan's
brood series titles by

heather poinsett dunbar &
christopher thomas dunbar

there are more stories to
tell, so look out for them

published and future works

Title	Synopsis
Morrigan's Brood Morrigan's Brood Book I	Éire is under siege by blood-drinkers seeking a powerful artifact. The island's only hope is Marcus Galerius Primus Helvetticus, a former Roman general who once aided Gaius Julius Caesar in invading Britain but now fights to protect Éire. Can the Deargh Du (ᛁᚢ—ᚻᚻᚠᛁᚢ—) rally in time, or will the invaders reclaim their lost power?
Rise of the Lamia A Story of the Morrigan's Brood Series	Marcus Galerius Primus Helvetticus, once part of Caesar's invasion of Britain, is now a Deargh Du with a mission to stop Gaius Julius Caesar Augustus Germanicus—known as Caligula—from repeating history. Infiltrating the Lamia in Rome, Marcus must avoid a former become his enemy, lest he realize Marcus is alive. Will Marcus succeed, or will history repeat itself in blood and conquest?
Crone of War Morrigan's Brood Book II	The Lamia (Λαμία) have forged an alliance with an Irish chieftain and his malevolent mother, gaining a foothold in Éire. With a massive army on the way from Rome, their conquest seems inevitable. Can the Deargh Du and their new allies thwart the invaders, or will their mistrust lead to their downfall?
Madness Short-Story	Madness overtakes one of the Lamia's most pivotal leaders after the events of 564 CE. Will this descent into insanity ignite a devastating civil war, or can unity be preserved despite the growing discord?
Reckoning Short-Story	In the wake of 564 CE, the Deargh Du must face the challenges of change or risk old strife resurfacing, which could shatter their unity. Will they adapt, or will past grudges tear them asunder?
Dark Alliance Morrigan's Brood Book III	A new menace threatens the Holy Roman Empire, spreading murder and chaos among both mortals and blood-drinkers. A fragile alliance between sworn enemies must confront this threat. Can they overcome their hatred, or will the empire succumb to darkness?
Curse of Venus Morrigan's Brood Book IV	The Strigoi (Стригои), cursed by Venus, ravage the Holy Roman Empire. Pope Leo III seizes the chaos as a chance to settle an old score with Charlemagne. Will their rivalry plunge the empire further into destruction, or can the Deargh Du angels intervene before it's too late?
Shards of Light Morrigan's Brood Book V	In the shadows, many watch as a dark alliance hunts for an ancient device to undo the corruption that plagues the Holy Roman Empire. But not all who watch remain passive. Will this unseen presence help or hinder the quest to restore the Balance?
Dynasties of Night Morrigan's Brood Book VI	For centuries, a brother and sister have manipulated two dynasties of blood-drinkers: Japan's Kyonshi (キョンシー), striving for independence, and China's Chiang-shih (僵尸), determined to maintain control. As their intricate game unfolds, will jealousy and vengeance continue to fuel this endless cycle, or will one dynasty triumph over the other with the help of an unexpected game piece?
Odin's Chosen Morrigan's Brood Book VII	Odin grants immortality to a starving king who seeks vengeance against those who condemned his people. Leading his army of blood-drinkers, the Einherjar (ᛗᛁᛏᚻᛗᚱᛩᛏᚱ), Runolf wages war on Britain, Scotland, and Ireland, unaware that other blood-drinkers inhabit these lands. Can Morrigan's Brood maintain the Balance, or will they be swept away by Runolf's wrath?
Hera's Wrath Morrigan's Brood Book VIII	In realms thought beyond mortal and immortal reach, dark horrors lie imprisoned, sealed away by the Tuatha dé Danann. Hera, Greek Goddess of Motherhood, holds the keys to their release. Will she use them to restore her vision of Greek family values, or will she unleash these ancient evils upon the world?

Title	Synopsis
It's In the Cards A Lusty Librarian Adventure	Cheri's mundane life as a basement librarian takes a wild turn when a professor and a collection of rare tarot cards and other artifacts enter her world. Join Cheri on a quirky adventure that defies the ordinary—because sometimes, even the quietest lives can be shaken by a little magic.
Bitches Love Unicorns Within *Dark Constellation: Origins*, Book 1 of the Dark Constellation Series	At a wild party, Kayleigh discovers unicorns—and other fantastical beings—are real. Bob the Unicorn sweeps her away on a magical journey through time, space, and realms unknown. As they dance through dimensions, Kayleigh finds herself falling not just for the adventure but for the unicorn himself. But as the night wanes, the lines between fantasy and reality blur. Even magical parties must end—will Kayleigh's new reality be as enchanting as the dream, or will she be left longing for the magic to return?
Dudes Love Faeries Within *Dark Constellation: Origins*, Book 1 of the Dark Constellation Series	Teddy, a pixie librarian, takes a job in the unseelie realm, hoping for fulfillment at Tír na nÓg's largest and most prestigious library. But his dreams are dashed when he realizes his new boss is evil incarnate. Demoted to the lowliest position of book-duster, Teddy and his inept yet secretly ambitious boss stumble upon a magical gateway hidden in the depths of the library that leads to ancient machines on another plane of existence—machines that could reshape the very fabric of the Otherworld. Can Teddy prevent the unseelie's malevolent ambitions from unlocking their power, or will doom come to all realms?
One Fat Witch Book 2 of the Dark Constellation Series	Hazel's topsy-turvy life in Houston takes a darker turn when her husband is kidnapped by a unicorn. With the help of a pixie hiding from an unseelie lord, Hazel must protect a key that controls powerful machines in the Otherworld. Can she save her husband and prevent a catastrophe, or will the unleashed magic consume their souls and plunge both worlds into eternal darkness?